COLD

HEARTS

TROUBLED

SOULS

COLD

HEARTS

TROUBLED

SOULS

Ashley Joel Osma

To the resilient woman who took a leap of faith, crossing the Atlantic in search of a better life.

To the brave girl who had a far from ideal childhood and had to grow up quickly.

To the self-conscious boy whose uniqueness made him a target.

1 / *Shannon I*
Not too old for a claat—beating—from Mum & Dad

Shannon's head was down, but down wasn't where he was looking. He was straining to peek at the muscular man sitting opposite. He hoped no one could tell, but he was in plain sight, hardly anyone standing in that particular carriage of the Victoria line train.

The man was dressed for summer in October, his tight clothes leaving nothing to the imagination. The white T-shirt he was wearing might as well have been sleeveless, his pumped chocolate arms devouring the sleeves, and his rocks for pecs threatened to destroy it with each breath he took. His three-quarter length bottoms were just as tight. And that damn bulge was hard to miss, even in Shannon's periphery. Muscle Man, sitting there with his legs open beyond the confines of his seat, must've been intentionally bringing attention to his crotch, to himself. One wrong move and everything he was wearing would just rip.

His cheek started tingling, enough to divert his attention from Muscle Man to the stray braids brushing the tiger-striped lap of the woman sitting next to him. The ends of her braids were caressing tiger stripes just beyond the point where her black jacket couldn't hide her above-the-knee animal print skirt. He tried to get his heart under control before making eye contact. He only locked eyes with the woman for a split second before looking down at his book. Good thing the hurtling train was loud enough to drown out his strained breathing. Needed time to get himself together. The woman was still staring at him though; his cheek was still tingling.

Movements opposite made him look that way again. The woman's fingers interlocked with Muscle Man's. Confirmation. They were together. More than that, they were both wearing rings on their wedding fingers. All those times he'd told himself to make sure a man was into men *and* interested in him before showing any interest . . . He never learned. He dared to look into the eyes of the person who wouldn't stop staring at him. *Don't look at him again, faggot*, her eyes were saying.

Tingling spread to another part of his face. More eyes were on him—Muscle Man's. The thirst trapper raised his eyebrows, then his forehead lines shifted lower so that his eyes narrowed as he played with his chin hair.

Another surrender in the staring contest. Made the book his focus again. It was shaking. His hands were shaking. That was the reason. He held the book tighter.

Moments passed, but two pairs of eyes were still on him. He stared back, this time with a piercing look, first at Muscle Man, then at Tigress. He surrendered again. The train was slowing down anyway. Almost time to get off.

Tingling remained as he prepared to alight for Highbury & Islington Station. His hands were still trembling. *Invisible Life* slipped out of his clutches, ended up by the tigress's black leather high-heeled boots, while the bookmark played with his fumbling fingers as it gracefully fell to the floor, as if going down an invisible spiral slide towards Muscle Man's Vans slip-ons.

Reading *Invisible Life* on the train was always going to be risky. Making it fall on the floor, dirty from all the footwear that trod on it, face up, proved that taking it out of his rucksack had been a mistake. The tigress just couldn't resist staring at the cover when she picked it up. As big as the world was, it was small enough for him to see a familiar face unexpectedly. His parents would've lost it if they knew he was reading that book.

The train stopped, but it was black outside the carriage, the window distorting reflections.

Tigress had an I've-caught-you-red-handed look, no urgency to hand the book over. The bitch knew what she was doing, delaying things, slanting the book so that anyone nearby could see the front cover.

She finally leaned over the space between them, tossing long stray braids back over her shoulder, to give the book back, but she was still holding it the same way, giving people nearby a good look at the front cover: a woman and two men, an obvious—but different kind of—love triangle, the two men looking at each other longingly while the woman clung to her man, the man in the middle, facing the prospect that he might want another man.

Sweat was trickling down his face. He reached over with a trembling hand and grabbed the book, but she wouldn't let go. She raised her eyebrows, her smile growing as his breathing intensified.

The train got moving again. That must've distracted her, because surprise replaced her smug countenance when he managed to snatch his secret from her grasp. The train was going to shoot out of the darkness at any moment; he got up quickly.

The married couple got up too.

Someone touched him. Had to be one of them. He turned his head, not too much to make it obvious he was looking around, but enough to see over his shoulder. Tigress was right behind him. She'd touched him. She probably couldn't help it; the train was jerking to a stop, like it wanted to punish anyone who wasn't holding on properly. She touched him again. Another look behind. Tight space. More passengers standing by the doors, ready to exit.

3

He knew she was close, but *that* close? In her high heels, she towered over him. He squinted as her exhales hit his eyes. Her sweet scent, some ocean fragrance mingling with whatever hair product she'd used, made him want to sneeze.

She leaned into him until a few of her braids slid along her shoulder and tickled his cheek. "Your bookmark."

Of course.

"Thank—"

"I love E. Lynn Harris."

He must've looked shocked; his pounding heart always betrayed him.

"He was a great writer." She smiled, an E. Lynn Harris fan happy to meet another.

"He was." He forced a smile back, then he took one last look at Muscle Man. Body of The Rock. Not the face to match. He locked eyes with the tigress. "Have a nice evening."

"Have a bad one."

He frowned.

She narrowed her eyes. Confirmation he'd heard correctly.

When the doors opened, he bolted out of the carriage, as if escaping from an airtight container.

He followed the crowd leaving Homerton Station until he neared the T-junction between Berger Road and Barnabas Road. He fumbled in his pocket for his phone. Last he'd checked, it'd been flashing red, his battery life at seven percent. About an hour ago. He unlocked his phone with merely a finger swipe up the screen. Two percent now. Three missed calls. WhatsApp alerts. He went into his call log. The missed calls had come from Elise. He would settle down, eat whatever his mum had made, then call Elise later. Funny she'd rung when she knew his phone would be on silent. He'd told her his schedule via WhatsApp yesterday, Elise a couple of hours from boarding Virgin Atlantic

4

in Orlando while he was getting ready for bed. Then again, maybe the time difference had confused her. Good thing her job kept her on the go. His parents would've expected to see more of her otherwise. There was only so much pretending he could do.

The WhatsApp messages were from her as well.

Call me before you get home.
It's important.

He frowned at the message, just as the battery went down to one percent. Elise would have to wait until he was home. He sent her a WhatsApp message.

Sorry I missed you. Can't call right now. Low battery.
I'll charge my phone when I get in. Give me an hour.

The phone rang moments later.

"Hi, Elise."

"Shannon, where are you?"

"A few minutes from home. What's—?"

"Don't go home! They know."

"Who knows what?"

"Your parents. They—"

A vibration tickled his hand. He looked at his phone. Black screen.

His parents knew? The only thing he didn't want them to find out was . . . It couldn't be that. But what if . . . ? He froze, pressed a clenched fist against his chest, ignored people who passed him then peered back at him wondering why he'd stopped. Suddenly, the buzzing and beeping from the traffic sounded far away, as if he were underwater.

It had to be something else, but if it wasn't, he couldn't go home. Wouldn't be safe. But that was his home, his only home.

Too cold to dilly-dally. And he'd been on his feet all day, his shoes digging into his ankles. The worst time for his phone to abandon him. He could've had more answers from Elise, or called his uncle.

Uncle Lionel. Maybe that was it. Maybe his parents had found out he was in touch with him. A dead giveaway, on top of everything else.

A wall covered in graffiti was paces away. Legs weak, he stumbled to it, leaned against it, crushing *Invisible Life* and everything else that was stuffed in his rucksack. He closed his eyes and tilted his head back, withstanding the whistling wind whipping his face. He opened his eyes once it stopped, stared through people padded in winter wear as they rushed past.

It had to be something else. It *was* something else. He sighed and shook his head. So stupid. Always fearing the worst. He started walking again, his legs still unsteady.

Glyn Road was like a ghost town compared to the buzz of Homerton High Street. Even the street lights were near dead. Something sprayed his cheek. He looked up. The street lights illuminated drizzle. He needed to hurry before it started pouring. But home was the last place he needed to be if his parents *did* know. They had an idea when he'd be home. Knowing them, they were probably following him.

He stopped, turned around, scanned. Just vehicles streaming along Homerton High Street.

It was something else they knew, not that.

He reached the silver Hyundai i30. Flickering in the bottom bay window. Someone, probably his dad, was in the front room.

If they really knew . . .

He wrapped his hand around the cold black gate. He tried to open it quietly. The longer he took, the longer it squeaked, but opening it quickly would make it scream. Should've followed his mind and oiled it on Sunday. Anyone could hear the gate, no matter how quiet, from the front room. He should've given himself more time to steel himself. Now, he would have to open the front door immediately. Any delay would make things worse. The porch light lit up the fog from his rapid exhales as he took out his keys, his hands shaking. Between the shaking and the coldness, he could barely feel his fingers. The keys slipped out of them; they crashed to his feet. He picked them up, his shaking hand making them jingle. He made a fist around the keys he didn't need, probably cutting himself, and brought the one he needed to the latch. Visible breaths. Numb fingers. The key wouldn't go in. He squinted at it. It was upside down. He was taking too long now. His mum was probably in the kitchen, watching his blurred form through the front door's two-panelled glazed glass. He fought to get the key in properly, but he didn't turn it. He still needed time to get himself together.

It's not what you think, it's not what you think . . . He'd lost count how many times he'd repeated that before turning the key.

Pots and pans knocking about, and drawers opening and closing, drowned out the wind. He left the front door on the latch then closed it with his back. If his dad charged out of the front room on the left and pounced on him, at least he'd see it coming. Had to be prepared for anything.

He cleared his throat. "Mum! Dad!"

The banging in the kitchen stopped.

Sounds were coming from the front room, but the light was off. If his dad was in there, he was ignoring him.

He quickly unzipped his jacket, his heart pounding, closer to knowing what the deal was with every passing second. No point taking off his shoes yet. He had to face his parents though. Maybe it was something else they'd found out. He took a deep breath then strode to the front room doorway.

No one was in there. Nothing but the furniture, the flickering TV watching itself. Maybe this was meant to throw him. He knew his parents.

He spun around, jumped at the short and stocky figure in the kitchen doorway. He gulped then looked his mum up and down as she swivelled the frying pan in her hand. He hadn't been beaten in ages. Back then, it would've been the belt or bare hands. Being twenty-four meant it was a different ball game. Being twenty-four meant he could fight back and stand a chance of winning. As he stared at his mum, he fumbled for the light switch. Dim light washed over the passage.

He let out a shaky breath at the improved view of his mum. Her lips were trembling and her cheeks wet. Something on the floor was pulling for his attention. He looked down. Refuse sacks, three of them, all stuffed.

"M-mum." Too meek. Guilty. He heaved a sigh. "Mum, what's wro—?"

Creaking from directly above stopped him. He looked up. The creaking travelled further along the upper level towards the back of the house and settled there. His bedroom.

He looked at the black bags again. "Mum . . . those bags . . . w-what's . . . ?" He knew the answer, but he needed to hear her say it. "What's inside them?"

"My . . . my . . ."

"Your what, Mum?"

"My only child. . . . How could you?" She dropped the frying pan then brought her hands to her face to stifle her sobs.

His throat was becoming immense with pressure, the kind that only led to tears. He couldn't let his mother see him cry. He couldn't stand there and watch her break down either. He had to go over to her, hold her, do something, anything, to keep her from shattering.

She put a hand out, her eyes menacing. "No!" She hauled up her brown pleated skirt as she bent down to retrieve the frying pan. "Me'll claat you with this if you come near me." She

8

swivelled the frying pan again and kicked one of the black bags. It bounced off the banister then stopped short of his feet.

Another glance at the black bags. His clothes had been shoved inside.

The moment he'd dreaded for years had actually come.

A tear tickled his cheek, then another.

Dead phone. Should've charged it in the frigging morning, or the previous night. Of all the days to have forgotten to pack his charger. The universe had it in for him.

Creaking from above again. "Vi, him reach?"

He jumped.

"Yes, Leroy!"

His dad didn't respond.

The silence was torture. Not knowing what would happen next was torture. He couldn't keep his secret forever—he'd never intended to—but it wasn't supposed to come out yet. He was meant to have his own home first, finish his master's . . . just be set in every way, and then his parents could find out. But *this* wasn't supposed to happen *yet*. How did they find out anyway? Elise probably knew how.

He backed up as a shadow started sweeping down the stairs. His father's Adidas slippers came into view, then the bottom of his jeans . . . then another refuse sack. His dad's other hand was behind his back. He was seeing more and more, faster and faster, until he could see his dad fully. The way his dad was looking at him made a chill run through him. It was a look worse than his mum's, worse because it was expressionless, almost as if nothing was wrong. He'd seen that look many times before—his dad was up to something.

He backed up until his rucksack was squashed between his back and the front door. His dad stepped over the refuse sack his mum had kicked, like it wasn't there, and he put the fourth with the other two, and— Shit. No wonder his hand was behind his back. He knew his dad, and his dad knew him.

His thoughts must've transmitted to his father's brain in that instant, because his dad charged at him like a bull, ramming into him. Between his unstable legs, the heavy rucksack and his father's strength, he ended up on the turquoise carpet, by the banister. Before he could register what was jingling, the belt came down on him. Whack-grunt. Whack-grunt. Barely stung. Because of his jacket.

Something came down hard on the side of his head, made him see stars for a moment, made it feel like water was blocking his left ear.

"Chi-chi? Not my pickney." That was his mum. The frying pan was primed above his head, ready to make him see more stars.

She whacked again and again. Whacks to his head, to his body, to the hand he was using to protect his face.

He writhed pointlessly as his father twisted his left arm and pinned him down. His other arm was restricted. It was his mother's doing, her effort to hold him down, to stop his one flailing arm, so that her frying pan had better access to every part of him.

The belt was hurting more. His father had found a way to his skin. All he could do was writhe and scream from every whack, every lick, every claat. His parents grunted as they punished him.

"Shoulda"—whack—"done"—whack.

"Dad!" He writhed as his skin sizzled. His abdomen was exposed.

—"this"—lick—"long"—lick.

"Daaad, stooop!"

—"time"—claat—"ago." Claat, claat, claat, . . .

"Daaad! Daaaddy. Da—"

A hand covered his mouth, nails digging into his cheeks.

"Beat"—whack—"this nastiness"—lick—"outta you."

He gyrated with each claat and flailed his legs about, faster and faster, matching the pace of the belt pelting his skin. Faster and faster, and more and more erratically until . . . thud-grunt.

"Leroy!" His mum was so close to his ear. "Look weh yuh do to yuh father! Nasty wretch yuh!" She was quickly back at it with the frying pan.

"Mum . . . please!"

"Me bring you into this world—me can take you out."

"Mum . . ."

He struggled for breath as he let his arms take the blows from the frying pan, his mother looming over him. He grabbed the frying pan when she brought it down, grimaced at the pain in his palm but held on. She started choking him. He grabbed a chunk of her hair, hair that had been done the previous day. He pulled until she let go of his neck.

He sprang up, skin sizzling, his rucksack and frantic legs nearly making him fall back down, just as his father wrapped the belt around his hand.

"Stay there, Dad." His voice was trembling.

They were ready for round two. Him against his own parents.

"You too, Mum. I'll use it if I have to." Chest heaving, he swivelled the frying pan, nearly dropping it. He stopped swivelling it.

All they had to do was get out of his way and he'd leave. But they weren't budging.

"I—" Trembling still in his voice. Would be frigged up if he ended up crying in front of them. He clenched his eyes shut for a moment. "Fuck this!" He grimaced.

He'd never sworn at his parents before.

His mum must've been deaf in that moment. She lunged at him, screaming, a deadly look in her eyes.

No time to wait for her to be all over him. He just had to do it. He swung then turned his head just before contact.

Slam. She was down.

His busted-lip-trembling father was wide-eyed, had never imagined he had the nerve. Shannon hadn't either. But his mother was on the floor, clutching her face as if to keep it from falling off.

"How dare you turn out like this?" His father roared and charged at him.

His legs were still wobbly and the rucksack didn't help. He stumbled backwards, fell on the stairs. He dropped the frying pan, his father all over him. Huffing. Puffing. Saliva dripping. Eyes bulging. Hard to move. His dad raised his hand with the belt in it. Buckle end. He reached for his father's hand. His dad struck his thumb. He flinched, pain radiating. His father struck him some more, got his cheek, his neck, his belly . . . new levels of pain with every claat. His hand took blows as he tried to grab the belt. Fucking useless. Couldn't do anything, legs trapped underneath his father, belt coming down faster than he could move his arms. Could barely writhe as different parts of his skin got pelted. No end to the torture in sight. Nothing to do but block and hope his dad would quickly grow weary. Forearm, neck, other forearm, neck again, wrist, navel, forehead . . . Felt like fire discovering new parts of his skin to ravage. Fighting to take the blows like something his parents used to tell him he needed to be—a man. Fighting the blurry vision in his teary eyes. He couldn't move much, things in his rucksack digging into his back, but he flailed his arms, risking his face being torn up. Tried to do the same with his legs. Screaming, fighting the pain and shock of the belt striking his lips, nose, new parts of his forearms, his palms . . . He was getting somewhere, amidst the claats, because his father had shifted. Legroom. He drove his knee right into his dad's balls. His father wailed, screwed up his face, brought the belt down faster, harder. But Shannon wasn't trapped like before. He could flail his arms and legs just as fast. His father was no longer the only one inflicting pain. Shannon was giving claats back.

One last kick changed things. His legs kept going even though they were kicking air. His father was down.

But his mother was getting up. She was disorientated, skirt ripped, hair messed up, but she must've known what he was thinking, because she looked at the front door then scowled at him like a zombie about to pounce on its next victim. She was approaching him. Nowhere to go—but upstairs.

He fought the weight of the rucksack to get up then raced up the steps for his life, bucking his toe. He couldn't get into his room and shut the door fast enough.

Footsteps were getting louder, closer. He fumbled to turn on the ceiling spotlights. A bulb was blown; half the room was illuminated. He tripped over a few books scattered on the floor as he dashed to his desk in the darker section, then he opened the top drawer. He fumbled for the key attached to a key ring with his name on it. Another dash back to the door as he yanked the rucksack off his back, careful not to trip over again, just as the handle came down. The door opened a crack. He stopped it with his foot, heart racing. He pushed into it with all his might and closed it. Someone kissed their teeth on the other side. The door handle moved up and down amidst grunts as he tried to get the key in the latch, but too much was happening. His hand was shaking. Someone—had to be his father—was slamming into the door from the other side, grunting, as he was trying to keep the handle still.

The key got in somehow, but the handle came down and the door opened again. He screamed as he pushed the door, trapping his father's arm in the gap. His father grunted and pushed some more. He thumped, thumped, thumped, thumped his father's arm until it was no longer wedged between the door and the frame.

He slammed the door and turned the key.

The handle moved up and down, constantly clicking, driving him mad, his back against the door. The door was locked though.

The books on the floor . . . He hadn't left them there. An Eric Jerome Dickey book was facing upwards.

A bang on the door made him jump. More bangs created vibrations, tickled him. He lurched from the door, drew closer to the books on the floor, books his parents had managed to find. He went to them, hands over his ears to drown out the banging. He picked up the Eric Jerome Dickey then gasped.

His parents had found the one book they were never meant to know he owned.

2 / Elise I
Torment

Countless calls since Elise's last conversation with Shan, and she still couldn't get through to him. His parents were probably mashing him up.

All her fault.

What was his mum supposed to think when she saw her son's girlfriend kissing someone else?

Actually, Aiden had kissed her, at the Homerton High Street bus stop. Just around the corner from Shan's house. Of all the pissing places.

She shook her head at her carelessness. What was done was done. She just needed to speak to Shan, needed to hear his voice, be sure he was alright. She was about to call him for the umpteenth time when the door to the flat opened.

"Elise!"

She sighed as she got up from her dressing table chair, then she peeped out of her bedroom, clutching the door frame, and acknowledged Tempest.

"Blasted rain . . . messing with my braids. You're lucky you missed it and . . ." Tempest frowned then strutted to her. "You've been crying."

Elise flinched. She tucked strands of hair, loosened from her ponytail, behind her ears, took some tissue out of her cardigan pocket, and dabbed her eyes.

Tempest turned on the passage light. "What's wrong?"

"Nothing."

"Could've fooled me. You look awful."

She turned away from Tempest and walked to her bed.

Things were knocking in the passage then dropped on the wooden floor. Soles of feet slapped against the floor. Louder. Closer.

Tempest stopped at the doorway, frowned. "Getting those calls again?"

Elise had forgotten about those. "No."

"Then what is it?"

She slapped her butt on the bed. "My friend's in trouble."

Tempest tossed her waist-length braids back as she bent down to remove her tights. "Why do you keep calling him your friend when he's more than that?"

Elise frowned. "What are you talking about?"

Tempest strutted to her, her lavender scent floating through the room, then sat on the bed too. "Aiden. You keep calling him your friend."

Elise grimaced. "I'm talking about Shannon, not Aiden."

"Oh. . . . What's wrong with him?"

She barely made eye contact. "How would you feel . . . about him moving in with us?"

Tempest had an I-don't-think-so countenance.

"I mean, you know him."

"I've *met* him."

"But he's—"

"Sorry, Els, this is a two-bedroom, and you know how I am about my space."

"You won't even know he's here. It would be temporary anyway. He can stay on the sofa and—"

"I don't know. Because of Carl, we don't have to pay much rent. Having someone else here wouldn't look good."

"Can't we work something out?"

"And he's a guy. Carl wouldn't be happy about that."

"But . . ."

"But what?"

She clenched her eyes shut briefly. "Nothing."

Tempest's eyes narrowed. "He *is* gay, isn't he?"

She abruptly turned her head from Tempest.

"I knew it. Is that why he's in trouble? His family found out?"

She sighed. "Yes."

Tempest slapped Elise's leg playfully. "Why didn't you tell me?"

"Wasn't my place."

"Is he alright?"

"I really don't know. Can't get through to him."

She called Shannon again. Still nothing.

"You worry too much. What's the worst that could happen, in this day and age?"

All she could do was stare at Tempest.

"Why you looking at me like that?"

"Doesn't matter what year it is and that more people are out now. There are still people who can't be."

"At least he doesn't have to pretend anymore. Must've been so hard for him."

"It's not that simple. He wasn't ready to come out. And the way it all happened . . ."

"How did it happen?"

She shook her head.

"Els, tell me."

"I met Aiden at a bus stop earlier, on Homerton High Street. Thought nothing of it, but I should've."

Tempest looked dumbfounded. "Why?"

"I'll get to that. Anyway, Shan lives nearby, and his mum saw me and Aiden. She saw us kissing—well, he kissed me."

"He did?" Tempest's eyes lit up like she'd been told she'd won an endless supply of beauty products.

"Yeah. But it was the worst thing that could've happened."

"Why? He *is* your boyfriend."

Elise grimaced. "Shan and I agreed that I . . ."

Tempest elbowed her. "Go on."

". . . that I'd . . . pretend . . . to be his girlfriend."

Tempest put one hand over her mouth, but that didn't hide her cheeks as they lifted, her eyes growing animated.

"It's not funny, Tempest."

Tempest cackled, collapsing onto Elise's lap.

She pushed Tempest off. "It's not funny."

Tempest started rolling on the bed.

Elise kissed her teeth then got up and stormed out.

Tempest followed her. "Wait, Els!" Her laughter was abating. "Sorry, it's just crazy."

She rang Shannon again as she entered the front room. "Damn it!" She pulled the curtains back and looked out of the rain-spattered window, as if he would suddenly appear three levels below.

"He's still not picking up?"

"No."

"Why did you pretend to be his girlfriend?"

"Was meant to be temporary. He was always complaining how his parents—actually everyone around him—kept asking him why he had no girlfriend, so I came up with the idea to—"

"It was your idea?"

"Yeah."

"Chile, bye."

She rolled her eyes and slumped down on the black leather sofa.

Tempest joined her. "What happened after his mum saw you with Aiden?"

"She was at the other bus stop—can't believe I didn't see her. She crossed the road like a madwoman and cussed me off. The way she came at me, I thought she was gonna box me."

"So how did she figure out that her son is really gay?"

"She kept accusing me of cheating. I told her that I wasn't, that Shannon and I had just broken up."

Tempest chuckled. "Chile, bye."

"Judge Judy always says that when you tell the truth you don't have to have a good memory."

"That's right."

"I forgot I'd spoken to Shannon just the day before, and we were talking as if we were . . . together. His parents must've been nearby. We finished by saying we . . . love each other."

Tempest's head went back and one of her legs up as she cackled.

Elise picked up a cushion and whacked Tempest with it.

"Oi!" Tempest hit her back with another cushion. "Don't be hitting me. You're the little sis. You fi know your place."

"Stop! I only hit you once."

Tempest stopped after the fifth hit. "Seriously though, she knew you were lying?"

"She didn't say it, but it was written all over her face. You know I can't lie."

Tempest raised her plucked, but thick, eyebrows.

"I can't."

"I guess."

"Maybe it was intuition. She's gotten to know me. She knows Ma by face and—" She grimaced, breaking eye contact quickly.

Tempest's exaggerated exhale confirmed her disdain.

"Anyway, she knows I'm not the type to go from one guy to the next. She must've put it all together."

"Parents know their children; she had to know deep down that her son's gay. Shit, *I* knew!" Tempest ran her fingers through her braids.

"But you've hardly been around him."

"Fine, I suspected. If I suspected without being around him that much, then his parents had to know."

"That makes sense. Maybe they did know deep down. Maybe they hoped it was a phase."

"Phase my batty."

"We know that, but maybe they didn't. Not in their family."

Tempest stopped playing with her braids. "How was Aiden with everything? How did he feel about his girlfriend possibly cheating on him? Was he pissed?"

"That's the thing. He seemed confused more than anything. Just quiet. Almost like he didn't know how to react. Even after we got on the bus and I let him know that I wasn't cheating, he didn't seem . . ."

"What?"

"Bothered. It was strange."

"He must've been bothered."

"I don't know. To be honest, if I did cheat, it wouldn't feel like cheating."

"Why not?" Tempest suddenly looked like she was anticipating the news of someone's death.

"I just don't know if . . ."

"Spit it out!"

"Don't worry, Temp. If Aiden isn't the one, then so be it."

"Why wouldn't he be?"

"Calm down. It's not like I've been seeing him that long."

Tempest got up from the sofa then went to the window in a trance-like state.

"Tempest?" Elise joined her sister by the window.

"He's just so fine, has that swag, has a steady job. Guys like him don't come around often."

"True." She tried to look Tempest in the face; Tempest kept turning away. "But we're probably better off as friends— Why are you breathing like that?"

Tempest stomped to the other side of the front room, putting her waist-length braids into a bun.

"I know you introduced us, but some things aren't meant to be."

"But . . ." Tempest finally turned around when she finished with her hair, a smile on her face. "He kissed you, didn't he?"

"Yeah, but . . ."

"But what?"

"The kiss was weird."

"How?"

Elise shook her head, couldn't find the right words.

"Couples kiss. Couples fuck."

She put her hands up, her palms facing Tempest.

"Don't know why you're making that face, like fucking is a disease. It's the most beautiful thing."

"I'm sure that's something I'll know when I'm married."

"Come on, Els, most people our age aren't virgins."

"I don't care about most people. Last I checked, Yvonne Orji is still a virgin, and she's in her thirties."

"Well, something's up there, especially with that surname."

"Her surname isn't even pronounced *orgy*."

"Forget her. What if Aiden's the one and you give up on him? What if he's your only shot?"

"I doubt he is."

"Why?"

"Don't get worked up."

"I'm not!"

Elise jumped.

Tempest laughed nervously, her braided bun threatening to collapse, as she walked over to Elise. "Don't give up on him yet."

"Whatever happens, happens. It really looks like we're better off as friends. Girlfriends even."

Tempest snarled. "Girlfriends?"

Before she could respond, Lianne La Havas's "Unstoppable" emanated from her jeans pocket. Had to be Shannon. She scraped her knuckles as she tried to get her phone out. Lianne had finished verse one. That meant plenty of rings. It would go to voicemail, or Shan would soon hang up. She could see more of the phone as Lianne became louder and clearer. Heart racing, she yanked the phone out then answered so quickly that she didn't even process the identity of the true caller until it was too late.

"Ma."

Tempest humphed then stormed out of the front room.

"Nice to hear you too."

"Sorry, Ma. I thought it was someone else."

"Nearly most me hang up. Everything alright?"

"Yeah. Just my friend. Having a rough time."

"Hush. Anyway, me just call to tell you me make the appointment for tomorrow."

"What time?"

"Twelve."

No lie in after all. "Well, thanks. I'll see if I can—"

Tempest was putting her tights back on.

"Ma, hold on." Elise held the phone against her chest. "Tempest, where are you going?"

Tempest put her almost knee-high boots back on. "To see Carl."

Elise flinched.

Tempest noticed, judging by her frown.

Elise paused.

Just as she'd thought—taps on the window. "It's still raining."

"I know, but right now I need dick, and not the electric kind."

"Tempest!" Elise pointed at the phone.

Tempest smiled. She knew what she was doing. "See you later." She left the flat.

Elise sighed and brought the phone back to her ear. "I'm back, Ma."

"Vulgar bitch."

"Ma, don't say that."

"No manners to rahtid."

"Ma, please."

"Just make sure you don't get here late."

"Whatever." She didn't mean to say that.

"Beg your pardon?"

"I won't be late."

"Awoh! See you ah morning."

"Bye."

Ma and her cantankerous ways. This thing between her and Tempest needed to end. If anything, it was about time Ma treated Tempest a bit better. She owed her that much.

They all did.

Maybe Elise more than her ma and their father. No, not maybe, definitely. Moving in together, bonding like full sisters, rather than the half-sisters her ma kept reminding her they were, was a start.

She jumped at the sudden music. Lianne La Havas. One hand on her chest, as if some energy could be transmitted to get her heart to behave, she looked at her phone screen and froze. *Number withheld.* No such calls for ages, not since . . . No, she'd changed her number. Couldn't be anything funny. Probably the wrong number. Her hand was shaking anyway, cautiously reaching for the phone.

By the time her index finger brushed against the screen, the phone stopped ringing. She couldn't take her eyes off it. It was bound to ring again at any moment.

But minutes passed and there was nothing. No noise except for her breathing, banging from next door, and rain tapping the window. The pressure in her chest eased. Wrong number it must've been. She released tension through a deep exhale and got up.

She was about to turn on the television when the phone rang again. *Number withheld.* Deep breath.

She answered the phone before Lianne's vocals joined the instruments. "Hello?"

Nothing except rustling and knocking.

"Hello?"

Still no response.

She hung up.

The "Unstoppable" ringtone didn't take long to return.

She slid her finger across the screen, underneath *Number withheld*, and waited a few moments before bringing the phone to her ear. "Hello?"

There was a familiar sound on the other end now—deliberately exaggerated breathing.

Her own breaths became short as she took the phone from her ear. All she had done to convince herself that history wasn't repeating itself, that changing her number hadn't been in vain. The breathing on the other end dashed her hopes.

She put the phone on loudspeaker and rested it on the coffee table. "Hello?"

"Don't hang up on me again, bitch!"

She gasped, backed away. The caller, his voice disguised, was about to come out of the phone to torment her, trap her, like the girl coming out of the television in those *The Ring* movies. Her calves bumped into the sofa. She fell on it.

"I'm coming for you. That's a fucking promise." *Beep.*

Everything was swimming. She wrapped her cardigan tighter around her body, heart racing, throat tight.

The phone rang again. She didn't budge.

3 / Shannon II
Out the window

Pain was plastered across the left side of Shannon's face. It burned just above his eyebrows. Sucking his busted lip didn't make the stinging go away. Just left a metallic taste in his mouth.

"Open the raasclaat door!" his dad said.

Heart pounding, hands shaking, he adjusted his jacket and shirt and tie, fabric inflaming the wounds from the belt. "W-what's going on, Dad? Why's my stuff packed?"

The answer to that question was obvious. Buying time, like someone held at gunpoint knowing that their time to meet their maker was imminent, but delaying things anyway.

"Open the door make we finish claat you!"

He dashed to his desk where his phone was charging. He pressed the power button. Nothing.

Banging on the door.

He stared at it as if it were about to burst open, then he glanced at his phone, willing it to charge faster.

More banging.

"Dad, stop!"

"Stop calling me that! Just hurry up and bring your funny self out here!"

He clasped his hands over his head, pressing down hard, as if that would wake him from a nightmare, but the banging continued. Relentless. He looked around the room, seeing everything and nothing at once. Of all the books scattered on the floor, most were ones his parents weren't supposed to know he owned.

His father grunted as he used more force.

Another phone check—still not enough power. No let up with the pounding on the door or of his heart. "Dad, I said stop!"

"Stop calling me that!" His father grunted amidst what sounded like kicks, making the key vibrate.

"Hello. Police please. . . . My parents . . . they're trying to kill me. . . . Shannon Horne. . . . 50 Glyn Road, E5 0JD. . . . Hurry!"

The banging stopped.

He heaved the chest of drawers to the door anyway, the legs squealing along the hardwood floor. He checked his phone, pressing the power button for the screen to light up. Still nothing.

The banging had stopped, but he wasn't out of danger. They were still on the other side of the door, probably plotting, pacing, waiting. He had to think of a way out of this before they realised he'd been bluffing. Couldn't be long to go before the phone had enough power. He needed to call his uncle to come and get him. He needed to pack first.

He went through all the drawers, each up to half-full. Same for the wardrobe.

The black bags downstairs.

"Me know we shoulda send him back home," his father said. *"Him woulda come back right."*

They'd actually considered sending him to Jamaica, as if that would fix him.

As if he needed fixing.

"You and that bitch lied!" His mum sounded like she was about to cry again.

He took out a wad of cash he'd stashed in one of his desk drawers. "Don't call her that!"

Either his mother didn't hear him or she pretended not to. *"Girlfriend? What a trial. Take we make poppyshow. She must be in that nastiness too. Imagine, Leroy. Imagine all the other lies him tell."*

"Bwoi, you let man touch you?"

He ignored that question, went to get the suitcase on top of his wardrobe. He hauled it down, dust showering him, invading his mouth and eyes. He chucked all kinds of footwear inside, scooped up toiletries and dropped them in there too. He extended his rucksack and stuffed some folders in there, with his laptop, then chucked the rest in the suitcase.

"Answer me, bwoi!"

He stumbled to the phone and pressed the power button. Still nothing. Could've thrown the useless thing against the cream wall.

"The police ah take them time."

He froze.

"Hold on a minute. . . . Him never call them. Him phone switch off."

His heart rate must've reached a new record in that moment. His dad had tried to call him. Another button squeeze. The screen lit up. He let out a deep breath.

The banging resumed.

"Open the bloodclaat door!"

He pulled out a duffel bag from under his bed, and watched his Samsung, waiting for the home screen to appear. He couldn't leave his E. Lynn Harris and Eric Jerome Dickey books behind, but he couldn't take so many bags at once. Then there were the ones downstairs. This was no longer his home, but there was no way he could get out of the house, unless his parents got tired and

28

eventually fell asleep. If they were sprawled out right in front of his bedroom door, he could step over them then creep down the stairs.

Maybe the banging on the door was making him think like an idiot, or the frying pan had knocked sense out of him.

The home screen, finally. Countless alerts. Some of them were probably from Elise. He would get back to her later. Had to try his uncle first. He brushed the screen with his trembling fingers, going way past *Uncle Lionel*. When he found *Uncle Lionel* again, he tapped it. The pounding seemed louder with each ring.

"Wha'gwaan, stranger?"

"Uncle Lionel!"

"Shannon?"

"I need you to come and get me."

"Can't hear you through the bangarang."

The furniture was rumbling.

"Shannon!"

"I'll explain later! Just come quickly!"

Rip. A slice of light hit the desk. The door was slashed, just above the chest of drawers.

He looked at the window then shuddered. "The f-front door should b-be unlocked. Go all the way to the garden. The b-back door key should be in the latch or on the ledge. Bring P-Peter if you want. Just don't—"

More rips. More slices of light. Thicker slices.

"Shannon!"

"Hurry! Dunno what they're gonna do to me!"

"Why would they . . . Me soon come."

Rips.

"Got to go!"

"Shan—"

Shit. What if his uncle didn't remember the address? He would phone him ag—

Light struck his shoes. Whatever his dad was using to rip the door down would soon be used on him. He ran to the chest of drawers and pressed his weight against it. Vibrations with each bang. His dad was determined; he'd always been that way. It would soon be the three of them in the room. What they'd said ages ago when they'd accused him of staring at a guy too long and hard, that he better not do it again, or else they'd claat him to death . . . they'd meant it.

Movement in the window startled him. Just his reflection. Blinds still up.

The window.

He rushed to his desk, snatched his phone from the lead and stuffed it in his jacket pocket. He went to the tilt and turn window, turned the handle as far as it needed to go so that the window opened like a door. Wind and rain accosted his face, drowning out the banging instantly. He peered out, his face turned away from the rain. Had to squint. Grabbing the ledge with his right hand and shielding his face with his left arm, he looked as far out and down, and left and right as possible.

A glance back at the door. The furniture barring the door was still shaking.

Only a matter of time.

He poked his head, at an angle, out of the window again, the wind and rain drowning out the pounding. One floor above ground. Doable, especially with the grass, most of it shadowed, and his padded clothing. And the pipe was right there. He heaved his suitcase, rested part of it on the ledge for a moment, then pushed it out some more. He had to let it down slowly, by the handle, so that it wouldn't have far to drop, but he couldn't take the weight for long. It was pulling him out, the wind hurling rain at him. He let go before the suitcase could pull him, head first, out of the window.

It had really come to this. He'd really just thrown his suitcase out of the frigging window.

Throat tight, tears were blurring his vision again. He covered his mouth, muffling his sobs. Tears hit his shoes and the hardwood floor as he picked up the duffel bag. Lighter than the suitcase. All he had to do was—

Tumbling from the door nearly made him look there. Looking would delay things. His periphery was enough. Furniture legs scraped the hardwood floor as more light entered the room. He threw the duffel bag out. The same with his rucksack. If his laptop or anything else got damaged, so be it. He stuck his left leg out of the window, then straddled the ledge. It was bad enough that it wasn't made for straddling, but the miserable weather and his distressed heart made it hard to stop swaying. All he could do was hold on tight and concentrate on getting down before his parents got hold of him.

Something made him look before he could stop himself.

"You lose your mind fi true." His father was limping towards him, hammer in hand, his mother stumbling right behind.

His father raised the hammer. He wouldn't do it. No way.

Everything that had happened downstairs, minutes earlier . . . yes, he frigging would.

He leaned into his room and pulled the window with his fingers. He pulled it until it was jamming his thigh. All he had to do was hold on to the handle for as long as— Shit. No frigging outside handle. As if any window would have one.

Something hit his shoe, his ankle, his shin. He flinched each time. He flinched until he went too far to the left, his distressed heart and tingling stomach torturing him as he nearly fell.

So much happening—moving the leg stuck inside his room to dodge his father's hammering, preparing for sudden gusts, cold rain pricking his exposed skin. A miracle he hadn't fallen—yet. He was going to end up hurt somehow, either from falling or being hammered senseless.

He lost his grip of the window. His mum was helping his dad pull the window away. They were about to do something, either push him off or pull him in to finish him off. His mum reached for him. He pushed her with all the strength of one hand as he gripped the window ledge with the other. She fell back into the desk.

The hammer was raised. He kicked his father, who grunted and went down.

The impact forced his own body backwards and down. No ledge underneath his sore backside all of a sudden. Felt like his heart was about to fall out of his chest. He flailed his arms and clawed at cold air and raindrops. His stomach dropping, heart at its limit, he grabbed something with one hand, slammed into bricks.

He was dangling, had the ledge by the fingers of one hand, his left hand, his weaker side. He closed his eyes as the rain hit his face, tried to figure out which direction was easier to look in. Didn't seem to matter, with the wind choosing the wrong moments to pick up. All he could do was try to keep still. The moment the wind died down, he tried to get his other hand up. . . . Too damn hard. Bad enough that the ledge was cold and slippery, and raindrops, sharp like icicles, were pelting his fingers. He turned his head one way, towards the pipe. Rain crashed into his face, made him turn his head from it. He squinted and tried again. Just enough light struck the black pipe, which blended with the claw-shaped shadows of moving trees. It was too far away though, impossible to reach. Too much movement would make him drop. His arm was aching and his fingers were going numb; dropping was inevitable. The wind and rain were unpredictable, kept him from assessing the distance to the garden. Maybe he could make it, like Sansa and Theon. They'd definitely jumped from a higher point. And those crouching tigers and hidden dragons had always landed on their feet.

What the fuck was he on about? This was real. A drop would hurt. Just a question of how much.

Movement above, in his periphery. His father was looming.

A squealing door then footsteps below. His mother must've made it to the garden, ready to finish him off, if his father didn't do it first. Shouts from the garden. Didn't sound like his mother. Maybe the wind and rain had something to do with that.

Something gripped his wrist. He strained to look up. His father was trying to pull him in, would rather kill him with his bare hands than let him fall.

His heart was trying to escape his chest. He couldn't let his dad kill him.

He writhed and writhed until he was out of his father's clutches.

Until he wasn't holding onto anything.

A scream from the garden. Again, it didn't sound like his mother.

Or maybe it was his own scream as heavy rain battered him on the way down. It seemed his body was falling too fast for his insides.

Then he landed hard.

4 / Tempest I
Too bad mind

The wind and rain were fucking with Tempest. She held her Burberry umbrella one way then the other as she battled the wind, only for rain to make its way through her chiffon head wrap to her braids and skin. Her new D&G handbag was getting wet too. She stomped the way she wanted to stomp on the asshole she was about to meet, probably stepping where there'd once been spit and shit. She cursed the wet night air and the vehicles that splashed her as they sped by, but she was almost deaf to her own voice, nature and her boots drowning it out.

She raised her umbrella, then squinted and turned her head far enough to avoid getting rain in her eyes but not too much that she couldn't see ahead. A lamp post craned over the bus stop, its light bright. The shed looked like a glass that was overflowing. Hard to tell if anyone was there. She sped up, the shed's interior becoming more visible, the red seat blurred beyond the wet glass.

She lost her balance. Unstable slab of concrete. Splashed a-fucking-gain. She gritted her teeth, trudged the last few metres to the bus stop, filthy water soaking her tights.

She closed her umbrella once she reached shelter. No one else around. The inclined seat looked clean enough. She sat down, unzipped her boots and stretched her tights, giving her skin temporary relief from clamminess. She pulled her jacket tighter around her body and rocked back and forth. *Eastway Local Express* was right behind. Maybe it was warm in there, but she wasn't in the mood to be hit on by those ugly, fat, mashed-up, could-barely-speak-English fuckers.

Cars were passing, heading towards, or coming from, Wick Road, but none showed any signs of pulling over. Traffic was running smoothly on the main road ahead otherwise. Fuck him for being late. She would show him.

Another car turned from Wick Road. Between the windscreen wipers putting in work and the rain having its way with the windows, the driver's face was a blur. The familiar blue Volkswagen Polo was slowing down though. It had to be him.

He stopped the car on the other side of the road. This meeting was his fault. She wasn't going to cross the road to get to him. She motioned for him to come to her. He did a turn-in-the-road.

Not bothering to re-open her umbrella, she cursed as she braved the few steps from the bus stop to the car. She had to leave her warm, dry flat for this meeting, a meeting that would've been avoided if he'd been doing his job properly.

She cut her eyes at him as she entered, then she got comfortable in the front passenger seat. Lines were in his forehead though. Cussing her through his facial expression. Fucking cheek. He never showed her those lines when they were cool. He was on her shit list now, with his funny self. Finest batty man she'd ever laid eyes on—finest man, full stop—even with the unkempt beard. Damn waste.

"You closing the door or what?"

She jumped, putting his good looks to the back of her mind. She rested the umbrella by her feet and kept her handbag in her lap, then she slammed the door.

"Shit! You trying to mash up my car?"

"Maybe."

He kissed his teeth. "Hurry up and buckle up. Can't stay here."
She complied with a huff.

"You must be trying to fuck up my seat belt too."

"Get a move on! I have a real man to see later."

He kissed his teeth again and stomped hard on the gas pedal, making her lurch as far forward as the seat belt allowed then bang her head against the headrest.

"Watch it! And where the fuck are you going?"

The way the car was positioned once he stopped it, no other cars could pass in either direction.

"I need to find parking."

"Not that way. Why do you think I told you to meet me so far from the flat? You want her to see us? Go the other way." She pointed.

He was aggressive with the pedals as he reversed the car then sped to the T-junction between Eastway, Wick Road and Chapman Road. Drivers beeped at him for not making his mind up. He beeped back, then he muttered something.

"What was that?"

"Nothing."

Headlights of an oncoming vehicle dazzled her. Must've affected him too.

"Don't know why you're upset," she said.

He turned onto Chapman Road, then he took the first exit at the mini-roundabout onto Trowbridge Road, slowing the car down, looking for a parking space. He didn't have to go far to find one.

"Let's make this quick." She took off her seat belt. "Taken up enough of my time already."

He turned off the engine. "*You* called *me*, so what the fuck is up?" His jaw was clenched, and his nostrils flared.

"She isn't sure of you as a boyfriend. And why would she be? Three months and you still haven't fucked the bitch."

His left leg was shaking.

"Get the ball rolling. If I don't see progress soon, I'll play the recording to your fam." She leaned into him. "You know I will."

His full lips trembled. "Bitch!"

She leaned back a little then slapped him square on his lips, making his head reverberate against his headrest. She couldn't have made better contact. He put his fingers on his lips. He was bleeding.

A blow to her face disorientated her out of nowhere. Her nose was suddenly runny, needed blowing. She rushed to put her fingers underneath her nostrils to stop the flow. She didn't have to look; there was only one explanation for the sudden stream.

She was losing her mind with each ragged breath and her heart was getting out of control. His busted lip needed busting some more.

Something clicked as she took off her jacket. She looked in the direction of the sound. He'd unbuckled his seat belt. He knew her too well.

She repositioned herself and tucked her handbag behind her back, as he unzipped his jacket. He started to quicken his pace the moment she found her umbrella with a brush of her fingers, as if he knew what was about to happen.

She screamed as she unleashed on him.

He shielded his face with his arms.

She hammered away at him with the umbrella handle and her fist, the drenched weapon getting her wet. "Move your fucking arms!"

She changed hands. It worked at first, getting him twice in the head with the umbrella and once in his side with her fist, amidst his desperate grunts. He caught up with the pattern of blows after that.

"I'm . . . gonna . . . fuck you up . . . bitch!" she said as she struck and he blocked.

He roared, took his chance and stopped shielding his face, deciding to unleash punches.

She kept hitting, but he was the personal trainer, bigger, stronger, fitter. It was like hitting a brick wall that hit back. His speed. His timing. She was the one with a weapon, yet she had to retreat backwards as he punched his way to her side of the car, until she couldn't go back any further.

She was too predictable with her movements. He managed to shackle her wrists with his massive hands.

"Get . . . off me!" She kicked him in the gut.

He grunted and grimaced from the blow, and his grip loosened, but only momentarily. He gritted his teeth as he squeezed her wrists and trapped her legs under his body.

"You're . . . hurting . . . me!"

"Then let . . . go of the . . . fucking . . . umbrella!"

"No!" All she could do was twist the umbrella around in her fingers so that the handle dug at his thumb. "Just get off me!"

He kissed his teeth then banged her hand against the glove compartment, their grunts drowning out the knocking. The pain made her drop the umbrella.

She had nothing. She was at his mercy, trapped, her hand throbbing and wrists shackled. He looked like he could go all night, his eyes almost a fiery-brown, his face frozen in a menacing glare, shiny with sweat. He was breathing heavily, his breath stifling her nostrils and tickling her lips. She looked around for some way, any way, to free herself. Nothing but steam on the windows and a flood of light with each passing vehicle.

"For . . . the last time . . . get off me!"

"No fucking chance!"

She flinched when his spit sprayed her.

That was it.

She spat at him. She managed to get herself too. At least it was her own spit. He wiped his zaddy beard. Her chance to fuck him up some more. She slapped him repeatedly until she could move a leg from underneath him. She kicked him off her completely, back to the offside. But she wasn't done yet.

She climbed over the handbrake and was about to straddle him when he kicked her, right in her titty. The woman-beater grabbed her chiffon-covered braids before she could recover, undoing her bun. He dragged her until her head was in his lap. Anyone passing would've thought she was giving him head. She thrashed like a bull determined to get the rider the fuck off her, but the handbrake was digging her hip and the steering wheel restricting her left arm. Her hair was on the verge of being ripped from her scalp. She freed her arm from under the steering wheel then flailed both arms blindly, one knocking parts of the dashboard, the other near his face. She raked her fingers through facial hair, and then something wet. Could've been his lips, maybe his tongue. He was moving too much for her to bury her nails in his fucking face.

He was pulling harder, and her wrap had shifted and reached just above her eyebrows. Her skirt was twisted, way up her thighs. The way she was flailing her legs about the nearside she might as well have been drowning in the Thames. Couldn't get them anywhere near him. Needed to be a contortionist. Fuck his face. She clawed his hand, digging right into bone. He wailed. Her hair was finally free from his grip. She shot up and backed into the nearside as he reached for her. She kicked him in his balls. Her foot was bootless.

He grimaced as he grabbed himself. "Bloodclaat . . . *bitch*!"

She had to give him one last punch, confirmation that she'd won the fight. And another one, for calling her a bitch again. The one before hadn't connected properly anyway.

She slumped against the nearside door, her heavy breathing matching his. "Have you . . . forgotten . . ." She patted the top of her head, as if the stinging would magically disappear. ". . . who the fuck . . . I am?"

He was still holding onto his balls as he gingerly got himself upright. He snarled at her. "The fuck's wrong with you?"

"The fuck's wrong with *you*?" She raised her batty off the seat, head pressed against the headrest, as she adjusted her skirt. "Putting your fucking hands on me."

He let go of his privates and ran his fingers over his scratched hand. He gave her a look only the baddest people could give, a hideous frown, like he was possessed by the devil. She stared back, giving whatever evil look she could. He looked away eventually. Maybe he remembered she was the one in charge.

He wound his window down, bringing in the sounds of the wind and distant traffic, and stuck his head out.

He hawked up phlegm and spat.

She flinched. "Nasty shithouse."

His head still stuck out the window, he gave her the middle finger.

"Fuck you back!"

A chill was seeping in, spreading over her chest. She looked down. Her blouse was undone. She felt for the top button then the next. They'd come off. There were blotches of blood on her blouse. A shadow too. No matter how much she shifted, it wouldn't move. She ran her hand over it. It was the mark from where he'd kicked her. Motherfucker. She looked further down her body.

"Look what you've done to my fucking tights." She filled some newly-formed holes in her tights with her fingers.

"You made me leave my yard for a fucking fight?"

She flipped down the vanity mirror then grimaced at her reflection. She had blood for a moustache. She rubbed it. Didn't go completely. Her chiffon head wrap was ripped and her hair looked like it had been braided by a toddler. She'd only had the braids in for two weeks, and they were meant to last at least until Sunday, her mum's birthday.

What would've been her mum's birthday.

Something dropped on her lap. A pack of wet wipes.

"You look like shit."

"Not as bad as you." She snatched out a wipe and scraped the blood off her skin.

He rolled his window almost all the way up. "What's this all about?"

"You're fucking it all up. She thinks your relationship isn't going anywhere. Your gayness is coming through."

He let out a deep breath like air was trapped in his throat. "I ain't—"

"Gay? Yeah, keep telling yourself that. Anyway, she knows something's off."

"Did she say?"

"No, but she suspects."

"How do you know?"

"I just do."

He cut his eyes at her then said, "Why you doing this to her?"

"Don't worry about that. Just do what you need to do to keep me from outing you."

"This is pure fuckery."

She quickly turned her head, igniting a jolt of pain along her neck. She grabbed the back of it. "When Carl finds out what you just did to me . . ."

"Bring him come."

"I'll tell him that."

"Elise doesn't deserve this."

She turned her head, slowly this time, until Aiden was clearer in the corner of her eye. "You have no idea."

"Bullshit!"

"She's evil!"

He muttered something as he waved her off.

"She is."

"No way she's worse than you."

She'd thought that most of her life, would've kept thinking that if not for what she'd overheard months ago. "Just hurry up and shove your dick inside her."

"You're sick."

"Sick?"

"Yeah. As fuck!"

"That bitch is sick! Because of her, I have no mother, and—"

Her expression must've been betraying her because his eyes had become slits.

"What? . . . She died when you were little. Or was that a lie too?"

"Course it wasn't!"

"What the fuck you mean then?"

This was too much. She'd shared more than she was ever supposed to.

"What's Elise got to do with—?"

"Just stop!" She put a hand on her forehead. It was getting hot, despite the air coming in.

Aiden grabbed her. "What's going—?"

She snatched herself out of his clutches. "Nothing for you to worry about. Just fuck her real good." She turned her head slowly again and looked at him through the corner of her eye.

Aiden opened his mouth to speak but changed his mind. He shook his head instead.

They let silence settle, Aiden probably rueing the day he'd met her.

All she'd wanted from him was friendship at first, even after their sexual encounter. It had been for fun, a test to see if he could make her come. He'd passed with flying colours. Face, body and dick . . . ten, ten, ten. Aiden would've been hers if he hadn't revealed his sexual fluidity to her. They would've remained cool if not for what she'd overheard Elise, their father, and Elise's shithouse mother discuss. Maybe she would've even sat on his humungous dick again for old time's sake.

Worst of all, she would've still been under the illusion that Elise was an angel, the better daughter.

"She's your fucking sister!"

She jumped out of the past. "Stop calling her that!"

"Think this through—"

"I have." *And this is only the beginning.*

"Come on, Tempest, just stop . . . whatever this is." His tone was soft but desperate.

"Aiden, if you don't do what I want, I'll tell your family everything about you. Don't risk losing your family just because you think Elise doesn't deserve it."

Aiden kissed his teeth.

"In a way, I'm doing you a favour."

"A favour?"

"Yeah. You don't want anyone to know that you're gay."

"Stop saying I'm . . . *that*."

"Fine, you don't want anyone to know that you're *not straight*, so what's wrong with having a beard?"

A moment went by, then he flared his nostrils.

"Funny you know what a beard is."

He rubbed his hand over his face, flinching as he touched his cut lip.

Good thing he wasn't out.

"You need to fix this, Aiden. The next time I ask Elise about you, I want to see her blush. I know what you're packing and what you can do with it, so I don't know what the hold up is."

Aiden frowned. "How do you know we ain't . . . ?"

"Don't give me that. I know she's not fucking."

He sighed. "You'd really have your own sister—"

"Stop calling her that!"

"—*half*-sister lose her virginity to *me*?"

"Yeah. She'll only lose her virginity to you if she's fallen."

"So out of all the ways you could ruin her, this is what you came up with? And you've brought *me* into this fuck-shit?"

"Yeah." He'd find out the best she could do later, though it was looking more and more impossible since he hadn't fucked the bitch yet.

He looked at her as if she were crazy.

Maybe she was. Desperate too.

She put on her jacket, gathered her things and opened the door. "I promise, as long as you get her to fall for you and open her legs, your secret will be safe with me. I'll even destroy the recording. Then you can dump her."

Aiden stared at her. No forehead lines this time. The staring alone was venom enough. She hated it. It was like the ungrateful clients to whom she gave makeovers and undeserved politeness when she really meant *fuck you, bitch.*

She opened the door and swivelled her legs out of the car. One leg felt different from the other.

The boot.

Before she could turn back around, strong hands pushed her. Nothing to clutch but air and raindrops. She fell on the grimy ground. Her brand new D&G handbag was tainted, its contents spilling out, drowning in filthy puddles. She struggled to her feet, squinting against the wind and rain, as the door slammed.

The motherfucker still had her boot.

Aiden did a screeching turn-in-the-road. She tip-toed on her bootless foot, bringing it level with the other. Aiden opened his window some more and chucked the boot at her. It hit her neck, forcing a dry cough. He sped off, taunting her with a long, loud beep.

She opened her umbrella then checked her phone. A message from Carl. He'd made the prank call to Elise, but he was going to have to cancel. Emergency surgery. She took a moment to catch herself, to keep the words *fucking* and *liar* from settling in her mind, before thoughts of Elise and Aiden took over.

She put her boot upright and stretched her foot like a ballet dancer to get it in. Her supporting leg started to wobble, and a gust of wind yanked at her umbrella. She squealed as the cold rain attacked her face. She lost her balance and ended up on her batty again. She screamed Aiden's name in vain.

He was lucky she needed him.

5 / Aiden I
Dark place

The rain had held up. Aiden had been parked on Powerscroft Road for ages. He ran his hands slowly up and down the steering wheel, scratched hand still sizzling. Licking his bottom lip made the stinging worse. The spit was the worst part. That bitch had skimmed his beard, but even so . . . He had to stop her. He would stop her.

Somehow.

Pain was settling across his forehead. He must've been frowning most of the drive home. Fucking dickhead, trusting Tempest with his secret. There was no denying it—the bitch was good. That thing with her mum and Elise though . . . Tempest hadn't said shit like that to him before. The way she'd stopped herself, refusing to get into it . . . something was off. Bitch was shook. Getting to the bottom of that shit had to be his way out.

His grandma always said, just because someone looked good on the outside didn't mean they were good on the inside. Instead of heeding her warning, he told her that Tempest was different, that she was as nice as she looked. She seemed that way at first when they met in the gym and, unlike the rest of the clients, who gave zero fucks about the ring on his wedding finger, she wasn't checking for him like that, even though they ended up smashing.

He should've known something was up with her when she'd challenged him to fuck her after he'd made it clear he wasn't strictly clit, but they remained cool. She was genuine, the way she treated him, opening up about losing her mum young and being only two months older than Elise because their dad was smashing their mums at the same time. Elise this, Elise that.

And then things changed out of nowhere. That day Tempest called him, crying like crazy, saying she was done with Elise, and he asked her what was up and she couldn't tell him. Then asking him about his same-sex attraction again, as if he'd imagined telling her about it the first time. It was around that time things changed, when she turned into a cunt.

And what about Elise? They'd been going out—no other way to put it—for a few months. She seemed cool. Maybe she really wasn't, otherwise Tempest wouldn't have hated her.

Maybe Elise was a bitch too, and he just couldn't see it. Probably worse than Tempest. No need to feel bad about doing what Tempest wanted. Wasn't like he hadn't been with females before. They got him hard, so there was nothing to sweat about.

Who was he fooling? Elise hadn't done shit to him, no matter what she'd done to Tempest. Elise was her problem.

But the two of them were now *his* problem.

A passing car, its headlights on full beam, dazzled him back to the present. Pain kept him from moving properly as he got out of the car. No light was coming from any of the windows; they'd all gone to bed. He wouldn't have to explain his busted lip or the scratches on his hand.

The gate squeaked as he opened and closed it, as if it were cussing him for waking it up. He hobbled to the front door, his movements and the wind shaking the leaves of the plants on each side of the lawn, balls sensitive and arms throbbing from Tempest's onslaught. His movements activated the porch light. He unlocked one lock and then the other and slowly opened the door, ready to stop and change tactics in case it wailed. A sudden gust of wind snatched the door handle from his grip. The door slammed into the passage wall. He cussed, grabbed the door, jerked it shut then double-locked it.

The only light came from outside, straining through the front door's frosted glass.

Taking off his jacket was a hassle; he couldn't set his arms properly without the pain screaming at him. No problems getting off his trainers. Light from outside was striking his slippers. Didn't need any light for the coat rack or for going upstairs to his bedroom. Used to the layout of the house.

He crept up the stairs, holding onto the railings, creaks irritating him as they grew longer and louder. At the top, he stretched his arm as far to the right as he could to feel for the bathroom door. As soon as he found the door knob, someone shuffled. He spun around. Pain halted him. There was a moving outline of someone in the darkness. Scraping along the wall didn't last long before the light came on. He squinted.

"What you doing in the dark?" Ethan's voice was gruff, knife in hand, and he was squinting too.

Aiden turned around to hide his face. "A knife? Really?"

"Yeah. I keep telling you to turn the light on."

"Didn't wanna wake you lot."

"Thought you'd be back tomorrow . . . night cap with your girl."

He checked the time on his phone. Twelve-fifteen. "Well, technically it is tomorrow." He stepped into the bathroom. He couldn't let his brother see his face, and he wasn't up for talking about females.

"You know what I mean. Get any pussy?"

He shot around. "Watch your mouth. They"—he motioned at their grandfolks' room—"might hear you."

"Don't worry 'bout them. They're sleep— Bro, your lip's busted."

He quickly tucked his bottom lip in and turned his face to the bathroom.

No point hiding though. "Elise . . . When I was at Elise's, her fridge door slammed into my face. No biggie."

"As long as I don't have to fuck anyone up for jumping you, then—"

"Ethan, watch your mouth."

"Sorry. Can't help it sometimes. You cuss too."

Couldn't deny that.

"Guess I'm still piss—*mad*—after what happened earlier."

"What happened?"

"Some fag checked me out on the train."

Shock gripped him. He hoped it wasn't showing on his face.

"Can you believe it? Some batty man checked me out!"

"Alright, alright, enough!"

Ethan fell silent.

Aiden shook tension away. "For true?"

"For true."

"Look, don't sweat it. Coulda been worse."

Ethan frowned. "What could be worse than that?"

Another fucking hole. "Well, some man actually coming onto you."

"True, but I could've knocked him out."

He nearly asked why. "Just let it go. You probably won't see him again anyway."

"I guess. Just can't take this gay shit."

"Ethan, just go to sleep."

"Yeah. Did you double-lock the front door?"

"Yeah."

"Good. I'm going back to bed."

"Night, bro."

"I better not dream 'bout gay shit."

Maybe you should then wake up with come all over you. "Just let it go, man."

Ethan sighed.

"Night, bro."

"Good night, bro."

As soon as Ethan switched off the light he'd turned on, Aiden switched on the one in the bathroom. He closed the door with his back and leaned against it for a bit. *Batty man . . . gay shit . . .* Silence except for his breathing and the humming ventilator activated by the light. He clenched his fists and pounded his thighs.

After a while, he limped to the sink, washed his hands and bent down to let the cold water run along his lips. In spite of the stinging, he rubbed the bloodied part of his lip hard, as if rubbing Tempest out of his mind, his system . . .

Out of existence.

That was the only way to get rid of his problem. He had the physical ability to kill her. Could've strangled the bitch earlier.

Prison wasn't an option though. No one else in the family needed to be locked up. It was just the four of them now. He had his brother and grandfolks. No mum and no dad. There were relatives all over the place—from England to the West Indies— and cool people who weren't blood, but he needed his brother and grandfolks more than anything. And they needed him.

That night . . . He shook his head like a drill was making it vibrate, shook it till unwanted memories were lost deep in his brain.

He stared at his reflection then screwed his face up. What Tempest was doing was madness, but he couldn't let his family find out about him. Things were different now though. People were checked for saying offensive shit about gays. Not like years ago, when people got away with it. Even secondary school kids seemed different, more free and open, compared to when he was their age. That guy from school, bullied for being gay . . . he could've saved him from those motherfuckers. He should've.

He was doing it again, thinking too much, feeling things only a gay person was supposed to feel.

He wasn't gay. Never would be. Never, ever, ever.

He *did* like females. They still got him off. Doing what Tempest wanted, there was nothing to it. He'd been with females before. All he had to do was woo Elise, bed her then dump her. Simple as that.

SATURDAY

6 / Shannon III
His Fineness

The whispering wouldn't end. Couldn't tell where was it coming from. Nothing in sight. It was getting louder, following Shannon from his dreams to reality. The whispering became clearer.

"Shit! Me wake him."

That voice was familiar.

"Morning, Shannon."

He jumped up. His neck screamed for him to rub it.

"Rough night?"

His father was looming over him. He flailed his legs about, his heart racing, but they were trapped.

The blanket.

"Easy, man."

Recognition made his heart settle. They really looked alike, down to the receding hairlines, but his father was almost bald. His uncle had dreadlocks. They were hidden under a bulging wrap.

"Uncle Lionel . . . it's you."

"Then nuh mus'!"

The photograph in a silver frame standing in the centre of the glass coffee table; the photos dominating each cabinet shelf; the

Ghanaian artwork flanking a clock in the shape of Jamaica, a massive flatscreen mounted just below; the *The DL Chronicles* and *Noah's Arc* DVDs; the space; whites and creams washing over the room; plants that looked like miniature palm trees; the beige sofa bed he was on . . . It was all starting to make sense.

"You really look like—"

"Don't say it."

He yawned.

Uncle Lionel told him to get up then turned the sofa bed back into a sofa before they both sat down.

"Sleep good?"

He took in his uncle's cooking scent, yawned some more.

"Stupid question. And it look like me wake yuh."

He rubbed his sore neck. "Don't worry."

"Was just telling Pete fi get sinting. Me usually go with him, but . . . Yuh neck really ah hot yuh."

He let go of his neck. "Must've slept badly."

"Look like you forget what happen last night."

"Course I haven't forgotten falling out the window, but I didn't sleep properly."

"Me did watch you while you sleep. You did toss and turn to rahtid."

"Must've been dreaming. I don't think it was nice. I can't remember it—"

"Try not to. It did look bad, how yuh twist up yuhself."

Another yawn. "What time is it?"

His uncle leaned to the left, rummaged through his jeans pocket, then took out his phone. "Ten o'clock."

Shannon slapped his feet on the hardwood floor.

His uncle grabbed him by the shoulder. "Weh you think you going?"

"It's late."

"Late?"

"Yeah."

"But it's Saturday."

"I usually get up early, and . . . Where's my stuff?"

His uncle's face tightened up. "Behind us. This"—he motioned at the sofa—"is temporary. We'll fix up your room."

"Room?"

"Ee-hi. Should be ready by tomorrow, but you haffi use an inflatable bed for now. Hope that's alright. You soon feel at home, and— Do, nuh start bawl."

The acknowledgement of the tears made the pit in his stomach deeper, the lump in his throat bigger, the trembling sudden and uncontrollable.

"Don't do it, Shannon."

He turned his head to keep Uncle Lionel from seeing tears trickle down his cheeks.

"Shannon."

"I just—" His voice broke.

"Me seh you fi stop."

He wiped his tears, head still turned away. "How did this happen?"

"Me know how you feel."

He gazed at his uncle.

"Me come out long time." His uncle shook his head as memories came to him. "Things did worse back then."

Things had been hard enough for his parents. Must've been doubly hard for his black *and* gay uncle . . .

"Times not as hard now, compared to when me was your age. You never know, yuh parents might come to them senses."

Seriously?

Uncle Lionel must've been reading his mind; he gave a dismissive hand gesture.

Hell was going to have to freeze over first. If his uncle hadn't been close to Glyn Road when he called him, and if not for fate being on his side when he bumped into his uncle and took his number those few years ago . . .

"Me nuh see Leroy this long time till yesterday, but me know him. Me did always wonder if him righted—although people did wonder the same 'bout me—but me sure him was going pull you in."

No consolation, no matter how he looked at it—if his dad had tried to make him lose his grip, then that was attempted murder; if his dad had tried to pull him in, it was probably so he could hammer him senseless.

His uncle shook his head. "The X-ray was fine. What a good thing not one part of you mash up. Not even a sprain."

"I was lucky. Fell right on the mud. If it hadn't rained . . ."

He flinched at the memory of the instant he'd hit the ground. Lying there, eyes closed to the rain, bracing for the onset of pain, paralysed from not knowing if moving would've made his bones crumble, paralysed by the quick footsteps of his mum, who was sure to finish him off, only to open his eyes a little when something tickled his cheek—Uncle Lionel's dreadlocks.

"Me well want go over there and beat them backside."

"I know."

"Well, you have me and Peter now, nuh true?"

Peter's smile—which made him look more like Colin Jackson than he already did—in the photo with Uncle Lionel, on the coffee table, was welcoming, wider than Uncle Lionel's, like he was echoing what Uncle Lionel had said.

"I just don't know what I'm gonna do. Doesn't feel real. Things were fine in the morning, but then in the evening . . ."

"Maybe it needed to happen."

He frowned.

"Living a lie like that drive you crazy."

"But it wasn't supposed to happen yet."

"Maybe it was, Shan. Remember, me tell yuh from time fi make sure yuh prepare."

Jill Scott's "Prepared" came to him. He hummed the chorus. His uncle joined in soon after, singing the words. Sounded like Uncle Lionel needed to clear is throat.

"Wah sweet yuh?"

He sucked his lips in, but his cheeks were widening.

"Me dare yuh fi seh me can't sing." His uncle bumped him in the shoulder.

One look at his uncle's cantankerous expression and he couldn't contain his laughter any longer.

His uncle kept poking him in his side until he nearly fell off the sofa.

"OK, OK! Stop!" He continued laughing amidst the pokes.

Uncle Lionel chuckled then said, "Seriously, Shannon, are you prepared? Even a likkle?"

"What do you mean?"

"Can you cook, clean . . . ? Suppose smaddy kill me and Peter, could you take care of yuhself?"

Uncle Lionel and his morbid ways.

"You haffi find yuhself, be a man. It's a tough world, and it nah go get easier, being black and gay."

Even after all this, being called *gay* was going to take some getting used to.

"Go upstairs sort yuhself out. Breakfast soon ready."

The sizzling and familiar smells kicked up Shannon's appetite.

"Good timing." Uncle Lionel put a plate next to the stove, and napkin-wrapped cutlery on the round, tan brown table for four. "Guess what me make."

"Ackee and saltfish?"

"You soon look like ackee and saltfish."

Uncle Lionel took the lid off the frying pan and stirred with such energy that the food threatened to spill over, but it never did. "It's ready. A whole heap deh yah. Yuh hand them clean?"

"Yeah."

Uncle Lionel pulled out a seat for Shannon then handed him some butter and a plate of fried dumplings.

"Uncle Lionel, I can't manage all this."

"Them fi the three of we. Peter soon come. Just butter them fi me."

"You waited for me? Peter left without having anything?"

"No, me nyam a slice of bread, and him probably have crackers. We do *Insanity* together first thing ah morning, leave the heavy stuff till later."

Something scratched at the front door as a forkful of food was primed for Shannon's mouth, the steam kissing his lips. Scratching soon became clicking.

"Soon come." Uncle Lionel rushed out then came back with Sainsbury's bags.

Peter followed, put more bags down then left the kitchen for the toilet.

He came back, put groceries away, made himself a plate and sat at the table, to Shannon's left, the scent of the manuka honey and milk hand soap he'd used dancing. "How you feeling, Shannon?"

He sighed and shrugged.

Peter massaged his shoulder. Uncle Lionel grabbed his other shoulder. The combined strength of their hands was overwhelming. Couldn't have gotten up if he'd tried.

"It's tough, but you haffi push through. You have your master's fi finish."

Master's. He grimaced.

"You've come so far. You have to get it done."

"I know that, but . . . it's a lot. Dunno if I'm coming or going. Some of my things are still at ho—I mean, where I used to live."

"Like we said last night, this is your home now." Peter gave an encouraging smile. "When we leaving, Lionel?"

"When we eat done."

"Leaving to go where?"

Peter avoided eye contact, and Uncle Lionel looked coy all of a sudden.

"Where are you going?"

"*We're* going to your house to get the rest of your things."

His fork crashed to his plate, and his heart galloped.

"Shannon, the sooner we do this, the better. When you nyam done, call yuh parents. Tell them we soon come."

"I c-can't do—"

"Yes, you can. We'll be there with you."

"But there's a lot—"

"It's fine. We'll use a lorry."

"A lorry?"

"Yes, your wardrobe, chest of—"

"They won't let me have them."

"Nuh fi yuh sinting dem?" Wild eyes and Jamaican patois. His uncle was just like his father whenever he was no mood for games, except the latter usually delayed his menacing expression.

"I've had them for years."

"And?"

"They paid for everything."

Uncle Lionel rubbed his forehead, and Peter sighed.

"Even most of my clothes, they paid for. I only ever paid a bill here, a bill there."

Uncle Lionel closed his eyes, as if meditating, then he reopened them. "He's not righted, but neither am I. With me and Peter around, him better not come up with no fuckery."

"Whose lorry is it?"

"Lolita's . . . good friend of ours," Peter said.

58

"Just nyam done and call them. We need fi let her know when fi bring the lorry."

Just oil splatters and cutlery were left on his plate before long. His belly wouldn't need anything for the rest of the day.

"Call them now."

Uncle Lionel had been watching him the whole time.

He huffed and took his phone out of his pocket.

"Put it on loudspeaker."

He scrolled down slowly as he braced himself. *Dad* came before *Mum.* "They'll recognize my number. I doubt they'll pick up."

"Use mine then." Uncle Lionel took out his phone. "Gimme the number."

Shannon called out the number.

Loudspeaker. One ring, two rings, three, four . . .

"He doesn't usually pick up if he doesn't recognize the number, so—"

His father picked up, his voice gruff.

He must've jumped or widened his eyes, or gasped or something, because his uncle gritted his teeth at him, nostrils flared.

"Hello?"

Uncle Lionel made a hand gesture, his eyes wide, for Shannon to hurry up and speak.

His father said hello again, irritation in his voice this time.

He opened his mouth, but only a hitched exhale escaped.

"Leroy, it's me."

Shannon gasped.

"Who?"

"The brother you dash weh."

No response.

"Leroy, yuh hear me?"

Still no response. Just background noise.

"Talk, nuh man!"

"Humph. Me just ah consider."

"Consider what?"

"Ah which brother you ah talk 'bout? Me nuh have no brother."

"Me neither. Look, we soon come fi the rest of yuh pickney tings."

"Ah no my pickney dat. Nuh know where him spring from."

The certainty in his dad's voice. He hadn't changed a flicker since the confrontation. What about his mum? Shit, why was he even calling them *Mum* and *Dad* after they'd told him to stop calling them that, and after what his dad had just said?

Dad again.

"Look, we soon come."

"Good, the sooner the better, before me set fire to him ting dem."

Peter leapt from his seat, chair legs torturing the floor. "You better not!"

"Ah the wife that?"

Uncle Lionel scrunched up his face. "Ah weh Viola deh with her sour face?"

"Who the bomboclaat you ah call sour, pervert?"

"Just make sure you don't touch yuh pickney ting dem."

"Ah nuh my pickney! Just hurry up and get unu raasclaat yah so!" Leroy hung up.

"Fuck!" Uncle Lionel banged, banged, banged the table, making everything on it shake and Shannon flinch.

Peter rushed to Uncle Lionel. "Take it easy."

"Can't help it . . . well want claat him, and . . . Sorry, Shan." Uncle Lionel calmed himself down, eyes closed as if he were meditating.

Or maybe having his shoulders massaged by Peter calmed him down.

"She nuh really sour-faced. And he is my brother, no matter what. It's just . . . the situation. Been dreading it. Me did *know* it would happen. Just never know when. Me see it coming, because is the same thing me go through with him and our parents."

Peter bent down and put his forehead against Uncle Lionel's.

Shannon reached for his uncle's hand, which clasped his.

They were like that awhile, before Peter said, "I'll call Lolita."

They stretched and sighed deeply, as if they'd dozed off.

"Ready, Shan?" Uncle Lionel gave a warm smile, the exact same kind his dad—Leroy, for frig's sake—gave whenever he was in a good mood.

"I guess."

They'd reached the place Shannon used to call home. He should've looked into finding a place of his own ages ago. He had nowhere near enough money though, and hardly any friends who were roommate material.

Maybe he had no friends.

No, that wasn't true. Just happened to lose touch with secondary school and university friends. Some moved south of the river, some to the suburbs, some abroad. There were a few in the inner city, but they weren't in regular contact. He had Elise, but that friendship was new.

This shit happened at the worst time. He was meant to complete his master's, settle into a well-paying job as an accountant or actuary, and eventually get to a point where he could afford living in his own place by himself. Everyone his age seemed to be doing their own thing. Even Elise could afford to move out of her parents' home and into a flat with her sister. Flight attendants couldn't earn that much. Maybe he should've thought of that. Not necessarily being a flight attendant—that would've set off alarm bells—but maybe working on a cruise ship, something to get out of England, at least temporarily.

"Shannon, we nuh have all day."

"Huh?"

"We reach!"

Peter grabbed Uncle Lionel's arm. "Try and calm down before you go in there."

"I'm calm."

Uncle Lionel snatched himself from Peter and got out of the car. Peter got out next, from the front passenger side.

A strong breeze hit the nape of Shannon's neck; Uncle Lionel had already opened the boot. All that banging. Still fuming from the phone call. Shannon had better hurry up. Didn't want to be on the wrong side of the gay version of his da—Leroy.

He opened the door just as someone appeared out of nowhere. Nothing could've prevented the collision. He cringed at the bone-smashing thud, and the person grunted expletives and grabbed his hip, doubling over.

He scrambled out of the car and rushed to the tower of a man he'd slammed the door into. "I'm so sorry."

The man was still holding his hip and grimacing.

"You alright there?" Peter approached him.

Still no response.

"I can take a look at it."

"It's . . . cool."

Shannon shook his head, reaching for the man. "I'm really—"

He tensed as chills assaulted him. The man was staring at him, teeth gritted, but he was *fine*. His thick eyebrows, eyes a stunning shade of brown, height, full lips—scrumptious even with the bottom one busted—his unkempt facial hair making him look rugged, the pierced right ear with no earring in—maybe both ears were pierced; for some reason, if a man pierced one ear only, it would be the left—his pumped chest, shoulders and arms pushing through his grey hoodie effortlessly, his—

He was doing it again, staring too long. The guy was standing straight, rubbing where he'd been hit. He'd stopped grimacing, but he wasn't smiling. Nothing but an intense gaze which was making everything spin. Wouldn't see it coming if the guy punched him. How quickly he'd forgotten what had happened on the Victoria Line train. He just couldn't help himself. All those times he'd promised himself not to look at a man twice, to let men stare at him instead. He must've looked fool-fool, so obvious, his lips trembling and eyes probably bulging out. Light-headedness worsened as his heart sped up. This tall Adonis was going to cuss him off, maybe even—

"No worries. Wasn't looking where I was going. Had all that space." *His Fineness* motioned at the inner pavement.

"Well, uh—"

There was movement in his periphery, from the front door.

Shannon got a proper look. He gasped. "Mum!"

She looked like she was about to collapse. She was at the front door, staring, hugging herself to fight the cold air.

Then her countenance changed. That look, the one from yesterday when she was claating him with the frying pan, forehead lines making her look possessed. "Leroy! Leroy! Come here! Quick!"

She sounded like she didn't know he was coming.

Leroy appeared.

Viola pointed. "Him bring man to we yard. Him bring him bwoifriend. Jesus have his mercy!"

"Hold on now!" Peter stepped forward.

Leroy gave His Fineness then Shannon the once-over. "You can't be righted, bringing yuh nastiness here so."

"Throwing it inna we face. Kiss me rahtidclaat! Look how him holding him."

Holding him?

Shit. His hand was on the guy. His Fineness didn't seem to notice at first, but something must've clicked; he backed off, giving Shannon the once-over.

"Sorry, I didn't realise I was touching you." That must've sounded nasty.

His Fineness was still staring at him. His gaze lost its intensity momentarily, as if he were in a trance, then it returned, making Shannon's stomach flutter and chest tighten. He fought to get rid of the butterflies and control his heartbeat. He lowered his head, focused on His Fineness's grey Skechers.

"No worries," His Fineness said before part-hobbling, part-swaggering away then disappearing onto Ashenden Road.

"Viola, stop the foolishness. Him nuh have bwoifriend—yet."

Peter backhanded Uncle Lionel's chest. "Don't say that."

Viola and Leroy snarled as Uncle Lionel approached them. Uncle must've been giving it right back.

Viola disappeared back inside the house.

"Make it quick!" Leroy cut his eyes at Shannon then at Uncle Lionel, before following Viola inside.

No change at all. His house was no longer his. Just like that.

"Shannon, Peter, come on!" Uncle Lionel, empty boxes in hand, was more than ready.

Shannon bit his lip. "What about—?"

A vehicle was humming, getting louder, closer. He turned around. A white lorry was bouncing towards them, the driver looking at them. She flashed her lights. Peter waved at her. Lolita.

Everything was happening too fast. He wasn't prepared for this. Pressure was building in his throat.

Someone squeezed his shoulder when the lorry pulled up by the gate. He turned around. Peter winked at him.

He gave a wan smile then entered the house. Had to keep the lump in his throat at bay as long as Leroy and Viola were nearby.

7 / Elise II
The root of it all

Elise bucked her toe on a leg of her chest of drawers. She kept pacing though, kept staring at her phone screen. She had to turn her phone back on, even if she wasn't convinced there would be no missed calls or messages from that bastard.

She stopped, took a deep breath then pressed the power button. The phone vibrated, made her flinch. Her heart thumped harder when the screen lit up. Plenty of notifications. She scrolled down, bracing for the sight of *Number Withheld*.

Nothing of the sort. Mostly missed calls from her ma. She tapped *Ma*. The phone rang just about once.

"Elise, don't ever do that to me again. What happened to you last night and this morning?" Ma was out of breath when she was done.

She turned the volume down. "Sorry. My battery died, and I couldn't find my charger."

"Well, me glad fi hear you. What time you getting here?"

Silence.

"Elise?"

"We'll try to get there by half-ten."

"That's cutting it fine—wait a minute. *We*?"

She grimaced. Ma was going to be more pissed off, but the state of Tempest's hair after whatever had transpired last night . . . She would have to understand.

"Elise, who's *we*?"

She rolled her eyes.

"Elise! You and who?"

"Me and . . ."

Ma was silent.

"You know it could only be me and Tempest." She moved the phone from her ear.

Rustling. The other side of the door.

Ma was saying something animatedly.

She brought the phone back to her ear. "What was that, Ma?"

"Your ears hard all of a sudden?"

"Just got distracted."

"Why? Is that wretch with you?"

"Ma, stop it," she whispered. "She hasn't done anything to you."

"Elise, don't give me that. Just make sure you get here soon—with*out* her."

The rustling kept coming and going.

"You hear me?"

"But her hair's a mess. Tricia wouldn't mind fitting her in last minute."

"Her hair looked alright when the two of unu did deh yah the other day."

Sharing the encounter fit for a Zane or Eric Jerome Dickey novel Tempest revealed she'd had with Carl mere hours ago would definitely set Ma off. "It's a mess now."

"Must be the out of wedlock dick she gets."

"Ma!"

"Ah lie me ah tell?"

She checked the time on the phone. "We should reach yours by ten-thirty, and—"

"*We*? She can't come!"

"But—"

"No!"

She kissed her teeth, regretting it immediately.

"Humph! Make me call Tricia and cancel then."

"No! Don't."

"She *can't* come."

"How am I supposed to tell her that? And don't act like you don't know her name."

"Tell *her* Tricia is booked up."

She huffed.

"You know we have to book from the day before."

"I booked the same day last time."

Ma kissed her teeth. "Me nuh know wah do you, ah come tell me fi make the gyal come with us."

She nearly kissed her teeth back. "Can't believe you're putting me in this position."

"Gyal, me soon ready. Nuh take long fi come." Click.

Charming.

Knocks on the door. "Els?"

Tempest had timed that perfectly. She'd been listening.

Elise opened the door. Tempest's eyes were narrowed.

"Tem—"

"So, what did she say?"

Straight to the point. She cringed at Tempest's facial expression until she couldn't take it anymore. She walked to the window, increased the distance between them. "Maybe I shouldn't have come up with the idea. Tricia's fully booked, and—"

"That's all I needed to know."

She spun around. All that greeted her were quick, heavy footsteps before another door slammed.

S he held the hood of her jacket snugly to her head as a gust of wind tried hard to blow it off. The wind helped her open the gate to her parents' house. She scurried to the front door and pressed the doorbell hard due to her numb fingers. Her teeth chattered while she waited.

Pa opened the door then hugged her, not as tight as usual.

"Everything alright, Pa?"

He was looking through her, fidgeting with the zip of the navy gilet he was wearing over a cobalt blue plaid shirt. Took him a while to snap out of it. "Yeah. Come in quick. It's frigging cold."

"So nice and warm in here. Shame I won't get to enjoy it for long. Where's Ma?"

He rolled his eyes. "Upstairs getting ready. She soon come."

"Thought she would've been ready by now."

They went into the front room, both of them brushing against a kentia palm plant on their way to the beige fabric sofa. Pa, at six-four, would've hit his head on the candle chandelier if not for the new glass coffee table directly below it. Used to happen to him often.

"Were you two arguing again?" she said when they sat down.

Pa made a dismissive hand gesture then slapped the armrest. "Yes."

Nothing new. They'd been married since before she and Tempest were born. People always praised them for lasting so long. No one knew her parents weren't happy. They weren't affectionate unless they had company, and even then it wasn't genuine. Things clearly hadn't changed within the last two months, since she and Tempest had moved in together. All marriages couldn't possibly be like her parents'. There just had to be better ones.

"I don't want you or your sister worrying about us."

Her sister definitely didn't care, which was understandable.

"Well, I doubt Tempest would be worried." He must've read her mind. "None of this is your fault."

"Feels like it is. If you're not arguing about me, then you're arguing about Tempest."

He frowned, as if an alarm bell had rung. "She alright? Vex me miss her the other day. She shoulda did wait till me reach home."

She took her eyes off him.

"Is she OK?"

"She is."

"You don't sound sure. Wha'gwaan?"

She turned to the door, listening. No activity on the stairs. She turned back to her pa then leaned into him and whispered, "It's this *thing* with her and Ma."

He flared his nostrils then rubbed his thick, more-salt-than-pepper beard.

Bringing up the tension between her ma and sister always led to a conversation about Sylvia. The last person she wanted to talk about, or even think about.

"What *thing*?"

The door to bad memories was opening. . . . Her pa's affair . . . *that* day. . . . "Uh . . . Let me check on Ma . . . see if she's ready." She got up.

He grabbed her wrist. "Elise, tell me."

She didn't know how to say it.

"Elise!"

"They don't like each other. Never will." She squeezed her eyes shut. Not what he wanted to hear, but that was the reality.

"Damn it! What did your mother say?"

She sighed. "The usual."

"From you was a pickney, me tell that woman not to talk bad 'bout Sylvia make unu hear." He kissed his teeth. "Sit back down and tell me exactly what she said."

She sat down, Pa still holding her. She looked towards the door again. Ma would be down any moment.

"Elise!"

She told him.

"So, you mean to tell me that making Tempest stay with her aunt all that time was for nothing?" He let go of her, rubbed his beard again then stared into space.

"I don't know what to say, Pa."

He buried his face in his hands. He only needed one, as big as they were.

She held his forearm.

"How it come to this?" he said to himself, rather than to her. "It's me Marietta should be vex with, not Tempest."

"I keep trying to tell her."

"Shoulda did leave her fi true." He was deeper in his own world. He probably couldn't even feel her hand on his arm. "If she did never get pregnant too, me woulda gone 'bout me business and—" He snatched himself out of whatever world he was in, regret in his eyes as he turned to her. "Elise, me nuh mean—"

She took her hand off his arm and scooted away from him, photos intruding on her line of vision to be noticed, photos of herself, Ma, and Pa, photos of all the family except Tempest. Pa, Tempest, and Sylvia would've been one big happy family if not for her. He would've divorced Ma, who probably would've found another man to be with—she was stunning back then, so she could've had anyone she wanted. Tempest wouldn't have had the childhood she'd had, and Sylvia wouldn't have died.

All because of her.

"Elise." Pa grabbed one of her hands and sandwiched it between his mammoth ones. "Didn't mean that."

She shook her head.

He pulled her towards him, the impact into his solid chest making her want to sneeze. His cologne went to her head.

"I'm glad I'm your father. No regrets there. None of this is your fault. *Me* cause this mess. *Me* cheat on your mother. *Me* get her and Sylvia pregnant same time."

"But I kill—"

"No!"

"But—"

"No!" As wide as his eyes were, wider than usual, he didn't blink. His nostrils were flared again. "We've been through this. Me not going tell you again."

"Pa, you're hurting me." Her eyes were glistening.

He loosened his grip then cupped her face, his calloused thumbs acting as windshield wipers on her lower eyelids. "Why you keep bringing this up?" His tone softened. "The last time you bring it up, nearly most Tempest hear."

She didn't need reminding. She would never forget feeling as if her heart had stopped a moment too long before it suddenly raced, when Tempest appeared in the middle of her conversation with Ma and Pa about Sylvia, no clue that Tempest was even coming to see Pa, unaware she hadn't shut the front door properly. Those few moments Tempest stood there staring, she had to have heard everything, but she hadn't. Hell would've broken loose otherwise. Still, keeping the secret from Tempest was torture.

"I thought I was ready to spend more time with Tempest, but that picture keeps reminding me of everything."

"What picture?"

"There's a picture of Sylvia in her room."

Pa nodded wistfully.

"I have to pass Tempest's room to get to mine. Sometimes, I see the picture. I feel like she's staring right at me. I don't know why Tempest doesn't always keep her door closed."

"I can't believe it." Pa let go of her as he shook his head. "The therapy was pointless. Shoulda did follow me mind and nuh let you move in with Tempest."

"You really expected therapy to do the job when I couldn't even talk about *everything*, had to pretend it was just about the broken family, that it was more than just *seeing* and *hearing* Sylvia die—"

Pa's menacing countenance came out of nowhere, made her skin crawl. His face went back to normal within moments.

"As for being flatmates with Tempest, I guess I wasn't ready. Maybe I never will be. You and Ma were right. Just the other day she told me it was a bad idea."

"Humph. Only because of how she feels 'bout Tempest." He kissed his teeth. "Maybe you should go back into therapy."

"What's the point if—?"

"We have to do something."

She grimaced then looked at him out of the corner of her eye. "Maybe I should do what I should've done ages ago."

Pa played with his salt-and-pepper beard, waiting for her to elaborate.

His gaze was penetrating, intimidating. She looked away, wrapping a strand of hair around her fingers. His breathing was becoming audible, not helping.

But she just had to say it. "I think I have to . . ." She peeked at him; he was still fiddling with his beard. She looked away again. ". . . tell Tempest the truth."

"For God's sake!" He thumped the empty part of the armrest a few times.

Pa paused and shut his eyes, as if counting down in his head.

"It's too late to tell her. We shoulda tell her there and then. She *can't* find out now. She's been through enough. It was an accident anyway."

"You know it wasn't."

"Elise, just stop."

She got up and headed to the bay window. Her legs disturbed the leaves of another kentia palm plant. His breathing tickled her ear in no time. She sat on the arm of the armchair next to the plant, her legs forcing leaves out of position.

"Sylvia saved you from being hit by the car, and that's that."

"But—"

"But nothing!"

But it wasn't as simple as that.

He knew.

She knew.

"Elise!"

She jumped.

"Don't mention it again." He sprayed her cheek. "Tempest would be upset . . . with you . . . with me . . . I can't afford to lose her, not again. Like I said, it was an accident. You were a pickney, didn't know any better."

"It's just so hard. Tempest shouldn't have lost her mum so young. It's not right that she doesn't know the whole truth, that I timed it so that—"

"Elise, I'm telling you—"

"And then all she went through after that—and still goes through—with a wicked stepmother—"

Coughs. They snapped their heads towards the door.

Ma was standing there, hardly any make-up on. Her hair was in a ponytail or bun—hard to tell, looking at her straight on, hat on her head. Her black, shapeless, thigh-length jacket was zipped up. Besides the off-pink fluffy slippers on her feet, she was ready to hit the road.

"See you in the car." Then she was gone.

The front door rattled open, the wind and distant traffic spilling into the house. Either the wind or Ma made the door bash into the wall.

Not even a hello. No goodbye for Pa.

Things were really bad between them. And her ma was pissed at her.

She got up.

Pa hugged her like he didn't want to let go. "Remember what me tell you."

"Alright, Pa." Hopefully her response was convincing.

Mica Paris's vocals mingled with the engine as Ma drove along Marylebone Road, buses and black cabs passing them constantly in the bus lane. Elise had been staring at her ma for most of the drive. Ma had been ignoring her, singing or humming along to the songs playing on Mi-Soul. She tried the same tactic when a red light caught them, but Ma's humming was drowning out Mica.

Enough was enough.

Ma snapped her head at her and frowned. "Why you turn it off?"

"To get your attention. I know you're upset with me."

Ma looked away. "First your father, and now you."

"What have I done?" She feigned obliviousness.

Ma looked at her through the corner of her eye. "'Wicked stepmother'?"

Elise shifted in her seat.

"Humph!"

She rolled her eyes as she turned her head to her door window before turning back to her ma again. "Sorry for saying that, but you've never been nice to Tempest."

Ma looked like she was about to go into a tirade. She opened her mouth, but she decided not to say anything. She looked into the road to the right then into her mirrors. She signalled right then forced herself into the right-turn lane, making a hand gesture to thank the driver behind.

"Ma, what are you doing?"

The light was turning amber as Ma turned onto York Gate.

"Why are you going this way?"

Ma parked the car just before a side road with a barrier and turned off the engine.

"Of all the places for you to park."

"What you talking about?"

"Look ahead . . . that bridge . . . where Sylvia was hit."

"Oh . . . of course." Ma paused, kissed her teeth. "That was years ago."

She widened her eyes at her ma. "Could've been *fifty* years ago . . . I was right there."

"Bet your father planned to see his tramp that day."

"Well, that *tramp* saved *your* daughter."

She'd succeeded in doing more than just hurting Sylvia. She'd killed her. Sylvia had been taken from her daughter. Sylvia had sacrificed herself to save her enemy's child.

"Ma, please . . . the blood, the way she looked, all twisted on the ground . . . I can't take it! I—"

"Fine, fine, fine." Ma restarted the car then did a U-turn between two islands. She parked by a lamp post with a parking sign mounted on it.

"Ma, look at the sign. We can't stay here."

"I need to get this out, so just listen."

"What is it?"

"You know about your father and . . . that woman."

"Yes, Ma."

Ma took off her hat, ran her hand through her shoulder-length hair, grey eating away at the tan brown hair dye in the roots. A few hours from now, her roots would match her skin tone again.

"Nothing to do with me and him has anything to do with you and him. I don't want you to love him any less."

"I know that, Ma. I can only imagine how much he hurt you, but he's still my pa."

"Good. That man has done me *wrong*." Ma clutched her chest, grimacing, then took a deep breath. "But he's a great father."

"I know."

"Anyway, you don't know why me never leave him."

"You stayed with him for me."

"Yes, but there's more to it." Ma slowly turned her head until she was looking straight ahead, towards the trees, which had started to shed leaves, and the church, as grey as the sky, but she was probably looking beyond them, into distant memories only she could see.

She placed her hand on top of her ma's. "What do you mean?"

Ma turned to her. "You know your grandparents weren't married and that your grandpa had other children besides me, Verna, Colin, Frederick, and Ursula."

"I know. There's Uncle Gerald and Auntie Stephanie."

Ma sighed. "And four more."

"*What?*"

"Four more—at least."

Her mouth was open, but words were trapped.

"Me speak to Ursula the other day. Is she tell me. She find them on Facebook. You know how she is."

"We only just found out about Uncle Gerald and Auntie Stephanie."

"Me know."

"Grandpa had *eleven* children?"

"At least. And Lord knows how many women he had them with."

"Damn."

"I'm five months older than Gerald."

She leaned into the door. "What?"

"You heard. Five months."

"But . . . you said you're two years older than him."

"Is lie me tell."

"That means . . . Grandpa cheated on Granny?"

Ma grimaced then looked away.

Elise pressed her free hand against her chest. "Poor Granny."

The church, traffic and trees faded as an image of Granny came to her. Granny's smile, warmth, peacefulness . . . The most gentle woman. Maybe the most unfortunate, most cursed. There was probably so much she never revealed to anyone, so much pain she took to her grave. No break from suffering, even towards the end. Cancer had come out of nowhere. Or maybe the diagnosis, because the cancer had to have been eating away at her for months or even years, or else she wouldn't have been given a month. And she was gone in less than a month. Snatched. Had to leave the earth to know true happiness.

A car pulled up next to theirs. Traffic had formed.

Her eyes were flooding. She blinked repeatedly. Tears tickled her cheeks. She turned away from Ma as she dried her eyes.

"I miss her too." Ma's voice was shaky. "Always will."

They both sniffled for a few moments.

"So, Granny and Uncle Gerald's mum were pregnant at the same time. Just like you and . . ." A flush tickled through her as everything started to click. "Does Pa know?"

Ma tightened her face as she nodded.

All that time thinking it was as simple as being cheated on, and for Pa to have betrayed Ma, knowing what Granny had suffered . . .

"This is a lot, Ma."

"That's not even the worst." Ma's voice was trembling, her eyes glistening. "Them stay together, Mama and Dadda, until . . ."

She squeezed her ma's hand as if she were in labour.

"Them stay together until . . . me did just turn one. Better check Mama's book when we reach home—she did write everything down. Anyway, me just turn one . . . when . . . when Dadda . . . God in heaven . . ." She put her hand over her mouth then shut her eyes, her demeanour stiff. ". . . when him leave Mama . . . all ah we . . . for Gerald and Stephanie's mother."

Her grandparents had separated long before she was born, but finding out the circumstances of their split . . .

"Him leave Mama with five pickney." Ma paused, her chest heaving as she rested her head against the headrest.

"How could he?"

"God only knows. Just turn one when Dadda leave, seven when me see him again. Mama did reach England. Me never recognize him, never remember him, never know him. Next time me see him was in '91 when me take you home for the first time. The only other time me see him was in '93, just before him dead."

"The picture of me and him at Auntie Ursula's house. We were on the veranda. I was sitting on his lap— Wait, you went that long without contact?"

"Yes. Ursula did find him. Me never care fi see him. If him never leave us, maybe . . ." Ma sighed.

Granny couldn't take her children with her to England. She had to make a life there and save up for them to join her. Ma had long shared what she and her siblings had suffered in the care of so-called family while Granny was in England.

"Lord have mercy," Ma whispered as she stared ahead. "Mama had a tough time, but she did everything she could for all her pickney—without Dadda."

"I'm sure she did."

"My childhood . . . it was . . . If him never leave . . . Lord help me." Ma burst into tears, her hand stifling her sobs.

Elise unbuckled her seat belt and hugged her trembling ma.

"It was so hard," Ma continued, struggling for breath.

"Ma, don't go there if it's going to get you in a state."

Ma released herself from the embrace like a frail elderly woman. "How Mama managed, God only knows. Dadda leave her fi smaddy else, humiliate her, and the dutty woman—Massa forgive me; me know she dead and gone—know him deh with Mama. Just like your half-sister's mother—that bitch!"

"Ma, she's dead—"

"That bitch give *my* husband him first pickney."

"Ma—"

"Him jook me, then jook her then come back fi jook me some more. What kinda filthiness is that?"

"Ma, please."

"But she get pregnant first." Ma squinted as she shook her head. "The embarrassment. People hear seh him have pickney, then when them see my big belly, them put two and two together and look 'pon me like me is the biggest ass. Big old, fool-fool wretch."

Something she had never considered. So focused on Ma's petty ways and treatment of Tempest. She hadn't ever put herself fully in her mother's shoes. She had never thought beyond the affair. So much more complicated than a mistake. A lot had come with it. A lot was still there. Elephants she could finally see as clear as ever.

"Can you imagine, Elise? You know a man deh with smaddy, him have pickney, and you want him. And you as a man with woman and pickney . . . it come in as nothing to leave them?"

"Times were hard enough. I always wondered why Granny never said much about Grandpa."

Ma dabbed her face with tissue. "Now you know, chile."

"All that time, I never knew what made her come to England, and why Grandpa stayed in Jamaica."

"Dadda was the breadwinner. Then him leave. England was looking for workers from overseas, and . . . well, you know about the Windrush."

"I can't imagine how you all felt when Granny left Jamaica. She came here in 1963. You and the rest came in 1969. All that time without seeing her. She must have felt so alone. No children; no man."

"It still hurts me. And we were split up, as you know. And the beatings, the chores, the duppy dem . . . Lord have mercy." Ma clenched her eyes shut and tightened her mouth. "Mama never beat any of her pickney."

"Duppies?"

"Whole heap of them!"

She stared ahead, until the stop-start traffic along Marylebone Road, blocking the trees and the church, became a blur again. The thought of her granny reaching cold, foggy England, probably worrying about, and crying for, her children the entire sea journey. There had to be a silver lining somewhere. Wherever it was, she had to find it quickly. Being beside herself like this was torture. Wasn't going to change the past.

"And Mama was proud. She didn't like asking for favours." Ma sighed. "But your aunt Ursula had it the worst. She never got along with Aunt Alice, so she ended up staying with Norman, and . . ." She slapped her hand over her mouth.

There was no need for Ma to say the rest. It was common knowledge. Everyone stopped calling him *Uncle* long ago.

"Wish I could've seen Auntie Ursula the last time I went to Jamaica."

"We soon see her."

"Yeah."

"Elise?" Ma's voice was stern.

"Yes, Ma?"

Ma looked at her out the corner of her eye. "Me did never want tell you all of this, never want you to feel a way about your grandfather."

She was blindsided, couldn't lie while her ma was looking at her that way.

Ma turned her head some more until she was looking at her square on. "I don't want you to hate your grandfather. Mama eventually made peace with everything, and so did we."

"I don't hate him. Hardly knew him. It just hurts . . . what you went through, especially Granny. Her life was hard enough."

Ma's face softened into blankness. Another memory.

They both sighed.

"Elise?"

"Yes, Ma?"

"Now do you see where I'm coming from . . . with your father?"

She closed her eyes briefly as she took it all in. "Yes, Mummy. You wanted to keep your family together to avoid suffering what Granny did."

Her ma smiled. "When last you call me *Mummy*? Sounds better than *Ma*."

She smiled back.

Sternness returned to Ma's expression. "Me know me tell you this before, but make me tell you again. Don't just go having children. Get married first. Me know it's hard in this day and age, but you've done well so far. Better to be a virgin than to give your body to the wrong man."

Blindsided again. Her belly tingling, she broke eye contact and shuffled in her seat.

"Maybe if Mama and Dadda were married, he . . . Then again, being married never stop your father." Ma shook her head, distant memories drawing closer, her eyes widening and glistening. "Good thing me did marry him, otherwise him woulda leave me one fi raise you . . . same way Dadda leave Mama, and—"

A knock on Elise's window made them jump.

"Shithouse!" Ma said, as a frowning traffic warden peered inside the car.

Ma rolled down Elise's window. "Please forgive me. I'm leaving now. It slipped my mind that I've been here all this time."

Elise turned her head so that the warden couldn't see her face as she stifled a laugh at Ma's transition to the Queen's English.

The warden kissed his teeth. "Make sure it doesn't happen again."

"Thank you," Elise and her ma said in unison as the warden walked off.

When it looked like he was far enough, they chuckled.

As the remnants of laughter trickled out, something came to Elise that threatened to ruin the mood. She fastened her seat belt, bracing herself for her ma's reaction to what she was about to say.

"Life is so short."

"You're telling me."

"Don't you think it's worth making an effort?"

"Effort?"

"To make amends . . . with Tempest."

Just like that, a snarl replaced Ma's smile.

"Please try."

"Can't make any promises."

Not what she wanted to hear. Ma had been hurt and humiliated though. Maybe the moment they'd just shared was the first step. There was more to Ma than just being stubborn. Not that she'd only just realised that. Just that Ma hadn't opened up like that for some time. She had to put herself in her mother shoes, truly understand her pain.

"Just please—and not in a bad way—be careful."

"Careful?"

"There's something about that girl."

"That she's Syl—that woman's daughter?"

Ma's nostrils flared.

"I know Tempest reminds you of what Pa did, but Tempest is no villain."

Ma opened her mouth, closed it, sighed. Whatever was on her mind wasn't going to leave her mouth.

She turned the engine back on.

Elise turned the radio back on as the car started to move. The lights turned red. Left turn only. They needed to go right. They'd figure out how to get back on track. They sang along to a Donny

Hathaway and Roberta Flack song, back on track in the way that mattered most—their relationship.

8 / Tempest II
Mother dearest

Everyone thought Tempest favoured her late mother. They had the same heart-shaped face complemented by naturally contoured cheekbones. That bitch Marietta saw her mother in her, the woman her daddy loved more. And why wouldn't he? Her mum was more beautiful, despite her patchy complexion and unplucked eyebrows. If only Tempest had inherited her father's smooth complexion and eyebrows fit for a beauty queen, like the other bitch, Elise, had.

She took the photo of her mum out of its silver floral frame and leaned it against her dressing table mirror. She strained to recreate the shot. A slight head movement triggered neck pain—she'd struck the last blow, but Aiden had really mashed her up.

She tried again, slowly. It hurt to stretch her already long neck almost to its limit. She turned her head slightly, struggling to keep her eyes on her mum. Something in her reflection was bugging her, insisting on being noticed. A mark on her neck. A bruise. She kissed her teeth. A filter was her only hope.

Her mum was pouting. It was subtle. Whatever Tempest was doing wasn't working. She relaxed, studied her mother, tried again . . . That was more like it. She caressed the part of her neck that met her collar bone, her wrist bent as much as possible. The bruise was hidden this way. With her other hand, she picked up her phone, darting her eyes to the screen to make sure her face and neck were well within it. With the sunlight piercing through the window and smudging the frame of her face yellow, no one seeing the pictures would see how fucked-up her edges were. She looked into an imaginary distant place and snapped photos in quick succession.

The pictures came out almost all the same, besides blurriness here, squinted eyes there. She picked up the photo of her mum and held it up next to the photo she'd chosen of herself. Could've done with more intensity in her eyes. A mystery how her mum had pulled it off. Probably nailed it in the first shot. Pointless trying to recreate her mum's look exactly. She should've taken the pictures as soon as she'd put in the extensions. One of the pictures would have to do.

Jill Scott's "Blessed" pulled her away. Her ringtone. She answered her phone. "Hi, Daddy."

"Hi, Temp. You dash me weh."

"Hasn't been that long."

"Been long for me."

"Maybe we could do something tomorrow."

"Humph!"

"What was that for?"

"I know you don't like coming here."

"Humph."

"It's my yard, not just your stepmother's. And my yard is your yard."

Stepmother? *Mari-heifer* was just fine. "I know that."

"You can come over if you want. Marietta's out." Her daddy sounded excited.

"Maybe another time. Tied up right now."

"Well, I can come over."

"No." That response was too quick.

"Fine." He sounded dejected. "Look, I know it's coming up to . . ."

". . . Mum's birthday." She stiffened up.

"It still hurts me that she's not here."

She clenched her eyes shut. She fought the lump forming in her throat.

"This foolishness with you and Marietta must stop."

She opened her eyes as if she'd awoken from a nightmare.

"Me know you hear weh me seh."

"Daddy, too much has happened. Being cordial is the best I can do."

He sighed. "Just want unu to get on. Me know you had it rough growing up—"

"You think?" she thought aloud then grimaced immediately.

Daddy kissed his teeth.

"How would you feel growing up the way I did? My main . . ." She squirmed. "My main mother figure treated me like shit."

"Watch it."

"Can't help it. That heifer is —"

"Your ears hard?"

"Being cheated on is the worst, but she shouldn't have blamed me. That whole thing was on *you*, and on *her* for staying with you."

"For God's sake!"

She gasped.

"Sorry." His tone softened. "Didn't mean to shout. You're right. It wasn't fair on you, but she did try."

She kissed her teeth.

"She did."

"I can't believe what you're saying, knowing the shit she put me through."

"Tempest, me and you is not size."

"Everything was fucked-up—"

"Tempest!"

"Stop forcing me to like that bitch."

"Tempest, you're—"

"I don't care! She is a bitch!"

"Tempest!"

"No! I get so angry when I think about it."

"*You're upsetting me.*"

"You brought her up."

"She's your stepmother."

She clenched her eyes, transported to her younger self.

"You hear me, Tempest?" Her daddy cut childhood memories short before they could be planted. "She's your stepmother. Don't you ever forget."

"She's one hell of a stepmother, not like the one Julia Roberts played, but a *wicked* stepmother. I'm stuck with her instead of my own mother, all because of Elise!" She grimaced. She'd said too fucking much.

"Weh you just say?" His voice was almost a whisper.

"I . . . I . . ."

"Tempest, don't *ramp* with me!"

She looked all around her room, as if some item of furniture or upholstery had the answer.

"Tempest!"

His voice made her tremble. Her breathing was heavy, trying to keep up with her rapid heartbeat. She put distance between the phone and her face. Couldn't let her daddy hear her distress.

"Tempest, answer me! Weh you mean 'because of Elise'?"

Her hearing would've been fucked-up if the phone had still been against her ear. Daddy usually paced the room whenever he was in this kind of mood, just like she did. He had to be doing it then.

"Tempest!"

She stifled a gasp. *Think, you stupid bitch.*

She fumbled to put the phone on loudspeaker, then she placed it on the dressing table. "Daddy, please—"

"Tell me, damn it!"

"OK. OK. I . . . I just meant . . ." *Tempest bomboclaat Cunningham, get your shit together.*

"You just meant what?" He was still too loud, every syllable making her flinch.

"Well . . . if . . ." *Breathe.* ". . . Marietta never got pregnant . . . with Elise . . . you probably . . . would've left her . . . for my mum . . ."

Nothing from Daddy besides heavy breathing.

"I would've grown up with my *own* mother and father."

He was still breathing heavily. No telling if she'd said the right thing, the right way.

"Daddy?"

"Still here." He sounded calmer. "Marietta being pregnant has nothing to do with it; Sylvia would've . . ."

. . . been hit by the car anyway. "Maybe not."

No response from him—still not convinced.

She fanned herself. "There'd be no Elise . . . and Marietta wouldn't have been in the picture. Mum saved Elise, remember? No Elise . . . no one to save."

He was still silent.

She picked the phone back up. "Daddy?"

"Never consider that before."

She formed a fist with her free hand and pressed it against her chest, mouthing a silent *thank you*, eyes closed.

"You're right. . . . Sylvia shouldn't have even been there," he said wistfully.

"Can't undo the past. Gotta move on." *Not from what Elise did and got away with.*

"I loved her, still do. If I—"

"Daddy, don't."

"Shoulda never make you stay with Janice."

She shook her head and tightened her face. Fuck-shit had reached its limit. A choice had had to be made—her or Mari-heifer. The two of them couldn't live under the same roof any longer. It was that bitch's house. All that time thinking it was as simple as Mari-heifer treating her like shit when Elise's betrayal was so much worse.

She clenched her eyes shut to keep tears in, fought to regain her composure. "Living with Auntie Janice was for the best."

"Fi true?"

"Yeah. . . . Daddy, I've got to go, but I'll see you soon."

"You promise?"

"Promise."

"OK. Love you." Daddy sounded distant.

"Love you too."

Call disconnected. She cussed as she threw the phone on the bed. If she kept this shit up, there would be no revenge. Maybe involving Aiden was a reach, but he was her best option. If everything happened the way she wanted it . . . He would have to do his part—asap. Worst case scenario—Elise, Daddy and Mari-heifer would find out everything too late.

She retrieved the phone and called Aiden.

She'd forgotten to withhold her fucking number. She hung up.

She pulled at her braids, frayed thanks to Aiden. With everything at stake, the shithouse couldn't avoid her forever. As long as she threatened to out him to his family—and she would do it—he had no choice.

She sat back down on the dressing table chair, rested her elbows on the table and ran her hands through her braids as she stared at the photo of her mum. She picked it up and traced her fingers over her mum's face. Mari-heifer couldn't hold a candle to her.

"Why did you have to chase after that bitch?" she whispered.

Would've given anything for her mum to turn her head, look at her and answer her. Giving everything wouldn't make that happen. She clenched her eyes shut.

Moments later, she removed her hair band. Waste of time putting the extensions in. She took out a pair of scissors out of a drawer.

She brought the scissors to her braids then stopped. She rang Carl. Countless rings, then voicemail. She tried again. He answered.

"Carl, I need to see you."

"Uh . . . I'm driving. Call you back later."

"But—"

He hung up on her.

She called him again.

"The person you're trying to call is unable to—"

"Fuck you!"

Carl never seemed to have time for her lately. It was going to be her and him the next time she saw him, but her hair needed sorting out. That fucking Elise, telling her she could tag along to Tricia's house. Then again, after the last time she let Tricia do her hair, she shouldn't have agreed. She was desperate though. She couldn't show up at work looking the way she did. She searched the Internet for Vanessa Andar's number. She dialled it.

Three rings before someone picked up. "Vanessa Andar. How can I help?"

"Hi. I need my hair done today. Four-thirty, five."

"How would you like your hair done?"

That was a good question.

"Hello? Are you still there?"

"Course I am!"

"Sorry, Madam."

"Right. Be more patient."

"Well—"

"Look, I have braid extensions in, and I want them out."

"Uh . . . I'm not sure I can fit you in to unbraid—"

"I can take them out myself. I'm not an invalid."

The woman mumbled something.

"I can't hear you. Speak up!"

"I . . . I—"

"I haven't got all day!"

The woman was struggling again.

"I tell you what, can you book me in for a wash and trim?"

"Uh . . . let me see. Please hold."

"Don't be long."

The woman put her on hold quickly, as if dying to cuss without being heard.

She tapped her fingers on the dressing table.

The woman came back. "Hello, Madam. Thanks for holding. There's—"

"Like I had a choice."

Silence.

"Carry on then!"

"Uh . . . there's a five-thirty slot available."

"Five-thirty it is."

As soon as she hung up after giving the woman her contact details and Elise's name, her phone rang.

"Hi, Auntie Janice."

"Hi, Temp. Just checking up on you. You alright?"

"Yeah. Just about to take my plaits out."

"What? You only just put them in. Tomorrow's meant to be special."

"I know."

"Then why you taking them out so soon?"

"They got messed up. Long story. I'm gonna take them out and then go to Vanessa Andar."

"Vanessa Andar? They're so thief."

"Aren't they all?"

"Tempest, this is silly. Make you nuh take them out, and wash and condition your hair yourself?"

"I'm cutting my hair. I tell you what, are you free for the next few hours?"

"I suppose. Just at home."

"Can you help me take the extensions out?"

"You sure you *have* to take them out?"

"Yes, Auntie. Besides, we can catch up."

Her aunt sighed. "Alright then. Come over. Don't forget your combs and things."

"Who did you fight?" Auntie Janice traced Tempest's neck with her fingers.

Tempest flinched. "That tickles."

"You have a bruise right here as well." Her aunt poked the top of her spine.

"Really?"

"Yeah. You sure you won?"

"Very sure."

"Well, you must've given her a good beating because your hair is really in a bad state. And look at all these bruises. How did it even start?"

"Don't feel like talking about it."

"Suit yourself."

She adjusted her position on the carpet, between her aunt's legs, batty sore.

Auntie Janice handed her a cushion to put under her batty.

Auntie's boyfriend—or *man*friend as she called him, since she was no girl and he was no boy—was sitting on the plastic-covered armchair watching football. The volume was low. She'd forgotten he'd moved in recently. She needed to finally tell her aunt what she'd discovered about her mum's death, but not with Reggie around. So tacky of him to be in the room with two women. There was a TV in the kitchen. He needed to take his batty there.

"Fifty-five tomorrow."

"I know."

Her aunt sighed, taking a moment's break from undoing the braids.

Tempest stopped too, relieving herself from the cramp in her arms. She turned to face her aunt, who was rocking a fringe and a plait as long as that tomb raider heifer's. Auntie Janice was wearing a wig, unlike the flesh-bearing action woman, but unlike the heifer, her aunt's big chest was natural. Somehow, her titties were bigger than she'd ever remembered her mum's being. Auntie Janice had put on a bit of weight though. The smoking couldn't have helped. Certainly didn't do her teeth any good, gums getting darker. Identical twins. Different personalities. Just one plait, but it was something, her way of remembering her twin, who'd died rocking braids, with their birthday coming up.

She took out her phone and went to her most recent photos. "Look at these pics. Keep scrolling left." She passed the phone to her aunt.

Auntie Janice gasped. "You're the spitting image of her—me. Reggie, come here! Look how much she favours Sylvia!"

He barely looked at the picture, his focus on the football match, as he muttered, "Yes, yes. Them favour."

"Tried copying her in that photo over there." She pointed to the top shelf of the cabinet next to the TV, where a smaller version of the photo in her bedroom stood.

Her aunt gasped again. "Send me a copy of this, Temp, so I can put my niece and twin next to each other."

I t was after three. The extensions were out after three hours. Auntie Janice came back into the kitchen after giving Reggie some leftover Chinese food. She found somewhere on the congested table to put two plates of shrimp fried vermicelli then sat opposite Tempest.

"Thanks, Auntie."

"You're welcome, babes."

"There's something you should know. Couldn't say anything earlier because of . . ." She pointed towards the living room.

Auntie Janice frowned, patting her wig. "OK . . . What is it?"

"It's about Mum."

The distant clinking of Reggie's fork on his plate and the murmur of the fridge were the only sounds for a moment before her aunt said, "What about her?"

She needed to tread lightly, somehow.

"What is it, Temp?"

"The way she died."

Auntie Janice grimaced, pulled her plait over her shoulder and ran her hand over it, her lips trembling. "Why do you want to talk about that?"

"There's something you don't know, about how she died."

Her aunt frowned. "What do you mean? Some shithouse cabbie ran her over—help me, Jesus."

The thought of being hit at high speed made pain radiate throughout her stomach for a moment. Good thing she hadn't seen her mum actually get hit. But the image of her mum sprawled out on the ground, her braids soaking in blood, was her last glimpse of her. Wasn't even allowed to view her body in the casket.

Auntie Janice grabbed her hand.

She swallowed, got back on track. "I know *that* part . . ."

Her aunt's head was shaking, almost vibrating. "There's no other part. She was hit by a black cab and that's that."

Tempest put her fork down and leaned back in the chair.

"Tempest, what's going on?"

"There *is* another part."

"What?"

"Months ago, I found out what really happened."

Her aunt clutched her heaving chest, her eyes glistening.

"Mum didn't just step into the road without checking. Elise ran into the road and Mum saved her."

Her aunt broke the eye contact.

"Auntie Janice?"

Maybe her aunt hadn't heard her.

"I never knew Mum had flung herself into Elise to keep her from being hit."

Still nothing from her aunt.

"All this time we thought she was just careless, and come to find out it wasn't as simple as that. And then . . ."

Her aunt put her elbow on the table, chin in palm.

All that time not knowing her mum had run into the road to save Elise, and this was Auntie Janice's reaction. Maybe something had gone over Auntie's head. Maybe . . . It couldn't be.

"Auntie?"

Her aunt looked at her reluctantly. "Yes?"

"Auntie!"

Her aunt darted her head towards the sink, as if the pipes had suddenly burst.

Tempest pushed her chair out, the legs screaming as they scraped the tiles. "You knew!"

Her aunt shot out of her seat. "Can't believe Oliver told you and didn't give me a heads-up."

"This is fuck-shit!"

"Watch it!"

"I'm not watching anything! You should've told me!"

"No one wanted you to hate Elise."

She was shaking. "I knew that Elise was on the other side of the road, but . . ."

"Not that Sylvia saved her." Her aunt finished her sentence, leaving out the other part.

Reggie walked in, belching quietly, hand to his mouth like he was holding a mic. "Everything alright?"

"Yes, Reggie. Just go back inna the front room."

Reggie narrowed his eyes at them then left the kitchen.

"You've known all this time, and you're OK with it?"

"Tempest, it was an accident."

"What are you talking about?"

"Me know how you feel. Me feel a way 'bout Elise when me find out, but I couldn't hold malice for a likkle girl."

"Likkle girl or not, she made sure my mum—your twin—died."

"Made sure? It was an accident, Tempest. Sylvia would've done the same thing for any other pickney."

Auntie kept calling it an accident, like Elise hadn't . . .

"Tempest, stop looking at me like that."

"Accident?"

"Yes."

"An accident."

Her aunt took her hand. "Come, Temp, sit back down. Finish the food before it gets cold. Sorry I didn't tell you the truth, but—"

"Stop, Auntie. Just stop." She sat back down.

Auntie Janice did the same. "I lost my sister. Can't lose you too."

She stared through noodles, shrimps and green chilli until her aunt's voice snapped her out of it.

"I can't take you being vex with me."

"I'm not vex, just . . . You knew she actually *saved* Elise?"

"Yes. She ran into the road without looking. Sylvia saved her."

Auntie Janice really didn't know the other part. Better to keep it that way for the time being. Auntie Janice knew how vengeful she could be. Better to ruin Elise first, tell Auntie after. Aiden was the key to everything working out perfectly. She took a deep breath at the thought of it. She would ring him on the way back home, keep ringing until he answered. He was stuck with her.

SUNDAY

9 / Aiden II
Unwanted invitation

The front door slammed shut. Would've made Aiden wake to a start if he hadn't already been awake. It was too dark, through the slit of his bedroom curtains, to be after ten. A draught was creeping up his neck. He didn't want it to catch his limbs, any part where skin was exposed, or else he would've shifted to check the wall clock or feel for one of the phones on the bedside table.

Taps. He listened closely, breath held. They were coming from above, behind and to the right. The window. Pitter-pattering rain. That explained the darkness. It probably was after ten. The time his grandfolks usually left for church. Only thirteen, fourteen hours till it was time for bed again, early start the next morning. Another Sunday that would race by, especially with that bloodclaat dinner Tempest came up with out of nowhere. Couldn't deny the bitch was as good a cook as his grandma.

His grandfolks always left home early for church. Besides slamming the front door, they weren't as loud as they used to be, around the time he'd stopped going to church—not that he'd ever gone regularly or enjoyed it. Maybe he was too old, tall and broad, as Grandma kept saying, to be told what to do. Or maybe age was catching up with them faster, too fast for them to force their hardback grandson to go to church with them.

Probably worth going once in a while to keep the grandfolks happy. He was taken anyway. Once church members learned this, they'd stop trying to marry him off to girls who deserved better than him.

Maybe Elise deserved better. Maybe not.

He snuggled tighter under the duvet. It was all phoney, but only he and Tempest knew that. In Elise's eyes, he was her man. She had to see him that way. Anyway, if he decided to go to church with his grandfolks again, he wouldn't be chatting shit—at least not completely—about having a girl.

But why would he go back to that pastor's church, the same pastor who'd talked shit about gays? Filthiness and nastiness—those were the words he'd used.

He was doing it again, being offended. He wasn't gay though, so he shouldn't have felt some kind of way about the pastor's words, or Ethan's the other night, or when his father . . .

The last fucking person he needed to be thinking about. And it was *Arthur*, not *his father*. He thumped himself in the head, kept doing it, beating unwanted thoughts back to wherever they were coming from. Luther Vandross, on the radio feet away, was enough of a distraction, though "Never Too Much" was finishing, the DJ chatting shit over the song.

He snatched his other pillow, knocking something off the bedside table, then arched it over his head, blocking out noise, and changed position. The draught snuck under the duvet, found his lower back and bare arms. He tightened the duvet around his body so that the draught only hit his neck, but there was a coldness in his boxers, a slimy coldness. Hand in undies. No sign of the tissue that was meant to be covering the tip of his dick. Whatever come had soiled his boxers wet his knuckles.

He hadn't come more than once in one night before.

He'd heard the two o'clock news, jerked off to the dude who'd bashed the car door into his hip. He had to jack off to him before sleep caught him, the memory of his face—lips as full as his, smooth skin, Janet Jackson cheekbones, and neat goatee—still fresh. Then the dude came into his dreams, kissing him, sucking him off with those full lips then giving up his hole. It was pitch black when he woke up the first time, his dick tingling into another eruption, dream and reality clashing. He had no control, the darkness not helping, as shaking took over his body. He had to bite a pillow, like a tiger trapping prey in his teeth, climax threatening to be noisy. His abs were sore when it was over, as if he'd just done a thousand pull-ups. Managed to catch some come in his hands. Some of it soiled his string vest, got to his abs. Too spent to give a fuck. Just took time to recover from that high, let the tremors leave his system when they were ready. Then he fumbled for the tissue box on his bedside table.

That dude had made him come.

Twice.

Movement in his underwear. Because of the memory.

He tossed the pillow somewhere, kicked the duvet off and shot out of the bed, the cold assaulting his bare arms and seeping through the holes of his string vest. He stepped on something. A phone. What he'd knocked off the bedside table. He kicked come-glued tissue on the way to the door, rubbing his bare arms, sore from weights and Tempest, then he yanked his dressing gown off the hook and put it on in a hurry.

He picked up the phone and pulled up Tempest's text again.

Dinner @ mine & dear Els's 2moro @ 4. Bring ur batty here . . . or else!!!

He gritted his teeth, chucked the phone on the bed, then went into the texts in his other phone, found Elise's text.

*Hey. My sis is doing a big Sunday dinner. 4pm.
I know it's last minute, but come if you're free.
I'll call before church x*

Some sister act.

He went to the bathroom, pissed, washed his hands and face, rinsed out his mouth. A sudden vibration in his dressing gown pocket made him cuss. His phone. He took it out. Elise was calling.

"Yo."

"Morning," she said. "Sounds like I woke you."

"No, I'm up," he said, leaving the bathroom.

"Good. . . . Just seeing if you're coming later."

"Yeah, I'm coming."

She was silent for a moment, then she said, "You don't sound enthusiastic."

"It's out of the blue, that's all." He started traipsing down the stairs.

"Don't have to come if you're not up to it. To be honest, I'm not crazy about it either."

"For true?"

"Just not in the mood. All Tempest's idea."

Clearly. "You tell her that?"

"Yeah, but she's so insistent. She just wants us all to get together. She's bought food specially."

"Your birthday soon come. Why couldn't she wait till then?"

"She thought I might like to spend it with my boyfriend."

He missed a step and grabbed a railing. "Shit!"

"What's wrong?"

"Nothing."

"Oh. . . . Can I ask you something?" She sounded serious.

"Yeah."

"Uh . . . what's hap—? Hold on."

She started talking to someone else in the background. Must've been that bitch. Then a door shut. He reached the kitchen.

"Sorry about that, Aiden. Just left the flat." Her voice echoed.

"No worries. What you wanna ask me?"

"Never mind. It can wait. . . . See you about four then?"

"I guess."

"OK, bye."

"Bye."

A note greeted him on the kitchen counter.

Grandpickneys, turn on the oven at 11.30 to gas mark 2. Will be back in time to do the rest. Grandma

He'd just started on his Weetabix when his other phone rang. He gritted his teeth as *Pussyclaat* flashed on the screen. She'd forgotten to withhold her number again.

"Yeah?" His mouth was full.

"Humph. You didn't answer, or return, my calls yesterday. What's up with that?"

"I was busy."

"I bet."

"I'm still busy, so hurry up."

"You're always busy doing something, busy with everything and everyone—except your fucking girlfriend."

He banged his fist on the kitchen table, his spoon bouncing on the rim of his bowl and some cereal spilling on Grandma's good tablecloth. He cussed.

"Remember where being wrenk got you last time?"

He ripped off more paper towels than intended and let them soak the mess. "Yeah—I boxed and choked the shit out of you."

"You did, and Carl's pissed about it."

"Bring him come."

"You really think I wouldn't out you if it came to it."

Everything rode on his secret. If not for that . . . "Maybe I'm done."

"Done?"

"Yeah, done hiding. Maybe I'll tell the fam."

She cackled. "Boy, bye."

Course he was shitting her, but he had to fuck with her, see what she would do. "I mean it. I'll tell Elise everything too."

"Aiden, who are you trying to fool?"

"Nobody."

"Listen to me . . ." Her voice was shaky.

He'd gotten to the bitch.

"Don't fuck with me on this. You and I both know you don't want anyone knowing shit about you, so make sure you show up at the flat later. Don't fuck this up!"

He smirked.

"Aiden, do you hear me?"

"Loud and clear, bitch."

She kissed her teeth then hung up.

He put his bowl of cereal on a tray and went to the front room.

He switched on the TV. A damn news report on gay marriage in the USA. He rushed to change the channel, then he stopped, his fingertip hovering over a button on the remote. No one was around to groan or kiss teeth. He turned the volume down. Ethan had a way of coming down the stairs so no one could hear him. Aiden listened out. . . . All clear.

Images of couples kissing and hugging. Nothing but white couples. Tell a lie, a mixed couple: Asian and white. No blacks yet. Like it mattered. He liked females. He liked Elise, just not the circum— A black couple! An Asian couple. Some of them were crying.

That was enough. He pressed a button on the remote control so hard that it didn't come back up on its own. Channels were changing every half-second. It didn't matter what they changed to. It could've been one of the home shopping channels, horse-racing, Welsh . . . anything that wasn't gay-related. He finished his cereal as he fixed the remote and found the BET channel. Adverts.

He sat back in the red velvet armchair, tilted his head back and sighed. Another morning—like so many others, and sometimes afternoons and evenings—spent reminding himself that he wasn't gay. He'd always been able to put it down on females. They still got him off. Elise was a looker, and even Tempest had gotten the business at one point.

There'd been males though, going back to his childhood.

Too far back. He slapped his forehead. That memory needed to fuck off somewhere quickly, before it brought back the memories of everything that followed. Slap, slap, slap. Thump, thump, thump. Out. Of. His. Mind.

Tray in hand, he got up and rushed back to the kitchen, the spoon rattling against the bowl in time with his quick steps. He dropped the bowl and spoon in the sink then caught water. The blast of water helped. He rubbed his stinging mouth, his breath heating his fingertips. He caught a whiff of cocoa butter. It was from the hand soap he'd used upstairs.

Cocoa butter.

That dude on Glyn Road had smelled of it. He was gay. And that woman thinking he was his boyfriend . . . Those men he was with, they were probably gay too. Gay knew gay, he'd heard before. That wasn't him though. It was just that he'd never seen dude before, but he'd only just started going to that barber's house. As long as he kept going that way, he had to bump into him again.

The toilet flushing directly above brought him back. He'd forgotten about the tap. It was turned on high, water wasting. He turned it off. He was about to head upstairs, ready to shower as soon as Ethan came out of the bathroom, when voices emanated from the front room. He went there to turn off the TV. About time

Ethan came through with the money for a flatscreen. He jabbed the button until the two pictures on top moved out of position. He straightened them. Ethan in the first photo. Raine's Foundation School uniform. Maybe year nine. His forehead was covered in spots. He looked like Arthur. People said Ethan and Aiden favoured; if Ethan favoured Arthur, then so did Aiden. But Ethan was so much like Arthur, down to his hatred of gays, gay dudes anyway.

He stared at his seven-year-old self in the other photo. May 1996. He was hardly smiling in the picture. Looked like he was in a dark place. The marks on his back would've been fresh back then. They'd long gone, but he didn't need to see his back to know when he was tracing his fingers over the same areas where the marks used to be, marks caused by a belt buckle.

The front room had turned into his bedroom in his old house. He was seven all over again, his back sizzling as he writhed half-naked on the carpet screaming for his daddy to stop, all the while Daddy shouting, most of the words ending *-claat*, calling him a batty boy. One moment Daddy was beating him senseless, and the next . . . A fucked-up time. The tears everyone had shed over Arthur . . . He'd cried too, cried a lot. Not over Arthur.

Other pictures were scattered around the room in different cabinets. He almost fucked up, nearly looked at the only picture in the cabinet next to the TV, a picture of his dad.

He made his hands into fists. *Dad* around everyone else, *Arthur* the rest of the time.

Arthur.

Ethan's voice came out of nowhere. He was telling someone *laters*. Aiden bounced his shoulders then clenched his glistening eyes, wiping his eye corners just in time.

"Morning, bro." Ethan put his phone inside a pocket of his navy robe.

"Morning, bro."

"Your eyes are red."

"For true?"

"Yeah."

"Oh. . . . Had su'um in them."

Ethan frowned for a moment, adjusted his durag. "What you up to?"

"Nothing. Just ate. Gonna shower now."

"Need to start getting up early on weekends like you."

"Early?"

"To work out. Wish I had your discipline."

He had no intention of working out. Still, he said, "Plenty hours left in the day."

"I guess," Ethan shrugged. "Seeing your girl today?"

He clenched his jaw; he hoped he'd caught himself, that no forehead lines or flared nostrils betrayed him. "Yeah, later."

"Lucky you."

"Gotta get ready. Grandma left a note to turn on the oven in . . ." He checked the grandfather clock above the TV. ". . . ten minutes."

"I'll remember."

Ethan was going to start chatting about females. Time for that shower.

10 / Shannon IV
Seating partners

The front door didn't close until Shannon was a few doors away.

Uncle Lionel and Peter had looked at him like he was mad when he'd told them about Sunday dinner with Elise, a friend of hers, and her sister and her sister's boyfriend.

"You've had a rough time."

"You must be shattered."

"You sure you've recovered from that fall?" . . .

They'd had a point, but he wanted to see Elise. It was either: accept the Sunday dinner invitation or wait until the next weekend, Elise flying out in less than twenty-four hours. They had to catch up properly before she left. Would be a chance to get to know her sister better and meet Elise's boyfriend. She'd never actually called him her boyfriend, just her friend, but the way she'd said *friend* was suspect.

The frigging 236 cut across Richmond Road to the next part of Queensbridge Road. When Richmond Road was clear where he was, he dashed across, then continued to the crossing on Queensbridge Road. The bus was at the stop across the road, a good sprint away. The road was getting clear from the right. The break of traffic from the left— Too late. The bus's right indicator light started flashing; its left side rose until it was level with its right. The traffic stopped all around as the green man lit up. He took off a glove, took out his phone and checked TfL. The next 236 was due in eighteen minutes. Too long to wait, especially in the cold. An off licence was further down, on his side of the road, right next to the tower block. Enough time to get a bottle of something there.

Blossom Hill Rose. One of Elise's favourites. She wasn't much of a drinker. He purchased it then refreshed the TfL webpage. Six minutes. Didn't feel as if twelve minutes had passed. Would be four minutes by the time he reached the bus stop. The lights had just changed for the vehicles to get going again, but gaps were forming from both sides, saving him a trek to the lights. He jogged across. A red single-decker bus emerged in the distance soon after. He checked the time. The bus was early.

The stench of fish hit him as soon as he got on. The culprits must've embarked at Ridley Road Market, two stops earlier. He held his breath for as long as he could. Most of the seats were taken, and a woman was standing with her pram in the wheelchair area. A few people were standing by the exit doors. At least two empty seats in the back row, a couple more behind people's shoulders in the back section. He headed there, many eyes on him. People usually stared when someone got on the bus, and only he had gotten on. Most of the other passengers stopped looking and continued doing what they'd been doing before—looking at their phones or out the window, or staring into space—but there was one who hadn't. A guy in a red jacket in the middle seat at the back of the bus. That guy won the staring contest quickly.

He made it to the seats two rows after the exit doors without tripping over trolley wheels or bumping into anyone standing, despite the jerky bus.

The tingling of someone looking at him was too relentless to ignore. The guy in the red jacket was still staring, but there were others who'd joined the staring contest. Two other guys in the back row, one by each window.

He was tingling elsewhere. A fourth pair of eyes was on him. He glanced, looked away, had to take another look.

A fourth guy, this one fine, finer than fine, toe-curling fine. Familiar too. Eyes a kind of brown that could only be explained by contacts. The guy he'd opened the car door into, right outside his house—his old house. It was His Fineness.

His Fineness narrowed his eyes, making them ten times more devastating. Mutual recognition. He couldn't put a finger on it. Then his facial expression relaxed. He made that gesture, that quick movement of the head, that manly alternative of saying hello.

Shannon tried to return the gesture, heart racing. His Fineness was squinting, even though there was no sun. Shannon must've looked stupid trying to pull off something he couldn't. A simple *hi* would've sufficed, but the word caught in his throat as he stared at His Fineness. He looked even better than before. Slightly different, but better, if that was even possible.

The shape-up. That explained it. Probably a fresh haircut underneath the woolly hat. He had a tiny hoop earring in each ear. His full lips were even more pronounced by the sharp geometry of his shape-up. His beard was thick like before, and the cut on his lip healing—funny how imperfections could be sexy—and those thick eyebrows were fit for an Egyptian king.

Lines were forming between His Fineness's eyebrows.

Promise broken. Again. Could frigging hear himself breathe. He must've looked crazy standing there all that time. Even other passengers were staring at him again. His Fineness's intense gaze had weakened him, kept butterflies active in his stomach.

The bus pulled into the Middleton Road/Queensbridge Road bus stop. One whole stop—too long to have been standing there staring. He unzipped his jacket and wiped sweat from his forehead with the palm of his hand. He finally sat down. He was to the left of His Fineness, but one row behind. He looked ahead, but he could tell in his periphery that His Fineness, head turned, was staring at him. Something was about to happen. He'd been lucky that time on the tube, because it had been a quick journey. This time, he was stuck all the way to Eastway, unless His Fineness got off before. Or maybe Shannon needed to take matters into his own hands. It was still early. *He*'d get off, walk away from the bus stop until the bus moved off, then return to wait for the next 236.

It was Sunday though; the 236 never even ran that well on weekdays. And it was cold. More importantly, £1.50 had been deducted from his Oyster card.

His Fineness had turned back around, was facing forwards. Breathing and pulse could return to normal.

His Fineness leaned to the left. Shannon did the same, right into the person next to him. He apologised and straightened up. He faced forward but turned his eyes as far right as possible. His Fineness was struggling to get something out of his right-hand pocket. Would've taken it out already if he were going in the pocket of his black hoodie. Whatever he was after must've been in his pants pocket. He was wearing snug-fitting denim jeans, a bit of his white sock exposed. His grey Skechers must've been a size twelve at least.

He finally stopped leaning, had taken out his phone. Shannon had to turn his body to the right for a better view, but not too much to betray himself. That *no staring* vow was about to be broken one last time. He shifted in his seat, the bend of his right leg extending over the aisle, so that the woman standing behind her pram in the wheelchair area dominated his view. His Fineness looked behind. Shannon made sure he didn't get caught looking this time. His Fineness turned to face forward again. Shannon waited a few moments before straining to look to the right once more. The guy was tapping away on his phone. He was communicating with someone. Probably had a girlfriend, maybe more than one. With that face, build and height—he had to be at least six-three—there was no way he was single. Whoever had him to go to bed with and wake up next to—or under, or on top of—was a lucky bitch.

A distraction from the left. The woman next to him pressed the bus stop button in front of him. As the bus turned onto Mare Street, she got up, just like that, no *excuse me*. He got up, just as His Fineness did the same. The guy was getting off.

Or not.

He stepped back, right into the woman Shannon had let out, as he let the woman he was sitting next to get past. They sat back down at the same time. Neither one of them moved to the inner seat. The seat next to Shannon needed to cool down after that woman's big backside had been on it. His Fineness must've remained on the outer seat for the same reason. Or maybe he was getting off soon.

Passengers off. Passengers on. Hard to tell if staring at, or away from, a new passenger deterred them from sitting next to him. He didn't make eye contact with anyone, just used his peripheral vision. The first person sat at the front. So did the next. The third didn't. He was coming, then he stopped at the exit doors, where he found space to stand.

The bus skipped the next stop. Shuffling all around as people prepared to alight at Hackney Town Hall. Plenty of people at the bus stop stretched their arms out. The bus was going to get full. He shifted to the inner seat as more people got on than off. The empty seats were filled quickly; people slumped as if they'd been on their feet for hours. An elderly couple approached. Most of the people sitting at the front were elderly. The couple was looking at the passengers they passed, their eyesight probably not great, as if to assess who was able to give up their seat. His Fineness stood up, got their attention, offered his seat. There was more to him than just his looks. His girlfriend was a really lucky bitch.

His Fineness was approaching. No frigging time to prepare. His Fineness slumped down right next to him, bringing a divine scent with him. He smelled as good as he looked. Shannon clenched his fists and strained to control his breathing as they stared at each other. The guy's gaze was too intense. No help in the fight to control his breathing, which he could hear again. His Fineness had to hear it too. Shannon broke the eye contact. He closed his eyes as he became light-headed. His Fineness's scent was fabric softener. It was intoxicating. Something pressed against his leg.

He opened his eyes. Their legs were touching.

His right leg shook at the contact, while His Fineness's left was carefree and solid. It was a strain to break the contact then maintain the distance; each time he moved his leg, His Fineness encroached more of his space and made contact again. Maybe he couldn't help it, with his long legs and broad shoulders, and someone standing next to him where the aisle was narrowest. A bit of a piss-take though. Looked like His Fineness wasn't that considerate after all.

The limited space and the effort to prevent contact with His Fineness were taking a toll, groin aching and right leg shaking. His only option was to intensify the contact between their legs.

Made no difference. It was as if His Fineness was numb to him, just like when they'd first met, when Shannon's hands had been on him and he didn't pull away immediately. But the closeness was a dream come true. He'd been this close to his former barbers, but none of them had been his type. His Fineness though . . . a different matter completely. This was something to savour while it lasted. Knowing his luck, His Fineness was about to slip away, out of the seat and off this bus.

By the time the bus reached Homerton Hospital, it no longer mattered that their legs were still touching. His Fineness might as well have been someone familiar, like Uncle Lionel, Peter or Elise.

The Glyn Road stop was coming up. He couldn't look out the window as the bus passed. He couldn't look right either. His seating partner would weaken him with that gaze of his. He was going to have to close his eyes, and listen out for the bus pulling away and speeding off before opening them again.

"Coming up to that road where you tried to kill me," His Fineness said out of nowhere.

His Fineness was smiling at him. And it was some smile, especially since it looked like smiling wasn't something he usually did. It was a rugged smile, seductive, the right side of his top lip curled up.

He was losing it, his heartbeat frigged up. "I-I-I . . ."

Lines between His Fineness's eyebrows again. He was still smiling, but the lines made him look evil. Was never good to be looked at like that. Only dangerous people could make that face. His Fineness must've had him figured out. Funny it had taken so long. Straight men usually picked up on Shannon's interest in them quicker than that. His Fineness must've realised his countenance was unnerving, because his face became expressionless.

"Hope I . . . didn't hurt you."

"Needed help getting out of bed. Big old bruise in my side."

"Sorry. I don't know what's wrong with me. I—"

That rugged smile again. "Just ramping with you."

Ramping. Caribbean. Perhaps Jamaican.

The driver shouted at people to move down, more people getting on than off. His Fineness leaned into him, the fabric softener coming to life again, as people passed. Funny how he could prevent contact with the people passing him but wasn't aware of his contact with Shannon. If this were a dream, he would have straddled His Fineness and let him have his way with him. Movement in his pants . . . He snuffed that fantasy out.

"It's funny." His Fineness was no longer leaning, but his upper body was somehow closer.

"What's funny?"

"Seen you twice now. Never seen you before." Not much lip movement from His Fineness, as if his top and bottom teeth were stuck together, or his lips were too heavy to part. His lips were full, but not necessarily big.

"I know." All he could manage.

A glimmer from below made him look there. He gasped at what he discovered.

"Look's bad, innit?"

He jumped, blinking repeatedly. Couldn't afford to let even one teardrop escape. "W-what?"

"The scratch on my hand."

He looked at His Fineness's hand again. A scratch indeed.

His Fineness squinted. "You alright?"

Something needed to happen for him to get over the disappointment, before he ended up crying. The pressure in his throat was trying to take him there. He couldn't let tears escape. Didn't even know the guy.

"I'm . . . fine."

His Fineness squinted again. "You know what else is funny?"

"What?"

His Fineness broke eye contact for a moment, as if wondering if he should continue, then looked at Shannon again, still squinting. "What that woman said."

Felt like his heart was about to burst, everything around him swimming.

That smirk returned, making him weak again.

The bus stopped vibrating.

It was as if his ears had been blocked and suddenly cleared up. Complete silence for an instant, then murmurs, followed by an announcement from the driver that the bus had broken down, then expletives and teeth-kissing. It was going to take forever and a day for everyone to get off.

When there was space, His Fineness got up quickly and let him out in front. People in front got up, blocking the aisle. His Fineness's breathing tickled his ear and neck; he scratched where he'd been tickled, zipped up his jacket and pulled up his collar as he willed the space in front to grow faster. He got to the front of the bus, tore a transfer ticket from the machine then looked to see if the bus stop showed bus times. It didn't. He took out his phone and checked the TfL webpage. Fifteen minutes until the next 236.

His Fineness was approaching, the hood of his Nike zip hoodie up, foggy breath clouding his face.

He looked at His Fineness's left hand again, just to make sure the ring was on the finger between the middle and baby fingers.

It frigging was. Just his luck to crush on a married man. He started walking.

"Where you going?"

"Uh . . . it's too cold. The next 236 is fifteen minutes away."

"Shit. That's too long."

"Have a nice day." He barely looked at His Fineness, proceeded to cross Lee Conservancy Road.

"Hold up!"

He grimaced then turned around. His Fineness looked hesitant then seemed to be studying him, as if seeing right through his River Island jacket to his denim shirt, through that to his vest, and through that to his skin.

"Where you get your hair cut?"

"My hair?"

"Yeah. It looks sharp."

"Could say the same for yours."

"My barber's alright, but he's too thief. How much does yours charge?"

"I do it myself."

His Fineness laughed, puffs of smoke from his mouth and nose clouding his face. Then he stopped. "Ah lie!"

Definitely Jamaican. "Seriously."

"Damn. Maybe I should come to you."

"Oh, I'm not a barber. No qualifications. No nothing. Just—"

"I'll pay you."

"I don't even have the time to—"

"Gimme your number." His Fineness took out his phone.

Felt as if something had gripped his heart and started shaking it.

"Your number."

What was going on?

"Alright, I'll give you mine and you can gimme a missed call."

"I don't even cut hair. What if I mess up?"

"Then I'll claat you."

He flinched.

"Just ramping." His Fineness snickered. "Just take my number. I need another barber. Can't keep throwing money away. And he smokes too much weed, and . . . Just save my number."

This straight man, who was married, was insisting on exchanging numbers—something wasn't right.

"You ready?"

"Uh . . . OK." This was all happening too fast.

His Fineness said his number, and Shannon keyed it in, for whatever reason.

"Got it?"

"Uh . . . I've got to go." He stumbled across the road then headed to a pathway in Mabley Green, His Fineness calling out to him.

He didn't know his name.

Didn't need to know. He was never going to call the number that was waiting to be called. He was going to delete it.

He needed to get away from His Fineness first.

11 / Shannon V
Mabley Green

Well into Mabley Green, it was as if Shannon had entered a different time zone, darkness falling upon him suddenly. Shadows were visible, lighting along the footpath weak under the indigo sky.

Footsteps from behind came out of nowhere, as if someone had been running. He looked behind. Three guys, one in a red jacket, the other two in beige ones. The same guys who'd been sitting at the back of the bus. They were peering at him. The one stuffed in the red jacket was in the middle like before. Shannon turned back around and quickened his pace.

They quickened theirs.

His heart started frigging about. He turned around again. They were still staring at him. He stared back at each of them as he walked backwards. Didn't recognize them. If he stopped, maybe they would pass. Or perhaps he could walk on the soggy grass—the friggers took up the width of the footpath—and head back to Lee Conservancy Road.

But if they moved to the grass too, blocking his way . . .

He couldn't take that step. If something was going to happen, he needed to be prepared. His heart was thumping too hard, the smoke leaving his nostrils too thick, for him to be ready. He turned around and walked even faster, almost tripping over his feet, legs shaking as if he were on stilts. They sped up too, their frigging shadows getting closer to devouring his, with every lamp post. So many football goal posts and no one playing football. Just one person way out to the left—a woman, judging by the long, swaying hair—with her dog. The wind was picking up, competing with the road noise from the A12 in the distance. Sounded like wind disturbing the ocean. Lights in the reddish-brown houses on the right were off, trees with leaves the same colour blocking some of the windows.

He was alone. No one would hear his cries for help.

He looked behind again. He gasped. Their eyes were narrower. One of them was smirking. One of the Beiges, the white one. The other two were black. The bottle of Blossom Hill in his hand wasn't going to reach Elise's flat. Not a drop of it would be swallowed. He could run fast, but they were probably just as fast, or faster, fitter. It seemed that running away, hiding or submitting was all he'd ever done, running from his parents countless times as a child and accepting punishment when caught. Even two days ago when he ran from them, locked himself in his room—old room—and fell out of the window . . . the desperation.

At least he didn't have much money on him. Nothing but change in his wallet. No repeat of what had happened that time he withdrew £200 from Barclays. Two hundred fucking pounds down the drain. *His* money. A knife pressed into his throat while some frigger laid hands on him—as if he owned him—looking for the wallet he'd put the £200 in. Shaking to the point that the knife actually pricked him and drew blood. Shaking from wanting to claat the fucker, but not being able to because that would've meant being stabbed to death. Shaking to keep the tears from falling down his face. And when they did fall, the fucker's eyes lit up.

Something like that wasn't going to happen to him again.

No matter what his three followers intended to do to him.

117

He turned his head slightly to the left, straining to look as far as possible. If he stopped there and then, one of them would bump into him instantly. He didn't have much money to lose. He'd be the one laughing when they realised he had change that probably didn't even come to a fiver. He tied the plastic bag handles around the neck of the Blossom Hill bottle and wrapped his cramped, yet gloved, fingers around it, as if gripping the handle of a tennis racket. He slowed down.

One of the friggers darted in front of him.

He stopped. One of the other two bumped into him.

He swallowed. "S-scuse me."

His heart was beating too fast, and his breathing too strained. At this rate, they were going to do as they pleased with him and hardly break a sweat. He needed time to muster up the courage to claat one, two, or all of them with the bottle, but time was almost up.

Time *was* up. He was surrounded.

One of them behind mimicked him.

Fuck you too, you frigging shithouse.

"The fucking faggot cut his eyes," Red said.

They could actually tell.

One of the Beiges got him in a chokehold. His heart was going wild, everything swimming all around again. If not for being choked, he would've probably fallen, as weak as his legs were.

The choker started patting him down.

"I . . . have . . . n-no m-money." He sounded so pathetic, his speech as wobbly as his fucking legs.

The choker found the wallet immediately and tossed it at Red, who looked inside, stretching it as if £50 notes would magically appear. The choker patted him some more.

"I don't . . . h-have . . . anymore m-money. Just—"

His phone. He'd forgotten about that.

Couldn't break free.

"Batty man's desperate." That was Black Beige; the choker was White Beige.

In an instant, White Beige's hand was inside the pocket with the phone. Shannon grabbed his arm.

White Beige squeezed tighter around his neck. "Let go, you cunt!"

Felt like his head was about to burst. White Beige took out the phone then pushed him into Red.

Red played with his beard then backhanded him. "Watch it, pussyhole!"

Free hand in the right place at the right time. Would've ended up on his backside otherwise. A wonder he hadn't dropped the Blossom Hill. God knew how he managed to stand up straight again, as much as his legs were shaking. He was shaking all over, the lump in his throat unbearable. He wasn't going to cry though. Couldn't let that happen. Wasn't going to touch his stinging cheek. Maybe if he just stood there and pretended he hadn't just been boxed . . .

"Do it again," White Beige said.

He clenched his fist, brought it to his prickling cheek. He was shaking too much, pressure in his throat getting the better of him. A tear fell. Then another. He clenched his eyes shut.

"Crying like some pussy!"

All three fuckers laughed.

He gritted his teeth, could feel his lips tremble and hear himself struggle to keep from bawling as he breathed.

Someone hit his shoulder.

"Box him again," Black Beige said. "Give the batty boy su'um to really cry about."

He opened his eyes. Tears and fog from his staggered breathing blurred his vision. That didn't keep him from seeing Red coming towards him, hand raised. If it were just Red, he would've boxed him back ages ago. He hadn't been in many fights, but he'd been taught to hit back. Hornes fought back.

This situation was no exception.

He was going to do what he'd seen Zhang Ziyi's character do to Chris Tucker's in *Rush Hour 2*. Red was the right distance from him. He had to do it before Red got any closer. It had to work despite his weak legs. Missing would be a disaster, an embarrassment. He tightened his face then jump-front-kicked. The first kick got Red in the stomach—no good because of the red padded jacket—but the next got him right in the face, Red going down like someone attempting a backflip but landing on his back.

Movement behind. Shadows combined. The other two friggers were about to pounce. He had to be as quick as his heartbeat. He swung around and claated one of them with the bottle, like Serena Williams crunching a forehand. The crack of the impact echoed. The frigger crumpled to the ground, as if dropping dead that instant.

The last one standing, White Beige, took something out of his jacket pocket.

A flick knife.

"You're dead, faggot!"

Footsteps scraped the gravel behind, then there was a roar. Before he knew it, someone hauled him down to the grass from behind. He landed right next to Black Beige, who was motionless.

Someone forced him onto his back.

"Look at my fucking mouth!" Red said, spraying blood on his face.

He turned his head to wipe his face on his shoulder, but Red had him pinned. Red started punching him, getting him on the forehead and cheek, before he blocked with his forearm.

"Let's kill him!" White Beige said.

He started kicking wildly to no avail.

He hit Red with the broken bottle, as much as the bag, slippery with blood and leaking Blossom Hill, and being punched, allowed.

Red's blows were faster and more brutal than before. A kick to the head. Then another.

White Beige.

He tried to reposition under Red's weight, amidst blows from different directions, as he blocked punches with one arm and protected his head from White Beige's kicks with the other. Frantic movements. Something kept shimmering then disappearing.

The knife.

His heart was on the verge of giving out. It took everything to keep from crying again, to keep from screaming for help, for mercy. He had to keep moving, yet blocking, keeping close to Red so that White Beige didn't have a fixed target as he slashed and punched. But there was only so long he could keep this going.

Two against one.

Soon three against one once Black Beige got back up. They were going to finish him.

Exhaustion—physical and mental—was slowing him down. Writhing, blocking and staying close to Red was all he could do.

Something blue was near his hand . . . *in* his hand. . . . The Blossom Hill bag. He squeezed what was left of it, glove protecting his hand from the shards, and noted as best he could, amidst the punches and flailing and writhing, where White Beige was. Too much was happening, but he couldn't go on like this. He had to act quickly, change tactics, even if it meant not blocking.

Red pinned one of his arms to the ground, moaning and grimacing with demonic effort. Couldn't keep hold of the bag with the broken bottle.

"Come on!" Red said, pinning his other arm to his chest. "Cut him the fuck up!"

White Beige crouched, blade glinting.

Writhing, as if on fire, wasn't enough; Red was too strong, too heavy. His cheeks tickled with tears as White Beige brought the blade down to his throat. He flinched then trembled against the ice-cold blade, heart rate sky high.

He closed his eyes to Red's shithouse face and the indigo sky, stopped resisting, let his nose run, just wanted them to get it over with. He'd lost everything anyway. They were doing him a favour. The wind picked up, gave him permission to bawl.

He swallowed as the back of his head was pressed into concrete and the blade scraped his throat. As he mumbled for them to hurry up and kill him, there was a thud. A second thud when something dropped on the grass. Then someone grunted before something else dropped.

The knife fell off his neck and rattled on the concrete. He opened his eyes. Red was looking up, forgetting to maintain his stronghold.

An opportunity taken to knee Red in the balls. He flailed his legs about, getting Red everywhere he could until the fucker was off him completely. He struggled to his feet, tripped over White Beige, who was sprawled on the footpath and holding the back of his head, and fell on the sodden grass and footpath, right next to someone's Skechers.

He looked up.

Wind blew the hood off the person's head, revealing a woolly hat. The top of his head was framed in gold from the nearest lamp post. The earring in his right ear glinted.

The person shifted until his face was clearer, his left earring glinting.

His Fineness.

Shannon struggled to his feet once more.

Red had fingers under his bloody nose as he got up. White Beige picked up his flick knife, hand still on the back of his head, his eyes on a brick, then he got to his feet. Red took out a knife of his own.

Shannon widened his eyes then glanced at Black Beige. He was still lying motionless, but something was different—the grass around his head was drowning in blood. His stomach churned.

The other two pricks followed his gaze, looked at each other, then shot looks at him that made his skin crawl.

His Fineness took something out of his pocket.

Shannon stumbled back at the sight of it, its blade glinting under the lamp post.

"You ready?" His Fineness had that devilish look again, worse than before, because he was snarling rather than smiling, nostrils flared. He was in no ramping mood.

Neither were Red and White Beige, knives wielded.

His Fineness and White Beige approached each other, legs slightly bent, feet shoulder-width apart, knives primed to end life.

Red was staring at Shannon like he was going to give him an excruciating end.

Hardly any life in his legs still. Needed to do something about that quickly because His Fineness and White Beige had started scuffling, had ended up falling to the concrete, fighting to stab and to keep from being stabbed.

Something snatched his attention from His Fineness and White Beige.

Red was charging at him.

12 / Elise III
News

"No answer." Elise ended her umpteenth call to Shannon. "He would've let me know if he couldn't make it."

Tempest was pacing from one side of the kitchen to the other, her head shaking, eyes vacant.

"Tempest!" She grabbed her sister by the wrist. "Aiden sent his apologies. He just couldn't make it."

Tempest scowled at Elise's hand around her wrist then slowly lifted her head until eye contact was made, as if to tell her to let go—or else.

"It's not like Shannon to—"

Tempest snatched her wrist out of Elise's grip, pulling her off balance.

"Tempest!"

Tempest was back to acting like she was the only one in the kitchen.

"Fine." Elise stormed to the sink. "Getting on my nerves," she muttered as she shoved her hands into washing up gloves.

"Damn it!"

She jumped.

"All for nothing!"

"Temp, didn't you hear what I just said? Aiden apologised for not showing up, and—"

Tempest put out her hand to shut her up.

Elise turned around, continued washing up.

"I guess I'll go now." Carl nearly made her drop a glass.

He'd spent ages in the bathroom. If he'd done a number two . . .

"OK then. Take care." She forced a smile.

"I'll walk him out."

"Yeah, whatever."

Could've sworn Tempest cut her eyes at her. Difficult to tell with the half-fringe Tempest was now rocking, accompanying her pixie cut.

With Tempest and Carl gone, the only sounds came from the radio, and the crockery and cutlery as she scrubbed and rinsed them under a burst of hot water.

Tempest didn't need to be so worked up. She'd put in a lot of effort, but she'd come up with the get-together out of nowhere. It could've waited. Shannon and Aiden's absences looked bad on Elise anyway. Didn't make sense for Tempest to have an attitude—unless she was still riled up from the hair appointment mix-up.

Some nerve if that were the case. Tempest knew Elise had planned on getting a pixie. Clearly she was no longer tired of people saying how much they favoured. Tempest had her mother's heart-shaped face, wide mouth and Nefertiti bust complexion, yet with short hair, anyone could've seen Pa in her. Funny how she favoured Sylvia so much, especially with the braids in, yet people thought she and Elise favoured, and Elise looked nothing like Sylvia.

Sylvia.

It was her fault Sylvia wasn't alive, her fault Tempest was motherless. Tempest's mum was never coming back. At least Elise had hers. The copycat hairstyle didn't compare. She could live with it. Besides, she was never going to rock a half-fringe, long set on an upsweep.

She flinched as something wet ran down her forearms. She yanked her gloved, soggy hands out of the water-filled sink, some of the soapy water splashing her face and blouse, and the tiles.

"Damn it!"

"That's what happens when you daydream."

She gasped and spun around, making more of a mess. She flinched when water spilled over to her feet. "Shit, Tempest! Didn't hear you come back."

"I know."

Silence lingered as Tempest stood there staring at her. Elise broke eye contact, turned back to the sink. She took off the gloves, made them dry out, then used a knife to unblock the sink.

"I'm off to bed."

"Good—"

Tempest's quick, fading footsteps kept the rest of Elise's sentence stuck in her mouth, her pursed lips frozen. Music from the radio filled the silence.

Aretha Franklin's "A Rose Is Still A Rose" had barely started when the ten o'clock news came on, the washing up done. Something about Mabley Green. She drew closer to the radio and turned up the volume.

". . . the victim died from his injuries. Police are in the process of tracking down the anonymous caller who made the 999 call at approximately 5.45 pm, hoping to get some answers . . ."

The rest of the news went over her head as she browsed the latest news in Hackney. One headline after another gave her the same information, in different forms. The message was clear: an incident—something to do with a knife, a brick and a broken Blossom Hill bottle—resulted in the death of a young man. Practically on her doorstep.

Her heart was starting to pound. The pounding radiated to her head, as if she had a second heart right between her ears.

Her hand shaking, she rang him again. One ring. Two. Three. Four. . . . Chest clutch. . . . Six rings. Seven. . . . Ten. She stopped counting long before voicemail came on. "Shan . . . I . . ." She swallowed. "Call me back . . . as soon as you can. . . . Been trying you . . . all evening. . . . I'm worried that . . . Just call me . . . text me . . . something . . . please."

A blocked sensation in her ear, the kind she experienced during flights, took over when she ended the call. She collapsed onto a stool.

Blossom freaking Hill. He knew she liked that. Mabley Green was too soon for him to get off though. The news couldn't have been about him.

But he wasn't answering his freaking phone.

He was good when it came to responding to calls. If he took long, it was with good reason, just like Friday evening.

Trouble had kept him from responding that time.

Trouble.

She didn't have his uncle's number, otherwise she would've called him long ago. She searched through her contacts for Shannon's home—former home—number. Her finger hovered over the record when she found it. Couldn't bear his parents' wrath. They'd disowned him though. He had no reason to go anywhere near them after everything that had happened, and— Damn it. The screen was too pissing sensitive. She was calling Shannon's house. She was about to hang up when a gruff voice answered.

"Hello?" Shan's dad said again, his voice thick with impatience.

"Hello."

"Who is this?"

"It's . . . Elise."

"Elise? . . . Elise!"

"Hi. I—"

"You nuh fi call this number."

"It's Shan—"

"The two of unu take we make poppyshow—"

"I think something's happened to him."

Silence.

"Hello?"

"I . . ."

"I'm hoping you've seen him."

Silence again.

"Hello? Are you still—"

"He's not our concern anymore. Nuh call this number again."

"But I'm worried about him . . . and so should you."

A strained breath came through from the other end. Hard to tell if that was worry or irritation.

"He's your son. Please, just—"

He hung up on her.

Eleven-thirty. Unanswered calls, one after another. Her cheeks were wet and sticky. She dragged herself, using the support of the kitchen table, then the washing machine, then the fridge door handle, to the kitchen door. Head spinning. She stumbled into the passage table, shifting the candle holder out of position then grabbed hold of the radiator.

Almost at Tempest's bedroom door. "Tempest!" she called, sniffling. "Tempest!" She knocked.

Nothing.

"Tempest!" She put her ear against the door and stopped sniffling.

Painful groans.

"Tempest?"

Distressed moans.

"Tempest?"

Tempest shrieked.

"Tempest!" She burst into her sister's bedroom.

The piercing shriek stopped abruptly when eye contact was made. Buzzing filled the silence. Tempest's body was shaking, one hand in the bust of her leopard-print nightie, and the other . . .

The light from the passage that the open door let in was hitting the buzzing vibrator. A slew of curse words betrayed Tempest further. The same light was weaker on Tempest's face, but not weak enough to hide the contortions, her head thrashing from side to side. She couldn't control what she was feeling, even with Elise standing there. The waves weren't going to stop sweeping through until they were ready to. A long time since Elise had played with herself. Even longer since someone had been inside her. Not the virgin everyone thought she was, but as good as. No one's business. She would be taken as a wife by her husband next time.

"Why-the-fuck-are-you-still-here?"

She flinched.

"Get— Aaaah!"

She scurried to the front room then slumped down on the sofa.

"Elise!" Tempest staggered towards her, snarling.

"Tempest, I'm so sor—"

Tempest pulled her to her feet. "Stupid bitch!" Clap. "What the fuck?"

Elise grabbed hold of the armrest. She would've fallen on the coffee table otherwise. She put her free, shaking hand to her cheek as if the sensation of a thousand pins pricking her skin would disappear instantly.

Her cheek suddenly felt as soiled as it did prickly, the places Tempest's hand had likely been moments ago making her skin crawl.

"What the *fuck* is going on?" Tempest said, her eyes wild, Listerine breath stifling.

The box had messed with Elise's upsweep, strands in her eye.

"The . . . news . . ."

"What news?"

"Someone died in Mabley Green."

Tempest crossed her arms, waiting for more information.

She rubbed her cheek some more, as much to rub sex from it as to quell the pain. "I've been phoning Shannon all evening."

Tempest's expression hardened some more. "And?"

She flexed her cheek, still rubbing it. "What if it's him?"

Tempest leaned into her. "Are you fucking joking?"

Elise stepped back. "He hasn't called back. It's not like him. I'm worried that someone robbed him or hurt him because—"

"Bitch, please!" Lines appeared like claws on Tempest's forehead, her fringe tucked under her golden head wrap.

Stunned into silence.

Tempest took a deep breath, her eyes closed. "It's a coincidence, that's all." Just like that, she was calm, her forehead line-free. "Maybe he's lost his phone."

All she could do was squint at Tempest, no idea what was coming next.

Tempest snapped her fingers in her face. "Stop staring through me."

"I just—"

"Look, I have to wake up early, and so do you. What time is Daddy picking you up?"

"At five."

"Then you really need to get some sleep."

"I . . . suppose."

"Shannon's fine."

"He is?"

"Yeah. You'll hear from him soon."

"I will?"

"Yes. Say you will."

"Say it?"

"Yes, like you mean it."

"I'll hear from Shannon."

"Yes."

"He's . . . OK. "

"Like you mean it."

"He's OK."

"Good. Now go to bed."

"I will, but . . . the kitchen . . . just need to finish up."

"Fine. Goodnight."

"Goodnight."

The slap of Tempest's slippers along the wooden floor faded, stopped, then started again, getting closer. "Elise!"

"Yes?"

Tempest's head was down, keeping eye contact to a minimum, like a little girl about to confess to her elder that she'd misbehaved, nothing like the savage lioness—or leopardess—she'd been moments before. "Sorry for calling you a bitch . . . and for boxing you."

Tempest had crossed the line.

Didn't compare to robbing Tempest of her mother.

"Did you hear me?"

"I heard you." It was her turn to make minimal eye contact. "Sorry for—"

Tempest gave another stop signal with her hand. "Accepted. Night."

She stood still until Tempest's bedroom door clicked closed. Then came more clicking. Locking.

She went back to the kitchen and closed the door, paced as Tempest had done earlier.

Lianne La Havas startled her. She almost dropped the phone.

Shannon was on the screen.

"Shan! Thank God! Someone died in Mabley Green and I was scared it was you, and . . . Shan, why aren't you saying anything?"

Breathing. Then nothing.

"Hello? Shan?" Maybe his signal was bad.

She sat on one of the black-and-silver chairs around the matching round table, waited for Shan to ring again.

Her phone soon vibrated. A text from him.

Hey. Soz bout that. Soz 4 missing ur calls. Just a quick text 2 let u no im ok. L8r.

She frowned. It was his name and number above the message box, but that wasn't a Shannon kind of text. No *xoxo* at the end, the abbreviated words . . . and since when did he start writing *Hey*? No explanation or apology for his no-show. So unlike him.

Maybe he had no time for one of his usual texts. He'd been having a hard time lately. He deserved to be cut some slack.

She responded.

Thanks for the message. Glad to know you're OK. We'll catch up in the week. I'm going to bed. xoxo

She was about to switch off the kitchen light when her phone vibrated again. Another text from Shannon. A thumbs up emoji.

Again, so unlike him.

13 / Tempest III
Going for the jugular

A soothing René & Angela song, along with the eye mask Tempest was wearing, should've been enough to lull her into a deep sleep, but she was still wide awake. The damn mask was tickling her. She took it off and threw it somewhere in the darkness on the hardwood floor. She squinted at the clock on her bedside table. Seven minutes until midnight. Seven minutes left of her mum's birthday. Less than seven hours to go before she had to get up. Sleep wasn't going to come any time soon, especially as she replayed that bitch barging in on her then standing there like an ass, staring, just as she was coming.

Anita Baker was just getting started when the midnight news cut her off. End of Mum's birthday. She shifted to lay on her side. She grabbed one of her two pillows and hugged it close as she listened. The Mabley Green shit. Still no suspects. Dead victim unidentified. If it were Shannon . . . No. Not enough misery for Elise.

She changed position again when the news ended and Omar's vocals came through. She was on her stomach, her head on one pillow and her arm on the other, as if she were resting her arm on Carl's barrel chest, post-sex. He would've fucked her to sleep if he'd stayed—then Elise would've walked in on the two of them!

Everything had been just fine—indescribable intensity, the image of Carl deep in her mind—until Elise fucked it all up.

She pulled the duvet tighter over her shoulders, keeping herself from being exposed even though she was wearing a nightie and it was just her in the room. No masturbation again any time soon. Marvin Gaye and Tammi Terrell singing that there was nothing like the real thing reassured her that maybe no masturbation wasn't so bad after all.

Then she was gone.

She woke up to a chill on her neck. Her bed had always been by the window, but that was a strong draught.

Shuffling. Looked like something was floating. She rubbed sleep out of her eyes.

Something was definitely moving, approaching her.

Taps on the floor . . . like someone was walking without wanting to be heard.

Someone was sneaking up on her.

She flailed her arms and legs as far as the sheets allowed, the person like a shadow, blending in with the darkness. A hand was pressed over her mouth before she could say anything. Her heart accelerated. Her screams were muffled. The hand smelled familiar. Bath and Body Works. Sweet Vanilla Sugar. Elise. She writhed, but Elise's hand was like superglue to her mouth. Looked like the bitch wasn't over the slap. She had to be mad coming into her room unannounced yet again.

But the door was locked.

Or maybe she'd forgotten to lock it.

No, she hadn't. She'd turned the key, heard the lock click into place and checked that it was locked.

She thrashed her head, her head wrap slipping off, until she got Elise's hand off her mouth.

"What the fuck, Elise?"

She managed to snatch her arms from underneath the duvet and flailed them about until she grabbed Elise's forearm.

Elise's arm was fleshy, strong.

It wasn't Elise.

She fingered her way up meaty arms, brushed against big breasts, then clawed blindly at the person's face. The woman kissed her teeth then started choking her. She dug her nails into the choker's skin. The intruder made a sucking sound then let go of her neck.

"El—" She coughed. "Elise!"

The person climbed on top of her. "Yuh wretch yuh!"

What the fuck was *she* doing in her room?

She fumbled for the lamp switch to the right. The person slapped her hand, then her cheek. Before she could recover from the blow, the person's hands were around her neck again, nails digging in.

"Mari . . . etta."

"Shut up!"

"Let . . . go." She reached for the heifer's face again.

Mari-heifer wouldn't let her hands reach her face. Mari-heifer pressed her into the bed, choking her tighter, the bed springs crunching until they could crunch no more.

"I . . . c-can't . . . breathe."

Another go at the heifer's face. Held too firmly to reach it. Losing strength. Darkness had been against her from the start. She was gagging. Couldn't keep her arm up . . . let it drop to the bed. The other arm was dropping too. No strength to dig her nails into skin as she slipped away. Could only manage to scrape Mari-heifer's neck. Chest burning, head about to explode, body writhing, fighting the end.

One arm was still up.

Something was keeping it up. Her fingers had caught onto something, something hanging. Mari-heifer fell on her, one less hand around her neck. She could suck in air again. Mari-heifer moaned like she was in pain. Fingers still caught in something on Mari-heifer's head.

The bitch's earring. She yanked at it and scratched the hand that was still around her neck. Mari-heifer let go completely. Tempest wheezed, still yanking the heifer's earring. Leg by leg, she freed herself from under the duvet and the big bitch, then kicked, kicked, kicked. She kept kicking and pulling, roaring like a lioness, until the heifer fell off the bed.

The earring was still in her hand. She threw it somewhere in the darkness.

Mari-heifer screamed. Tempest stumbled out of the bed, still wheezing. So unsteady that she slammed into the wall. She fumbled for the light switch.

"You bitch!"

She turned on the light, just as Mari-heifer charged into her, bringing her down to the floor. She was underneath the big heifer again. So much movement. Had to squint whenever Mari-heifer's head wasn't blocking the light.

"Going kill you!"

A backhand to her cheek. Another one. A box in the nose made her see stars.

"What you're doing . . . to my one . . . and only pickney . . . stops now."

"Elise! Elise! Eliiiiise!"

She kicked Mari-heifer in her old pussy.

The heifer grabbed herself, grimaced. Tempest punched her square in the nose.

Free from that weight on top of her, she scrambled to the door, found the handle and pulled it down.

The door wouldn't open. It *was* locked, the key still in the hole.

She turned the key, but it wouldn't turn all the fucking way. She pushed her body into it and turned the key. That worked.

Growling from behind. She looked that way. Mari-heifer was getting up.

She turned to face the door again then pulled the handle down. She opened the door a crack before Mari-heifer brought her down to the floor again with the strength of a bear.

The door moved in her periphery.

Someone was in the doorway.

She multi-tasked, fighting and trying to get a better look at who was standing there. Could just about make out red attire. She elbowed and clawed at Mari-heifer as she took another look. Light wasn't shining on the face, but she glimpsed the upsweep.

She couldn't get comfortable, Mari-heifer pulling her hair, but at least Elise was in the room.

"Elise . . . help me!"

Her scalp felt like it was on fire. Didn't even know when her head wrap had come off. She found some part of the bitch's face to dig her nails into, made sure she felt the same fire. Another glimpse of Elise. It was as if she hadn't moved an inch from the doorway. Red pencil skirt. Ugly white blouse. Virgin Atlantic uniform. Couldn't be that time already.

"Elise, ple—"

Mari-heifer pressed something cold and sharp into her neck. She tried to tear skin off Mari-heifer's face. The bitch applied more pressure with the knife. The deeper she tore into the heifer's skin, the more the knife punctured her throat.

"This is for the best, sweetheart," Mari-heifer said. "Haffi get rid of this bitch."

"Elise . . . why are you . . . just standing there?"

Footsteps. Elise turned around. Daddy appeared. He put his hand on Elise's shoulder.

"Daddy! Thank God! She's trying to kill me!"

It was as if he didn't hear her.

"Daddy!"

"It's for the best, Tempest." His eyes were glossy.

"Daddy!" She moved too much. Tickling joined the stinging—she was bleeding.

"Me know you miss your mother."

"Daddy, please!"

Grabbing Mari-heifer's arm just made her push the knife even deeper. Any deeper and . . .

"Elise, let's go."

"Daddy! Elise!" She blinked as her tears fell. She let her nose run.

Daddy and Elise disappeared from the doorway, their footsteps fading along the passage. One last grab of Mari-heifer's arms.

"See your mother in hell."

The knife was on the left side of her neck, digging right into her jaw at an angle, paralysing her, stinging radiating, Mari-heifer too strong. The door to the flat rattled open then closed heavily. She tensed up, as if that would make her skin strong enough to keep the knife from going through it.

She was already bleeding though. She squeezed her eyes shut, starting to tremble. Tears seeped through, adding fresh wetness to her cheeks and to everything between her nose and lips.

"See that whore in hell. See that whore in hell. See that whore in hell. See that whore . . ."

Mari-heifer didn't stop, the blade going deeper, blood pouring out.

Mari-heifer's voice started to fade away, echoing, until her words were indecipherable.

Then there was nothing.

She was on her back somewhere, kicking in the darkness until there was nothing on top of her. She kept flailing her legs, struggling for breath, *keke*-ing. Her hands were around her neck to keep the blade from cutting her head off. She gasped for air, drenched—in blood.

Her blood.

Her throat had been cut.

She was going to bleed out.

The pain was taking long to come. Waiting made it worse. Slow onset of pain; slow death. She was struggling to breathe, her heart pounding like she'd run a marathon. Her head was pounding too. She let go of her neck. Still no pain. No blood gushing out either, it seemed. The faint house music from the radio and cars trudging along Eastway made it seem everything was alright. Still hard to be sure. Hand shaking, she fumbled for the lamp switch on the bedside table, knocking off the clock. She found the switch then turned her head blindly to the door. Needed to be ready for what, or who, she was about to see.

She turned on the light, flinched. She squinted as she scanned the room. The key was still in the door, and her mum still looked gorgeous and undisturbed on the dressing table, and she was the only living thing in the room, besides the fly that was flitting under the shade.

Everything looked normal.

She patted her skin, then looked at her hand. It was shiny, wet. No blood. Just sweat. She leaned against the bedhead, while she let her body dry off, her breathing and heartbeat settling down.

Her top and bottom eyelids were drawing to each other like magnets when the DJ announced it was three o'clock. Something was tickling her nose. She jerked herself upright just before sleep could catch her again as the fly—or maybe another one—flew away from her face then landed on her leopard-print nightie. She moved about until the frownsy fly fucked off. She touched the part of her neck where the knife had been, then she flinched. Mari-heifer was too fresh in her mind, likely to invade her dreams again and pick up where she'd left off. Couldn't let that happen. But she hadn't fallen asleep thinking of Mari-heifer. Hadn't thought about Daddy either. Only Elise had been on her mind.

The dream had to mean something. It had felt too real. The thought of that bitch being even remotely suspicious . . . Still no fucking clue how she was going to pull off what she wanted. Couldn't be so sure Aiden would even get Elise into bed. She could only blackmail him so long, and everyone had a limit. The last thing she needed was for him to brave coming out, or for Mari-heifer to discover something, be it everything or just a part of it. A part was more than nothing; it was too much.

Fuck it. The dream was a nudge to speed things up before Mari-heifer fucked everything up. If only Elise wasn't out of the country so much.

She paused, able to hear herself breathe despite a reggae beat coming from the radio.

She swivelled till her feet were off the bed, stepping on the clock that had fallen. She picked it up. Eight minutes past. She put on her slippers then paused again.

Slippers slapped. Too noisy.

She took them back off, put on her kimono-style dressing gown, then picked her duvet up off the floor and wrapped that around her body too, before unlocking and opening the door. No amount of gentleness would kill the door's squeaking. She peeped to the left, towards Elise's room. There was enough light to guide her there.

She turned the knob of Elise's bedroom door like an assassin opening a safe she wasn't supposed to have access to. The door squealed. She froze, heart pumping fast. Only open a fucking crack. She opened it some more, a little bit at a time, gritting her teeth as the squealing continued. A sudden movement made the duvet bump into the door, making it fart open some more, too quickly. She grabbed the handle before the door could knock into the wall. She unwrapped the duvet from around her body then placed it on the passage floor.

Movement on the bed. Couldn't tell if Elise was awake, the light from next door not hitting her face.

She crept to the bathroom, turned the light on in there, then returned to Elise's room.

Elise had turned to her side, her back to Tempest. The light from the bathroom caught her head wrap and the string of the eye mask she was wearing. Stupid bitch. Doing everything *big sis* told her to do. Just like that dumb whore in *Cruel Intentions* doing as Sarah Michelle Gellar's slutty, bad breed alter ego instructed.

She crept further into the room. Her knee knocked something. A suitcase. The handbag on top of it fell off. It landed in her hands with a slap. Sweat trickled down her face as she struggled to breathe quietly. A close look at Elise . . . Bitch was moving again, rolling onto her back. The light was now on her nose and eye mask. The light would seep through to her eyes and she would remove the eye mask and see Tempest holding her handbag.

She was doing it again, letting negative thinking take over. *Not long to go, not long to go, not long to go. . . .*

Didn't have to dig too deep inside the handbag to find what she was looking for; it was right there, separating sheets of paper. She opened it, strained to see the expiry date. She could've kissed it. She put it in her dressing gown pocket. Another look at Elise. Elise's chest was rising and falling slower than before, approaching the right speed for sleep.

She tiptoed to the chest of drawers, her left foot scraping a wheel of the blasted mirror. The unlit part of the room. It had to have been some intervention from God or her mum, the time she had seen Elise put what she was now looking for inside the top drawer.

She kept an eye on Elise as she pulled out the top drawer, making it rumble. Another noisy fucker. She stopped, continued, stopped again, kept going until her hand and wrist could fit through the gap. She ran her fingers along what felt like silk, careful not to make a mess. She stopped with her hand in the front left corner, keeping her fingers on something other than lace and silk lingerie that dominated the drawer, something smooth and hard and strong like card, its corners curved. She snatched it out, scraping her hand through the tight gap. She turned around, stretched her arms until the item was sprinkled by light, and she flicked to the important page.

Exactly what she needed to see. She squeezed it against her chest, taking another deep, quiet breath.

She stuffed it between the papers in the handbag, hopefully in the exact same place the one in her pocket had been. She zipped the handbag as she crept to the suitcase then put the handbag back and waited long enough to make sure it wasn't going to fall off.

She tiptoed to the door. Elise started stirring, her chest rising and falling faster. Her energy sensed a disturbance.

Tempest manoeuvred out then grabbed the doorknob. She braced herself for the squeaking. She wasn't moving the door much, but it wouldn't shut up. It would take forever to pull the door in at this point, her heavy breathing and the slippery doorknob not helping. Better off pulling faster.

But Elise was moving even more, her limbs like moving mountains under the duvet, head turning one way then the other. Elise was going to wake up. If she didn't find out what Tempest had done straight away, she would find out in a few hours.

Elise's hand came out of the duvet then reached for the fucking eye mask.

Tempest gritted her teeth, her heart beyond uncontrollable. Too eager to fuck with Elise. What she wanted Aiden to do was good enough. Everything was ruined now.

Elise was trying to find the edge of her eye mask. She couldn't find it, but she'd find it eventually.

Then her hand went to her neck, lingered there. It was on the move again, but it looked like gravity's doing, as it slid along the duvet till it landed by her side. Her chest movements were slowing down.

Tempest kept still. She stayed that way, barely breathing, a bit longer, just to make sure.

Elise's head turned to the right, away from the doorway and the light coming in. Still asleep.

Tempest grimaced as she brought the door in quickly, almost to a close. The door cried, but not for too long. One last look at Elise through the slit for a gap. No visible movement on the bed. She turned the knob, closed the door then delicately released the knob, the latch clicking into place quietly.

She picked up her duvet, turned off the bathroom light then crept back to her room.

She stayed awake in bed awhile. No sounds from next door. She'd pulled it off. Bitch needed all the sleep she could get, the morning she had in store.

She smiled as she snuggled under her duvet, whispered, "Happy belated birthday, Mum."

Hopefully another belated birthday present was in store, something bigger and better.

14 / Aiden III
Like mother, like son?

Aiden, breathing heavily, let the moonlight sneaking through the trees guide him as he scrubbed his knife. He was good at pretending, so pretending to be calm should've been easy. He'd never been in mess like this before though. Plenty of fights. A few knife fights. But shit was different this time. His knife, blood all over the blade, proved it.

He'd never killed anyone before.

Like mother, like son.

No, no, no. Just because they'd left those motherfuckers motionless didn't mean they were dead. He'd knocked them out, stabbed one of them too, but not every stab victim ended up dying.

The white shithouse had to be alive.

But what if he was dead?

No. He'd had enough experience with knives to know how to stab without killing.

But things had been different earlier. One eye on white dude, the other on Cocoa Butter.

Cocoa Butter was standing there wide-eyed, trembling. Shame he couldn't handle the fuckers on his own. He'd put up a good fight though, was about that life. Three—well, two since one of them had been down the whole time—against one. Pussies.

Good thing he'd let Ethan borrow his car. If not, Cocoa Butter would've been stabbed up.

But now Aiden was caught up in some shit. Served him right, trying to be slick and get dude's number.

That woman—must've been dude's mum—accusing them of smashing . . . dude had to be gay. Their legs had been touching the whole time on the bus. Maybe he was just too soft, needed toughening up. Would've been funny if dude had cussed him off. But he never did. Kind of . . . sweet.

That woman's mad remark had chased him away before he could get a name. Could've put that name—along with *Glyn Road*—in Google. Seeing him again on the bus, along with everything that followed—the seat change, the bus breaking down—had to be divine intervention.

He'd rushed off on Glyn Road; Cocoa Butter had returned the favour at Mabley Green. Insisting on exchanging numbers over a fucking haircut . . . Cocoa Butter had called bullshit on it. Dude's demeanour had said it all. Probably wasn't going to call him. Lightning struck twice, not three times. He would never see Cocoa Butter again. Had to let it go.

But those bloodclaat fuckers had gone into Mabley Green as well. Didn't look right. He had to follow them. Dude was so . . . delicate—funny calling man that—and not righted, going that way on his own in the dark. Aiden had had his knife and was ready to use it . . . for a virtual stranger.

And he did use it.

He gave his knife one last inspection under the moonlight and caught a glimpse of his bleeding knuckles before an endless blanket of clouds hid the moon.

His breathing was back to normal. "I never got your name."

Dude seemed half-dead, like he was ill and death was about to snatch him at any moment.

Aiden tucked his knife in his polo shirt pocket, zipped up his hoodie, got closer to Cocoa Butter and shook him by the arms.

Dude snapped out of it, his wide, glistening eyes fixed on Aiden's. The longest he'd managed to hold eye contact all day. His lips were trembling.

"Chill out!"

Out of nowhere, dude collapsed into him and cried.

He was no longer grabbing dude's arms, just supporting his head with his chest. His hands hovered over Cocoa Butter's upper back, went up, then down, then up again and hovered over the back of his head. He scanned all around—light from the lamp posts along the footpath; windows of people's houses, mostly hidden by trees, on the right; more lamp posts in the distance, craning over the A12, the endless stream of traffic sounding like the sea . . .

Fuck it. He put one hand on the back of dude's head. Nothing to sweat about, even though his heart was racing. He looked around again. Dude wedged his bobbing head into the arch from Aiden's neck to his chin. He'd held his granddad and Ethan before, but they were family. His heart had never raced then.

Dude stopped his head-bobbing and crying. He stayed still and quiet, snuggled into Aiden's neck for a moment, then suddenly tried to disconnect, as if he'd only just realised how close they were, had become uncomfortable.

Aiden let go, willingly and unwillingly at the same time, as something wet his cheek. He looked up. Thick cloud spread across most of the sky. His face was sprayed some more. He put on his hood.

"Sorry about that. I . . ." Dude put on his hood as the rain fell heavier.

Aiden bounced his shoulders, shook off their moment.

He registered something in the corner of his eye. Movement. He turned quickly for a better look. Someone in the distance, limping.

He turned to face Cocoa Butter. "Let's go through here." He pointed to the right-hand branch where their footpath split.

"Where are we going?"

"Out of here. Think I saw one of them."

"Shit!"

They ran to the end of the path then took stairs leading up to a housing estate. Dude stopped halfway up.

"What's wrong?"

Cocoa Butter patted himself down. "My phone."

"What about it?"

"They took it."

"Fuck!"

"I have to go back." Dude did a one-eighty and started going back down the stairs.

Aiden went after him, grabbed him and dragged him back. "You mad?"

"You . . . you . . . stabbed one of them—"

"Shut up!"

"And I hit one of them with the brick after you hit him, and I smashed the other one in the head with—"

"We can't go back!"

"We have to! The one I hit with the bottle . . . he was down the whole time. What if he's—?"

"Shut it!" Aiden leaned into him.

"And the one you stabbed, what if—?"

He choked dude with both hands. "No!"

Dude looked like he'd seen a ghost, reaching for Aiden's forearms, but not being able to grab hold, then flailing his arms until he grabbed the railing.

Being rough with him wasn't a good look. Aiden let go of his neck and was about to say something when sirens wailed from beyond the stairs. Didn't make sense for the police to just appear—unless someone had seen everything and snitched.

"My phone! They'll trace it back to me. If any of them died—"

He grabbed Cocoa Butter and pulled him back down the stairs. The sirens were getting louder. Hard to tell where they were coming from; left, right, or directly behind. Tyres screeched. Doors opened then slammed. Probably more than one vehicle. Hurried footsteps. He yanked the dude like someone pulling along his unruly pickney.

The same person he'd seen in the distance was limping closer, close enough to recognize. Didn't need to see the face. The red jacket was the giveaway. The fucker was staggering, one of the lights on the footpath illuminating his bloody face and head, blood from where Cocoa Butter had claated him with the brick, bloody from being punched up by Aiden. And there he was, on his feet, not knocked out long enough. Strong motherfucker.

No fucking sign of the other two.

Cocoa Butter started calling God's name in vain through the wind and rain. Aiden's heart was pounding. He needed to see the white one. Cocoa Butter needed to see the other one.

Cocoa Butter shook him. "We need to go! The police!"

The fucker just needed to get closer, close enough to get punched some more.

"Let's go!" Cocoa Butter yanked his arm.

He gritted his teeth as the shithouse cunt made a gun gesture with his hand before Cocoa Butter pulled him into a run along the path towards Eastway. Dude took the lead like he knew where he was going.

They ran parallel to a red cycle lane, constantly crunching fallen leaves, the traffic on the upcoming A12 getting louder. Fencing either side protected them on the bridge over the A12.

The rain made it hard to look ahead without squinting. The wind was fucking with both their hoods. Dude was slowing down, shielding himself from something on the right. Probably vertigo from the view of traffic speeding right to left.

They soon reached wooden fencing on the right leading to a beige brick wall of houses struck by light from lamp posts. Metal fencing, trees towering over it, continued on the left, A12 traffic coming from that direction now. They ran past the brick wall, then past more fencing on the right, vehicles disappearing into Eastway Tunnel.

They crossed the bridge, ran past another beige wall of houses then more fences, trees closing in on them. Temporary cover from the rain. A double-decker bus passed ahead, traffic getting closer, louder, the Hackney Wick bus garage emerging to the right, Eastway cutting across straight ahead. The opening to Eastway was like a door they needed to get through before it closed and locked. Needed to get there before police cornered them.

They got through the opening to Eastway, no surprises meeting them. They breathed heavily as rain battered them.

"What's the time?"

He took out his phone, his free hand shielding it from the rain. Missed calls from Elise, and even Tempest. The bitch must've tried getting him on the other phone.

"Nearly half-five."

"Shit." Dude was squinting to the left, pulling his hood tighter around his face.

"I know. I was meant to be somewhere too."

"Can't go again. Not now."

"If you need to call someone, then go ahead."

Cocoa Butter reached for the phone then stopped. "I don't know the number by heart."

"You sure you still can't go wherever you need to go, get your mind off—?"

"No." Cocoa Butter frowned. "I just want to go home."

Aiden nodded then texted Elise, apologising and wishing her a safe flight. "Let's keep going."

They turned right, headed to Wick Road, where the wind and traffic coming from all directions sounded like the sea. Enough activity for the two of them to go unnoticed, to blend in. The battle between the vehicles and the wind and rain made them shout at each other. The rain was hitting them from behind now; they could raise their heads.

"So, what's your name?"

Dude was staring ahead.

"I said, what's your name?"

Dude jumped then widened his eyes when they locked with Aiden's. "Uh . . . Shannon. Some people call me *Shan*. You?"

"Aiden. What should I call you?"

"Either."

Shan would make him look thirsty. *Shannon* was too distant. "Well, Shan . . . non . . . almost there."

"Where?"

"Your yard."

Lights from passing vehicles made Shan's frown look more sinister.

"You live on Glyn Road, right? Could've sworn it was Glyn Road where . . ."

The lines on Shan's forehead disappeared, then he looked away.

"Thought that woman was your mum."

"She is . . . was . . . is . . . was . . ." Shan muttered something else under his breath.

"What she said . . . 'bout us being—"

"She has a way of jumping to conclusions."

Maybe it was too soon to get personal, but getting into his business would take his mind off the fight and why the fucker in the red jacket was the only one to reappear. It would give them both something else to think about. They barely knew each other, but he had saved Shan. Shan had to know he could trust him.

"I'm just gonna come out with it and ask you."

Shan looked at him as if asking the wrong question might earn him a punch. Shan wasn't as soft as he seemed, not soft at all, but he was too jumpy. He didn't know how to give zero fucks. He needed to have that look, that demeanour, of someone not to be fucked with so that people left him the fuck alone in the first place. Worth teaching him new skills or enhancing the ones he already possessed. Anything to see more of him.

"Why are you staring at me like that? What do you want to ask?" Shan did it again; he made eye contact one moment and abruptly looked away the next, like he was too overwhelmed to lock eyes any longer.

"Sorry. Was just thinking. Was gonna ask you—I won't feel a way if you don't answer—what all that was about, that thing . . . with your mum . . . yesterday?"

Shan squinted, like he was trying to decide if he could trust some stranger, then he relaxed his face. "You saved me, so I guess I owe you something."

The people at the door were his parents and they were done with him now that they knew he was into men.

"So yeah, I lived on Glyn Road—until Friday. Live in Dalston now, with those two men you saw."

"I remember them."

"One of them's my uncle. The other is . . . his . . . partner."

"Partner?"

"I know. You'd never guess they were gay. Not like me."

"Not like you?"

"I've always been told I act a certain way, so I'm sure it's obvious."

Shan definitely *walked* a certain way, his butt wining a bit.

"Were your parents ever suspicious?"

151

Hard to tell by Shan's face if he was pissed or reacting to the rain hitting it.

"I mean, you said people always made comments about you. Parents know their children." He was talking to himself as much as to Shan.

"They probably knew deep down, or maybe they thought it was a phase. Besides, I pretended to have a girlfriend."

"Ah lie!"

Shan narrowed his eyes. "No lie. Her idea."

"Damn." Similar to his situation with Elise, except he was playing his family *and* Elise. At least Shan's pretend bae knew everything.

"You're Jamaican, right?"

"Yeah. I spring from Guyana and Trinidad too. How did you know?"

"Certain things you said."

"I realised you're Jamaican when I heard your mum. *Jesus have his mercy.*"

Shan actually managed to smile.

"*Bwoifriend.*"

Shan's smile disappeared and he tensed up. "Uh . . . I don't live on Glyn Road anymore, so where are we going?"

"Maybe get su'um to eat."

Shannon narrowed his eyes as they went under a bridge.

By the time they were out of its shadow, his expression returned to normal. "I *am* hungry. Haven't eaten since this morning."

"Fancy walking to Chatsworth Road? A few Caribbean places there."

"Yeah, let's—"

Sirens.

Shannon jumped, came to a halt. He looked like a dead person standing, no air coming out of his nose or mouth.

"Shan! Shannon!" Aiden shook him until his breathing created smoke again.

Shan's teeth started chattering, fog coming out of his mouth in regular bursts.

Had to rough him up again. "Get your shit together!"

Shan got going once more.

"Faster!"

The rain started coming at them from the right, heavier. The sirens were deafening, and blue lights more and more blinding. Police cars. Two ambulances. Approaching them. Fuck.

"They c-could be coming . . . for anyone." That last part was for his own benefit. "I mean, shit . . . probably not even a real emergency. Just wanna get past everyone on the road."

Regular vehicles turned one way or another to give way.

He put his arm behind Shan's back, pushing him to speed up as they went under another bridge. "We need to act normal, like we're just going 'bout our business."

The emergency vehicles were going to draw level with them or take the slip road entry to the A12.

They missed the turning.

"Oh God!"

"Shannon!"

"They've found the phone; they've tracked it back to me. Cameras must've been all over the place."

"Fuck this!" He forced himself in front of Shannon and to his left, closer to the kerb. "Look straight. Don't make me tell you again."

The vehicles would've long passed them if they'd maintained their speed, but they were feet away.

"Remember what I said, Shan. Look. Straight. Ahead."

He hid his busted knuckles in his pockets and hunched his shoulders so that his chin and mouth were hidden where the zip of his hoodie reached the top, as blue lights made him squint and turn his head to the right. The wind was blowing the rain to the right side of his face. He had to turn his head to the left a bit. He plugged a finger into his left ear as the sirens blared louder, flashed brighter, drew nearer. The first police car was at walking pace as they met. Could tell the occupants were looking in his direction. Tried hard not to make eye contact. Shannon wasn't helping, making those fucking noises.

"They know something."

"Wait till we pass them, Shannon."

"We won't. Any moment now, they're gonna come out and cuff us."

"For *fuck's* sake!"

"Just look how slow they're going." Shannon looked behind. "They have space in front of them."

"I swear I'll break your neck."

"But—"

"You're pissing me off to bloodclaat!"

They'd passed the last ambulance, but the police car in front was still slowing everything down.

He looked behind, just when the vehicles sped up, then they vanished around the curve of Wick Road. Right where he and Shan had come from. He sighed.

Cameras. If there were any in that part of Mabley Green, then the two of them were fucked. Their faces, clothing . . . no wonder the police had slowed down and looked their way.

Like mother, like son.

He shook his head wildly, fighting unwanted thoughts.

Maybe two blacks doing something as simple as walking looked suspicious to the police.

"I can't believe this is happening."

"Can't change shit now."

"If anything's happened to any of them and my phone is found with them, they'll trace it back to me, and your number's on it."

Shit.

"It's all my fault. I should've been wary of them from the time I got off the bus. Running from you . . . into Mabley Green . . . so stupid."

"Yeah, why'd you do that?"

Shannon's face tightened. He looked away as vehicles streaming along the slip road halted them.

"Tell me." What should've been a slap on Shan's shoulder ended up being a shove.

Shan frowned then shook his head. "Long story. Was in a similar situation not too long ago and . . . I just felt weird about it, like you were setting me up."

No green man, but there was a break in traffic. They ran across the A12 slip road.

"Let's go up Kenworthy Road."

"I'm used to straight men being funny around me, and with you being married, I just—"

"Married?"

"Yeah. Your . . . wedding ring."

He glanced at his hand. Was going to take off the ring when he reached Elise and Tempest's flat building. "What's the big deal about me wearing a wedding ring?"

"N-n-nothing really. I just—"

"Let's cross the road quickly while it's clear. A 488's coming." He almost put a protective arm around Shan as they crossed the road, but stopped himself. They were more visible now.

Only two other passengers were on the bus, a woman and a little girl. Aiden let Shannon get on first. Shannon let Aiden sit inside. Taking turns being the lady. First and last time being the lady.

"Where we going?"

"Making sure you get back home. Dalston, right?"

"I thought we were getting food."

"Shit! Um . . . we can get off at Homerton, then walk from there."

"Alrighty— Wait, I don't have enough money on me."

"I'll pay."

Shan grimaced. "I can't let you do that."

"You have no choice."

He burped a whole heap of cheat food as Shan put his arm out for an approaching 242 on Chatsworth Road. He let Shan get on first and sit inside.

"Where do you live?" Shan said.

"Powerscroft Road."

"That's good. This takes you straight home."

"Yeah, but I wanna make sure you get home."

"You can't go out of your way for me."

"Not going out of my way. Dalston ain't far from me."

"Alrighty. I'll get my uncle to drop you home then."

"I'll be fine."

"It's the least I could do." Shan suddenly frowned. "The 236 doesn't run near Powerscroft Road."

"236?"

"The first bus we—"

"Oh yeah. Just had some shit to sort out."

"Oh." Shan broke eye contact.

"What's wrong?"

"Nothing."

He elbowed Shannon.

Shannon elbowed him back, not as hard.

He elbowed Shannon again. "I won't let it go."

Shannon grimaced. "Tell me . . . about your . . . wife."

Aiden smirked.

Shan made a hand gesture. "What's funny?"

"I ain't married."

Shan furrowed his brow.

"Just wear this to make people think I am. People come at me at the gym—I'm a personal trainer—and it gets tired."

Shannon was about to say something when someone got on the bus in a frenzy, glad to be out of the rain, chatting on her phone. Of all the fucking places to sit—right behind them.

"Your . . ." Aiden looked at the woman behind him.

She paid him no mind as she continued to chat Jamaican patois about man.

He had to raise his voice, drown hers out. "Your phone situation."

Shan's eyes widened.

"Chill. Report it stolen. That way, if the police find it, you can just say someone stole it earlier today or something, or that you just lost it. No. Stick with it being stolen."

"I hadn't thought of that." Shan was considering the idea. "It really was stolen."

The longest Shan maintained eye contact . . . before uncertainty or awkwardness kicked in, making him look away.

"Good thing I insured it."

"Good thing."

Shannon grimaced.

"What now?"

"My phone has no PIN. Just a swipe unlocks it."

"*. . . Mabley Green.*"

That woman's words kept him from cussing Shannon. They both turned around. The woman frowned at them. They looked at each other again then turned back around. Eavesdropping had become important.

"*Ee-hi, them find dead body. Look like smaddy claat him inna him head.*"

Shan gasped, started shaking his legs.

Aiden gulped, almost touched Shan's thigh, let his hand hover close enough for Shan's thigh to tickle his palm.

"Aiden—"

"Shan, don't."

Could hear Shannon breathe. Sounded like he was going to have an asthmatic attack.

Couldn't blame him, hearing the woman reveal how the fucker had died in Mabley Green.

Dead from head injuries, not stab wounds.

Not like mother.

MONDAY

15 / Elise IV
Nowhere to be found

What Elise would've given for more sleep, especially after the previous night. At least she'd finally heard from Shan. One less thing to worry about while getting ready for work.

She pulled her bedroom curtains back; it was still dark outside, the only light coming from the lamp posts. Another few hours until it brightened up. She turned on the bedroom light then looked at her reflection in the six-foot-tall mirror-on-wheels, changing position as she adjusted her bright red jacket and matching pencil skirt. Still hadn't taken to the colour after all this time. Burgundy would've been better. The blouse was even worse—because of the hideous frills. She turned her head one way then the next, making sure no strand of hair was out of place at the sides. She patted her upswept pixie and pressed her nude lips together. She looked closely for a mark on her left cheek—nothing. The memory of the box made her skin prickle for a moment though. Tights check—no holes.

A vibration jolted her. A text from Pa. He was five minutes away. She picked up her luggage and handbag, slipped on her bright red hourglass-heeled shoes then stood in the doorway for a few moments, scanning the room. She shut the door, its moaning making her cringe.

Five minutes must've gone by the time she opened the door to the residential building. A car was approaching, its headlights illuminating the frost-covered cars either side. She click-clacked to the kerb. The familiar grey Nissan Qashqai stopped just beyond where she was standing.

Pa got out of the car. "Morning, little red riding hood."

"That's not funny."

"Just ramping," he said as they hugged.

"You look tired. You sure you'll be OK taking me to Gatwick?"

His expression let her know that was a stupid question.

He opened the boot and started to put her luggage in. "You all set? Passport, keys, phone, clothes . . . ?"

"Yeah."

She opened the front passenger door, got comfortable in her seat and shut the door before taking one last look in her handbag. Burgundy red was the main thing she needed to see inside.

Pa got in, did his mirror and seat checks, and started the car.

They entered the Blackwall Tunnel, a MiC LOWRY song playing on the radio.

"How long it take fi reach Cancún?"

Looking at the sides was dizzying. She stared ahead. "Ten hours and a bit."

"Jesus peace!"

"Not much longer than going to Jamaica."

"True."

"It took nearly ten hours the last time I went there, but the plane had to hover for a while before landing."

"What time is your flight again?"

"Nine something."

"Nine something?"

She picked up her handbag from between her feet, opened it, pushed some documents away from her passport until she could see the flight information. "Nine-thirty-five."

Odd. That mark wasn't supposed to be on her passport. Her old one, yes, but not this one.

"That's alright then. Right on— What?"

She must've put the two of them in her bag without realising.

"Elise?"

It was difficult to see into her bag properly, shadows and the tunnel lighting changing as the car moved.

"Pa, turn on the light please."

When the light came on, she stretched her bag to its limit, pushed things left and right, dug her hand in like she was digging up sand. Her breathing became unsteady.

"Elise, calm down."

Only one burgundy document in there, but . . .

"What is it?"

She took out the passport and opened it to the last page, her eyes closed. She would see that all was well when she looked inside, but even with her eyes closed, she knew something was wrong. She could feel the part of the document that had been clipped. She looked at the last page. A flurry of blinks wouldn't make the information change. The date was still the same, in English and in French.

"Elise, you leave something?"

They were out of the tunnel.

"I don't understand." She took out sheets of paper, her make-up bag, her purse, anything not resembling a passport, and dropped them in her lap. She unzipped the compartments and raked through them, brought her handbag closer to the light and looked everywhere inside it.

No passport besides the expired one.

"Weh you leave?"

She put back everything she had taken out.

"Well?"

"My passport."

"See it deh, in your hand."

"No, it's my old passport."

Maybe it was in one of her pockets. . . . No, not the left. Not the right either.

He sighed as he rubbed his hand over his face. "Me going take the next exit."

A few beeps came from behind as he changed lanes abruptly to exit the A102.

His breathing was ragged. "Wah do you?"

"Pa, don't."

"What you mean *don't*? You fi make sure you have everything you need. Look where we reach!"

"I know for a fact I packed everything. I—"

"*For a fact*—my batty!" The way his mouth twisted as he spoke, things were only going to get worse. "Can't believe me haffi take you back." He kissed his teeth. "You know what, me was going do a U-turn, but me change me mind."

"Where are you going then?"

His lip twitched into a momentary snarl, then he took the first exit at the roundabout.

He drove slowly along Millennium Way. The O2 contraption, its masts for a crown pointing to the sky, and skyscrapers in the Canary Wharf area loomed in the distance. Plenty of windows were lit up in the tall buildings, but that would soon change; the sky was getting lighter, lilac eating away at navy blue. Time was running out. Pa drove past the first road on the left and took the next.

"What are you doing?"

"Parking, so you can look properly."

"I'm telling you, I put it in my handbag—"

"Stop saying that!"

She jumped at his rage.

He got out of the car and slammed the door.

She tightened her jacket then got out. "Pa, we can't stay here. Double-yellow lines."

He ignored her and took her luggage out of the boot.

She hugged herself, rubbing up and down her arms, and hurried to him. "Pa, my passport's not in there."

"Gimme the padlock key."

"Pa—"

"Gimme the rahtid key!"

She kissed her teeth.

"Like me and you is size."

Her ragged breaths were coming out in small bursts of fog as she stretched her bag open and took out the padlock keys. "Can't believe you have my nice, clean luggage on the wet ground."

He snatched the keys from her.

"It's not in there."

"Then weh it deh?"

"I don't know."

"You don't know?"

"I'm telling you, I put it in . . . Forget it. Just open it."

He opened it, then stared at her.

"What is it?"

"You just going stand there?"

She bent over her luggage. "We won't find it here."

"We better. Too early for foolishness."

She wasn't looking for anything, but she fiddled around with the contents of her luggage to make it look like she was. Pa was just messing everything up. She hadn't gone mad. She hadn't dreamed putting her current passport in her handbag, and her old passport in her drawer. Right before she went to bed, she'd checked the inside of the passport she had put in her handbag to make sure it was the new one. That wasn't a dream either.

"Wearing this fi smaddy?"

"Pa!" She snatched a sheer, chiffon, ruffle thong from him, stuffed it back inside the Zpac packing cube. "Can't believe you went in there."

"Passport could be anywhere."

"Not in there!" She closed the luggage.

"Me really haffi take you all the way back?"

She'd definitely put the right passport in her handbag, yet it wasn't there now. "I . . . guess so."

Pa kissed his teeth again and put the luggage back in the boot, while she just stood there looking ahead at nothing in particular. Just like the smoke from her breathing clouded her vision, her mind was clouded by reasons why the new passport wasn't in her freaking handbag.

They should've been on the M25 by now, maybe even near the M23, but instead they were back at the flat.

"Me going look parking."

She didn't respond to her pa. His patois was still strong; he was still pissed.

She bumped shoulders with Tempest on the way to her bedroom. Only Tempest said sorry.

"What you doing here?"

"I can't . . ."

Tempest followed her into her bedroom. "What's going on?"

If her old passport was in her handbag instead of the new one, then the new one must've been in the drawer, but that made no sense. She hadn't taken her old passport out of her drawer for ages. She yanked the top drawer open, backing into Tempest.

"Els, what's happened?"

She slid her hand between the front left corner and the lingerie laid there. Nothing.

"Elise!"

"I'm looking for my passport." She slid her hand to the other end. Nothing but wood, silk and lace.

"Your passport? You usually check you have everything before you leave."

It had to have slipped under something.

"What time's your flight?"

"Nine . . . thirty-five. Oh God."

"It's after six."

"I know that, Tempest!"

"No need to take it out on *me*."

"I'm not. I just don't need . . . *Where is it?*"

"Is Daddy downstairs?"

It looked like a hurricane had ravaged her drawer, and still no passport.

"Elise!" Tempest grabbed her by the arm.

She yanked her arm away.

"I just asked if Daddy is down—"

"Yes, Tempest!" Seeing Tempest lean back made her stomach bite. She closed her eyes and breathed deeply. "Sorry. I—"

The buzzer went.

Tempest stormed out, her red-and-gold kimono-inspired robe almost sweeping the floor.

Elise went through another drawer, then another, and the one below that, which was stupid because she hadn't put her passport in any other drawer. Nothing, just as expected. She checked her jacket pockets again. Nothing. As expected.

She slumped down on the bed, slapped the handbag onto her lap and pulled it open. Maybe she'd misread the date in the car. She took the passport out. Maybe . . . Damn it. The clipped corner.

She flicked to the back anyway. Same date as before. She started shaking, struggling for breath, throat tight.

"Elise!" Pa was inside the flat. *"Find it yet?"*

She went on all fours and looked underneath the dressing table, then she crawled to the left side of the bed. She pushed the box underneath to the foot of the bed. Nothing else was underneath.

Footsteps stopped at the doorway.

"Well, it must be here somewhere."

She peeked over the bed. Pa was squinting at something. She got to her feet and followed his gaze, just as he walked to the foot of the bed, luggage in hand.

Damn it. She'd pushed the box out too far.

Pa picked it up.

"I . . . I—"

"You what?"

"I—"

Tempest appeared in the doorway. Her eyes widened at what Pa was holding.

"What you doing with this? You have one of these too, Tempest?"

"N-no, Daddy." Tempest made sure she didn't make eye contact with Elise.

Elise cut her eyes at her anyway.

"Me never know you inna this nastiness, Elise."

"That's rich, since you . . ." She grimaced.

Tempest raised an eyebrow without raising the other.

"Since I what?"

"N-nothing. Look, it . . ." Should've followed her mind and put the freaking box somewhere else ages ago. Tempest was about to shoot her a dirty look. ". . . it was given to me. I've never used it."

"You must think me fool."

"Just help me find my *damn* passport!"

Pa flared his nostrils.

She pressed her hand against her head then sighed. "Just help me, please." She avoided eye contact with Tempest, but she could tell Tempest's arms were crossed.

Pa humphed and cut his eyes when he dropped the vibrator box on the floor.

Tempest gave a cutting look as she sashayed over.

"Gimme the keys for the luggage," Pa said.

It was futile, but she gave Pa the keys again. She sat on her bed and emptied her handbag. A pack of tissues, sweets, chewing gum, hand sanitizer, hand cream, make-up bag, travel documents, itinerary, keys, phone, purse . . . no pissing passport. She held the bag above her head and turned it inside out as much as she could. She unzipped and emptied every compartment. Nothing besides loose change, more sweets and her Nectar, Sparks, and Tesco cards. She threw the empty bag at her dressing table, knocking over cosmetics, then buried her face in her hands.

"This is ridiculous, Els. Ruining your make-up for nothing." Tempest dabbed at her cheeks, retrieved handbag in hand.

"Elise, it must be here somewhere." Pa took things out of the suitcase, as if preparing for a snake to jump out at him.

"It's not in there, Pa." She sniffled.

"Els, don't give up." Tempest looked around. "Where are your other handbags?"

"In the wardrobe. Tempest, there's no point—"

"Too negative, too quick to give up."

Tempest came back with two Coach bags and three Kipling bags. "Now I know you use this one a lot." Tempest handed her the blue Kipling bag.

"You look in them for me."

"No. You should."

She snatched the bag then looked inside it, even though she wasn't going to find the passport in there.

"Elise, just retrace your steps."

"Pa, like I said, I made sure the right passport was in my handbag just before—"

"Obviously, you didn't put the right one in there."

"I did."

"Then is mus' duppy take it." He kissed his teeth again and closed the suitcase.

He was staring at her like she was losing her mind.

She knew what he was thinking, what he wanted to say, what he would've said without Tempest present.

He looked at his watch. "Half-six now."

She cringed. She would have been mere minutes from the airport by now. She looked around. Tempest was staring at her, both eyebrows raised, as she put the second of the two bags she'd searched through on the bed. Elise turned back around to find Pa shaking his head.

"Maybe the stress from last night . . ."

She shot around. "What stress from last night, Tempest?"

Tempest put her hands up. "Calm down!"

"What stress?"

Tempest put a hand on her hip. "You nearly had a fit about your friend."

She waited for Tempest to say the rest.

"What else, Tempest?"

Tempest narrowed her eyes at her then stopped as soon as Pa turned around to look at her.

"She boxed me."

Pa raised his eyebrows. "*Why?*"

"She was acting stupid, so I just slapped some sense into her." Tempest sauntered to the doorway. "I don't know what to say about your passport, Elise, but I need to get ready." She went to the bathroom.

Elise rested her elbows on her thighs, ran her fingers through her hair and pulled at it as she rocked.

"Elise, listen," he whispered. He looked towards the doorway, his silence stilling her. The burst of water from the shower gave him the go-ahead. "Maybe you should try therapy again."

She got up.

"Listen to me."

She leaned on the dressing table, tapping it with her nails. She grimaced at her reflection in the slanted oval mirror. All that time she'd spent on her hair only for it to be all over the place, and her cheeks were smudged with black streaks, as if ants had been squashed on them.

"Things like this don't just happen."

A tear trickled down her cheek, then another. "I should be at the airport by now."

"Haffi call in sick."

"No!"

"You have no choice. It would look bad, but this"—he motioned with his hands—"would look worse."

She scoffed at her sorry reflection.

"Just call in sick."

"I'll look so unprofessional."

"Maybe, but you can't go anywhere without the passport."

Funny how she'd been getting tired of being a flight attendant and yearning for something else, something better, bigger, wider and higher, as Jill Scott would say—if only she knew what—and now the idea of losing her job and the reputation she'd worked so hard to build . . .

"Call in sick." Pa said, bringing her back to earth. "Me haffi mention therapy to your mother."

She'd put the correct passport in her handbag only hours ago, and the older one in her drawer weeks ago. She was about to tell Pa that.

But what if she *was* wrong? Only she had been in her room. Carl had always been in sight—except for that time he went to the bathroom. But she'd checked right before getting into bed, and she hadn't forgotten how to read. She wasn't losing her mind.

Or maybe she was.

Her pa's concerned gaze met her defeated expression in the dressing table mirror.

She clenched her eyes shut then opened them again, her exhales deep. "Mention therapy to Ma."

16 / Shannon VI
Mess

Shannon was about to come but didn't want to. Coming meant the end, and he wasn't ready for Aiden to stop doing what he was doing. Never imagined being deep-throated and finger-fucked at the same time would feel so good. It didn't matter that his sphincter seemed to have a maximum circumference of a pound coin.

He glanced down at Aiden. Aiden noticed, kept on fingering, let Shannon's dick out of his mouth slowly as if it was never going to come out. Then it finally did, and Aiden gave him a devastating look, early morning sunrays slicing through the blinds adding gloss to his lips. Aiden was going to turn him out. Shit, he already was. Intense golden-brown eyes. Thick eyebrows that made him look devilish and beautiful at the same time. The way his lips twitched as he fingered away was so sexy. He'd had a shape up, making his lips all the more glorious, his face stunning in every way.

Aiden did something that made Shannon clench, Shannon's dick pulsing and hitting Aiden's chin. Aiden smirked. Had to break eye contact to keep from going over the edge. He fought not to release whatever sounds his soul was fighting to push out.

He lost that battle.

His dick was going through it, tingling all over, flooding with come. He shuffled as much as Aiden's firm hold allowed. He dared to glance at Aiden again. Aiden stretched his tongue out, a tongue that looked like it started in his chest, then licked his way around Shannon's dick, as if working his way up a helter skelter slide.

Closed eyes made it worse, which meant better. Licked and finger-fucked with eyes closed. Had to focus more on the build-up of come. Had to keep it in longer. Aiden had him flinching, sometimes clenching almost too tightly to delay climax. It was hard to know how to feel with so much happening to him, premature climax a constant threat, the tingles trapping him between urges to curse and thank Aiden. More flinching. More clenching.

Another close call, probably the closest yet, made him widen his eyes and mouth, every muscle stiff. He grabbed Aiden's head, his dick stuck in Aiden's mouth as he tried to make Aiden stop. Tears trickled from his eyes, his breathing hitched. Aiden wiggled his fingers out while Shannon clenched. Aiden knew that was a close call too, wasn't ready for it to end either.

"You squirted a bit in my mouth."

"S-sorry. I . . . I . . ."

Aiden looked like he was going to murder him, but then he gave a mischievous grin, started feeling up Shannon's erection as if looking for a pulse.

He clenched just in time again, grabbing sheets, probably tearing through them, as he experienced the closest thing to rigor mortis.

"Come as much as you want. I'm just getting started."

"No . . . not . . . yet . . . God . . . help me. . . . Aiden . . . you . . . fu— Aaah!"

More frigging teardrops. More embarrassing sounds.

Aiden snickered then groaned, squeezing Shannon's dick as if it were a near-empty tube of toothpaste. Shannon's foreskin tickled, pre-come seeping along it. He gasped; Aiden growled. He cried again as Aiden snarled and grinned.

Then Aiden switched things up, brought his face to Shannon's, his lips glossy with saliva and semen. Before Shannon could say anything, Aiden's tongue was in his mouth, lips pressing lips. Aiden let him taste himself. Breathy moans escaped from one mouth only to go down the other's throat. The only time hot morning breath was sexy. They tongue-wrestled and sucked each other's lips as they rubbed against each other on the inflatable bed, Aiden feeling up Shannon's backside like he owned it. Sweat was the only barrier between them as they tried to keep their leaking, slippery, sensitive erections connected. Tingles and waves were ravaging Shannon's body. Aiden was chanting like pleasure and torture were at war inside him, his body trembling.

Could tell the bedroom was bright, even with closed eyes. Surroundings as heavenly as the sensations. Never imagined his first time would be so intense. His first time had come now that he was free, no longer living a lie. And it was with His Fineness himself, fine in face and body, from hair follicle to toe nail.

Lips then tongues separated. Aiden sucked his way down Shannon's neck to his nipples, taking time as he sucked and bit each of them, then ran his tongue and beard down Shannon's abdomen to his navel. Tickles made him flinch and squeal, the inflatable bed trying to swallow him. They both chuckled.

Then his penis was in Aiden's mouth again. It was as if there'd been no break from the sucking that had come before. Aiden was moaning and slurping like nothing tasted better.

He'd long submitted; his body wasn't his own anymore. He wasn't Shannon at all. He was someone else, something else, head thrashing from side to side as he surrendered to the nerve responses ravaging him. His dick was getting closer and closer to falling off, his balls tight. He couldn't come yet, not before Aiden penetrated him, not before he went down on Aiden again and snorted the masculine funk of his manbush until the taste settled in his throat, not before Aiden ate him out again, not before he let Aiden hit it every which way, not before—

Shit. It was happening. Too weak to clench as much as he needed to this time. Wanted more . . . couldn't take anymore. Aiden knew it, or else he wouldn't have started bobbing his head faster.

Something started to vibrate. He flailed his bare legs, bringing his feet down hard on Aiden's strong, sweaty back without meaning to. He tried to grab Aiden's head. Aiden grabbed his wrists, pressing them into the bed with his big hands as he sucked faster and slurped louder.

And then it happened, as the vibrating grew louder. He arched his back and parts of his body took turns trembling, and then he grunted in a way he never knew he could, his eyes closed. Tears seeped through anyway.

The vibrating kept going. He competed with it, went wild as he came, didn't give a frig if Uncle Lionel and Peter heard him. His loud climax was his thank you to Aiden, his message that Aiden was the one.

His high was over. He opened his eyes. They were burning. Had to close them. He was still coming, spasms not over, but everything was different, besides the vibration, coming from the left. He was on his stomach, gasping for air, not naked anymore, barely able to move, dick still tingling mercilessly.

Climax over, heart pumping hard, chest heaving, he opened his eyes again. The room wasn't as bright as before. He patted for Aiden.

Nothing.

He made more effort to move, then he tensed up, stopped. His crotch area was sludgy. The damage had been done. Pointless keeping still. He kicked off the duvet so that it only covered him from the knee downwards, and he yanked his head away from the pillow, saliva coming out of his mouth, mixing with sweat. He wiped his mouth with a sleeve of his onesie.

Something was still vibrating. He sat up, finding his balance, on the inflatable bed, one hand on the sheets and the other on the drenched pillow. He moved his hand along the pillow until it reached a dry area. The vibrating was coming from the right now. He looked down at his crotch and shook his head at the mark that looked like a shadow.

It had all been a dream.

The vibrating. His phone. He hadn't lost it after all and—

He studied the vibrating phone.

Only some of it had been a dream.

It was a Samsung, but not his. It was Aiden's. Aiden had left it in Uncle Lionel's car. Maybe that was Aiden ringing, trying to locate it.

Could only shuffle so far in the bed before the wetness in his groin paralysed him again. Each movement made the come spread to his thighs and the shadow in his onesie grow. Aiden's phone stopped vibrating.

Aiden.

Aiden had made him come.

He unbuttoned the onesie all the way down, igniting the pain from either of his last two fights. He stretched the waistband of his underwear away from his skin then flinched as the cold air swept through his pubic hair and all over his sore and softening penis. A frigging mess. The way time passed in reality versus a dream, it was hard to tell how long he'd been laying and rolling around in his come, and if he'd come more than once. He opened a pack of tissues, pulled a few pieces out, caught a whiff of his mess as he wiped himself and threw them away. He took out another tissue and put it in the front of his underwear, come still draining out.

It was dark, as if it were night time. The clocks had gone back over the weekend. As dark as it was, it seemed earlier. Something to eight, according to Aiden's phone.

Shit. Work. He needed to call in sick.

But the number he needed was on his phone, wherever the frig it was—probably at some frigging police station. He headed back to bed, sat down, staring at nothing. His laptop right in front of him, on the desk, was no longer a blur. An email wasn't the best way to report in sick, but it would have to do.

He read the email one last time then pressed *Send*.

Prompt reply. Granted a week off from work to ease the pressure of his looming coursework deadline. Lucky for a change. Just what he needed after the last few days, even if there really was no deadline and it was just a reading week.

Just gone eight-forty. Daylight finally caught up, sunrays shooting through the now open blinds of his new bedroom. Rain didn't look imminent. A reason not to be cooped up in the house. If only he, his uncle and Peter had dropped Aiden off on Powerscroft Road, and not off it, he would've known Aiden's door number and been able to return his phone. Aiden was probably at work though.

Couldn't see Elise either. She had to be well into her flight. He couldn't contact her anyway. Maybe it was worth taking a stroll though. Dalston was transforming. It certainly had a lot more going on than Homerton. There was no reason for him to go back there. Only madness would make him go back.

He turned on the DAB radio. Beverley Knight's voice was fading, the hourly news about to begin. He couldn't risk hearing anything about Mabley Green.

But he couldn't avoid the news forever. Maybe the situation wasn't that bad. Just like Aiden had said over and over, he'd been fighting for his life. Could've been him at the morgue. Nothing could be traced back to him. He'd been wearing gloves the whole time. Things had happened so fast. Maybe the Blossom Hill bottle hadn't killed the prick. Maybe he'd hit his head on the concrete.

Before the newsreader could tell him otherwise, he covered his ears as he rushed to the radio to turn it back off.

He left his bedroom. Maybe his uncle and Peter had left him a note on the kitchen table, like his paren—like Viola and Leroy used to.

Aiden's phone vibrated when he reached the stairs. Aiden had beaten him to it. It must've looked so bad, taking long to return the call. The number was withheld.

He barely slid his finger across the screen before someone said, "You're not fucking righted."

It was a woman.

"Not showing up yesterday . . . Ignoring my reescleet calls . . . I swear to God, Aiden."

"Uh . . ."

"Cat got your tongue?"

She sounded familiar.

"What do you have to say for yourself?"

"Uh . . ."

"Aiden, I won't stop until I know you've gone through with it."

"Uh—"

"What the fuck happened to you yesterday?"

He was busy saving me.

"Fine. Don't answer me. Just remember I'm the one in control. I know where you live. I'll go to your house and tell your shithouse family *everything* if I have to. Why is it so hard for you and *sweet little Els* to go all the way? That bitch is your girlfriend, for fuck's sake!"

"Uh . . ."

The caller kissed her teeth then hung up.

Aiden *did* have a girlfriend then.

There'd been hope: their legs touching on the bus, Aiden's persistence to exchange numbers, pretending to be married—so many straight guys enjoyed female attention—and the way he'd held him in Mabley Green. Straight men didn't hold other men like that.

Looked like Aiden was an exception. Better to find out before falling for him and—

Maybe he'd already fallen.

Maybe the truth would help him get over Aiden.

But that dream . . . it wasn't his first wet dream, but it was different from the others. He hadn't prompted Aiden into his dream, as he'd prompted the other men he'd fantasized about, to take him like that. He brought his hand to his lips as he closed his eyes. His fingers were Aiden's divine lips for a moment.

He tingled, opened his eyes.

It had been a dream, but it had been the real Aiden . . . his scent, face, height, fresh haircut, build . . . A very late birthday present. Or Christmas had come almost two months early. Aiden, his dream man.

No, not his man. Aiden was someone else's man, some lucky bitch called Els. If Aiden could put it down the way he did—he looked like good sex—in the dream, then whoever he was sexing was a lucky bitch.

He wouldn't be able to look at Aiden the same. He'd barely been able to look at him before. Once Aiden got his phone back, that would be it. They wouldn't have to see each other again; he would be able to forget him completely.

But that caller, that rude bitch, had to be significant. She was bothered about Aiden's love life. Too bothered. And she knew his secret, whatever it was.

Mabley Green. The secret she was talking about. The woman with the dog.

But that woman had looked white, and the caller sounded black. Maybe it was something else. Had to be something that had started long before Mabley Green.

What secret then?

He shook his head and staggered to the door. No falling for anyone ever again.

Breakfast and shower out of the way, he went to the front room, a room whose owners showed how proud their were to be black and gay. Some of the same DVDs, novels and magazines had been in his old bedroom, the black non-LGBT ones on display, the LGBT ones hidden. He sighed then checked Aiden's phone. A few missed calls, all from the same number. Probably wasn't that facety bitch. She would've withheld her number. He sank into the beige leather sofa then returned the call.

"Shan?" Aiden said, his voice urgent.

"Aiden!"

Aiden's sigh messed up the connection.

"Glad to hear you."

"Same here."

"Sorry about your phone. Hope you haven't gone mad without it."

"Good thing it ain't my main phone."

"That's lucky."

"But it's still important."

"Oh . . . So, how are you . . . after yesterday?"

"Alright, I guess. How 'bout you?"

"I'm OK. Off work for the week."

"Makes sense."

"But I've got work to do for uni."

"Might help take your mind off everything."

"Maybe."

"Look, sorry for being rough and shit yesterday."

"Oh . . . no worries. Sorry for panicking."

"That's cool. . . . So, we're good?"

"Yeah."

"Cool."

Deep breath. "Aiden, there's something you should know."

"What?"

"Someone called your phone. She was really something else."

Aiden's breathing changed, sounded strained.

"Aiden? The line's crackling. I can't—"

"Who was it?"

"Some facety woman. Didn't get her name. She kept going on and on. I really wanted to let her know I wasn't you, but she wouldn't let me talk."

"What did she say?"

"She was pissed about not seeing you yesterday, and she was really threatening, angry. She also said . . ."

"What?"

"We never had this conversation before—well, we talked about your wedding ring—but I'm just wondering . . . if you're *seeing* someone."

"Why?"

"Something she said."

Nothing on the other end, not even breathing.

"Aiden, you still there?"

"Yeah."

"You don't have to answer the ques—"

"I am . . . talking to someone . . . I guess."

"Uh . . . hold on." He moved the phone away from his ear and covered his mouth, his throat getting tight.

No knowing what he was going to do. Could never control his emotions. Still a frigging fool. He'd only just met Aiden. Another guy he let himself get too excited about.

He clenched his eyes briefly, swallowed, brought the phone back to his ear. "Sorry about that, Aiden. Just had to sort something out."

"No worries."

"She sounded . . . gangster."

"Who?"

"The person who called."

"Oh . . . yeah."

"You in trouble?"

Aiden let silence linger for a moment. "No."

"Alrighty."

"Shan?"

Shannon was starting to sound better than *Shan*. "Yes?"

"If the phone rings and it ain't from this number, don't answer."

"What if it's someone else?"

"It would only be me—or her."

"You sure?"

"Yeah."

"But she's obviously mad at you. If she knows that I have your phone, she'll—"

"No!"

He flinched.

"Look." Aiden lowered his voice. "She can't know you have the phone. I don't want you involved."

"Involved?"

"Look, Shan . . . non, I lied just now. I'm caught up in some shit. She's . . . a problem."

"She sounded like bad news. She threatened to go to your house and tell your family your secret."

"She *what*?"

"If you don't *go through* with something."

Aiden came out with a string of all the curse words he could think of, in Jamaican patois.

"Aiden!"

"What?"

He had to do it. Would keep bothering him otherwise.

"What, Shannon?"

He needed to be convincing, because if it didn't work . . . "Like I said, she . . . she thought that I was you, so . . ."

"So?"

He swallowed, his heart speeding up. "She . . . she said what the secret is." He slapped his hand over his mouth before he could confess that was a lie.

Silence on the other end.

Heart going even faster.

"Aiden . . . you still there?"

"*What the fuck you just say?*"

Too much time had passed to take it back.

"She said what she said, thinking I was you. I know what's going—"

"That bitch!"

He jumped. His heart couldn't take it anymore. Aiden needed to hurry up and tell him his secret.

"Think I'm a dick now?"

"Well . . ."

"Shan, I ain't. I just . . . Fuck!"

"You just what?"

"My fam can't find out," Aiden whispered. "Knowing what you're going through . . . your parents dashing you away . . ."

Can't find out?

"Can't stand me now, can you?"

"I . . . I just . . ."

"I'm just me. No labels." Aiden was still whispering. "I mean . . . Course I like females, but . . ."

"But?"

"Whatchu mean *but*? You know."

No labels.

"Shannon?"

"I-I'm still here."

"I can't go through the shit you went through. My fam's all I got."

The embrace, lying about being married to keep from being hit on . . .

"Shannon!"

"I-I—"

"After what you went through, you've got to understand."

"It's just . . ."

"You think I like this shit?"

"N-no. I . . ."

"No one else can know about me."

"Know about you?"

Aiden kissed his teeth. "Why you acting all clueless and shit? She fucking told you."

I can't go through the shit you went through . . . Aiden wouldn't have said that unless . . .

"Shan?"

Course I like females, but . . .

"Shannon, say something!"

If Aiden ever found out he'd been tricked . . .

"Shannon, you're pissing me off!"

"S-sorry. I'm here."

"Disgusted?"

"N-no, I just . . . So you're . . ." He couldn't say it.

"The bitch told you, so stop fucking with me. Stop trying to get me to say it."

"B-but you're really—?"

"And you just couldn't stop her, tell her she'd called the wrong fucking number or something. You just had to find out what's going on. You slick . . . fucking . . ." Aiden took a deep breath, kept the rest of the insult in.

Aiden, this Adonis, was really like him.

"She really didn't let me get a word in."

"Bet she didn't."

"Damn it, Aiden. I'm sorry"

"He's sorry, he says."

"She must be really dangerous, because you're the baddest person I know, after yesterday."

"What's that supposed to mean?"

"Your bravery, the way you fought . . . You saved me, that's all."

"Wish I could've done it differently."

"I wish things could've been different, too." That was to both Aiden and himself, his mind going back to the news of the death.

Death from a head bashing, not a stabbing.

"Shannon, did you hear me?"

"Sorry, what did you say?"

"I'll come by later . . . get my phone."

"Alrighty."

"What's your door number again?"

"It's 50 Glyn—I mean 19 Richmond Road."

"Got it. I finish up about five. Should get to you by six."

"Alrighty. See you later then."

"Shan, hold up."

"What?"

Strained breathing from Aiden again.

"Aiden?"

"I'm leaving my girl soon."

"Alrighty. . . . And?"

"Just letting you know."

"Why?"

"Because . . . You know why."

Butterflies sprang to life in his stomach.

"Shan—"

"See you later, Aiden."

"Late—"

He cut Aiden off by hanging up. He was shaking. All that time thinking the likes of Leon Lopez, Michael Obiora and Boris Kodjoe were out of his league, that no one on their level of fineness would ever want him.

Then Aiden came along. Aiden the hunk. Aiden the Adonis. Lips, eyebrows, gaze, physique, swag, height . . . He had to have the dick to match.

His own dick was tingling, swelling. He shuffled free of arousal. There was no knowing what would happen, what he would let Aiden do to him, if neither Peter nor Uncle Lionel reached home first. He craved for Aiden.

Even scarier—Aiden wanted him.

17 / Aiden IV
Detour

Bishopsgate. Rush hour. Endless streams of people entering and exiting Liverpool Street Station. It looked like a dead end, the RBS building looming where the road bent to the left. Trail of vehicles with brake lights activated . . . the last thing Aiden needed to see. Those lights stayed on, even when the traffic lights turned green. The buses in the bus lane were at a standstill, too fat for the narrow lanes. Didn't help that other vehicles were straddling lanes, because the drivers were either selfish or shit at driving. Beeping cars ahead and behind were driving him crazy. He punched the horn, making pain tear through his bandaged hand, scaring the shit out of a woman passing in front of him. He'd forgotten his knuckles were mashed up from mashing up those cunts in Mabley Green. The pedestrian was looking at him wide-eyed. He beeped again, this time with his palm. She ran-stumbled out of his sight. More fucking pedestrians, crossing in front and behind like they owned the road. The bomboclaat cyclists and motorcyclists were just as bad, weaving through the gaps at will.

The knuckle pain was wearing away, but not the memory of Mabley Green.

The pussyhole had died from head injuries, not stab wounds.

The other fuckers were out there somewhere.

Shan could fight but wasn't cut out for street shit. That made those motherfuckers even bigger pricks for going after him. Shan could've died, but he'd killed someone instead. Hopefully that pep talk would keep his mind right. No need for police involvement. Too late for that anyway. Had to be settled in the streets.

The lights turned green again, but brake lights stayed red. He blasted the horn. Other drivers copied him. Being stuck like this was one thing. Being stuck with his thoughts was another.

He'd never lost the bloodclaat phone before. Should've felt it drop out of his pocket in Lionel's car. Shan knew more than he was supposed to. Shan must've thought he was a shithouse.

Shan was *Shan*, not *Shannon*, whether they were together or not. Dudes had come and gone. Quick head, quick ass, then on to the next. Couldn't have been anything more. But for the first time, someone he didn't want to just hit and quit had come along.

Maybe it had something to do with getting further away from twenty-five and closer to thirty each day. Everyone needed meaning at a certain point. Looked like he was at that point, otherwise he wouldn't have told Shan about breaking things off with Elise soon, as if they could just roam together in the fucking sunset. The whole thing with Shan and his parents . . . he couldn't let his family find out his secret—but he wanted Shan.

Tempest never knew when to stop. Shan should've stopped her. He was chatting shit when he said he'd tried to.

A beep behind. More space in front. Only a few car lengths of progress then another standstill. Couldn't be like this all the way to Kingsland Road.

His main phone rang. He paused at the name on the screen. Red lights caught him and vehicles in front again.

He turned on his Bluetooth headset. "Elise?"

"Hi, Aiden." Her voice was low.

"What's up?"

She let out a deep breath. "Just wanted . . . to talk."

He picked up the phone and looked at the screen. Just as he'd thought. It was a normal call, not WhatsApp. "Flight cancelled, or am I mixing up the dates?"

She took another deep breath. "No. . . . Should've . . . almost reached Cancún by now."

His headlights extended suddenly as the traffic in front got moving again. "Why—?"

A car horn interrupted him, just as he found the biting point. He looked in his rear-view mirror to find the driver behind rushing him with hand gestures.

He gave the middle finger with his bandage-free hand then lurched the car forward. "You off sick?"

"I . . . I've just had a bad day . . . and . . ." Her voice cracked between sniffs. "I just need to . . . talk to someone." She sobbed.

"What the fuck, Elise?"

She bawled louder.

"Is Tempest there?"

"No."

"What happened?"

"You're probably on your way home, but could you come round? I need someone to . . ."

Almost six, according to his dashboard. "When's Tempest coming back?"

"Don't know."

It was bad timing, but he couldn't leave her hanging. With all that was happening, he owed her.

"Traffic's bad, but I'll get there as soon as."

"Thanks, Aiden." She blew her nose. "See you soon."

"Cool."

One last sniff before she ended the call.

Another red light. He called his other phone when he stopped.

Shan picked up after the third ring. "Aiden?"

"Yo."

"Everything alright?"

"Yeah. Look, I'm running late."

"That's fine. I'm not going anywhere."

"Cool."

"Aiden, just so you know . . ."

"What?"

"The phone's been ringing a lot lately. All withheld numbers. Some calls around lunch time as well."

"Did you answer?"

"No."

"Good. Keep ignoring it."

"I will. I don't feel right about this though."

He restarted the car as the lights changed. "When I get the phone back, you won't have to worry."

"Alrighty. See you later."

"I'll call when I'm closer."

"Alrighty. Bye."

"Bye."

The intercom crackled. He told Elise it was him before she could ask who it was.

He twisted the fake wedding ring off his finger when she buzzed him in. When he reached her floor, a door clicked then rattled open. Elise stepped out of the doorway of the second door on the right. Looked like she'd rushed out of bed and thrown on the white dressing gown she was wearing. She was trying to say something, but she couldn't keep her mouth open long enough to say shit. She gave a wan smile as he drew closer. Incense was in the air. She looked down and stepped back into the flat. He closed the door behind him. Something was flickering. The lit candle on the entrance table. That explained the smell.

Sniffles made him focus on Elise. She'd taken out her weave, had short hair now. Strands were out of place, and there were bags under her glistening eyes.

Her phone dropped. She bent down to pick it up, her breasts about to tumble out, as if the dressing gown were all she had on, but the top of something cream, maybe her nightie, peeked out.

"Elise, what hap—?"

She wrapped her arms around him, squeezing him as if they were seeing each other for the last time.

He wasn't into this lovey-dovey shit, but he held her tight enough to kill the trembling in her body.

She pulled away slowly then frowned down at something. "What happened to your hand?"

"Accident at the gym."

She took him to the front room. They sat on a black leather sofa.

"Why you upset?"

Elise told him her passport was gone and that she thought she was going mad.

Had to be some Tempest fuck-shit. Shame he couldn't tell Elise that.

"The passport's got to show up. Couldn't have just vanished. You know for a fact you put it in your handbag."

Her expression was blank, like she didn't hear him.

"Elise, you wouldn't just forget . . ."

A picture of her and that bitch had been staring at him all that time, from the window sill. He looked away quickly, no chance for Elise to catch him shooting Tempest a dirty look.

He brought his leg further up the sofa, as Elise had done. Their knees touched for a few seconds before he broke the contact.

"You wouldn't forget putting your passport in your bag. I mean, we're talking 'bout last night."

"I don't know what to tell you."

"Maybe someone took it."

"No one's been here but me and Tempest. And her boyfriend."

He raised his eyebrows at her.

"But he was gone before I put the passport in my bag." She shuffled, her knee and thigh exposed. She didn't notice. "I put the old passport in my drawer ages ago, and . . . I just don't know how it ended up in my handbag. I . . ." She put her hand to her chest and looked up, as if the ceiling had the answers.

"At least you still have your job and you've got time off."

"I know, but it can't happen again."

"It won't."

"Can't be sure of that. What if I've really gone mad?"

"You ain't mad."

She shook her head. "There are things you don't know, things I've been carrying . . . for a long time . . ."

He couldn't become attached to Elise, and vice versa, be her counsellor. That would make him an even bigger prick. But she was staring at him, waiting for a response, permission to elaborate.

"What things?"

She opened then closed her mouth a few times, then she looked away.

He touched her knee, touched skin instead of cotton. He'd forgotten her dressing gown had come up. "Elise?"

She finally fixed her dressing gown. She faced him again, just about. "I . . . can't."

Because of her, I have no mother.

They were kids when Tempest lost her mum, so that made no sense, but Elise had done *something* to piss Tempest off.

"You can trust me."

"If you knew everything, you'd . . ." She shook her head again. "All that time and money spent on therapy."

"Therapy?"

Her eyes widened, like she'd said too much.

"When did you have therapy? And why?" *Because of her, I have no mother.*

Elise got up, walked around the shiny, brown coffee table; passed the on-but-mute TV and stopped at the DVD rack. A picture of two little girls was on top. She picked it up and chuckled as she ran her finger over it.

Looked like she'd forgotten she wasn't alone. "Funny how when one thing goes wrong, you end up thinking about other things that have gone wrong, and all you can do is cry, then cry some more."

He got up and joined her, towered over her. She did look a mess, like she'd just come out of bed, face not washed, but she smelled fresh out of a bathtub.

"Another picture of you two."

She turned the picture around so that he could see it better. "Yes."

Their complexions were different, Tempest's patchy and a shade of sepia like his, Elise's smoother and darker, but they favoured even more back then. They were both smiling, Elise revealing an incomplete set of teeth, Tempest with her mouth closed like she was too exhausted to smile. Elise's arm was around Tempest. Her plaits were countless, pink beads at the end of each. If Tempest's hair had been in plaits, it would've been just one, in a ponytail, no centre part.

"How old were you here?"

"I was almost nine; she had just turned nine." She frowned and became distant again. "Sylvia was long gone then." Her lips quivered.

"Sylvia?"

Elise's eyes widened like she'd jumped awake from a nightmare.

She put the picture back. "I . . . I can't . . ."

"Was Sylvia Tempest's mum?"

She broke down again then collapsed into him, her sweet scent as intoxicating as the candle's.

He wrapped his arms around her, his chest muffling her sobs. "Tell me what's wrong."

Either she couldn't hear him or she couldn't talk through her sobbing.

He shook her until she looked at him, then he cupped her face. "Tell me." He didn't flinch when her tears gathered at his thumbs. Worth it if it meant getting to the bottom of this shit.

"Aiden, I just need . . ."

"What?"

"I . . . feel . . . so weak. I want it to just . . . go away. I need to . . . feel good."

She placed her hands on his, staring at him wide-eyed, never blinking, then turned her head so that part of her lips were touching his left palm, the bandage-free palm.

He flinched.

She closed her eyes as she stretched out her lips against his skin. She was breathing through her mouth, warming his palm.

"El-ise?"

She opened her eyes and moved her lips away, frowning at him. He let go of her cheeks, but she put her hands behind his head and continued staring, more intently this time, like she was caught between two choices. He'd seen that look on her face before, in the beginning, when she was feeling him.

She tiptoed then brought her face to his. Something else she hadn't done in a minute.

Breathing was tickling him, either hers or his own hitting her skin and deflecting onto him. Her scent was sweet, made him crave doughnuts for a moment. Probably bathed in that Body Works stuff. He would sniff her all night if he could. She closed her eyes again. He closed his. Both of them were breathing louder. Breathing and Elise's lips tickled him, then breathing was muffled and tasted when her lips pressed against his. More than a peck, more than what he was used to getting from, and giving, her.

She broke the contact, leaving his lips wet and cold. He opened his eyes. She'd shrunk back to five-seven. Her fingers on her lips, she stared at him like she was reading him.

She put her hand behind his head, tiptoed and brought her face to his so that breathing tickled skin again. She was searching through his face this time, like it had something she was looking for. She pressed herself into him, woke his dick up. He moaned. She gasped. She moved her hands down his chest, kept one there while the other continued downwards and stopped at his waist. Her expression was blank.

"El—"

"Don't say anything," she whispered.

She moved, not much, but enough to get her hand on his boner. She squeezed it, made him moan again.

She took his good hand with her other hand and brought it to her breast then, eyes and lips half-open, whispered, "Squeeze me, Aiden."

He obeyed, heart beating faster. She moaned.

The picture of Elise and Tempest as children stuck out in his periphery. Even as a nine-year-old, the bitch was telling him to take this opportunity, or else.

Elise massaged his dick, stealing his attention from the photo on the DVD rack. He shook until he collapsed into her, his chin resting on her shoulder, as she made him harder. Her scent drew him to her neck. He rubbed his nose against it, snorted like a line of coke was there. She manoeuvred herself so that their noses touched. She pressed her lips against his, and he didn't—couldn't—tell her to stop. She wrapped one leg around his waist, and he automatically grabbed her thigh before she brought her other leg up.

They were joined like a pretzel as they tongue-wrestled, trapping groans. They bumped into the coffee table as they staggered backwards, knocking over whatever was on it.

His calves bumped into something else. The sofa. He turned around so that her back was facing it, held her as she undid her dressing gown. It was hanging off her. She struggled to get it all the way off. He ended up losing his grip, one hand not as good as the other. He dropped her without meaning to, her legs still around his waist, more exposed than before. Falling didn't hurt her; it got her excited, if anything. She put a cushion on the armrest, then she arched her back and started wining, her boobs resting higher up her heaving chest like they were about to tumble to her neck. He massaged her thighs. Fuck knew where that urge had come from. She sat up then yanked at his hoodie, the zip stuck. He took over from her, snatched his clothes off until he was shirtless. Elise widened her eyes as she looked up and down his torso, letting out a nervous breath. She'd never seen him like this before. Their first time.

Her first time.

She went back on her back, and traced her toes up and around his abs, pecs and nipples, making him flinch. She did the same to his Adam's apple and then his lips. Her nightie had bunched beyond her smooth thighs and some of her ass cheek. She had to be wearing panties. Commando didn't seem to be her style. Then again, she was holding the reins, like she'd had enough of being a virgin. She was a virgin freak. Probably owned toys from Bedroom Kandi and had porn star crushes.

He swallowed. "Elise, you sure—?"

She prodded his boner with the toes of her other foot till he doubled over and grabbed her calf.

"Don't say anything. Just . . . take me," she said breathily. "Please."

"But—"

She tucked her toes into the waistband of his Adidas tracksuits and pulled at him until he was on top of her.

His left hand found its way under her nightie. His heart was pumping faster than Usain Bolt's legs ever could. He swallowed, stiffened up, but her willingness and his curiosity were claating the part of him that didn't want this as his fingers brushed against a warm, rough fabric underneath her nightie. He pressed against the outline of her pussy through her panties. He prodded, circled, tickled, tried different things until she couldn't take it anymore, until she whimpered, bit her lip, clawed at leather, arched her back.

Strained breathing. He'd never been this close to taking her virginity before.

She sat up abruptly, forced him backwards, undid the string of his tracksuits and pulled them down. Boner was almost free. She put her arms around his neck and kissed him again. He kissed back, receiving and giving tongue.

She was fidgeting. He opened his eyes. Black panties were in her hand. She chucked it on the wooden floor.

She couldn't have asked him over for this.

She sat back, her nightie bunched up at her hips. Closer to seeing beyond her inner thighs. He hadn't seen her pussy, but he'd touched it, rubbed it, through her panties. And now her panties were on the floor. She'd started the process of giving herself to him. Too late to stop.

Or maybe that wasn't the reason. The picture on the DVD rack snatched his attention. Nine-year-old Tempest, staring back at him, was reminding him he had to do it.

Elise pulled at his underwear with her toes, struggling to free his erection. When she got his dick out, it slapped his abs then sprang to a stop like a diving board. Her eyes bulged out at it, then she pulled him down on top of her.

"El—"

She yanked his dick, teased the head and her entry, bracing herself, then opened up as he pushed gently.

They widened their eyes, and she gasped, when the head was in. His heart felt closer to bursting the deeper he went, the progress drawing out moans from them. Had to stop looking her in the eye. Bad enough feeling and hearing her as she lost her virginity to him, not knowing the fuck-shit she was in. She moaned some more, clawed at his back, clenched when he was at his deepest, damn near trapping him, like she was gauging if she could handle his length and thickness. Chills ran over him as she clenched. She was making him feel good. He didn't deserve to feel good. She grabbed his face, made him look at her, made him see her contortions, her lip-biting. Her chest was heaving, her nipples about to be exposed, the nightie bunched up above her waist. She was fidgeting and mumbling. It was her first time, so it had to hurt. He started moving in and out of her, nearly came out of her completely, maybe a chance to stop it, but she started squeezing and spreading his ass cheeks, her nails digging into his skin, thrusting him deeper and harder into her. She tightened around him, had him mumbling gibberish. He could still satisfy, and be satisfied by, a female. He still liked being inside a female.

He was finding his groove when something made him look at it again. The picture on the window sill. His eyes stayed on Tempest, didn't go to Elise. He growled.

"Aiden . . . deeper . . . harder . . ."

He was smashing with the kind of rhythm that made Elise sound like she was moaning next to a fan on full power. His good hand was massaging her breasts under her nightie, flicking and pressing her hardening nipples. She kneaded his ass cheeks, encouragement for him to thrust harder.

His eyes locked with Tempest's in the picture on the window sill again. She was smiling, pleased with herself. He sped up his strokes and grunted louder, his ass cheeks being squeezed as if chunks were going to come off like clay. Grunts from below, then chanting . . . low then high depending on how deep he was. Tempest's smile in the picture was pissing him off, their fight flashing before him, grunts and moans the background music, as he ploughed through walls harder and faster.

Then something made him completely present. Elise came up to him, grabbed his face and planted kisses everywhere, her tongue clumsy, sweat mingling as skin connected. She forced him onto his back, still keeping him inside, and started riding him, her right leg bent between him and the sofa, her other leg stretched to the floor. He could be as deep or shallow as she wanted him to be. His head was on an armrest now. No cushion. No more Tempest. Just Elise falling into him, light illuminating her like she was an angel.

She was an angel.

He was fucking an angel.

In this position, this angel was fucking him.

The angel in her was stripping away with each stroke.

Her nightie had come back down, tickling his thighs as she bounced, bounced, bounced. He felt up her ass, aggravating pain in his right hand, as she pinched his nipples, pulling hairs around them. Grunts each time she slapped down into him. Strands of hair had fallen to her forehead. She started breathing through pursed lips, eyes narrowed, like she was drifting into sleep as she rode him. She bounced and bounced until one of her straps fell, exposing part of her right nipple.

He couldn't take looking at her anymore. He closed his eyes. She was starting to sound like she was in distress, as if she didn't know what she'd gotten herself into, that journey out of virginity, that feeling of loosening what had always been locked tight.

Maybe Shan was a virgin too. Aiden could be his first, would let Shan ride his dick like Elise. His eyes were closed, but he could see Shan riding him. Shan's face was begging for pleasure and pain, dick flapping with each bounce, perineum rubbing against manbush, balls slapping groin, tight hole filled. If Shannon were a virgin . . .

Elise took a deep breath like someone who had come back to life. He opened his eyes. More strands of hair had fallen to her forehead, sticking. She let out a piercing squeal. Her head went back as she moaned to the ceiling, her neck at its longest. That did something to him, made him squeeze the shit out of her ass then her exposed breast, as his upward thrusts slapped into her downward ones at the same time.

Tingles were slithering up his dick out of nowhere, balls tightening, perineum getting sore. His dick was about to fall off. It was coming and he couldn't control it. She was feeling something too, digging nails into his clenched chest. She was getting wilder. He returned violent thrusts with savage grunts as her nails left marks on his chest. They sounded like they were trying to kill each other. He got in a few more rough thrusts as he gritted his teeth, tasting his sweat. Elise slammed down on him just as hard, a battle between pleasure and pain etched on her face. Her body started to shake; she looked like she was about to cry.

A few more hard thrusts and . . . "Fuck! Fuck! I'm-gonna-come!"

He screamed, arched his back and shook, his abs sucked in tightly like they'd remain stuck like that. She struggled off him, ripping their connection, his come chasing her, and spraying his torso and anything else in range.

Spasms worked him, from his feet to his thighs, from his abs to his chest, every muscle stiff, then back the other way, as he banged his head on the armrest. Couldn't stop moaning as long as he was coming.

The moans were finally gone; heavy breathing remained. Chest heaving, limbs weak, it took everything in him to shift even an inch. He moved like he was getting out of a car wreck. Elise was huddled on the other side of the sofa, her head to her knees, mumbling as she rocked. One eye was exposed. It widened, then she hid her face completely. She'd been staring at him.

They stayed in their corners, Elise huddled, Aiden sprawled out as coolness dried him when something vibrated against his ankles. He got up, paused, moved then paused again, sweat and come tickling his torso. His tracksuits were bunched at his ankles. He pulled them up, with his boxers, to just below his balls. Tissue was on the coffee table. He stretched for some, fresh come tickling his stomach. He pulled a few pieces out with his bandaged hand, made the box fall off the coffee table.

"I need . . . to use . . . your bathroom."

Elise was still recovering, but she managed a quick peek at him then a nod. He took his phone out of his pocket. A missed call from Shan. He zig-zagged, legs like jelly, to the bathroom, had a quick clean-up then phoned Shan back.

"Aiden, where are you?"

"I'm . . ." He peeped out of the bathroom. Shuffling in the front room. He ran his hand over the back of his head, clenching his eyes.

"Aiden!"

"Sorry, Shan. Was meant to call you again—"

"Where are you?"

He peeped out again. Elise was busy in the front room, the way the flickering candle was making her shadow dance on the passage floor and wall. He closed the door.

"Did you hear me? Are you at home?"

"No."

"Oh, God."

"What is it?"

"It's that person again."

He clenched his jaw. "What about her?"

"She rang again and . . ."

"And?"

"I . . . answered."

"*What?* Why?"

"I wasn't thinking. I didn't say anything—just like before—but it must've really pissed her off."

"What—?"

Quick slaps along the passage floor, getting louder . . . Elise was coming. Then a door opened.

"Shannon, hold on."

He opened the bathroom door and peeped out. The door opposite was open. Could see part of Elise's reflection in a mirror-on-wheels. Strength in his legs not fully regained. Walking back to the front room was like walking on a travelator, the candle's intoxicating scent getting to his head. When he reached the front room, he cringed at the black sofa. It was creased where he'd fucked Elise. She'd been a virgin, had saved herself all that time, only for him to fuck her life up. It was almost as if he were the virgin. He'd actually done it. They'd done it.

And without protection!

He was clean though. She had to be too; he was her first. If his come had gone inside her . . .

No. They'd disconnected.

He shook worries away. "Shannon, sorry 'bout that."

"It's OK."

"What do you mean she's pissed off?" He put his hoodie back on, zipped it up halfway, didn't bother with his polo shirt or string vest. Still hot.

"She's . . ."

"What?"

"She's going to your house."

"*What?*"

"Does she even know where you live?"

"She's been to my fucking yard before."

"Good thing you're not home then."

"But my fam's home!"

"Shit!"

"Gotta go. Good looking out."

"Alrighty. Let me know what's going on, and be careful."

"Thanks."

Aiden hung up first.

The photo on the window sill caught his eye again, Tempest smiling like she was up to no good.

"Aiden, is everything OK?"

He spun around. "Shit, Elise! I didn't hear you."

"Sorry."

"I need to go."

He looked around the room to make sure he had everything then dashed to the flat door. Couldn't stand looking Elise in the eye. The main thing was that he'd done what Tempest wanted.

"Aiden, before you go . . ."

He stopped in front of the door, then he turned around, careful not to look at her too hard. She couldn't look at him properly either, not like before. Things had changed—big time.

"Thanks for coming—I mean . . . you know what I mean."

He grimaced. "It's cool. Hope the passport shit gets sorted."

"Thanks."

He had his hand on the door handle when Elise called his name again.

"Don't be offended by this."

He frowned.

She took a deep breath. "You don't have any . . . infections, do you?"

"Course not!"

She put up her hands defensively. "Had to ask. I don't, in case you were wondering."

Course she didn't. He was her first. But she didn't know he knew. "Cool. Catch you later, Elise."

"Bye, Aiden."

He put his hand on the door handle again, paused. "Elise?"

"Yes?"

He grimaced, took his eyes off her, swallowed. "You gonna . . . take the pill?"

She looked confused at first, then she said, "Oh . . . the pill . . . y-yes."

He nodded. "Good. Catch you later."

"See you, Aiden."

Something made him lower his head to hers and go in for a kiss. they were both stiff.

Damn prick for doing that—he was going to end it soon.

He was barely out the door before she closed it—or slammed it.

Didn't matter what it was. What mattered was reaching his yard—before Tempest.

18 / Tempest IV
Trash

Tempest was in front of the gate to Aiden's house, without a plan, but her presence alone would tell him she wasn't ramping. His car wasn't there, but someone had to be home. Too cold for his grandparents to have their old batties outdoors.

She opened the gate. If she were a midget, the plants flanking almost the entire length of the lawn would've looked like trees. She manoeuvred past almost conjoined leaves, as if passing fragile items in a shop, to the front door. She couldn't remember it being so bad the last time she'd visited.

The porch light came on suddenly. Her half-fringe kept her from being dazzled. The light was on in the living room. She jumped at the sight of someone, veiled by the living room's net curtains, peering at her. Their fair complexion blended in with the light inside. Must've been the grandma. She smiled at the old woman, only to receive a frown asking who she was and what the raas she was doing there.

The face disappeared, the net curtains falling back into place. The passage light came on moments later. Someone with a hunched posture approached slowly. She sighed, and adjusted her hair and jacket when the person stopped, keys jingling.

"Who is it?"

"Uh . . ."

"Who is it?" The grandma's Jamaican patois was stronger, her voice deeper. "You nuh see the bell?"

"Was just about to press it. I'm Tempest, Aiden's friend."

No response.

Being made to wait was getting her heated, not hot enough to keep from shivering and rubbing up and down her arms.

"He's not here," the old shit finally said.

"Will he be back soon?"

"Me nuh know."

She was about to say something else when a much taller figure appeared. It was a man, his form blurred through the front door's frosted glass. Must've been the granddad. Mumbling on the other side. She tried to make out what they were saying, but an approaching car drowned them out. Keys rattled as the granddad unlocked the front door. She stepped back when the unlocking sounds ended with a click, just as the gate squeaked open then crashed to a close. She barely turned around before someone grabbed her.

"You mad bitch!"

The front door opened as she was about to unleash. The granddad was standing in the doorway, his head missing the top of the door frame only because of his slight hunch. Same old pot belly. He stared at her with a glint in his unusual eyes.

"Aiden, you make it just in time," Mr Gordon said.

"Hi, Granddad."

"Hi." Time for an innocent girl smile. "I'm Tempest. Remember me?"

"Of course me 'member you," Mr Gordon said, looking her up and down then making eye contact; he liked what he was seeing.

The grandma pushed past him then peered at her.

"Hello, Mrs Gordon."

"Hi." The grandma wasn't doing herself any favours, tightening her lips and frowning. It was bad enough her cheeks were sagging.

Mari-heifer would like her.

"Hi, Grandma."

*Grump*ma's face lit up at Aiden. "Hi, baby." Her voice was high-pitched. Then lines returned to her forehead. "Gwaan till you catch cold." High start, deep finish.

Grumpma was right. There Tempest was hugging herself, suede jacket covering her from part of her face to just above her knee, and Aiden was thirst trapping, wearing nothing underneath his halfway-zipped up hoodie, as if his pumped, somewhat hairy chest had busted the zip. He was sweating, a black top and white string vest slung over his shoulder. His Adidas bottoms were sagging, the string untied. That was a first.

"Chill out, Grandma."

"Humph."

"Bring yuh likkle friend in." Mr Gordon said.

"Soon come. Just need to talk to her."

"Bring her in, man."

Grumpma gritted her teeth at Mr Gordon. "It's late, and me tired."

"Cora, go to bed if you want to," Mr Gordon said.

She strained to keep smiling as Grumpma's face stayed sour. Cheeks aching too much to keep it up. Just when it didn't seem possible for more lines to appear in the old heifer's forehead, the lines squeezed together right at the top of her nose. The old wretch's top lip curled upwards to reveal healthy-looking teeth. Had to be dentures. Grumpma humphed and turned around, her batty swaying as she left them at the front door.

"Pay her no mind." Mr Gordon took her by the hand, bringing her into the house.

"Thank you."

Aiden's breathing sounded like a distant wind. He wanted to explode, but he forced a smile.

She peered into the living room. The same Windrush period-looking furniture she'd seen on her previous visit. The lighting in there was better than in the passage. A hand on her shoulder made her turn around.

"You want a drink?" Mr Gordon said.

"No tha— Actually, yes please."

Aiden needed to know she was sticking around. She smiled at him as his smile disappeared. His eyes were vacant, but his staring alone spoke volumes, screaming at her, asking what the fuck she was playing at.

"I'll get it, Granddad," he said suddenly.

"Actually, don't. Not staying long."

The glint in Aiden's eyes erased her smile. She wasn't going to let him, her enemy, get her a drink. He knew that.

"Alright then," Mr Gordon said.

She gave the nice old man a smile, but it disappeared like ink off whiteboard at the sight of Grumpma peering at her from the kitchen. The old woman's beige attire and tan complexion were camouflaged with the bright kitchen colours. CCTV in human form.

"Tempest, in here." Aiden motioned towards the living room with a bandaged hand.

Anything to be out of sight of that old heifer.

A picture in the wooden cabinet of an older version of Aiden—had to be his dad—held her attention before she was grabbed by the arm. Aiden practically threw her against another wooden cabinet. Crockery and glass shook and clinked behind her.

"Fucking cunt!" He was close enough to smell. Not the usual scent of fabric softener. A different kind of sweetness she couldn't figure out.

"Let me go, you prick!"

Aiden tightened his grip, keeping her from writhing. He was too strong, too mad.

"Stop *fucking* with me, Tempest!"

Her eyes widened at his deadly ones. His bushy eyebrows joined together. Face of the devil. Must've inherited that expression from Grumpma.

"Get. Out." His teeth were gritted.

"Aiden . . . you better . . . let . . . go of me." She managed to get her free hand in her handbag. "Your granddad will be back any moment now . . . or that shithouse nan of yours—"

"Watch it."

"And they'll wonder . . . why you're . . . hurting me." She stopped moving her hand, recognizing the familiar object in her fingers. "And then I'll play that recording to them." She took out her pocket knife quickly then pressed it against Aiden's dick.

The harder she pressed it there, the more he loosened his grip until he finally let go. She moved the knife away from him then rubbed the part of her arm he'd squeezed. Almost no life in it.

"Why are you here?"

"*Els.*" She put the knife in her jacket pocket, kept her hand in there, just in case. "And to actually hear your voice. Why'd you ignore me on the phone?"

Aiden looked away.

"What is it?"

"Yo."

She jumped, spun around, did a double take at the person in the doorway. Aiden's other double. She'd forgotten about Ethan.

"It's been a minute." He came to her, hugged her, squeezing her titties into him, his hands just above her batty. Slick shithouse.

His cologne was stifling. She struggled out of the embrace. "Long time, Ethan. Just stopped by to see my friend." She backhanded Aiden's solid chest.

"Grandma and Granddad still in the kitchen?" Aiden said.

"Yeah," Ethan said. He turned to Tempest. "So, he's just a friend?" He smiled then licked his lips, more like Maurice Green than LL.

He was no Carl. His grey hoodie looked too big despite his height, probably to hide a body that had a bit too much fat and too little muscle, but he was good-looking, like his blasted brother, especially with a fresh trim, facial hair like an anchor, and eyes a shade of brown unique to the Gordon men.

"Just a friend," she said.

"Well, don't be a stranger."

"Sure won't."

Ethan smiled at her then winked at Aiden as he left the living room.

"Now, where were we?"

"Where you fuck off."

Aiden reached for her. She slapped his bandaged hand. He winced.

"That shit with the phone calls earlier, something's off." She stepped closer to him. "What the fuck—?"

"Everything alright in here?"

She jumped at the high then deep voice.

"All good, Grandma. Tempest's going now."

Aiden was mocking her with his smirk. She nearly narrowed her eyes at him, but Grumpma was right there. She kept her eyes on Aiden, but there was that burning sensation of the old wretch staring at her. She gave her cheeks more exercise, forced a smile before finally looking at the woman. The stare from Grumpma was sharp enough to cut her resolve in half. She quickly looked at Aiden before she could let the old hoe know what she really thought of her.

"Clyde, Aiden's friend is leaving!" Grumpma said.

Shuffling, along with habitual throat-clearing signalled the old man's approach.

"Leaving already?" He was winded.

"Yes."

"I'll walk you out." Aiden was just too willing.

Grumpma wasn't a Tempest fan, but there were more visits to come.

She extended her hand to Grumpma. "It was nice seeing you again."

"Me hand them not clean. Goodnight." The old woman slid past her husband.

Mr Gordon sighed at Grumpma then shook Tempest's hand. "Hope to see you again soon."

That glint in his eye again. Seemed as if he didn't want to let go of her hand. He'd probably been a playboy in his day. He thought he still had it. Randy old man. A little cute though.

"Likewise." She maintained her smile as she tried to get her hand out of the old man's strong grip. "Goodnight."

"Goodnight." He finally let go.

Aiden followed her out of the living room. Grumpma was standing by the banister. Lines were busy all over Grumpma's sour face, especially in her forehead. The ultimate look of facetiness. Her sagging cheeks weren't helping. Tempest forced another smile, but the old heifer bent her head so that her eyes were almost completely hidden under her upper eyelids. Only a pair of glasses resting near the bottom of her big shithouse nose was missing.

Mr Gordon shuffled to the passage. "Tempest, you need a lift home?"

"She'll be fine, Clyde," Grumpma said, voice high, like she'd been waiting for Mr Gordon to ask that question so that she could check him. Then her Maya Angelou voice returned. "She bring herself here so without problem, nuh true?"

The things she could've told Grumpma . . . from her ugly face to her cobweb-filled, shrivelled pussy . . . "I'll be fine."

She gave Mr Gordon one last sincere smile, and the old heifer a final fake one and an imaginary middle finger.

"Went well, didn't it?" Aiden said once they were outside.

"Funny enough, it did. That thing may not like me, but—"

"Who you calling *that thing*?"

"But your male family members do."

"Keep coming here, make her work your bloodclaat."

"Please. That old thing doesn't want it with me." She headed for the gate. "And the lawn needs sorting out. You or Eth—"

"Tempest!"

She was met with Aiden's devilish expression when she turned to face him.

"It was you, wasn't it?"

"What?"

"Elise's passport."

She opened her mouth, words stuck, fog escaping. She clutched her handbag as she averted her gaze from his.

"I knew it!"

"How do you know about that?"

"She was in a bad way when I saw her."

"Oh, you went to see her? Good. Guys are supposed to *see* their girlfriends."

His jaw clenched, then he seemed to be looking through her.

"When you gonna fuck her?"

He turned his head, sighed fog.

She'd asked him that question before. He usually had a response.

"Just piss off." He turned around to go back inside.

A different kind of sweet scent. Sagging pants. Top off. He'd been to the flat, seen Elise.

Her stomach tingled. She rushed to him, grabbed his waist and yanked his tracksuits down. She went to her knees and pressed her face into his batty.

211

He spun around.

Even better.

He fought to get his pants back up, but they were below his knees.

"What the fuck, Tempest?"

She planted her face in his grey underwear and sniffed to the point of brief light-headedness.

She got up, hand over her mouth, short bursts of fog her excitement.

He yanked his joggers up, cussing under his breath.

"I smelled her on you when you were all up in my face. Your underwear . . . your dick . . . reeks of sex."

He turned his back to her.

"Did you . . . and Elise . . . ?"

Just another sigh, as he looked up, into blackness.

She could've cried.

"Just go, Tempest."

"You . . . actually . . . did it."

"And now, it's over." He opened the door.

"No, it's not."

He paused, turned to her again. "I did what you wanted, so now I'm gonna end it."

Maybe the next step wasn't a big reach after all.

"You hear me, Tempest? I'm done now."

"No, you're not."

He narrowed his eyes at her.

"You won't end it. You're going to *keep* doing it."

"What?"

"Fuck her again and again and a—"

"*Tempest*," he said, looking as if he was going to snap her neck. "I did what you wanted—"

"I know. Now, I want you to keep doing it . . . till I feel like enough's enough."

He gritted his teeth and jabbed his finger at the air.

"Keep fucking that heifer to keep me from coming back here."

"Tempest!"

"Keep fucking her."

He shook his head, his fists clenched.

"Keep—"

"Fuck you!" He stormed inside then slammed the door.

She practically floated to the gate. The crash it made after she went through it took her out of her daze.

Movement ahead, in the direction she'd come from, made her stop. A woman in black, camouflaged by shadows and breathing that came out in smoke, was staring at her. Seemed she'd been walking then stopped abruptly when she saw Tempest. A gust of wind blew her hat off. That took the woman by surprise. She scurried to retrieve the hat, the wind making her waist-length braids dance, but the hat was determined to get away from her. Tempest sped up, the wind messing with her half-fringe.

The woman had long given up on her hat by the time it reached Tempest's feet. Tempest picked it up, approached the woman then stopped. The woman had one hand on her hip and the other was pulling her jacket collar over her mouth. The rest of her face was exposed. They weren't close to each other, wind pitting lights against shadows, but she could've sworn the woman was giving her a facety look. Or maybe the woman was flustered and pissed that her hat had been blown off her head. Tempest kept going. The woman put her hand out, signalling for her to stop.

"What the fuck?" she muttered, her click-clacks dragging to a stop. She waved the hat around, fingers cramping.

She was close enough to the woman just as the wind blew the woman's collar out of place and revealed more of her face. Definitely someone she didn't know.

The woman gritted her teeth as she said something, so she couldn't have been that loud, but even if she were loud, the wind and traffic along Chatsworth Road would've drowned her out. The woman twisted her head with attitude. Tempest put a hand on her hip. The woman cut her eyes. Tempest looked behind. Nothing but parked cars and swaying trees. That look had been for her. She was about to cut her eyes back when the woman took out a phone then held it up. Flashes came and went before Tempest could hide her face.

"Oi!" She ran towards the woman.

The woman ran too, away from her, her waist-length braids floating like a cape. She was wearing flats and trousers. Tempest had on trousers too, but heels instead of flats. Hard to close in on the woman. The woman ran across the road then disappeared around the corner.

Cars were coming from behind, threatening to increase her distance from the woman. She kept running on the left until the cars passed her, then she crossed the road. At the end of Powerscroft Road, she went right like the woman had done. She stopped just past *William Hill*, looked as far ahead as she could, then she looked behind, even though the woman hadn't run that way. Other people were around, no one with braids, no one wearing all black. Plenty of parked cars, others moving. No sign of the woman. She went back to *William Hill*. It was closed.

She passed *William Hill* again then stopped next to a fancy, white BMW with tinted windows. It was parked next to a red Honda that looked like it was about to fall apart, a bin close to both. Made sense for the mashed up car to be parked by the bin, but the beauty deserved better.

She neared the bin, inspecting the wide-brimmed hat. Gucci. Tiger-print band around the bottom of the crown. This was for keeps.

She had to get rid of what was in her handbag though. Couldn't risk being seen with it. She'd come too far. She scanned all around, making sure no one was watching her, then took out

Elise's passport. One last look at the photo page. Couldn't deny that Elise was photogenic. Bitch had good skin too.

The most important thing—the passport was current. She shut the passport and chucked it in the bin.

THURSDAY

19 / Shannon VII
Coming together

I t was half-term, so Westfield Stratford was packed as if it were a Saturday. Shannon had almost told Aiden he couldn't make it to the get-together with him, his girlfriend and his girlfriend's sister. If only he hadn't phoned Aiden as soon as his new phone arrived. It was going to be hard to feign ignorance and happiness in front of someone he had feelings for *and* his girlfriend. But Aiden had sounded desperate to see him, to make sure they were still good despite the revelation. Maybe meeting Aiden's girlfriend was the one thing he needed in order to move on. It was bad enough to want someone, knowing he was taken, straight or not straight. Maybe he would become friends with the girlfriend. He would definitely have to get over Aiden then.

He continued towards TGI Fridays once the escalator brought him up to the Food Court level.

"Shannon!"

He stopped, looked around.

"Shan!"

He scanned the open area again. Someone who favoured Elise was looking his way. The same figure-hugging navy jacket. The same walk. Short hair. Hems of snug black jeans were tucked in black ankle boots. She made hand gestures as she strutted, asking him what he was doing there. It *was* her.

"Elise!"

"I messaged you earlier about meeting up."

He pulled her into a tight hug. Looked like she'd forgiven him for being a no-show on Sunday, the way she was hugging him back. The thought of bumping into Elise at the same place he was supposed to be meeting up with Aiden and his people. Maybe Elise could join them. Maybe—

Aiden, not too far away, wearing a red Champion hat and a black hoodie just about able to withstand his muscles, seemed to appear out of nowhere. He was frowning. Could've sworn his lips trembled for a moment. Maybe it was jealousy. Rich, considering he was the one with the girlfriend. Just him. No girlfriend.

Aiden's intense stare woke up butterflies. Even with the beard not looking as sharp as before, his fineness was unchanged. He made looking mashed up look hot, a tiny hoop earring in each ear adding to his swag. Those lips of his trembled again, like he was heartbroken by what he was seeing. He put Aiden out of his misery, let go of Elise.

"Hi, Aiden," he said.

"Shannon." Aiden was half-looking at him and half-looking at Elise.

Elise turned her head from one to the other. "How do you two know each other?"

"Uh . . . I—"

"Shannon . . . is the homie I was talking about."

Elise's lips stretched into a smile. She took Shannon's hand. "*Shannon*?"

He looked at Elise then Aiden, then Elise again.

"Yeah," Aiden said, shrugging his shoulders.

They'd been talking about him, and . . . It couldn't be . . . "Els?"

"What was that, Shan?"

He turned his back to them, towards people streaming on and off the escalators until ringing, deep in his head, deadened the clanging and chatter of hungry shoppers like bleeps over curse words.

Sweet little Els. "Els is Elise."

Someone spun him back around, back to the buzz floating throughout the top level of Westfield Stratford.

"What do you mean, Shan?" Elise turned to Aiden, smiling. "You call me *Els*?"

Aiden furrowed his brow then widened his eyes as if a memory had come to him. "Yeah."

Elise was the only one smiling. Aiden gave Shannon the same look he'd given to calm him down in Mabley Green and Eastway.

The last thing he needed to be thinking about. No police, no prison, no nothing, just—

"Anyone there?" Elise was waving her hand in his face.

Heart racing, fists clenched to fight trembling, he said, "*Elise* is your girlfriend?"

Aiden swallowed. "Yeah." Another swallow.

He managed to see sexiness in the mere up and down movement of Aiden's Adam's apple, despite the mess.

He looked away, shaking his head, Aiden's countenance terrifying.

Gone through with it.

"Shan, are you alright?"

"He's fine," Aiden said, threat hidden behind his smile. He stepped between Elise and Shannon then held Shannon by the shoulder. "Right, Shan?"

He tried to make Aiden nothing more than a blur, but Aiden's stare was penetrating him. Aiden wasn't going to look away until their eyes locked.

Aiden had that look, that frightening snarl and hideous tightening of skin between eyebrows. Even worse, Aiden was gripping his shoulder like he was going to pick him up and fling him over the glass barrier to the lower-ground level.

Looking at Elise wasn't much better—her eyes were narrowed.

Back to Aiden—the same murderous look. Couldn't take it. "Y-yeah . . . I'm fine."

"You sure? You're sweating."

"Yeah. A bit hot." He unzipped his jacket and wiped his forehead with the back of his hand. "Can't believe I know the both of you and didn't know you were . . . together."

"I'm just as surprised."

"That makes—"

He yanked himself out of Aiden's clutches then dashed to the other side of Elise.

"—three of us," Aiden finished, stare still intense.

"You said your girl—Elise's sister was . . . coming. . . . Tempest."

Looked like Aiden flared his nostrils for a split second.

"Tempest sent me a text . . . about ten minutes ago." Elise took her phone out of her handbag. "She was in Mile End."

"That's not far."

"Let's join the queue at TGI's . . . see how long we have to wait." Elise slipped her arm into his as the three of them headed to TGI's. "It's only been a few days, but it feels like I haven't seen you in weeks."

"Been meaning to contact you to apologise about Sunday."

"You texted me, remember?"

"What?"

"You texted me the same night."

"No, I didn't."

"You apologized for Sunday *and* Tuesday."

He stopped, bringing Elise and Aiden to a halt. "Tuesday?"

"Yeah, we were meant to meet up on Tuesday evening in Dalston Square."

"I haven't been able to contact you since Sunday morning."

Her cheeks rose as she frowned, her lips widening. "We texted each other up until yesterday—tell a lie, I sent you a text around lunch time earlier today, but you didn't respond."

"I thought I was hearing things when you mentioned something about contacting me earlier today. I lost my phone on Sunday."

She broke the three-person chain then fumbled in her handbag. "I must really be going mad." She exchanged a knowing glance with Aiden then took out her phone. "This is you, right?" She held the phone so close to Shannon's face that his breath clouded the screen.

He put some distance between his face and the phone then swiped up and down the screen. "Makes no sense. . . . I definitely sent the texts up until Sunday morning. I remember that Sunday text . . . but the rest didn't come from me."

"But it says *Shannon*."

"I know."

"I waited for you in Dalston Square, but you didn't show up. You just sent a text saying you couldn't make it."

"I see it, but I lost my phone on Sunday."

"Then who's been texting me?"

"I—"

"You were mugged, right?"

He met Aiden's prompting, wide-eyed gaze.

"Mugged." Aiden's expression was unchanged.

"Y-yeah."

"What?"

"That's why . . . I . . . ."

Aiden prompting him with a grimace, rushing him to come up with something, flustered him.

". . . didn't show up on Sunday."

Aiden's countenance relaxed.

"But someone obviously has my phone, and they've been messaging you, pretending to me." He glanced at Aiden.

Aiden understood. Elise was unknowingly caught up in the Mabley Green mess.

"I'm so sorry, Shan. Were you hurt?"

"I'm alright now."

"Was it one person?"

"No. Three."

Her hand went to her mouth.

He glanced at Aiden again. Usual intense gaze. Clenched jaw. Intimidating and sexy at the same time. Pointless trying to maintain eye contact.

"Did you see their faces?"

He searched Aiden's face for assistance. The only help Aiden gave was a raised eyebrow, a nudge to come up with *something*. "No."

"Where did it happen?"

"In Mab—"

"Dalston," Aiden said.

Aiden's widened eyes and nodding head scared him into going along with the lie. "Yeah . . . I'd uh . . . just left . . . my uncle's."

Elise was looking at him intently, waiting for more information, then she said, "What about the police?"

"Uh . . . uh . . ."

"They're investigating, right, Shan?" Aiden's voice was laced with irritation.

"OK—I mean, yeah."

"When are you getting a new phone?"

"Got it today. Thank God I had insurance."

"Thank God."

The queue wasn't too long when they reached the TGI's entrance, but just about every table in sight was taken.

"The person who took your phone has really been texting me. No wonder you wouldn't return my calls, and the texts were so . . . not you." Elise snarled. "I've been communicating with some scumbag all this time. Why would they even arrange to meet up with me?"

They let the chatter, near and far, and clanging cutlery fill the silence.

"Elise, what did you put in the texts?"

"Asked Shan how he was doing . . . stuff about my passport . . ." She looked at her phone again then grimaced.

"What is it?"

"I bet you don't delete your messages."

He shook his head.

"I texted you my address."

That made him snap his head at Aiden, whose eyes widened.

"We need to know the police's progress."

"No!" Aiden and Shannon said at the same time.

"They're already investigating. This might help them solve everything faster. Bad enough those scumbags are out there."

He and Aiden exchanged glances again, both of them mumbling before Aiden took the initiative. "Don't worry about shit. You're safe. And you have other addresses in your phone, right, Shannon?"

"Uh . . . right."

"See?"

"Can't be too sure."

"Has anyone been around?" Aiden said.

"No."

"There you go."

"But what about all your pictures and music and stuff, Shan?"

"Had transferred a lot to my laptop."

"That's good."

"Come on, you two." Aiden alerted them to the moving queue.

"Elise, you mentioned something about your passport. Is that why you're here, in England?"

She rolled her eyes. "Let's not even go there."

"What happened?"

She exchanged another knowing glance with Aiden.

"Tell me."

"I was supposed to fly out to Mexico on Monday," she said. As if seeing an image of something only she could see, she looked down and continued distantly. "I definitely had the passport in my handbag the night before. . . . I checked and . . ." She shook confusion away and made eye contact again. "Anyway, I don't know what happened to my passport, but I have a new one. Arrived today. I'm off this week. Flying out next Tuesday."

"That's strange."

"The last time I saw it, I had put it inside my bag."

"Could anyone have stolen it?"

They were almost at the front of the queue.

"I put it in my bag right before I went to bed—or so I thought. Turns out it was my old passport in the bag."

"So, what about the other one?"

She shrugged her shoulders.

"It must be somewhere in your flat."

She sighed. "Doesn't matter now. Got the new one."

He scanned the dimly-lit restaurant as Aiden asked the waiter for a table for four. It was packed, but it wasn't long before another waiter guided them to a booth table. Elise slid across the leather seat, and Shannon the seat opposite her. Aiden took a moment before deciding who to sit next to. Eventually, he gingerly manoeuvred his long, hard-bodied frame into the space next to his girl.

"Sorry, Aiden." Elise got up, her knees trapped under the table. "Just got another text from Tempest. She's in the shopping centre. I'll wait for her outside."

"What you having to drink?"

Elise scanned the drinks menu. "Coke, please." She smiled at Shannon then scurried through the dim restaurant.

He waited for Elise to disappear into the brightness outside the restaurant, before snapping his head towards Aiden. "What the fuck's going on? *Elise* is the one your lying to about your sexuality?"

Aiden reached over the table, grabbed Shannon by the scruff of his neck and swivelled his long, wide frame around the table to the chair next to him. Conversations died down, and Beyoncé's vocals were suddenly clearer. He scanned the restaurant then loosened his grip.

A waiter and waitress came over. "Everything good over here?" the former said.

"Yeah." Aiden feigned a smile and let go of Shannon.

The waitress narrowed her eyes at Shannon. "You sure?"

Aiden had it in him to do some damage, looked like he was in a claating mood, but there were witnesses.

"Yes," Shannon said.

The waiter and the waitress stood there a moment longer then nodded and left.

Aiden leaned into him. "Sorry."

"The facety bitch on the phone said something about you and Elise going through with it. What did she mean? Who the *frig* is she?"

"Shannon, for fuck's sake, just stop!" Aiden grimaced. Even his lips were quivering again. "How—?" He cleared his throat. "Why didn't I figure out you're Elise's friend?" He kissed his teeth. "Shan, stop looking at me like that."

He had to break the eye contact. So easy to be sucked in by Aiden's dangerous eyes. Had to fight it, especially since Elise was the lucky bitch.

She wasn't lucky, and she certainly wasn't a bitch.

"Shan." Aiden grabbed his thigh, started massaging it.

He pushed Aiden's hand away. "You must be not righted."

Aiden looked down at the table, like a child being told off by his parent.

"Hold on . . ."

"What?"

"You said you wouldn't be with her much longer."

Aiden took a moment to remember, staring through Shannon, then something clicked, made him lock eyes again before hanging his head, jaw clenched.

"What did you mean, Aiden?"

Aiden put his elbow on the table and massaged his forehead.

"Just tell me Elise won't get hurt."

Aiden was shaking his head.

"Say something!" He was so animated that his hand gesture ended up being a backhand to Aiden's rock solid arm, making Aiden flinch.

The leg contact on the bus had been intentional after all.

"Shan, just trust me."

"Trust you?"

"We'll be over soon. She's not even that into in me."

"Doesn't seem that way to me. At least not now."

Aiden waved him off.

"Before today, before Mabley Green . . ."

"What?"

"If I didn't know Elise was seeing someone, I would've thought she was single, but now . . . the way she looks at you . . . she's different. She's . . . into you."

Aiden gave another dismissive wave.

"Something changed. Something happened—recently."

"Maybe she's always wanted me, and you just never noticed."

"No, she's changed. She's . . . glowing."

Aiden rubbed his hands together, grimacing. "Well, I *was* there for her after the passport shit. That must've changed things." His last sentence was distant.

Another waiter appeared, took their drink orders.

Aiden thumbed through the food menu when the waiter left, his turn to avoid eye contact.

"Who is she, the caller, the bitch who's doing this to Elise?"

Aiden sighed his irritation. "You know too much . . . ain't supposed to know shit."

"Aiden, just tell me. Who is she to you and Elise?"

Aiden was motionless, except for his clenched jaw then puckered lips.

Even now, it was impossible to ignore Aiden's rugged sexiness. That dream . . . He looked away as tingles set in.

"I can't," Aiden finally said.

"Maybe I can help you."

"You can't, Shan. I have to do what she wants. Can't lose my family." He was pleading with his golden-brown eyes.

"Who would do this to Elise, knowing you're gay?"

Aiden shifted with enough force and speed that condiments shakers rattled and cutlery slid off napkins.

He looked around the restaurant, then leaned into Shannon. "I *ain't* gay."

"Kn-knowing that you like men?"

Aiden looked around again.

Then pain gripped Shannon's thigh.

"Keep. Your. Voice. Down."

"Let . . . go."

Aiden finally showed mercy; he let go.

"Fuck's sake, Shannon! You think I like this shit?"

"I have to tell her."

"What?" Aiden's satanic countenance returned, like he would've killed Shannon if they were alone.

"I don't know everything, but I'm gonna tell her what I know. Maybe then—"

Aiden squeezed his thigh again, forcing him to double over as far as the table allowed. "No, you won't, Shannon."

Aiden finally loosened his grip but kept his hand on Shannon's thigh. "Don't worry 'bout Elise."

He moved his hand up Shannon's shaking thigh then continued until it pressed against his dick. Aiden's touch had no mercy, creating tremors and tingles, and causing swelling and hardness.

Then someone yelled out, made him snap out of it. He forced Aiden's hand off as waiters, one of them carrying a cake with a sparkler candle in its centre, marched to a nearby table, about to sing "Happy Birthday", TGI Fridays-style.

"Don't worry?" he hissed. "You're *fucking* her life up."

Aiden banged his fist on the table, making cutlery bounce. "Fuck it, Shannon!"

Good thing the "Happy Birthday" song was playing.

"She likes you; you don't like her—"

"I do."

"Not the way *straight* guys like their girlfriends."

Aiden looked away.

"This needs to stop before she . . . sleeps with you."

Aiden grimaced.

"What is it?"

Aiden massaged his forehead.

"Aiden?"

Nothing from Aiden except a shake of the head, still grimacing, making no eye contact.

Then it came like a punch in the gut. "You haven't . . . you couldn't have . . . she wouldn't . . ."

Aiden finally made eye contact. His eyes were wide, glistening, as if pleading to be forgiven for cheating and getting his side piece pregnant.

Shannon's throat tightened and his pounding heartbeat exacerbated his heartache. He clenched his eyes shut.

"Shan, I'm sorry." There was a tremble in Aiden's voice.

Things had gone too far, couldn't get worse. Elise had mentioned that she was saving herself for marriage—even if it meant waiting until she reached forty. What she felt for Aiden was strong. She'd fallen, had been deceived into breaking her promise to herself. And Aiden wasn't frigging straight. She would find out eventually and regret it. She didn't deserve that.

The guy he was falling for, the guy who was interested in him, the guy who could've been the one to make up for all his pain, had bedded his friend.

"We're here, guys!"

He jumped. Elise. He nearly turned around, but tickling teardrops stopped him. Good thing Aiden's and his backs were turned to her.

Aiden cleared his throat then turned around.

Shannon blinked rapidly and wiped his eyes before turning to Elise.

"Hi," Tempest said, waving at Aiden then Shannon with the repeated downward movement of her fingers.

She bent down to kiss Shannon first, her half-fringe tickling him and her fruity scent hypnotic, and then Aiden. They held each other's gazes a split second too long, or maybe Shannon was seeing things.

Tempest was all smiles, black lip liner giving her a sultry look, as she strutted to the leather seat like she was on a runway, clutching her D&G handbag for dear life. Shimmering earrings, flawless face, spunk in her walk . . . Tempest would fit right in with those Atlanta housewives. She slid across the seat until she was right opposite Shannon. Elise sat next to her.

"Nice seeing you again, Shannon."

"Likewise."

He looked at Tempest then Elise, then at Tempest again. They looked more alike than he remembered, the both of them rocking pixie cuts. Jackets off. They were both wearing white tops, Tempest's a short-sleeved button down akin to the kind worn by a department store beautician, Elise's an off-white, long-sleeved, off-the-shoulder design.

"Was hoping to see you on Sunday, Shannon," Tempest said, scanning the drinks menu. "Els told you how worried she was?"

Her tone was brisk, familiar too, even though he'd hardly spoken to her before. He told Tempest the same lie he'd told Elise earlier.

"You not showing up . . . the news about the murder . . . had her in a fucked-up state."

Panic gripped both his chest and belly. Of all the things for her to bring up. It was all he could do to keep from looking at Aiden for a reaction. What he was feeling was showing on his face, from the look Tempest was giving him. The same look Aiden was capable of giving, that simultaneous satanic frown and snarl.

Tempest was about to say something else when Elise slid the food menu towards her.

"I know what I want. Checked on the bus ride here."

"That makes two of us," Elise added. "How about you guys?"

Aiden took one last look at the food menu then, showing Elise his choice with a pointed finger, said, "I'm getting this."

So influenced by each other's choices, so involved, as good as married.

"That looks nice. You ready, Shan?"

Elise and Aiden were holding hands, Elise running her thumb over the part of Aiden's thumb that joined his hand. The faded bruises on his knuckles brought back Mabley Green again.

"Earth to Shannon."

He jumped. Tempest was staring at him. Her half-fringe covering more of her right eye than before, she looked sinister, like she had a grave problem with him, a lioness about to devour her prey.

She motioned behind him.

He turned around. The waiter. *SHAWN* was printed on his name tag. Hadn't noticed it before. Shawn smiled, revealing braces. Probably in his late teens, judging by his slender build and boyish face. Was going to be fine in the years to come, giving the likes of Aiden a run for his money. The thought made his stomach flutter.

"Ready to order?"

"Oh . . . sorry. I'm ready."

When Shawn left with their food orders and Tempest's drink order, Elise said, "I never even asked how you two know each other."

"Met at the gym." Aiden was quick to respond as usual.

Frigging convincing liar. What else could he have said though?

Something from Tempest's direction was distracting Shannon. He moved his eyes without moving his head.

She'd been staring at him—only she knew how long for—appraising him, her eyes—or eye—narrowed.

"No offence, but what do you *do* in the gym?" she said.

That frigging voice of hers, its harshness familiar, was getting to him.

"It's just . . . your body . . . you're not . . . hench." Her visible eye became animated. "Which is fine. Not everyone needs to have muscles like this one over here."

Aiden laughed. Sounded fake. There'd hardly been any interaction between Aiden and Tempest since her arrival.

"Shannon just started going." Aiden to the rescue again. He made no eye contact with Tempest, even though he was talking to her.

"Lucky you . . . being surrounded by all those sweaty muscle men."

"Uh . . . I don't pay attention to—"

"Boy, bye. I bet action men are your type."

He waited for a flush to subside before looking at Tempest; then Elise, who looked like a deer in headlights; then Aiden, who was fiddling with his cutlery; then back at Tempest, who was waiting for an answer. One thing was for sure: any similarities between the two sisters ended with their physical features.

"Come on now, Shannon. From the moment I met you, I knew you were gay."

"Uh . . ."

"Obviously, these two"—she motioned at Elise and Aiden— "don't give a fuck. I definitely don't give a shit. Don't see why it's even a big deal."

"Why couldn't Carl make it, Tempest?" Elise's voice was laced with irritation.

Tempest shuffled in her seat. Something made her uncomfortable for a change. "Work. Operating room."

That damn voice.

Shawn brought the drinks over. All of them except Tempest thanked him. Would've thought she hadn't been the last to order her drink.

As if she'd had an epiphany, she said, "Excuse me."

"Yes, miss?" Shawn said.

"Are you single?" She gripped Shannon's forearm. "It's just that my friend here is single and—"

He spat out the lemonade he'd pulled through the straw, putting his hand to his mouth too late. Looked like some sprayed Tempest. Served her right, acting like she was trying to help. Damn bi— No, this was Elise's sister. He didn't know her well enough to call her anything other than *Tempest*.

"She's ramping with you. He ain't single." Aiden to the rescue for the umpteenth time. He looked irritated too.

Shawn forced a smile as he left, shaken, either by Tempest's stunt or Aiden's glare.

"Tempest, what's wrong with you?" Elise said. "Did you have something else to drink before you got here?"

Tempest didn't respond. She just used her napkin to wipe her bare forearms, sneering at Shannon.

"Sorry for spraying you, but you shouldn't have done that."

"Shannon, are you really seeing someone?" Elise said.

"Yes." He would tell Elise the truth—when Tempest wasn't around.

Elise squealed. "Since when?"

"Since the other day."

"Who is—?"

"I'll tell you later!" He grimaced. Didn't mean to sound pissed, not with Elise of all people.

She put her hands up defensively. "Fine . . . later."

He rolled his eyes. "Here, key in your number." He handed her his phone.

She keyed in her number and returned the phone to him.

He was about to put his phone away when Tempest said, "What about my number?"

He could barely look at her, ideas of how to avoid exchanging numbers with her not coming to him.

"You give Els your number and not me?"

Els.

Els?

Els.

Ringing returned, bleeping out chatter, clanging cutlery and whomever was singing.

Aiden's demeanour around Tempest, the face he'd made earlier when Tempest's name came up, their prolonged eye contact, her familiar voice . . . *Els.*

He'd shut his eyes at some point. His name was echoing. Sounded like Elise was calling him. Hands were on him, tight grips on his wrist, forearm, shoulder . . .

Someone was shaking him, made him open his eyes.

"Shan!"

Clanging cutlery, music and overlapping conversations were not so distant anymore. Aiden, Elise, and Tempest all had their hands on him. He tensed until they let go.

"Shan, you OK?"

"I'm . . . I'm alright, Elise."

"You sure?" Tempest said.

Fuck. It really was her. Her biting tone was ever present, even when she was being—or trying to be—nice.

"What happened?" Aiden was frowning.

"Uh . . . nothing. . . . I'm fine . . . really . . . just . . . uh . . . my belly."

Tempest and Elise narrowed their eyes. Aiden drew his top lip into a snarl. Another sexy thing he did. Something that couldn't go unnoticed, even at a time like this.

"Your belly?"

That voice.

"Can't believe none of you heard it. Just craving shrimp."

Elise chuckled. "We didn't hear."

Another glance at Aiden. No snarl. Just narrowed eyes. A glance at Tempest. Her lips were puckered. At least one eye was still narrowed. She was analysing him, fishing for truth. His body language must've been betraying him.

He summoned a smile. "Here, Tempest. Put your number in."

She snatched the phone from him then entered her number.

She thought she called the shots, used to getting her way.

It was down to him to keep the bitch from getting away with whatever she was doing to Elise.

He had to get close to her and find out what the frig was going on.

FRIDAY

20 / Elise V
Suspicion

Time off coming to an end, Elise was only just getting used to the break. Would've given anything to work less hours yet make more money, like Tempest, or even Aiden. Funny how she was missing work anyway. Boiling on the shores of Cancún would've been better than freezing in grey London. The only good thing to come out of the passport chaos was her upcoming catch up with Shannon.

Her pa had called her Little Red Riding Hood, as he sometimes did when taking her to the airport, just to ramp with her. Dressed entirely in blue—navy snug-fitting, thigh-length jacket; skinny ankle-length jeans; white slip-ons with flecks of blue; indigo Kipling handbag—Pa would've probably called her Smurfette, but he wasn't with her, walking where Shan had been mugged.

Maybe Shan should've come to hers.

Someone had died in Mabley Green though, so maybe his place was better. At least she would see exactly how he was doing in his new abode.

That one thing, that kiss with Aiden, had ruined Shan's life, forced him out of one home into another. Seven days since that evening and she still blamed herself.

Entering Richmond Road helped push unpleasant memories aside. A line of new houses painted dark grey and off-white were coming up on the right. Shan was now living in one of them. Nice upgrade from his old house—yet it was here he'd been mugged. She clutched her handbag to her hip, as if the Crown Jewels were inside, looking around for unwanted company nearby as the wind made strands of her upsweep tumble over her forehead. She sped up.

She reached number 19 in one piece. Shan opened the front door as soon as she opened the gate.

"You must've been looking forward to seeing me."

"Yep. Knew you'd get here any moment now since you operate on the *actual* time."

They hugged, Shan's familiar cocoa butter scent swirling around her with the wind.

He took her jacket. "The front room's more like the back room, right at the end. Want a drink?"

"Juice, please."

As the fridge door opened and closed, and glasses clinked, she let the beige leather love seat suck her in. She placed her handbag on the shaggy rug then scanned the room. The interior reflected the newness of the exterior. So different from Shan's old house. Plants that looked like miniature palm trees were by the window, and countless photos of the same two men—backdrops ranging from beach settings to landmarks like the Great Sphinx of Giza, Golden Gate Bridge, and Victoria Falls—filling the corner cabinet by the window and scattered along the white walls. The only dark colours were black, the colour of the flatscreen LG TV mounted on the wall, and mahogany brown, the colour of the wooden African art pieces flanking a Jamaica-shaped clock above the TV. Everything else was mostly beige.

Another picture, on the coffee table, got her attention. The same two men. The one with the dreadlocks had to be Shan's uncle; he really favoured Shan's dad. Two short stacks of coasters were either side of the picture, another set of coasters stacked behind. Coasters from Las Vegas, Punta Cana, and Fort Lauderdale topped the piles. *The Book of Night Women* by Marlon James was behind the picture. Magazines were overlapping on the shelf underneath the table; Kelly Rowland on the cover of *Pride*, Queen Latifah gracing *Essence*, and Michael Strahan on the cover of *Ebony* were outdone by a cover shot of a group of black men dressed in black for a magazine called *Clik*. Hadn't heard of *Clik* before. None of the men looked familiar. She didn't know all the black magazines after all. Maybe this one wasn't black; maybe it just happened to have black men on the cover. Just as she was about to pick it up, Shan walked in with two glasses of juice. He handed her one, and she put the *Punta Cana* coaster directly on the coffee table then rested her glass of what looked like pineapple juice on it.

"Straight to the magazines," he said as he got comfortable next to her.

She took a sip then said, "Yeah. Who are these men? They're kind of *alright*."

"They're from *Noah's Arc*. I mentioned that show to you a while ago, remember?"

"Rings a bell."

"Have a look through it."

"Later, but I want to know how you're *really* doing."

He gulped down some of his juice. "I've been better. Been worse too. I started writing down my thoughts and feelings."

"Like a journal?"

"Something like that."

"That might actually help you, Shan."

"Doesn't really feel like it's helping—nothing's changed—but I've been doing it."

"I know the situation hasn't changed, but hopefully when you look back at what you've written months from now, you'll see some progress."

"I guess. It was Peter's idea. Don't know what I would've done without him and Uncle Lionel. Still doesn't seem real."

"You haven't spoken to your parents since . . . ?"

"Since I went to get the rest of my things? No."

"I don't even have the words to this day."

"I knew it would come out, but I wasn't prepared for it. And the way things went down . . . I knew they'd be livid, but the frying pan, the hammer, falling out the window . . ." He hung his head.

She rubbed his knee. "Shan, you don't know how bad I feel."

He took a deep breath. "I couldn't keep it from them forever. All secrets rise to the surface."

All secrets. She shuddered.

"I think they always knew though."

"Really?"

"Yeah. They were just in denial, probably thought I would've grown out of my girly ways—not that all gay men are girly."

"I know what you mean. I learned long ago not to generalize."

Shan nodded.

"I get that the confirmation would've shocked them, but for them to do what they did . . . pack your things, chuck you out . . ."

"Yep. They dashed me away. It's as if that one thing about me negates the straight *A*s; being the only one in the family to graduate from university, getting a first; the birthday, Christmas and anniversary gifts; the times I cooked . . . Never been arrested; never fallen out of clubs like an asshole; never taken drugs . . . Just a good son in every way . . . except . . ."

"And then for you to be robbed and . . ."

Shan was shaking, grimacing, fighting tears.

"Enough of the bad stuff. Tell me about bae."

Shan frowned.

"Remember? Yesterday? TGI's? Tempest tried to set you up with that waiter, and Aiden said you had a man."

Shan rolled his eyes. "There's no man. Aiden was just trying to rescue me."

She chuckled.

"Just make sure you don't tell Tempest."

"I won't."

"Good."

She sipped some more pineapple juice then said, "Didn't know you were going to the gym."

That confused expression again, before self-consciousness made him relax his face.

"I'm not serious about the gym, as you can see." He motioned at his body.

He actually looked better than he thought. Compared to Aiden . . . Nobody's body could be compared to that of a fitness professional, but Shannon looked healthy, slim everywhere, except for his butt perhaps.

"But Aiden was there when I started going. He was nice to me."

No eye contact at that last part.

"How long have you and Aiden been together?"

"Over three months."

"You never really talked about him before."

She took a few more sips then said, "I know. At first, I wasn't really sure *what* we were to each other." She had to avert her gaze. "But now I can definitely say we're . . . together."

Shan shifted on the sofa, glass to his lips. "What do you mean?"

"Don't laugh, but at first I thought he was seeing someone else, or that . . ."

He raised his eyebrows.

She tightened her face.

Shan took another sip, not taking his eyes off her.

"I thought he might be into men."

He started choking, rushed to put his glass down.

"You OK, Shan?"

"Yeah." He coughed hard, thumping his chest. "Why'd you . . . think that?"

"Didn't feel like he wanted me."

"But you're sure he's into you now?"

"Yes." Of all the things for him to say—*into*. She started tingling as if Aiden had entered her, heat rising.

"How?" There was almost an edge to his voice.

"Well . . ." She grimaced, tingling, moistening—the last thing she needed in front of someone else, even Shan. She took short breaths as she became light-headed. "Jesus."

"What's wrong?"

She trapped her wrist between her thighs and rocked, barely looking at Shan. "Can't believe I'm about to say this."

"What?"

"We've been . . . intimate." She cringed, anticipating Shan's reaction.

Not much of a reaction from him. He just kept drinking.

"Did you hear me?"

His glass was nearly empty. "I heard. I'm . . ."

"What?"

"Not surprised."

"Really?"

"Yeah. Yesterday, you seemed . . . different."

"I did?"

"Uh . . . yeah."

"How?"

"You were . . . glowing. . . . Thought it could've been . . . to do with sex."

"I better watch it. If my parents knew I was fornicating—"

"You're nearly twenty-five. Not many people are virgins at that age."

That was the last thing they needed to talk about.

"It surprised me."

"I bet it did."

"You think I'm fast, don't you?"

"No."

"It's only been a few months. My parents wouldn't look at me the same."

"You might be their child, but you're not *a* child."

"I know, but I remember the look Pa gave me the other day when he saw my vibrator."

His eyes lit up. "Vibrator?"

"I've never used it though. Tempest got it for me."

He snarled, stopped snarling quickly, as if what he was thinking wasn't meant to show on his face.

"Sorry for what she did yesterday."

"It's whatever . . . Back to you and Aiden."

She sighed. "I never expected things to go that far with us, but Monday was awful. Didn't know what to do with myself. I needed someone to be there for me. Tempest was at work that day, I contacted you—or so I thought—and Pa was already upset with me for making him get up so early, and I knew Ma wouldn't let me hear the end of it. I was vulnerable. I never understood how people could blame having sex on vulnerability—until then. I was so low. I needed . . . something . . . saw Aiden in a new light, for whatever reason."

"You said you've *been* sleeping with him. You've done it more than once."

She couldn't answer; all she could do was get up and go to the window. Garden view.

"And you're sure he's not into guys?"

She turned to face Shan. "Well, the way he puts it down, there's no way he is." Tingling in that spot again. She needed to move, returned to the love seat.

"You don't think it's possible for a gay man to have sex with a female?"

"Well . . . I guess, but . . . What are you trying to say?"

He raised his hands as if to tell her to relax. "Just making sure that you don't get hurt."

"No need to worry about that." She rubbed his knee. "Besides, you're friends with him, so you can keep an eye on him."

Shan smiled awkwardly then said, "Using protection?"

"Of course!"

Shan took a deep breath then said, "Good. You can never be too careful."

A blessing they'd used the condoms Tempest had given her the last couple of times. The more they sexed using protection, the more that one time without would be insignificant.

"I just wish . . ."

"What?"

"That . . . Never mind."

"Come on. Say it."

She opened her mouth, closed it, opened it, closed it.

"Tell me."

"OK. But no one else knows this."

"Alrighty."

She grimaced. "Tempest wasn't careful."

"What do you mean?"

"She . . . started out young."

He frowned.

"Having sex."

"Oh! . . . And?"

She shook her head. It wasn't her place to chat Tempest's business, but she'd already started. "I'm serious, Shan, this stays between us."

"Sure."

"She ended up . . . pregnant."

"What?" His eyes bulged out.

A stronger reaction than when she'd revealed she'd been sleeping with Aiden.

"She was fourteen."

"She has a child?"

"No."

"No?"

"She . . . miscarried."

He grimaced and shook his head.

"She had a rough upbringing . . . more than anyone knows." Things were coming back to her, things including Sylvia.

"At least she has you."

"I'm lucky to have her."

"Are things getting better between her and your mum?"

"No. Maybe she wouldn't have gotten pregnant so young if things had been different. That was the worst time for her. Ma shamed her, and Pa was heartbroken. As bad as it sounds, it was probably a good thing she lost the baby. I thought that was a lifeline, but she kept on hanging around boys a lot. Ended up staying with her aunt because things worsened between her and Ma."

"I don't know what to say."

"I feel so guilty when I think about it."

"Why?"

"Because . . ." No, she definitely couldn't tell him why. She'd said more than enough already.

"Because?"

"Nothing."

"Come on—"

"No!" She grimaced.

Shan didn't know how to respond, wasn't used to that sharp tone from her.

"Sorry."

"I sort of snapped at you yesterday . . . guess we're even."

"I forgot about that."

Silence for a few moments.

"I know she was out of order yesterday, but she's really a good person."

Shan cut his eyes, caught himself too late.

"She's just had a hard life. She was a child caught up in big people's problems."

"Once you told me she's only two months older than you, I guessed your dad . . ."

". . . played around. Not only has he suffered for that, but so has Ma, and so has Tempest."

"Losing her mum so young, not having the best relationship with her stepmum, being separated from her dad and you, being the black sheep . . . some people would let that hurt consume them, harbour resent—"

"Not Tempest."

He shaped his lips to form more words, but he kept quiet.

"What is it?"

"There's something . . ." He was blinking rapidly, hardly able to maintain eye contact. ". . . something you should—" He jumped.

So did she.

Buzzing.

He took out his phone, looked at the screen, then glanced at her.

"Take it. I don't mind."

Looked like he was going to ignore it, but he rolled his eyes and slid his finger across the screen.

"Hi. . . . I'm alright. . . . Just have a *friend* over. . . . Hold on." He took the phone away from his ear then said he'd be right back.

She nodded. Shannon left the room, his cocoa butter scent lingering. A door—maybe the kitchen door—closed.

Straining to hear him was pointless. The men on the cover of *Clik* had been staring at her long enough. She flicked through the magazine, drink in hand. Most of the *Noah's Arc* cast members looked straight. Didn't really matter. She had Aiden.

Aiden.

She put the magazine aside, finished her juice and picked up her handbag from the shaggy rug. She took out her phone and checked the time. Perhaps Aiden was on his lunch break. She called him. Engaged. She took out her compact, checked her hair and put on more lip gloss. She tried Aiden again, just as a door opened in the far reaches of the house and footsteps approached. The phone was ringing now.

Shan came back in, just as Aiden answered.

"Hi," she said.

"What's good?" Aiden said through a deep breath.

"Just giving you a quick ring. Hold on." She took the phone away from her ear and mouthed *Aiden* to Shan.

His eyes widened then relaxed quickly, but not quick enough.

She put the phone back to her ear. "I'm at Shan's. Wanna talk to him?"

Aiden hesitated then said, "Why not?"

She passed the phone over.

Shan exhaled some tension then spoke. "Hi, Aiden." His smile was awkward, and he was blinking quickly. "Not bad thanks." He shook his head, glanced at her then continued. "Haven't decided yet. . . . Let me give the phone back. Trying to sort out some food. . . . Speak soon." He gave the phone back to her and almost stormed out of the room.

He hadn't waited for Aiden to say bye.

She brought the phone to her ear, TGI's coming back to her. "I'll let you get back, Aiden. Will I see you later?"

"Don't know yet. Might be working till late today."

"Oh . . . OK. Let me know."

"Will do."

"Bye."

As soon as she hung up, Shan returned with three different pizza packages.

"Which one, Goodfella's pepperoni . . ." He put the top box underneath the bottom one. ". . . Domino's ham and pineapple . . ." He rearranged the boxes again. ". . . or Chicago Town meat feast? They're all thin-crusted."

She considered the options then said, "You choose."

"Fine. I'll put in the Goodfella's." He rushed back to the kitchen.

When he returned, he said the pizza would be ready in twenty minutes, barely making eye contact again.

She sighed then clamped her eyes shut.

Her eyes were closed, but the memories were clear to see: Shan's reaction when he found out she was seeing Aiden, his discomfort seeing them hold hands at the table, his questioning Aiden's sexuality, his awkwardness when he spoke to Aiden moments ago on her phone . . .

She opened her eyes, clutched her chest, started rocking. "Shannon?"

"Yeah?"

"Is . . . ?" Deep breath through pursed lips. "Is something going on . . . between you and Aiden?"

His eyes widened. "W-what?"

"You . . . and Aiden."

"I . . . I don't . . . understand."

"Do I really have to spell it out?"

He nodded, not good at feigning confusion.

"Are you"—she tightened her face—"lovers?"

It was as if he didn't know whether to scream or gasp, pass out or pace the room.

"I could tell you didn't want to talk to him just now. You looked awkward. . . . You're awkward now."

Shannon picked up *Clik*, hands shaking, and turned the pages forwards then backwards. Something to keep his eyes off her.

"Shannon!"

"I'll pretend you never asked me that."

That wasn't convincing. She grabbed his wrist. "If something's going on, I need to know."

He screwed up his face. "Nothing's going on."

"God. . . . You're lying!"

"I'm not!" He pulled.

She tightened her grip.

It made sense now. She'd been an idiot. And she'd slept with Aiden! No, no, no. Aiden couldn't be . . . No. But what if . . . ?

"What's . . . wrong . . . with you?" He yanked and yanked. "Let . . . go!"

"You . . . the gym . . ."

He kissed his teeth.

"You said— No. *Aiden* said you'd met at the gym."

He pulled harder.

Her one-handed grip was weakening. She started using both hands, pulled him closer. "You've never . . . been interested . . . in . . . the gym . . . before. . . .What's . . . freaking . . . changed?"

He gritted his teeth as he used his fingers to pry her hands off him. "Have you . . . forgotten . . . what . . . happened . . . to me . . . on Sunday?"

"What's that . . . got to . . . do with—?"

He snatched himself out of her clutches, nearly making her fall off the love seat.

He got up. "Frigging hell, Elise! I'm trying to get stronger so that no one can fuck with me. Twice, I've been robbed. Twice! Happy now?" His chest was heaving, face crumpled and body shaking.

She'd jumped the gun.

He grimaced, shook his head.

"You were robbed before?"

"Yeah."

"Sorry."

"Happened ages ago." He rolled his eyes, took a deep breath. "Look . . ."

"What?"

"About me and Aiden."

She clutched her chest. "Yes?"

He rubbed the back of his neck and let out a strained breath. His grimace returned. "I might've had a . . . *thing* for him."

That was what she'd picked up on, something one-sided.

"But I don't anymore," he said, shaking his head. "It's just that . . . the two of you seeing each other . . ."

"Here I am, telling you that we're sleeping together, accusing you of . . . I feel bad now. I'm with someone you have feelings for."

"No, I don't *now*."

He was willing to sacrifice his own happiness, swallow his pride, for others, for her. It was an innocent crush; he could never have Aiden. No different from his crushes on Laz Alonso, Asafa Powell and Luke James.

It was obvious Shan still had a thing for Aiden, yet she still said, "Are you sure?"

"I'm sure."

"And he knows. Makes so much sense now."

He squinted.

"He seemed reluctant to speak to you."

"Really? Maybe he was busy or something."

"Humph. Maybe."

"Let's see what's on the TV."

He was the one to change the subject to get rid of the awkwardness. Anything would do if it meant making the things said in the last few minutes go away.

"Shan, put in *Noah's Arc.*"

"Alrighty." His eyes lit up, a genuine, excited smile spread across his face, unlike the smile he'd had when he was talking to Aiden. He got up and took out three different *Noah's Arc* DVD cases. "You wanna see the movie, season one, or season two?"

"Um . . ."

"Season one came out first, and the movie came out after season two."

"Might as well watch season one."

"Season one it is. We'll watch the pilot episode first, then the actual season."

"Great."

He gave her the case. She studied the images of the black gay couples: the one with the cornrows holding a thick-haired, pretty man from behind; the light-skinned, bald-headed character, who looked like Peter, lifting a darker bald-headed man, like a groom lifting his bride . . .

She peeked at Shan, gave him a smile.

He deserved his own Aiden.

SATURDAY

21 / *Aiden V*
Two visits

Hardly a sound in City of London Cemetery and Crematorium, besides cawing birds and footsteps crunching leaves, the wind wreaking havoc like it didn't give a shit. Aiden tugged at his jacket against the ruthless wind. Ethan had to keep putting Grandma's scarf back in place when the wind exposed her thinning, grey hair. The mud was wet from the rain earlier in the morning. No blue sky in sight. Aiden was wearing Nikes, plastic Sainsbury's bags tied around them. The only one not wearing wellies.

Three months since they'd last been to see Arthur. The birthday card Ethan had jabbed into a gap between a flower holder and the black granite headstone was still there. Rain, mud and bird shit had fucked it up. It favoured a bird's-eye view of mountains. It was the same card though; the *Happy Birthday* badge was undamaged.

"What's up, Dad?" Ethan said, putting the card in an empty bag.

The grandfolks hollered at Arthur next, like they were waiting for his response.

Aiden didn't have shit to say as he drew closer to the grave. He handed a bunch of roses to his granddad, and his grandma started singing some hymn. Granddad joined in with his aged baritone.

Would've kept his ass home if he could've. There was only so long he could stand there, not doing shit, before one of them complained, so he trudged closer to do something, or at least look like he was doing something.

It was taking forever to clear out the muck. He glanced at Ethan. Ethan had stopped at some point, had started running his fingers over the headstone, in a trance. He traced his fingers over Arthur's picture, then his name and life span underneath. His eyes were shiny. He was about to break down again. It wouldn't be right for Aiden to act like he understood what Ethan was feeling. It was fucked-up that he was even there, for him, and for the dead prick. Arthur was probably turning over and over, hell-bent on rising from the grave to pick up where he'd left off all those years ago.

Something grabbed him. He spun around.

"Your ears hard. Move, nuh man!"

He stepped out of the gap between Arthur and his Trini neighbour so that his granddad could get to the headstone where Ethan was.

Granddad grabbed Ethan out of his trance too, then emptied brown, slug-infested water from two flower pots and replaced them with fresh water, as he'd already done with two other pots that were back in their places at the foot of the memorial. Ethan got back to work, using stray branches to rake out dead leaves that were hiding the off-white chippings in the middle.

Grandma stopped humming. She was struggling with plastic the chrysanthemums were wrapped in. Aiden helped her then unwrapped the bunch of carnations.

"It look more lean, nuh true?"

He stepped back. She had a point. Arthur must've been falling for his Guyanese next door neighbour, Abigail Anderson.

"Dunno, Grandma." Anything to keep her from fretting.

Abigail, Arthur, Luke.

Guyana, Jamaica, Trinidad and Tobago—his mum's countries.

Not coming to the cemetery for months always made him forget the nationalities of Arthur's neighbours. Couldn't tell if the others ever remembered where his mum was from.

Ethan's breathing was strained, hand over his face, Granddad comforting him. Made no sense.

Or maybe it wasn't just about Arthur. Maybe it was everything—being bullied by bad breed kids at school for having no parents; Aiden fucking up the bad breeds so bad that he was expelled, his grandfolks struggling to find a new school for him; little bro without big bro to protect him, something those pricks made the most of till Ethan finally gave them what they'd been asking for, doing enough to be excluded but not enough to be expelled; their grandfolks raising boys that were a handful at times, being robbed of years they should've spent enjoying retirement.

Tears were catching; he was squinting to keep his tears back. That night.

The memory was too stubborn to piss off, throat tightness relentless. He swallowed then clenched his eyes shut as he held in sobs through gritted teeth. Tears were pushing through his clamped eyes. He wasn't going to make noise. Had to keep sniffing against the cold dampness.

Arthur's life over because of that night. Same for his mum's life.

Another strong gust of wind came, scattering his memories.

He let the wind dry his cheeks.

Someone grabbed his arm, turned him around—and his face wasn't fucking dry.

Grandma.

She took out tissue, wiped his cheeks, said, "All these years, me did think you hate yuh father." She pulled his head down to hers, turned it and kissed his cheek. "Come, son, make we put in the rest of the flowers them."

He couldn't tell her he wasn't crying for Arthur.

The grave's four corners were quickly blooming in reds, whites and yellows, amidst black granite and off-white stones. His family inspected the sight, searching for anything that didn't look right. A pointless last check. A delay for nothing. He was the first to walk away from Arthur's resting place.

Someone grabbed his arm, stopped his eager strides back to the car. One moment his grandma was lagging behind with the others, the next she was right behind him.

She glanced back at Ethan and Granddad, then she looked up to him. "Me need the toilet. Walk with me." Deep voice throughout.

"We can drive there."

"No. Make them gwaan."

He took out his car keys, gave Ethan a heads-up, then threw them at him. "You sure, Grandma? The chapel ain't close."

"Could do with likkle exercise. Clyde leg them worse than mine."

They both watched as Ethan became Granddad's walking stick, the actual walking stick still in the car.

"Besides," Grandma continued, "me want chat with you."

He frowned down at her as she leaned and tilted her head, pissing him off with that cantankerous look of hers.

She finally stopped staring, then she glanced back again. "We soon come!"

She interlocked her arm with his as the car doors shut. The chapel was looming ahead, older and more elaborate resting places in the section they were approaching.

"Me curious 'bout your *friend.* What was her name . . . Temptress?"

Hard to tell if she made her voice go from Nina Simone to La Toya Jackson on purpose that time.

He let out a breathy laugh, his smoke snuffed out faster by the wind. "*Tempest*, Grandma."

"I beg your pardon."

Didn't want to look at her too tough while she was digging for information. "Why you curious?"

"Me old, but me still have sense."

He let cawing birds, swaying trees, and the rustling Sainsbury's bags around his Nikes fill the silence. He stopped then took the bags off. The muddy section was way behind them.

Grandma squeezed his arm with her tiny hands. She kept squeezing until he looked at her. She had a determined grimace.

"Trying to pop my biceps, Grandma?"

"Something not right 'bout that gyal."

"What you on about?"

"Spirit nuh take her. Me know you did well want her gone the other evening. Is what the two of unu have?"

He brushed her jacket like there was something on it, buying some time to come up with a response.

"Me going tell you again—me old, but not fool."

"She's my girl's sister."

"So me notice. How come me nuh know nothing 'bout this ladyfriend?"

The car rumbled up to them.

"Grandma, you sure you don't want to get in?" Ethan said.

"Ee-hi. Go to the front and wait fi we." Grandma sounded as irritated as she looked. She didn't like repeating herself.

When the car was way ahead, she said, "So, the ladyfriend . . . ?"

"It's . . . new."

"Humph."

"What was that for?"

"Jus' ah consider how me see the ladyfriend sister, in *my* house, and not the ladyfriend. She have a name?"

He hesitated. "Elise."

"Pretty name. When we going meet her?"

He shrugged his shoulders.

"Something not right with her either?"

"Nothing's wrong with her."

"Well, Elise is better than Eddie."

He stopped walking, heart accelerating. "Grandma?"

"God is clearing the clouds," she said, like that was the first thing she'd said since they'd started walking.

She hadn't stopped walking. He took a giant stride to keep from being dragged by her.

"Anyway, back to Tempestuous," she said.

He snickered again. "You're doing it on purpose."

"Not keen on her at all, coming over uninvited, flaunting her dutty self inna *my* yard, giving me dutty looks. Facety wretch. Me ah tell you, she's the devil."

If only she knew.

"Me nuh know what you and that wretch have," his grandma said when they were footsteps from the chapel, "but me going find out, whether you tell me or not."

He opened the chapel door for her, avoiding eye contact. She was staring at him, but he knew better than to stare back. Her neck would eventually ache, well over a foot in height between them.

"Shoulda leave this in the car."

She one-upped him, tricked him into looking at her properly.

She smiled mischievously as she gave him her handbag, then she hummed her way into the toilet. The toilet door squeaked open then slammed shut.

The silence that followed left him trapped in his thoughts. The image of his grandma having a heart attack as she discovered everything was the scariest.

Almost three-thirty. Pushed for time. Wrong choice again. Public transport would've been less hassle. Looser parking restrictions on weekends than on weekdays meant less available spaces. He emerged left back onto Camden Road for the hundredth bloodclaat time. There was that orange building standing out again. He approached it, reached it and passed it. A piss-take that he couldn't park in the grounds. He gritted his teeth as he checked the time on the dashboard. 15:14. Should've found parking long time. Needed more time to prepare. He signalled left onto Chambers Road at the last moment, almost braking like he was doing an emergency stop. Pissed-off beeps from behind. He was just about to beep his horn a *fuck you back* when a car pulled out ahead. He pushed harder on the accelerator before the driver could change her mind and pull back in.

15:21 on the infotainment system. He needed, wanted, to holler at Shannon. Didn't matter if Shan was still vex. The time on his phone read 15:15. He took out his other phone, the Tempest phone, ignored the new activity alerts. The phones agreed on the time. No reason for both phones to show the wrong time.

He stopped someone who was passing, asked for the time. Three phones in agreement. He chucked the Tempest phone on the front passenger seat then adjusted the time on his dashboard.

He was about to call Shan when a beep came from the Tempest phone. He snatched it up.

A text had come through.

So glad ur coming thru 4 me with Els. Maybe I should give you a try again . . . not!

He squeezed the steering wheel, his knuckles not as painful as before and the bruises clearing up. That time he'd choked her, he shouldn't have let go.

If they ever fought again . . .

Drum beats made him cuss before Prince started singing that breakfast could wait. New ringtone. Not so new song. Shannon was calling.

"Yo."

"Just returning your call." Either Shan was irritated or one of them had a shit signal.

"Which one? I called you earlier. Called you a few times yesterday. What the fuck?"

"I can hang up."

"Don't!"

"Why were you calling me, Aiden?"

"Wanted to hear your voice."

"That's it?"

He half-kissed his teeth. "Didn't know you and Elise were gonna see each other. Hope things weren't awkward."

"Well, they were. She could tell."

"Tell what?"

"I couldn't lie to her."

Heartbeat up. Jaw clenched. Tighter phone grip. "Couldn't lie 'bout *what*?"

"I told her that I . . . had a thing for you."

"And?"

"Nothing about you."

He sighed.

"Aiden, you still there?"

"Yeah. Sorry." He rubbed his face in one fell swoop. "So, you told her you're feeling me?" He couldn't help grinning as his heart relaxed.

"No, I told her I *was* feeling you. What else was I supposed to say, that you're not really straight?"

"Stop saying that shit."

"Cut the crap, Aiden! The sooner—"

"Shannon!"

Shannon was breathing heavily. "I can't believe you're still sleeping with her."

"She told you that?"

"We're close like that. We tell each other everything. . . . Well, she tells *me* everything."

He massaged his forehead. "Look, I'll fix this—"

"I know you will. And soon."

"The fuck you mean?"

"I can't keep lying to her."

"Don't ramp with me."

"Not ramping."

"You think I'm gonna hurt her?"

"You already are. This needs to stop."

"Ain't that simple."

"Why not? Why did Tempest set the two of you up, knowing what she knows about you?"

"Tempest?"

"I know it was her who called when I had your phone."

He cussed through gritted teeth.

"That thing with me . . . at TGI's . . . being hungry . . . I was pretending. I recognized her voice, realised she was the facety bitch on the phone."

"I knew you were bullshitting."

"Why is she doing this?"

"Only she knows."

"You've never asked her?"

"Course I have. Won't tell me shit."

"How did this even start?"

"I'll tell you when we see each other."

"Tell me now. Tell me something."

He kissed his teeth, then said, "I met Tempest at the gym. Unlike other chicks, she wasn't after my dick, had respect for the ring on my finger. We hit it off real quick. Thought we were cool, so I told her the ring was just for show." He looked through the car parked in front until it became a blur. . . . "I opened up to that bitch."

"How?"

"I trusted her . . . felt comfortable telling her shit no one else knew 'bout me."

"Like what?"

He looked around. No one in the car but him. No one nearby.

He lowered his voice anyway. "That I'm *down* and that my fam ain't with that."

"And she's having you mess around with Elise?"

"She's blackmailing me. If I don't do what she wants me to do with Elise, she'll tell my fam. And that can't happen, Shan. They're all I have. My brother can't stand two men . . . and it'll kill my grandfolks."

"Wouldn't it be her word against yours?"

"Bitch recorded me telling her everything."

"Shit."

That one word was all Shan could come up with, a reminder that there was no way around the situation.

"How far does she want things to go?"

"Dunno. Thought all I had to do was take Elise's virginity then dump her. Now she wants us to keep smashing."

"That bitch."

"She hates Elise."

"But why?"

"I don't know, but something she said the other day . . . maybe it's got su'um to do with her mum."

"Tempest's?"

"Yeah."

"But she's dead."

"I know, but she said something like, because of her—Elise—she has no mother."

"She said that?"

"Yeah."

"Elise told me they were kids when Tempest's mum died. Why would Tempest blame her?"

"Been trying to figure that out."

Silence on the other end.

"Shan?"

"I'm here."

"What you thinking?"

"You mentioned your grandparents. What about your parents?"

"They're dead," he said quickly.

"Didn't know. Sorry."

"No worries. I'll tell you 'bout that another time."

"Alrighty."

"Shannon?"

"Yes."

"I'll fix this."

"Whether you fix it or not, I can't sit back and do nothing."

"Meaning?"

"If Tempest really does hate Elise—which she must do if she's doing all this—then Elise is in danger."

"I won't let anything bad happen to her."

"You don't think bad things are already happening to her?"

Out of ideas for a response.

"Look, I feel bad for you, but if you won't do something about Tempest, I will."

"Shannon—"

"I need to know why she wants to hurt Elise."

"You and me both, but let me handle it."

"Let you handle it?" Shannon kissed his teeth.

"Look . . ." No, he couldn't go there, couldn't threaten to go to the police about Mabley Green. Didn't want Shan to be more vex with him. Was never going to do Shan like that anyway. He was no snitch.

"What, Aiden?"

"Just promise you'll call me before you do anything crazy."

Shan sighed.

"Please."

"I don't want to make things harder for you."

"Then don't."

"Where does that leave Elise?"

"Just be patient with me."

"I'm out of patience."

"Please."

Shan sighed some more then said, "Fine."

"Thanks, Shan. Thank you, thank you, tha—"

"But you don't have much time."

Not much time, but it was something, time to figure out how to keep Shan quiet.

"I better let you go."

He took the phone away from his ear and looked at the time. It was 15:27. Nearly time.

He brought the phone back to his ear. "Alright then, Shan. Catch you later. Sorry for this."

"Whatever. Bye, Aiden."

He took a deep breath as the time on his phone changed to 15:28, then the screen went black. He checked for his car keys, licence and visiting order, then got out of the car. He sighed into the cold air.

One last look at Royal Holloway Prison before walking in. Hopefully his mum wasn't still vex with him.

SUNDAY

22 / Tempest V
Someone else to deal with

A pillow was pressed over Tempest's face, her nails digging into it. She was doing the pressing. Couldn't tell the wetness of her pussy from that of Carl's tongue; they had become one. The Simba to her Nala. His tongue was planted inside her; no matter how much she wiggled, he just wouldn't pull out completely. She squeezed his head tighter with her thighs without meaning to, because of his arrhythmic tongue. Ripples were intensifying. It was going to happen again, for the umpteenth time this morning. He knew it too. That was why he started pinching her nipples and feeling up her titties like he was trying to rip them off. He wanted it to be epic.

Then his tongue stopped moving, had become a mere bath plug.

Her eyes were closed, but tears were seeping out. Waves swept through her, had her rolling her stomach and hips, her moans into her pillow warming her face. Head wrap didn't feel right. Felt twisted. Could tell some of her hair was out.

Then he stopped working her. His fingers left her nipples wanting and her titties sore. His tongue wasn't as deep as before, and he was struggling to break free of her thighs. She wasn't going to let him go, not while she was on the brink of coming again. He had to get it out of her, take it in his mouth then share her taste with her like before.

But he was slipping away, extinguishing the fire in her as his breathing and facial hair tickled her. He was too strong. She was too weak, body ravaged by one orgasmic wave after another. Head and neck overcame thighs. His tongue and hands had left ripples inside. All she could do was continue to gyrate her hips and moan into the pillow. She needed to close her legs, tingles torturing her, but maybe he would get back to work any moment. She had to be open and ready for him. When her lion king decided to return again, she wouldn't see it coming. He was going to shock his lioness queen into an almighty climax. Removing the pillow would ruin the surprise, keeping her from coming like she wanted to.

But he'd abandoned her for too long, adrenalin waning, orgasmic waves receding.

She took some pressure off her pillow.

He was talking.

He was talking, but not to her.

Someone was in the fucking room with them.

She closed her legs and hid her nakedness with the pillow.

It was just the two of them, Carl standing nude in front of the wardrobe, his back to her, his massive muscles glistening with sweat. They were the only ones in the room, but he wasn't talking to her. He was on the phone. She hadn't heard it ring.

She gave an *ahem* and shuffled in vain. His bare, glistening batty was still facing her, clenching with every hand gesture. She threw her other pillow at the batty she'd kneaded most of the night. That shocked him, but not enough to get him off the phone. He continued with the hand gestures as he spoke, stressed. If she understood Spanish, she would've known exactly what he was saying. She crept up behind him as he mixed Spanish and English. She grabbed his semi-erect dick. He flinched; the condom fell off.

He elbowed her, right in her titty, made her stumble backwards. He turned to her, covered the phone and mouthed *sorry* as she recovered on the bed. First, he'd fucked up what would've been one of her best orgasms, then he elbowed her.

And now it looked like he was getting ready to leave.

He picked up his jeans and started looking for something. His eyes stopped at his Hugo Boss underwear. He reached for it, speaking Spanish. She got to it before he could, snatched it up then clutched it to her chest. He was frustrated, motioning for her to give him his undies while trying to pay attention to the phone call.

"Who is that, Carl?" She wrapped the duvet around her body.

Panic took over his face, and he covered the phone with his hands and the person—a woman—said something indecipherable.

He ended the call, the yapping on the other end cut off.

She. She. She.

"You better answer me. If I'm sharing you—"

"Tempest, give it to me!"

"Was that her?"

"Tempest, I said give it—"

"No!"

"Temp—"

"You swore you were done with that bitch."

"I am!"

She was shaking. "Fucking liar!"

"That was my fucking sister!"

"Oh . . ." She blinked back tears and took a deep breath. "What was she saying? And why was she speaking Spanish?"

"She's more into her Cuban side than her Jamaican side. She's still getting to know our dad, close to her mum."

"Well, what did she want that was so important for you to abandon me?"

"Can't explain now. I need to help her with something."

"What?"

"Tempest, I need to go. I'll make it up to you."

"You not gonna clean up, have breakfast before you go?"

"No. Need to go now."

"You sure?" She went down on all fours, letting her titties tumble out of the duvet, then used her chin to lift his semi-erect dick to her lips, the residue of his come dominating the air she was breathing. She gripped his foreskin with her teeth, then he somehow snatched the underwear from her.

"Tempest, I have to go."

Before he could bring his grey Hugo Boss trunks up past his knees, she boxed his dick. It spun around at least once before he grabbed it to sooth whatever pain she'd caused. He kissed his teeth.

She freed herself from the duvet, snatched up her nightie and thong from the floor and yanked them on, then she snatched her kimono robe from the door hook. "Get out!"

"Tempest, we fucked all night and all morning. What more do you want?" He straightened his tight jumper on his bulging torso.

"Hurry up and piss off!"

"You act like I'm not there for you."

"Because you're not."

"I am, down to this Elise shit."

"Why would you bring that up?"

He waved her off then started patting himself. He wasn't making eye contact. His brow became furrowed and his jaw clenched.

"What you looking for?"

He found whatever it was in the back pocket of his jeans, and relaxed his face. He bent down and puckered his lips.

She mushed him. "Don't feel like tasting myself now."

He muttered something then unlocked the door.

She stopped him before he could open it. "The condom."

He huffed as he went to pick up the condom.

He opened the door just as Elise was passing. She gasped.

"Morning."

"M-morning." Elise hurried off, to her bedroom.

Tempest walked Carl to the front door, sent him on his way then returned to her bedroom. The things she and Carl had done to each other . . . the funky smells they'd created . . . the tastes they'd left in each other's mouths . . . so sweet at the time. She'd been uninhibited, someone other than herself, as she savoured tasting herself on Carl's tongue and tasting Carl himself, and sucked in the mingling scents of sweat, sex and cologne. Her mood had shifted, as if an age had passed since she'd been turned on. Just left with a sore clit. Fucking prick . . . leaving her hanging.

She came out of her room the moment Elise left hers again. Awkward eye contact. Elise must've heard them through the night, going at it like Simba and Nala, even though the bed had been pulled away from the wall and pillows had muffled their moans. Couldn't have done shit about the bed springs.

"Nice dress." One of the few times she complimented the bitch and meant it.

"Thanks." Elise had the straps of her sea-blue-and-beige shoes dangling from her fingers, the blue matching her mini dress.

"Didn't think you'd ever wear it."

Elise's response was almost dismissive.

"Is everything OK?"

"Yes."

"You've been seeing Aiden a lot lately."

Elise paused for a moment, a moment too long.

She bent down to put her shoes on. "Is that a bad thing?"

Ouch. "No, just observing."

First the too-sexy-for-church dress and heels, then the defensiveness. Aiden was turning the bitch out. To think she was going to have to out him.

265

"Are you going to church together?"

"I invited him. I don't know if he's going, but Shannon is."

"Oh . . . Shannon. . . . That's nice."

"You wanna come too?"

"What time is it?"

Elise looked at her watch. "Ten-ten. Doesn't matter if you get there late. The service might take a few hours."

"You know me. By the time I'm ready, the service will have ended."

Elise took her navy jacket off the coat rack. "Alright then."

"Tell Shannon I said hi."

"Will do." Elise went through the door.

Shannon. Something was off about him.

Maybe Aiden had something to do with it. They were both into men. The vibes she'd picked up from that meal . . . there had to be something going on. They could've been playing footsie or grabbing each other's dicks under the table that day. Aiden taking Elise's virginity, dumping her for her male bestie . . . that would be epic, on top of . . . Too soon to get excited, to tell if the full damage had been done yet, but Elise was sprung. Only weeks ago, it had looked like Aiden and Elise would never fuck.

Shannon though . . . he'd become a factor. He could make revenge that much sweeter or fuck things up. Until she knew the full damage had been done, she needed to watch him. She had his number. Time to utilise it.

J ust gone three, according to the microwave. Maybe Shannon had reached home. She started a text message then deleted it. Texts could be ignored. She needed to hear his voice.

She rang him, keeping an eye on the flat door, the other eye with a view of her half-fringe.

"Hello?" He answered as if he didn't know who was calling.

Either he was playing dumb or he'd deleted her number already.

"Hello?"

This fool . . .

"Hello?"

"Shannon, it's Tempest."

"Hi, Tempest. Uh . . . everything alright?" He'd make a shit actor; his enthusiasm was as fake as what Elise and Aiden had going on.

"Yeah. You with Els?"

"Els?"

"Yes. Els. Elise."

"N-no. She should be on her way home. You trying to reach her?"

"No. Wanted to speak to you."

"Oh."

"Busy?"

"Uh . . . not really."

"Good. I need to see you."

Silence.

He was taking too long to respond, like he'd dropped dead.

"Shannon, you still there?"

"Uh . . . yeah. You told Elise about this?"

She rolled her eyes. It was either that or cuss him off for being slow. "Elise?"

"Yes. Isn't she working most of the coming week?"

"Yeah, but what's Elise got to do with anything?"

"Uh . . . she has a busy schedule, from what she told me, so if we're going to get together, *all* of us would need to be free."

"No, Shannon. Just you and me."

More dead silence for a moment.

"You have a problem seeing me, Shannon?"

Good thing they weren't face to face, though he could've heard her irritation over the phone.

"N-no. Uh . . . how does next weekend sound?"

"Awful. I was thinking maybe today or tomorrow."

"That's a bit short notice. I'm busy all week with uni and work."

"Twenty-four hours a day?"

He was struggling for words.

"Just joking." She feigned laughter. Not wise to scare him off, not before she figured him out.

He laughed back. Still fake.

"Maybe we could meet up tomorrow after work . . . have a coffee or something."

"Uh . . . I finish work at about five-thirty, but I don't usually feel like doing anything after work. You sure it can't wait until next weekend?"

That *uh* of his.

"I'm sure."

He sighed. "Alrighty. I'm surprised you wanna meet with me."

"It's not that I *want* to see you . . . I *have* to see you."

If he gave the silent treatment one more fucking time . . .

"It's serious."

"W-what's going on?"

Telling him why, over the phone, would give him time to prepare a case for his defence, and she wouldn't have full control during their meeting. "I'll tell you when I see you."

"If you insist."

"It won't take long."

"Well . . . if it can't wait . . . I don't see why not."

That was more like it. "So, you finish work at five-thirty tomorrow?"

"Uh . . . yeah."

"Where do you work?"

"Near Oxford Circus."

"Me too. Debenhams. Beauty department. I finish at five. Can we meet up at Oxford Circus Station, say . . . five-forty-five?"

He was lost for words yet again, probably thinking of a way to worm his way out, before he finally agreed.

"Which part of the station is best?"

"Uh . . . I don't know."

That *uh* . . . it was coming to her, then it slipped away. "I tell you what, let's meet by the Nike shop."

"Fine."

"Look forward to seeing you."

"Me . . . too," he said.

Fucking liar. "See you tomorrow then."

"Tomorrow."

"One more thing, Shannon."

"What? I mean, what is it?"

"Don't mention anything to Elise or Aiden."

His words and breathing were clashing in his confusion.

She repeated herself.

"Uh . . . fine," he said.

"Good. See you soon."

I t was tempting to play another passport trick on Elise, but doing the same thing only a week later, Elise would have to be dumber than dumb not to figure it out the second time around.

A knock on the door made Tempest jump, jolted her from her catch up with the Atlanta housewives. Someone had let her daddy in downstairs. She rushed out of the living room, nearly bumping into Elise, luggage in hand. Elise was trembling as she stared at her phone.

"What's wrong, Els?"

Elise didn't answer, just put her luggage by the coat rack.

Tempest rushed to the door when her daddy knocked for the second time. "I'm coming, I'm coming!" She skipped looking through the peephole, smiled as she opened the door, looking forward to being in her daddy's arms.

Her smile contorted into a snarl at Mari-heifer's ugly mug inches away. "Oh. . . . Hi."

"Humph. . . . Hi." Mari-heifer barely looked at her, and she forced herself into the flat, her boulders for shoulders knocking Tempest off balance.

"Hi, Ma." Elise forced a smile.

"Hi, hon." Mari-heifer perked up.

"I thought Pa was coming."

"You don't want to see me?"

"Of course I do."

"Borrowed his car. Mine playing up."

"What's wrong with it?"

"The brakes take long to work. Thought I was imagining things at first, but last night, on the way back from your mad auntie, it was really bad. Nearly most me hit smaddy."

The bitch should've crashed into a tree.

"That sounds bad."

"So, since your father has to get me around, me decide to pick you up for a change. You ready?"

"Almost. Just left something in my room."

"Your passport?"

Elise looked at Mari-heifer with narrowed eyes. "Definitely not that."

Elise went into her bedroom.

"You look nice," Mari-heifer said.

She scanned all over the passage then locked eyes with Mari-heifer.

"Your hair, it's nice. Short like Elise's."

"Oh . . . thanks."

"One thing about you . . . you have style. I'm sure Elise has a peach version of that cardigan you're wearing."

She looked down at her grey maxi cardigan. "She probably does."

The bitch was looking at her as if to see right into her soul, to figure her out, disarming her of her nerve. Mother's intuition.

Her neck prickled. She grabbed it as the nightmare came back to her. She headed to Elise's bedroom.

Mari-heifer was following her. She stopped, let the bitch pass her and go into the living room.

Tempest knocked on Elise's open bedroom door. Elise was looking at her phone then realised she wasn't alone. She stuffed the phone in her pocket like she was Rose hiding Jack's note from her mother in *Titanic*.

"What's going on, Els?"

Elise looked beyond Tempest into the passage, strode past her to the door, peeped out, then motioned her further inside the room.

"Well?"

Elise closed the door. "They stopped."

"What stopped?"

"The calls."

Funny Elise was only just mentioning it.

"And now they've started again."

"The prank calls?"

"Yes. First, the night before we got our hair done, and then last night and today."

"Hold on. Run that by me again."

"That's why I changed my number; I got a call last Friday."

"And you've had calls since then?"

Elise nodded.

Carl was meant to stop.

"The voice was clear this time."

"*What?*"

"And I just changed my number."

She looked around the room at nothing in particular as she tried to make sense of what Elise was saying. It was true. Elise had a different number, so how could . . . Of course. She'd given Carl the new number last night, just in case. He should've said something to her before going ahead.

"Hardly anyone knows my new number."

"What did the bastard say this time?"

"That's the thing. . . . The bastard was a woman."

She squinted at Elise.

"Why is this happening to me?"

"What did *she* say?"

"That she's coming for me."

"Why?"

Elise leaned into her and whispered, "For sleeping with her husband."

A flush tickled through her. "Aiden's married?"

"No!"

"You're getting wood from more than one guy then. You slut!"

"It's not funny!"

She held Elise's shoulders then made their foreheads touch. "Sorry. The dumb bitch obviously has the wrong number."

"She called me by name."

That put her heart out of sync.

"And she knows my address."

She held up her hands for Elise to stop.

"Well, not *this* address, the old one."

"What do you mean?"

"I told her she was mistaken, but she had Ma and Pa's address."

A stronger flush ran through her system, reaching her calves this time, as she tried to remember giving Carl that address.

"Exactly. She said it word for word."

"This woman knows your name and *old* address?"

"Yes."

"What about *this* one?"

"She said nothing about it."

This was good work, but she was going to kill Carl. She went to the door, opened it and peeked out. Nothing but the passage and Mari-heifer telling NeNe Leakes to tell someone about their *muma*. She closed the door then brought Elise closer to the window.

"What is it, Tempest?"

Fucking with Elise's head gave her life. "What if your mum's cheating on Daddy?"

Elise looked at her like she'd gone mad.

"No, I'm reaching. But . . ."

"But what?"

She turned around. "Daddy did cheat on her with *my* mum, so she could be getting even."

Elise narrowed her eyes and put her hands on her hips.

"Alright. She wouldn't do anything like that."

"I *know.*"

"Elise!"

They both jumped. Mari-heifer was right outside the room.

Elise picked up her handbag and rushed to the door. "Coming, Ma!" She opened the door.

"You ready?" Mari-heifer said.

"Yes, Ma."

"And you're sure you have your passport?"

Elise took her passport out of her bag, opened it and showed it to Mari-heifer.

"Good," Mari-heifer said, inspecting it. "Let me hold on to it till the day you fly out."

"No!" Elise put her passport back in her handbag.

"What time's your flight?" Tempest said when they were all close to the flat door.

"Something to twelve."

"OK. If I don't speak to you tomorrow or early Tuesday, safe flight."

"Thanks."

"Thanks again for leaving tonight, giving me and Carl some alone time today and tomorrow."

They hugged. A few more fuck sessions between Aiden and Elise, and hopefully she'd be done hugging the bitch.

She wasn't the only one who hated the hugs. The mother bitch had her back turned to them the whole time.

"Bye," Mari-heifer said.

"Bye." Barely a look at the heifer.

She leaned against the door as soon as she closed it then took her phone out of her cardigan pocket. She didn't know if she was going to cuss Carl off for pulling another prank on Elise without a heads-up, or proclaim her undying love for him for having her back. She pulled up his name anyway then tapped the screen, just as something Elise had said came back to her. She cancelled the call before it started ringing and walked away from the door slowly, to wherever her feet felt like going.

She stopped in the living room doorway then leaned against the door frame, clasping part of it.

The woman Carl had gotten to call Elise knew Daddy's address. Elise was the one who had just moved out of her parents' house.

Tempest had moved from her aunt's. Hadn't lived with her daddy in years.

She put her hand against her head as if that would make her remember why she'd given Carl that address, but nothing was coming. Nothing at all.

There was nothing *to* come.

She'd never given Carl Daddy's address.

MONDAY

23 / Shannon VIII
Muscles & braids

With a never-ending trail of Christmas lights along Oxford Street, Christmas could've been two weeks, rather than two months, away. The shops had gone all out to attract customers. Tourists were going from one window to the next to take pictures or videos for Instagram or Snapchat.

Londoners were rushing to catch buses and trains, drained after a hard day's work. Some were caught up in slow-moving crowds.

Shannon was one of those unfortunate ones, his patience tested, close to cussing, desperate to escape the people jams and beat Tempest to their meeting point. And he was on the phone. Pressing down the tragus of his free ear didn't make it easier to hear Aiden. The chatter all around; impatient drivers beeping and revving away; sudden gusts of wind; trying to keep from being dazzled by the festive lights; doing everything not to bump into anyone, or be bumped into . . . He told Aiden he'd call back.

When the crowd finally pulled him to John Prince's Street, he continued until the evening rush hour buzz on Oxford Street seemed worlds away.

Shuffling. He snapped his head towards the movement, heart rate and breaths speeding up. Someone, beard unkempt, was curled up in a sleeping bag, had been asleep perhaps. The narrow street, buildings either side of it keeping most of the light out, made for a good hiding place. Just enough light to see the ground was wet where the sleeping bag was. Poor drainage, or something had spilled. The man moved some more, shivered, wrapped up in the sleeping bag like it was a straitjacket. Fog was coming out of his mouth. He made eye contact with Shannon. Shannon hurried away from him, past Evening Standard stands, then crossed over and turned right onto Great Castle Street. He stopped in front of a restaurant with outside seating, gathered himself.

Homeless. Approaching the worst of winter, Christmas weeks away . . . the worst time to be in that predicament.

That could've been him if he hadn't managed to get hold of Uncle Lionel.

Or maybe a prison cell.

Thick, endless fog from his mouth dimmed his view of the dazzling Christmas lights on Regent Street ahead.

Prison wasn't out of the question.

Prison at Christmas.

Music in the distance distracted him from unwanted thoughts, bringing him back to why he'd ended up off Oxford Street. The music was coming from Regent Street. Someone was playing a trumpet. Sounded like Janet Jackson's "I Get Lonely", one of his favourite songs of hers. Probably a different song though. Whatever the song, he lost himself in it until the trumpeter played the final notes as slowly as possible. Distant, scant applause, then another beautiful song. Sounded like Soul II Soul's "Keep on Movin'". Maybe the trumpeter did share his musical taste.

He called Aiden.

Aiden answered after half a ring.

"I'm about to meet . . ." He looked around. ". . . you-know-who."

"What the fuck's she up to?"

"Who knows?"

"I know you weren't comfortable at TGI's, but there's no way she knows that you know."

"I really can't see how she would've found out."

"Fuck. What we gonna do?"

"You mean what am *I* gonna do?"

"I'm in this, deeper than you. I've *been* in this."

"I shouldn't even be in this. I should be heading home right now, not to some meeting with this bitch. It's not like I don't have things to do. And it's freezing."

"Just chill."

"I'll try."

"Always be a step ahead of her. Don't make it look like you're hiding su'um."

He wasn't good at pretending.

"Did you hear me?"

"Yes."

"Sit on ready. Don't be fooled by her, like I was. She ain't your friend."

"You're right about that."

"Can't let her get to you."

"She already is."

"This *serious* thing probably ain't that serious."

He sighed. "Maybe."

"Let me know how it goes later."

"Will do. We probably need to talk about Elise's birthday anyway."

Aiden hesitated. "OK . . ."

"You *do* know when her birthday is?"

Aiden breathed heavily into the phone. "November the . . ."

"It's on Sunday."

"Thanks for reminding me."

"You're meant to know that. You're her frigging boyfriend."

"Cut it out, man."
"It's true though."
"I better let you go before I go off on you."
"Let me go? Maybe that's a good idea."
"More like the other way round."
All he could do was breathe fog into the darkness.
"Humph. Call me later."
"Whatever."

1 7:48. He was breathless when he reached Niketown. Black-and-white photos of athletes, including Serena Williams, dwarfed him at the entrance. He was the only one waiting there. People were entering or exiting, none of them Tempest. He'd arrived first. Better him than her. She seemed the impatient type. Nothing to do but watch and wait in the frigging cold, amidst sounds from everyone and everything around him, and the dazzling Christmas lights under the navy, early evening sky. Could count on one hand how many times he'd seen Tempest. Had never seen her with hair so short until that meal. Between her hairstyle—one eye hidden by her half-fringe, as if inspired by Gabrielle—and her resemblance to Elise, he couldn't miss her. He looked around, as people rushed down the stairs into Oxford Circus Station.

He took out his phone. 17:52. A missed call from Tempest. He went further into the entrance of Niketown and called her.

She answered after the second ring.

"Hi, Tempest. Sorry I missed your call." He pressed down the tragus of his free ear.

"I bet."

"Uh . . . come again?"

"Humph."

"Temp—"

"I think . . . Yes, it's you. Can see people walking past you."

He proceeded to step out of the entrance, but a stream of passers-by stopped him. "People are blocking me, so maybe it was me you just saw."

She could see him, but he couldn't see her. A lioness, hiding in her domain, waiting to pounce on her lost prey. So much for being a step ahead.

"It's you. You're the only one on a phone looking flustered."

He took the phone away from his ear and looked at it as if he were looking at Tempest herself, then he searched for her between passing people. No sign of her.

He brought the phone back to his ear and said, "I'm not *flustered*. I'm just trying to find you."

"Don't get agitated. It's not cute."

"I'm not agitated." He sighed, beyond caring if his tone was betraying him. He was out in the frigging cold because of her. Would've already reached Highbury and Islington Station. "Where are you?"

"Try and find me."

The bitch had him confused with Colin Farrell's character in *Phone Booth*.

There was a break in the rush of people. He darted to the kerb, then scanned from one end of Oxford Street to the other, as far as possible.

Someone stood out in a black jacket with furry lapels, looking in his direction, phone in hand, the multi-coloured Christmas lights making her look magical. The person smiled and finger-waved at him. People walked past, this time on her side, his view blocked again. She moved back into his view.

"We could go to Costa on Argyll Street, or the Caffè Nero off Regent Street, though I prefer Costa."

"Well, let's go to Costa."

"I'll wait for you over here, then we can go together."

"Alrighty."

"Be quick."

"Huh?"

"You heard. Bye."

Being inside Costa—just being indoors—was better than being outside in the cold, in people jams, underneath a sky dark as if it were midnight. He waited for his and Tempest's orders while she found a table. She'd offered to wait for their orders and let him find a table, but that was too risky. What she was doing to her own sister was beyond foul. No limit to what she could do to the likes of him, like tampering with his food and drink.

He took his and Tempest's orders to their table. As he approached, he caught her staring at him out the corner of her eye, her half-fringe not covering either eye as much as it had at TGI's. She flashed a smile too late.

"Thanks," she said, taking her chai latte and ham-and-cheese toastie out of the tray. "How was your day?"

"Alright."

She stared at him, her head tilted just enough for her half-fringe to hide more of her right eye, as she waited for him to say more.

Enough time had elapsed for her to realise he wasn't going to elaborate.

She glanced at his muffin. "That's all you're having?"

"Yeah. Don't want to ruin my appetite. I'll eat proper food when I get home." He braced himself as his stomach cramped. His digestive system must've thought he was sitting on the frigging toilet. This bitch needed to make it quick.

She took a small bottle out of her handbag. Sanitizer. She rubbed the gel in her hands. She offered him some. He accepted. She multitasked, eating her toastie and talking.

"How did you and Elise become friends?"

The person all smiles before him was the demanding wretch he'd spoken to the previous day, the devil who'd spoken to him like a gangster thinking he was Aiden. Pointless guessing what she was going to say.

Having his mouth full bought him time. "We went to the same sixth-form, but we never saw each other again until about a year ago."

Her half-fringe completely over her right eye now added more intensity to her countenance, her mouth barely moving as she ate her toastie.

"She was walking and dropped something without realising. I noticed and got her attention. It took me a moment to realise it was the same Elise from sixth-form. Kept in touch ever since."

"What about Aiden?"

His heart started pounding for his attention, and it succeeded; it drew his hand to his chest. His mouth was empty at the worst moment.

Lines formed between Tempest's thickly-plucked eyebrows, and her mouth stopped moving. That devilish look, the ultimate look to kill, was something she and Aiden had in common. He took a sip of his hot chocolate. It burned his lips. His hand jerked, making some of the beverage spill over the mug onto his hand and the table. He made more of a mess as he put the mug down.

"Go and run your hand under cold water."

As if she really cared.

As if he would leave her alone with his muffin and hot chocolate.

"I'll be fine." Another bite of the muffin.

The devil lines disappeared, but her left eye narrowed, and it looked like her right did the same through the breaks of her half-fringe.

"How did you meet Aiden?"

Chew and think. Chew and think . . . "Uh . . ."

Lines in her forehead again, but this time she wasn't looking at him. She mumbled to herself, then she looked at him again, her forehead lines still there, like she would claat him if he didn't give the right answer.

The answer he needed to give came to him. The bitch had tried it. "At the gym. Remember? TGI's? Aiden told Elise."

"Right . . . I forgot." She sipped her latte. "What gym was it again?"

"Uh . . . pardon?"

"What gym?"

"Uh . . . uh . . ."

That damn facial expression accompanied by moving lips, words inaudible, again.

"Oh yeah, easyGym," she said.

"Yeah . . . easyGym." That didn't ring a frigging bell.

There was a glint in her eye, and she was smirking. "easyGym."

He shrugged his shoulders. "easyGym."

She maintained her smirk moments longer, as if she were making sure he noticed in case he hadn't before.

"It's nice that the two of you are friends."

"What do you mean?"

"A straight man being secure enough in himself to be friends with a gay man. Very big of Aiden."

This was his cue to sip some more hot chocolate. There was no mirror in front of him to see his reflection, but Tempest was expressionless this time, so he must've barely reacted.

After a couple of sips, he said, "It is nice. . . . So, what did you want to talk to me about?"

She put her elbows on the table then rested her chin on her clasped fingers. "Don't play dumb with me."

He swallowed, stopped looking at her, then took another bite of his muffin.

"Shannon, give it up."

He shrugged his shoulders.

She chuckled.

"Fine. I'll just leave—"

"No." She grabbed his wrist, looking desperate for the first time, like *she* was at *his* mercy.

He sat back down.

She let go of him. "I'll just say it. You like Aiden, don't you?"

His heart couldn't take it. His hands were starting to shake. He put them in his lap.

"Gone deaf all of a sudden?"

"Uh . . ."

"Spit it out!"

"Course I like him! We're friends."

Her lips turned up, but not in a smile. "Don't do it, bitch. Don't play dumb."

"Come again?"

She wagged her finger. "Tell a lie, you don't like him."

That made his heart settle.

"You're in love with him."

Even without paying attention to any changes in Tempest's countenance, he knew the answer to her question was written all over his face and demeanour. Heart back in distress, hands shaking, café spinning, he shut his eyes and clenched his fists.

"It's alright," the bitch said.

He opened his eyes. "Look, Tempest, I don't—"

"Bullshit!"

He looked around the café, as if something or someone could rescue him. Tempest had only been around them once. His feelings couldn't have been that obvious. But Elise had picked up on something too.

And love. It was definitely more than *like*. But *love*?

"Shannon, you're a shit liar."

He fidgeted, café still spinning.

"It's not like you're a threat." She cut her eyes up and down him. "Aiden's straight. He'd never feel the same way. That's why it's alright." She put a finger over her lips, looking distant. "Actually, it's not alright. You're in love with your friend's man. You nasty, shithouse heifer."

"Wow." So rich of the bitch. He couldn't say that though, not even with his countenance. "I'm not after Aiden. And I'm not what you just called me."

She flicked her half-fringe away from her eye. "Glad to hear that—because you can never have him."

"Is this the *serious* thing you needed to talk to me about?"

She raised one eyebrow without raising the other. "Something else going on? Why did you think I wanted to see you?"

He took a few more sips of his hot chocolate then said, "Nothing."

He looked at her for a reaction, for a change. There was none.

"It's just that ever since we spoke yesterday, I wondered why you wanted to see me. Could've done this over the phone."

"No. I needed to see your reaction. Would've been easier for you to lie and deceive over the phone. In person, your only option is to tell the truth."

He sighed. "Elise is my friend. I'm not after Aiden. He likes females anyway." That was good. No pause. He'd committed to that last sentence.

"Glad we're clear on that."

She'd eaten over half of her toastie. He'd finished his muffin and only had a few gulps of hot chocolate left. Her latte mug was half-full. He gulped down what was left of his lukewarm beverage.

"That was fast," she said. "Or am I slow?"

"A bit of both."

"And I still haven't said why I wanted to see you."

He frowned. "What?"

"I better get on with it."

"You just told me. You wanted to confront me about Aiden."

"Yes, but there's another, more important, reason."

His heart started picking up pace again.

"Elise's birthday is coming up."

He nearly put his hand to his chest. Good thing his hand was in his lap, hitting the table from below instead.

"Sunday to be exact."

"I know."

"I was thinking of doing something for her. She'll be twenty-five, so nothing too big."

For someone who was trying to harm her sister, this was a nice gesture—too nice.

"Sounds good to me."

"Great! You can come early, help with the preparations."

"How early?"

"Well, let's say the party officially starts at four o'clock—everyone has to work the next day—then that would mean getting there for two-thirty, two-forty-five latest."

Something about this wasn't right, but he had to make sure he didn't betray his suspicions.

"I've asked my boyfriend to help as well. And I'll get Aiden to help too."

"So, it would be just the four of us?"

"Yeah. My boyfriend hasn't confirmed, but I'll make sure he comes."

"And Aiden?"

"I'll let him know," she said, her expression pensive for a moment and back to normal the next. "I'll make sure he's on board."

"Alrighty."

"As long as it doesn't make you uncomfortable."

"Uncomfortable?"

She cut her eyes then took final bites of her toastie.

"Why would I be uncomfortable?"

"I couldn't face being around someone I was feeling, who wasn't feeling me back." She was enjoying this.

"It won't make me uncomfortable, because I don't want him."

"Whatever," she said before finishing her latte. She was about to say something else when her focus shifted to her handbag.

Jill Scott's "Blessed" was emanating from it. An insult to Jill Scott to have such a bitch as a fan.

Tempest took things out of her D&G handbag frantically and slammed them on the table: her Oyster card; sheets of paper; and her purse, which fell off the table and landed completely open. Some coins tumbled out and rolled away. While she took the call, he stretched his legs to stop the rolling coins. He crouched down to recover them, picked up her open purse and started putting the coins back in.

He paused at a photo of her, her hair in braids, and some man. Must've been her boyfriend. Looked like she had taste in men too.

No. He was doing it again, checking the wrong guy out. He had to snap out of it, convince himself he'd seen better.

Aiden was better.

Back to the photo.

The man's upper body swallowed Tempest's. He took up most of the photo, Tempest's hand resting on his massive chest. He must've been a bodybuilder, his neck and chest straining his black muscle shirt. Tempest was tall, probably six-two in the heels she was wearing for this meeting, but looked so slight compared to her boyfriend.

He brought the purse closer and narrowed his eyes at the man. . . . Something familiar about him. . . . Facial hair like an anchor.

He'd hung out with Tempest properly for the first time at TGI's. Other than that, he'd never seen her with a man.

But the man in the photo . . .

Not handsome as such. The body—at least the chest and shoulders—made up for that.

Muscles.

Braids.

He squinted at Tempest in the photo.

It couldn't be.

It wasn't.

He studied the boyfriend again.

Moustache not connected to the beard. Body of The Rock. Not the face to match.

Fuck.

But this made no—

Someone snatched Tempest's purse out of his hand. He jumped, stumbled, nearly ended up on his backside.

"I know he's fine, but he's *mine.*" Tempest loomed over him as she zipped up her purse.

He stood up. "Uh . . . I w-wasn't—"

"Don't try it. You were checking him out; your eyes were bulging out." She mimicked him, making her eyes look like they were about to pop out. "I swear, if you do that on Sunday . . ." She dropped what she'd taken out of her handbag back in. "*He actually checked him out in front of me.*"

They couldn't have been ready to go at a better time. His eyes must've have bulged out at the photo as they probably had when he'd first seen him.

"Remember to keep Sunday free," Tempest said as they headed for the café's exit.

When they were outside, she said, "We'll catch up before Sunday."

"Sure."

"I'm taking the bus home. I never take the tube, even though its quicker."

She never took the tube.

Confirmation. Not that he needed it.

"You still thinking about my man?"

"Yes—I mean, no. I . . . uh . . . I'm taking the tube."

She snarled at him, nostrils flared.

"I really wasn't checking him out."

"I believe you, Shannon," she said, her voice thick with sarcasm.

He watched her walk away like she was on a catwalk until she blended with the other pedestrians.

He started for the underground station, that frigged-up evening his parents became as good as dead to him, and vice versa, coming back. Could've had another showdown earlier that evening, with that couple on the train.

Muscle Man on the train was the same Muscle Man in the photo with Tempest.

Tempest's hair was braided in the picture.

The woman on the train had had long braided hair.

But that woman was not Tempest.

WEDNESDAY

24 / Aiden VI
Thinking hats

The front room light was off, but the TV was on, and light was seeping in from the passage. Shannon was sprawled in one of the armchairs, asleep, flashes from the TV lighting up his face. Shannon's lips parted.

Aiden could've filled that gap with his tongue.

Throat clearing from the left. He snapped his head there, towards the beige two-seater sofa next to Shannon. Lionel and Peter were sitting there. He couldn't maintain eye contact. The TV was in front of them, yet their heads were turned to him. He locked eyes with one, then the other, as his heart banged around. The two of them staring at him, Peter with mischief etched on his face, Lionel with his lips turned up, was pissing him off. Lionel just had to be extra with his *mmhmm*. He'd been sloppy, letting the lovebirds catch him.

Better them than the fam.

He looked away, back at Shannon. Shan's mouth was open wider, his body leaning to the right, his head about to lose support from the armchair. Suddenly, the TV flashed even brighter. Either that or Lionel, cracking up, jolted Shan awake. Too confused to pull off looking like he'd been awake the whole time. Lionel's laughter was booming. Peter cackled. Aiden joined in.

"Shannon, what a trial," Lionel said. "Fall asleep and company deh yah."

"Sorry, Aiden." Shan adjusted himself.

"It's cool."

"Let's go to the kitchen."

Aiden yawned. He got up and picked up his empty glass from a Punta Cana coaster.

"Looks like this sleeping thing is catching," Peter said.

Peter and Lionel snuggled closer to each other, Lionel rubbing Peter's bald head as he winked at Aiden.

The thought of having that with Shannon, that closeness, the hand-holding, sharing a bed, fucking . . .

His brother came to him, followed by his grandfolks. He shook the fantasy away.

He had to squint when he entered the kitchen.

"They're cool people." He sat on the end stool by the counter.

"They are." Shan took Aiden's glass and put it in the sink. "I don't know why I'm so tired."

"First week back at uni and work, and seeing Tempest."

Shan rolled his eyes.

"You sure she doesn't know that you know what's going on?"

"Yeah. She just wanted to make sure I wasn't trying to turn you gay—stupid bitch—and to talk about Elise's birthday."

"So, she thinks you're after me?"

Shan got all flustered, couldn't take the eye contact. "That's what she said."

Shan's ass jiggled while he washed up. Could've walked up to him, grabbed him and done all kinds of nasty shit to him right there.

"She asked you about helping out yet?"

He shifted on the stool to make his dick behave, then he took out his Tempest phone and searched for her latest facety text. He put it on the counter for Shannon to read when he finished washing up.

Shan paused by the two empty stools. He kept his distance, choosing to sit on the furthest one. Close enough to give off a whiff of that cocoa butter scent.

Shan screwed up his face as he read the text.

"Nothing about her fazes me anymore."

"Do you really have to go through with this, Aiden? It's gone too far."

Aiden shrugged.

"And we don't even know what else she's planning to do. How do you know she won't expose you anyway?"

"She won't. It would kill my folks if they knew . . . 'bout me. Granddad had heart surgery last year, and Grandma had a mini stroke the year before. Couldn't live with myself if . . . I just can't lose anyone else.".

"Anyone else?"

"Forget I said that."

"Aiden, who—?"

"Leave it!"

"F-fine."

He massaged his forehead. "Sorry."

Shannon hesitated, thinking on something. "But don't you think your family suspects?"

He peered at Shannon then shifted to the middle stool and grabbed him. No one was meant to clock him, but maybe people could see something in him that he couldn't.

"Aiden, what's . . . wrong with you?"

"Why'd you ask me that? Do I talk funny? Am I feminine?"

Shannon broke free and got up.

Aiden shot up from the stool. "Tell me!"

"B-because of my own experience, that's all. Your family knows you . . . better than most . . . c-could've picked up on something."

His bloodclaat cousin had picked up on something, or else . . .

He ran his hand over his face. "I've had females. Maybe that's why nothing's come up."

"Lucky you then." Shan turned his head towards the cream blinds over the window.

"What you thinking?" Aiden sat back down.

"Everything." Shan sat back down, on the middle stool. "Here I am, telling you to come out, yet look at me. My parents . . . Need to stop calling them that. . . . They want nothing to do with me." Shan closed his eyes like he was meditating.

Aiden didn't have to worry about being chucked out of his house—his income helped keep a roof over his folks' heads—but his grandfolks wouldn't take this kind of revelation well. Age was taking them closer to their graves. No need to speed up the process. And Ethan . . .

"Back to what you said Tempest said, about being motherless because of Elise."

"What about it?"

Shan turned in his stool, kicking up that cocoa butter scent of his. "Did she say anything else?"

"We were fighting and—"

"Fighting?" Shan said, making fists.

"Yeah—don't ask—then she just said it."

Shan frowned.

"I know. Some weird shit."

"Elise told me about Tempest's mum being dead. They were children back then, so why does she blame Elise?"

"I don't know, but when Tempest said what she said, she was all shook. Never seen her sweat till then. She got so worked up that she let it out before she could catch herself."

"I know what you mean." Shan was looking through him. "Elise was upset when she told me about Tempest's mum's death. Thought she was being Elise, you know, being sympathetic, but she didn't elaborate, like she didn't want to talk about it."

"When did she tell you?"

"Couple months ago."

"How'd she die?"

"She was hit by a car."

"Fuck."

Losing a parent. One thing they had in common. Existing and being alive were two different things. His mum wasn't alive; she was as good as dead, had been for most of his life so far. She existed.

"Aiden?" Shannon was shaking him by the shoulder.

He'd slid forwards, the counter digging between his shoulder blades instead of the middle of his back. He sat up. "Just thinking 'bout how her mum died."

"Yeah. That's all Elise told me."

"Whatchu mean *that's all*? If someone's hit by a car, then they're hit by a car."

"I know. It's just . . . Elise's demeanour when she told me . . . it was like she was reliving something she'd seen, like she'd forgotten I was with her, and instead of telling me, she was telling herself about the accident, remembering it . . . frightened."

"Some mystery shit."

"Right."

Because of her, I have no mother.

"You don't hurt people for no reason, especially your own sister. The way Tempest said what she said, it's got to do with her mum's death."

"Talking like Elise *killed* the broad."

"I know she never did *that*."

No one said shit for a moment.

"You said she was hit by a car?" Aiden said.

"Yes."

"Then that's not on Elise."

Silence again.

"It's frigged-up what you're doing to her."

He looked Shannon up and down. "What?"

"Sleeping with her."

Didn't see that coming.

"Don't have shit to say about that?"

"What you expect me to say?"

"Something."

"Sounding like wifey interrogating her man after she smelled some other broad on him."

Shannon kissed his teeth.

"Jealous?"

Shannon widened his eyes, words stuck in his throat, then looked away. Aiden reached for Shannon's hand, but Shannon pulled away. He grabbed Shannon's thigh, massaged it as he worked his way up, grip tight. Shannon put his hand on Aiden's. Aiden massaged shaky whimpers out of the guy he had his way with in his dreams, making dream bae's hand slide off and his head snap back. Aiden kneaded as Shannon squirmed.

"Aiden . . . please . . ."

He got up, leaned over Shannon, got close enough for them to heat each other's skin with breath. He started kneading both of Shannon's thighs.

"Aiden . . . I . . . can't . . . do . . ."

"Don't act like you don't want this," he whispered.

Shannon's eyes were glistening, and his lips quivering. He shut his eyes to trap tears.

Aiden buried his face in Shannon's neck, rubbed his beard against it as he snorted cocoa butter.

Something was moving against his left hand. He looked down. Movement beyond Shannon's zipper. Shannon's dick was approaching ten o'clock.

His own dick was swelling, probably trying to reach two o'clock from Shannon's point of view.

He started feeling up Shan's dick as Shan took short breaths.

He squeezed harder. Shannon grabbed his hand. They hand-wrestled. Aiden won, started squeezing Shannon's hardening dick with his other hand. Shannon grunted, grimaced in embarrassment, confusion or something else, went forwards, then threw his head back, taking his torso with him. Aiden was gripping one hand, while the other hand was pushing his head away. A chance to kiss Shannon's palm. He got carried away, starting sucking fingers and groaning as he felt up dream bae's dick some more.

Then Shannon fell off.

Ass on the tiles, Shan looked like he'd just woken up from a nightmare. His trapped tears escaped. He wiped his eyes quickly then looked up at Aiden as he wiped his other hand on his grey jumper.

"Shannon—"

"Stay there!" Shannon backed up, ass sweeping the tiles, till he reached the door.

"Shan, wait." Aiden repositioned his dick to get it soft faster.

"What the frig was that?"

"I . . . dunno."

"Elise is my friend. How could you?"

"Don't put it all on me."

"I . . ."

"You what?"

"I . . . You were . . . too strong. . . . I was stunned, con—"

"You liked it!"

Shannon's mouth was open, his lips changing shape as he tried to talk, before he finally looked away.

"You know how I feel about you—"

"Don't!"

He started to move around the circular, tan brown table that separated them.

"Stay there! Actually, go!"

"Shan, look, I'm sorry."

Shan was shaking his head.

"Come on, Shan. I don't wanna leave like this. Just sit back down."

Shan was still shaking his head.

"I ain't dangerous."

"You are."

"I won't do it again."

Shan peered into the passage.

"I'll go back to the stool. You can sit at this table, or keep standing. I won't come near you."

Shan didn't take his eyes off him as he pulled out a chair.

"Stop looking at me like that."

"You and Tempest are hurting Elise enough already." Shan took something out of his pocket, a small bottle of something green, squirted some of it into his hands, rubbing most of it over the fingers Aiden had sucked. "And now you're trying to get me to do the same."

Aiden ran a finger and thumb over his eyebrows, eyes clenched.

"And to think that you took her virginity."

"Ain't like I raped her."

"You might as well have."

"It takes two. Wasn't like I wanted it the first time, but she . . . I couldn't reject her."

"And what about the other times?"

"Tempest changed the rules, wanted us to continue."

"You do know you're letting Tempest make an ass out of you?"

"Course I know. . . . If you were there that day, the way she was after the passport shit."

"I'm just glad she's back at work, away from you and her bloodclaat sister."

"Shit, Shan. That *bloodclaat* was posh."

"It's not funny."

"I know, I know."

"Is she even safe?"

"Safe?"

"With Tempest."

"She's abroad, so she's alright."

"But she's coming back tomorrow."

"Tempest ain't trying to . . . put a bullet in her."

"Doesn't make it alright."

"Just be glad Elise still has her job."

Shan cut his eyes.

"Tempest took her passport."

"Tempest?"

"Yeah. When I asked her about it, she didn't deny it."

"I knew something wasn't right. Made no sense when Elise told me about it."

"Bitch is trying to fuck with her head."

"For frig's sake. What else has she done that we don't know about?"

"Your guess is as good as mine."

Shan was struggling to say something.

"What?"

Shan was still struggling.

Aiden got off his stool and went to Shan, surprising him. He drew out the chair next to Shannon and straddled it. "Spit it out."

"Aiden, I meant what I said. Don't try anything."

"Just hurry up and tell me." He punched Shannon's arm, harder than intended. "Sorry."

Shan rubbed his arm and frowned. "You can't tell Elise what I'm about to tell you."

"OK."

"She was nearly hit by a car when she was a child."

"What?"

"You heard. She didn't go into detail . . . hard to talk about."

"Maybe what happened to Tempest's mum reminds Elise of what happened to her. She ever mention therapy to you?"

Shan frowned. "No."

"She was in therapy once. Dunno when. She blurted it out the other day."

"What was she doing in therapy?"

"Dunno."

Shan had a far-off expression. He got up and started pacing, cocoa butter dancing in the air.

"What's up now?"

"Nothing." Shan kept on pacing.

He got up and blocked Shannon's path.

"Really, it's nothing."

"I wanna know."

"There's no point."

"Shannon!" He backhanded Shannon's chest.

"OK! OK! It's probably far-fetched. . . . Elise and Tempest, they're the same age, right?"

He nodded.

"And Tempest lost her mum when she was young."

"Yeah."

"She was hit by a car, right?"

"Yeah."

"And Elise was nearly hit by a car."

"Yeah . . . and?"

Shan started frowning, mumbling, in his own world again.

"Say su'um."

Shan rubbed his head like he was having a migraine.

"Shannon."

Something was coming to Shannon, his eyes widening as it got closer, became clearer.

"Shan?"

"What if . . . ?"

"What?" He grabbed Shannon by the shoulders.

"What if it's all connected?" Shan shook his head. "God, what if Elise . . . what if Tempest's mum saved her? What if that's how she died?"

Because of her, I have no mother.

Elise, nearly hit by a car.

He grabbed Shan's face. "You fucking genius!"

Shannon put his hands on Aiden's, excitement in his widened eyes. They stayed like that for a moment, then Shan stiffened up. Aiden could've trapped Shan's face in his hands, could've forced a kiss—wanted to—but he let go.

Shan made a swift move to the middle stool then sat there. "You think that's what happened?"

"Yeah." Aiden went back to the stool he'd sat on before. "Makes sense."

"Then it was an accident. How could Tempest hate Elise because of that?"

"I don't know, but I can't come up with shit else."

"When Elise gets back, I'm gonna ask her some questions."

"Me too."

"Remember you're not supposed to know she was almost hit by a car or how Tempest's mum died."

"Same for you and the therapy."

"Right."

"In the meantime, *we* need to watch out for Tempest. We have to play it cool."

"I know."

"You sure she didn't pick up on anything . . ." He couldn't help grinning. ". . . besides you feeling me?"

There Shan went again, getting all flustered and shit.

"You need to work on your poker face."

"The main thing she said is that I better not try and come between you and Elise, and there's no point trying to turn a straight man gay."

That wiped the smile off his face. He was about to remind Shan he wasn't gay when Shan screwed up his face.

"You look like you have more shit news for me."

"Which gym do you work at?"

"Fitness First."

"Shit."

"What?"

"She tricked me."

"How?"

"When she asked me how we met, I said, the gym."

"Good, just like I told Elise."

"But the bitch went on to ask *which* gym."

"What did you say?"

"She came up with easyGym . . . and I agreed."

"Shit! If it comes up again, just tell her you got confused."

"No, she kept saying it and I kept agreeing. She knows I wasn't confused."

"Fuck. . . . Look, the main thing is she doesn't know *you* know what's going on."

"She's suspicious of me, but she can't know I know."

Shan widened his eyes.

More shit news.

"Her boyfriend—you know him?"

"Not like that. He's a surgeon. Can't stand the fucker. Why?"

"I think—no, I *know* he's married."

"For true?"

Shan talked about some couple he'd seen on the train and that Tempest had a photo of herself and the same man.

"She probably knows."

"What if she doesn't?" Shan said.

"If she knows, she knows. If she doesn't, she doesn't. Not our problem."

"Shit! He'll be there ... at Elise's birthday ... early like us. What if he recognizes me?"

"Maybe he won't."

"But what if he does?"

"Then act normal."

"But—"

"Look, Shan, if Tempest doesn't know that he's— Did you say he's married?"

"They were both wearing wedding rings."

"Then he has a lot to lose. He won't do anything stupid, and I'll be there. I bet she knows though."

"I hope you're right."

"We'll fix this."

"Fix what?"

"This Tempest-Elise thing. I'll end it."

"Shouldn't have even started."

"I know that, but I'll ... break up with her. Sounds crazy saying that, like we're actually together."

"But you *are* together. You *slept* with her. You've *been* sleeping with her."

Couldn't tell if Shan was disgusted, hurt, or both.

"Even if you know it's fake, she doesn't. She smiles at the thought of you. You make her happy."

He looked down at the pristine tiles.

"How do you do it?"

He looked at Shan. "Do what?"

Shan grimaced, rolled his eyes, let out a distressed sigh then finally said, "Have sex with her?"

I could show you better than I could tell you.

No, he'd allow it, keep that shit in his head; Shan was just getting relaxed again. "Elise ain't the first female I've had."

"How do you do it though? How do you get aroused by a female, when you like males?"

"Come on, Shan."

"How?"

Aiden kissed his teeth. "I guess I like . . . both sexes." He'd actually said it—to someone. No whispering, even though everyone else in the house was gay and his folks weren't around. But still . . .

"You're bi then?"

"I ain't nothing."

Shan rolled his eyes. "Are you black?"

"The fuck you mean?"

"Are. You. Black?"

"Look at me!"

"Another question: are you male or female?"

"Where you going with this?"

"You'll see. Male or female?"

"Female."

Shan sighed.

Aiden grinned.

"Whatever. Last question: are you gay, straight, or bisexual?"

Words were caught in his throat. Any other time, he would've said *straight*.

Shan broke the silence. "So, you're sure of your race and gender, but not your sexuality?"

He still couldn't say it, what he *and* Shan knew.

"I'm not doing this to mess you up. I'm the last person to judge. Until recently, *I* faked being straight, especially for my parents' benefit. . . . God, my parents . . ."

Shan's left thigh started shaking, his forearm resting on it. Aiden reached for Shan's forearm slowly, trying not to scare him, then finally made contact. He squeezed right into muscle and bone to stop the shaking.

"Talking about them just . . ." Shan noticed Aiden's hand on him, then he stiffened up.

He put Shan out of his misery, let go.

He didn't let awkward silence last long. "What about you?"

"What about me?"

"You gay, straight, or bisexual?"

"Well, I'm definitely not straight or bi."

"That leaves *gay*."

"I guess."

"You don't sound sure."

"Trying to think of another way to identify."

"And you're giving *me* grief about labels."

Shan let out a deep breath, surrendering, then his face turned serious again.

"What is it?"

"How will you end it with Elise?"

He paused.

"Well?"

"Maybe I'll tell her there's someone else."

Shan's eyes widened, his breathing caught in his throat. He was fighting to put on a poker face, but he was losing. "Don't tell her that."

"Don't tell her I want you?"

Shan rested his elbows on the counter top and rubbed his head from back to front and front to back. If he'd had dreads, like

Lionel, he would've gone back and forth between tidying them and messing them up.

"Just ramping. I won't say it's you, but at least . . ."

"What?"

"We can . . . you know . . ."

Shan tensed up like he was fighting to hold a stinkie in. "We can't . . . just like that. Elise is my friend, my *good* friend." He sighed. "Of all people, why her?"

"You know why—Tempest."

"What you gonna do about Tempest once you end it with Elise?"

He shrugged.

"I don't have a good feeling about Elise's birthday. Feels like Tempest is up to something. Maybe we should tell Elise everything we know before then."

"No!"

"The longer this goes on, the more Tempest continues to hurt her. What if—?"

Peter came into the kitchen. Couldn't have timed it better.

"I better get going," Aiden said.

"But . . ." Shannon shook his head. "Alrighty."

Aiden and Peter fist-bumped.

"Don't be a stranger," Peter said.

Shan followed Aiden out of the kitchen and to the front room. Aiden told Lionel bye as he put on his camouflage jacket, then Shan followed him to his car.

"Really, Aiden, what if . . . Do you think Tempest would . . . kill her?"

Aiden dismissed that shit with a wave in the chilly night air.

But what Tempest was doing to Elise wasn't far off killing someone.

"Elise isn't safe."

"Tempest wouldn't do that."

Shan shook his head. "We have to tell Elise everything."

That would fuck Elise up. She'd hate him.

And the recording . . . if his fam ever heard it . . .

He took a deep breath, his fog kissing Shan's. "Fine. Let's do it."

Shan sighed.

"But *after* her birthday."

"After? How long after? A day later, two weeks later, a few years—?"

"*Soon* after."

"Why not before?"

"Maybe nothing bad is gonna happen on her birthday. There's still shit to figure out anyway. Let her enjoy her day."

Shan looked towards the approaching stream of traffic lighting up Richmond Road. He kissed his teeth.

"Come on."

"Monday then. We can tell her together."

"But . . ."

"What?"

He sighed. "Nothing. Monday."

Monday was good, meant more time to figure shit out, because Elise was due back out of the country early Monday.

SATURDAY

25 / Tempest VI
Change of plan

The sky was almost clear, no part of Victoria Park spared the sunlight, the mostly leafless trees giving the rays larger gaps to strike through, but Tempest's own breath fogging her vision was a reminder of the cold. Clear view otherwise, half-fringe tucked under her sweatband. She checked her running watch, wheezing, her thighs and calves burning with each stride. Below *08:37* was her running distance. Not even a mile yet. Didn't seem right. She scanned the surroundings for something familiar as she ran along Central Drive. And there it was—Old Lake. Her running watch was working just fine. She'd fucked up, not running the previous Saturday. Four miles was the goal, but she wasn't feeling up to it. She would finish where she'd started, at Royal Gates.

A stocky, golden dog was running from the right as she was passing the Band Stand. Plenty space ahead. The dog could've been heading anywhere. It seemed to be looking her way, but she got close enough to spot what it was really looking at—a tennis ball at the wind's mercy, balancing on the camber of the footpath. It reached the ball as she was about to pass. Either the dog didn't slow down soon enough and made the ball roll into her path, or the sudden gust of wind, fucking with her hood, pushed it further along.

She fought gravity in vain, the dog barking as if laughing at her. Her palms stung, pain radiating to her stomach. The dog kept barking, right at her ear, drowning out her heavy breathing. Something started blowing her fingers. Or wetting them. If she'd landed on spit or shit . . .

She snatched her hand away. The wet sensation returned with a vengeance. She turned her head the other way.

The dog was licking her hand! She sprang to her feet, cussing. The frownsy dog kept jumping to pick up where it'd left off.

"Fuck off!" She scraped her hand against her cardigan. "Piss the fuck off!"

The ugly, muscle-bound bitch kept barking and jumping.

A man in a burgundy hoodie was jogging towards them. "Vixen! Vixen, no!"

The dog ran to him as Tempest continued scraping her hand against her cardigan. Scraping was making no difference, hand still tingling where the dog had licked it.

"Bad girl!" He was rough with the dog, almost choking it as he put its leash on its collar.

Most of his face was hidden; his hood was up and an Arsenal scarf was covering his mouth. She was about to cuss him off when the wind blew the hood off his head and he pulled the scarf down. Beneath evidence on his face that he'd been in a fight—top lip sunken and one eye red where it should've been white, the lower eyelid darker than the other, darker than his predominantly honey complexion—he looked familiar.

"Tempest?"

"Marvin?"

"Whatchu doing here?"

"Running." She wiped what dirt she could off her jogging bottoms, her palms still stinging. "Didn't know you had a dog."

"My bro's dog."

"Oh."

She was scowling at the funny-looking dog. It wasn't entirely golden, vitiligo trailing from the middle of its forehead to its belly, and on the paws. It must've been a bulldog, its legs short but muscular, its nose pushed in and up, its mouth shaped like the Gateway Arch. Its cheeks were droopy. Should've been named Cora, after Aiden's grumpma.

"I ain't used to her."

Wiping and wiping, and the sensation of her hand being tainted with dog saliva remained.

"I'm not a dog person. It *licked* me." She wiggled her fingers.

"*She's* clean. Hope you're alright."

Instead of wiping the dirt off, she made it spread over her clothes. "I'll live."

"Like I said, I ain't used to walking her, but she needed to come out. Had to clear my head anyways."

A glance at her watch. The timer was still going. The rest of the run would be fucking pointless.

She sighed. "What's . . . ? Wait a minute . . ." She brought her hand to her mouth and stopped abruptly, so close to putting her dog spit-infested hand on her mouth. She tugged at her bottoms. "It was your cousin who died in Mabley Green, wasn't it?"

Marvin pursed his lips, looked down at the dog, rocking to control his emotions.

"Condolences."

"Thanks."

"Whoever killed Jason will get what's coming to them."

He became stiff, like he'd stopped breathing, his lips barely moving when he spoke. "They will?"

No wonder the funny-looking top lip—two missing front teeth.

She tried not to stare too hard. "Yeah. Feel like I should know more about it; it happened just round the corner from me."

The dog was ready to go, excitable, pulled at its leash, wanted to play some more. Marvin wrapped more of the leash around his hand, like he was trying to break the dog's neck, until the dog kept still.

"Any leads? The police made any progress?"

"Fuck the police. I know who did it."

She was about to clutch her chest. The filthy sensation on her fingers stopped her. "How do you know?"

"Saw 'em."

"Them?"

"Two batty men."

"If you know who did it, you should tell the police."

Marvin snarled.

"Or not."

"Got unfinished business with those pussies. There was a fight, and . . . I've said too much. Just know I'll handle it."

"Be careful. No need to end up like Jason, or in prison. Let the police . . . Just don't do anything stupid."

"Whatever."

"Everything comes out eventually."

Hopefully not what she was doing to Elise. At least not until after her birthday, until things were too far gone. Bad enough Shannon had become involved, fucking things up.

"It's my *sister's* birthday tomorrow. You should pop round."

"I don't even know her."

"So? Just come. My place. Starts at four."

"Guess I have to buy her something."

"Not really."

"I could buy a card later. What's her name?"

"Elise."

He frowned, looked through her. "Elise?"

"Yeah. You must've seen her around. Probably the chocolate version of me since people say we favour. We're flatmates."

His frown disappeared.

"Everything OK?"

"Yeah. Gimme the address."

"I'll text it to you. What's your number?"

Marvin gave her a missed call, then she texted him her address. He read her text aloud, while she nodded.

"See you at mine tomorrow then?"

"Yeah." He grinned then caught himself, part of his top lip sinking into the gap where two teeth once were. "Can I bring someone?"

"Why not."

"I'll bring Callum. He's fucked up too 'cause of what happened to Jason."

"Yeah, bring him."

He had an energy about him, his body rocking like he was warming up for a boxing match, looking through her. "See you tomorrow."

"Tomorrow." She jogged away, the dog barking its goodbye.

She staggered to the bathroom as soon as she reached home. She washed her hands. Two times. Vigorously. Two different soaps. Could never be too clean. She was spent, her legs sore and wobbly from what had ended up being a three-mile run. No pain, no gain—her batty. She was in pain and there was no gain. Even factoring in the interruption to her run, she knew she hadn't come close to her target time.

She peeled off her sweat-soaked, turquoise jogging bottoms and matching cardigan, no energy or patience to put them in the laundry bin properly. She left a leg and a sleeve spilling out, almost reaching the floor. She snatched off the sweat band, could barely toss the hair that had fallen to her eyes. Stripped down to a white vest and black thong. She staggered to the living room, hot and sweaty, then collapsed on the sofa, sprawled herself. She spotted the sweat band on the floor, close to the doorway. No idea she'd dropped it.

She was half-asleep when muffled music made her jump. Jill Scott was singing "Blessed" from somewhere. Her phone. She hadn't taken it out of her jogging bottoms. Maybe it was Carl, but her muscles were too sore and the sofa was sucking her in nicely.

The ringing stopped then started again immediately. She cussed as she hauled herself from the sofa, huffed and stomped to the laundry bin as Jill Scott kept singing about how bloody blessed she was. By the time the pocket finally let the phone loose, Jill stopped. Missed calls from her daddy.

Cooled down, she went to her room and put on a black maxi skirt. She was about to call her daddy back when a WhatsApp alert appeared. She almost tapped the WhatsApp icon when she remembered Elise had sent her a message. Going into WhatsApp would let Elise know she was online. *That woman contacted me again* was all she could read without going into WhatsApp. She'd been meaning to turn off read receipts. WhatsApp could wait.

Keeping up the act was draining, and Shannon had become an issue. Still, Aiden and Elise were having sex, hopefully using the condoms she'd given Elise. No more of the fake shit after Sunday, and by that time . . .

She sighed, called her daddy back.

Background noise came through when Daddy picked up, but he wasn't talking.

She was about to say something, but she was beaten to it. All she could do was look at the screen to see if she'd called the heifer by mistake, but she didn't even have her number.

She brought the phone back to her ear. Even though it wasn't her daddy, she still said, "Daddy?"

"No, it's me."

She cut her eyes. From where she was, it looked like her mum was doing the same thing in the picture on the dressing table.

"Yes, it's me."

The bitch could've easily handed the phone over.

"Tempest, why you so quiet?"

Deep breath. "Is my daddy there?"

"Your *daddy*?"

What a dumb fuck. "I'm returning his call."

"He's not here."

She frowned. "He just called me."

"No, *I* called."

"With *his* phone? Where is he?"

"Never mind that. Is me did call you—for a likkle chat."

"What is it?"

"Just letting you know . . . if you do anything to my pickney—me and you."

She stumbled backwards, her calves bumping into the side of her bed. Either her unstable legs or the knots forming in her stomach forced the contact between her batty and the bed. The dream—the nightmare—must've been a warning. Too intense to have been a coincidence. Maybe Mari-heifer suspected something.

"You hear weh me seh? Anything bad happens to her—me and you."

She moved the phone from her ear like it was burning her. Couldn't let the bitch hear her heavy breathing and realise she was getting to her.

Mari-heifer was saying something else.

She brought the phone back to her ear.

"Tempest!"

"Why are you so loud?" She clasped her neck with her free hand. She gulped tightness down.

"Listen good. Come for me if you want to, but don't hurt Elise." Mari-heifer's voice was thick with threat, but there was something else, a hint of desperation, like she'd been reduced to asking her enemy for a favour, knowing that there was no other option.

Fuck knew where this was coming from. Maybe Mari-heifer was a bigger problem than Shannon. She had come too far for everything to backfire. She needed to calm down, to sound like she hadn't just finished a run.

"You hear me?"

"I rang to speak to Daddy. He's obviously not there. I have things to do."

She was about to ask the heifer if she was still there, when Mari-heifer said, "Fucking with my pickney better not be one of those things." Click.

"Fucking dry-pussy bitch!"

She squeezed her phone like it was some part of the bitch—her neck, face, one of her sagging titties . . . squeezed till her palm hurt. Then she banged, banged, banged the phone on the bed. She let it slip out of her hand and slide to her batty. Her hands were shaking, a new lump in her throat starting to grow. She shook her head like the psycho in *Orphan* did in a toilet cubicle. The past was hurling the things the bitch had done to her, at her: making sure that Elise had the nicer dolls and clothes; paying more attention to Elise's hair, while Daddy, who couldn't plait, did hers; showing no interest in parents' evenings when it came to her; slut-shaming her for starting to fuck so young, like other girls her age weren't doing the same thing; trash-talking her mum for her to hear . . . So much shit. Good thing her aunt had taken her in when she had. Probably saved her from prison. Probably saved them all: Mari-heifer from being dead, Elise from being motherless, her daddy— Well, maybe it would've saved him to kill her.

The things Mari-heifer had done to her—and was still doing to her—were bad enough, but the fucking worst . . . the things the bitch had said about her mum to her daddy and Elise, none of them aware she was in the house. Homewrecker this, slut that. *Thank God Elise lured that tramp bitch into the road. Thank God Elise had the mind to do it.*

313

Bitch could fuck herself, just like her daughter.

She didn't know how long she'd been motionless. Spent, her eyes wide and hardly blinking, she let her upper body fall to the bed then brought her legs up and lay on her right side. Her fringe tickled her eyelids. Tears from her left eye tickled across her nose then blended with the tears falling from her right eye. She didn't bother wiping them, just waited for time and the draught to dry them.

She needed Carl.

No sooner did she open the flat door than she wrapped her arms around Carl, snorting his hypnotic cologne.

"What's wrong?" he said.

"I've fucking had it." She led him by the hand to the living room.

"Why?" he said as she sat down.

He remained standing, hands in the pockets of his leather jacket.

"Sit down then."

It was as if he'd gone deaf.

"Take off your jacket and sit down." She patted the space next to her on the sofa. "How come you're so covered up? It's not as cold as it was earlier. Heater's on."

Carl took off his jacket slowly, and he sat down just as gingerly on the other side of the sofa. "What's wrong?"

She squinted at him, regarded his green turtleneck, her hand still resting on the space between them.

She scooted closer to him. "That heifer called me."

He started to turn his head towards her but stopped himself, moved his eyes without moving his head. "What did she want?"

She told him about the conversation. He wasn't giving his full attention; he was facing straight ahead, even though she was beside him. And his clothing . . . he wouldn't have worn a turtleneck in Antarctica.

"You must've slipped up."

"There's no way she knows anything."

"What if she does?" He was still staring straight ahead, at the TV, which wasn't even on.

She sighed, grabbed Carl's face and turned it towards her. "Why you acting so—?"

He stiffened up. There were rough patches on his left cheek. She held his face firmly with one hand and traced the outline of the roughness with the other, then she hauled up her snug-fitting maxi skirt and climbed on top of him for a better look. He'd been scratched.

"How the fuck did that happen?"

He pushed her off him, back to her side of the sofa. "Had an accident at the gym yesterday."

She kicked his thigh.

"Shit, Tempest!"

"What kind of gym accident?"

"I was helping someone lift something . . . and there were nails sticking out. The man I was helping, he lost his grip and the next thing you know . . . it fell and the nails fucked up my cheek."

"Sounds like bullshit and looks like someone scratched—"

"I'm getting sick of telling you I'm done with her."

She closed her eyes, did a woosah in her head until it suppressed the words *fucking* and *liar* .

"Tempest, do you hear me?"

She opened her eyes. "Lucky it missed your eye. Is that why I couldn't get you yesterday?"

He hesitated. "Yeah."

"It looks bad."

"I'll live."

Another woosah. "Is everything sorted out for tomorrow?"

"Tomorrow? . . . Oh, yeah. Yeah."

"You don't sound sure."

"Everything's sorted."

"It has to work out perfectly."

"It . . . it will."

She swallowed.

"You said that Shannon's slender."

"Yeah."

"And you're sure he knows what's going on?"

"That time I phoned Aiden, and he wouldn't talk . . . it was Shannon. Don't know how the fuck he got Aiden's phone and . . . Doesn't matter how. What matters is he knows, and he needs to be handled. The two of them do. They're up to something. Have to get them before they get me, even if Elise isn't . . . No, I won't say it. She has to be. Don't know for sure yet, but she has to be. Everything else has worked. Why not that?"

Carl scratched his head.

"Did you hear me?"

"Yeah."

Her heart rate picked up; shit was getting real. "You sure they won't . . . die?"

"They won't."

She pursed her lips for a few exhales. "And the timing will work out perfectly?"

He shrugged. "Told you before . . . hard to say. Just do what you're supposed to do."

"A lot's riding on this. Why do you sound unbothered?"

"Tired."

"This can't go wrong. I have to get them. I can't be the only one to go down, not if Elise . . . What's wrong with me? I keep putting that into the universe."

"I've done what I can."

His body language was worrying, but if he said everything was sorted, she had to believe him, whatever was going on with him.

She closed her eyes, took more deep breaths. "I'm worried about Mari-heifer fucking things up."

"She coming here early?"

"Elise is supposed to go to Daddy's first, then the three of them will come here."

"Then they should be out of the way long enough." He leaned forwards, like he was about to get up.

"Speaking of Elise . . ."

He rested his forearms on his thighs, still leaning forward. He gave her a hand gesture, hurried her up.

". . . she messaged me."

"And?"

"Haven't read it yet."

"Might as well read it."

She opened the latest message from Elise.

That woman contacted me again, but I think it's over now. She said she was wrong about me, because I'm out of the country and she saw her husband with someone else recently. Poor thing. Anyway, I should be back late afternoon/early evening.
xoxo

"As much as I like her shitting herself, I'm glad you ended that prank. She was pissing me off."

Carl didn't respond.

"I'm still trying to figure out how you know where Daddy lives." She thumped his leg playfully. "After tomorrow, if this works . . . It has to work. It will. And I'm gonna make it up to you, cater to you like crazy." She went to lean on him, but he shot out of the sofa, making her upper body slap into the warm space he'd left.

"I have to go."
"Carl!"
By the time she collected herself, all that was left of Carl was his cologne.

SUNDAY

26 / Shannon IX
A tenant

Shannon could've told Aiden to turn around and continue towards Eastway, but he needed to get it over and done with. This stop had been on his mind all day, a day he had to start early so that he could give himself and—finally—Aiden a haircut. Too late to back out. Tempest wanted them at the flat for two-thirty. Getting there at two-forty-five was more realistic. A fifteen-minute delay was nothing.

Maybe his parents had tried to reach him on his old number. They had to have calmed down by now, over two weeks later. It was time to find out where they stood.

Or maybe he already knew, deep down. Growing up, his parents had warned him against being gay, as if he had any say in whom he was attracted to. The idea of sending him to Jamaica to make a man out of him had been thrown around a few times, as if possibly liking men made him less of a man, as if going to Jamaica would've changed anything. Getting Elise to pretend to be his girlfriend must've given them hope. Maybe they would never get over it, too set in their ways, but he had to be sure.

"Lemme go down a bit more," Aiden said, his feet keeping the car at the biting point, his stare as intense as usual.

"No. I'll be fine. I won't go in. I'll ring the bell and rush back to the gate so that you can see me from here. Remember the signals?"

Aiden shrugged his shoulders. "I guess. . . . Why don't I walk down with you?"

"No. If they see you, it'll make things worse. Remember what happened when we first met, what my moth—what *she* said?"

Aiden furrowed his brow.

"She said we were boy—"

Aiden cracked that devilish smile of his. That widening smile and fresh trim brought about fluttering. Probably showed on his face.

Couldn't take it anymore. Pulling, pulling, pulling the door handle wasn't making the door open. Then Aiden did something to make all the doors unlock at once. He leaned over to open the door, his solid arm pressing against Shannon's chest, familiar fabric softener scent coming alive. He wouldn't move his arm. Shannon met Aiden's intense gaze, held it for as long as he could, before he removed Aiden's arm—or maybe Aiden let him—then stumbled out of the car.

The cold outside was welcome for once, as hot as it had been getting inside, Aiden doing what he did best—making him weak.

Elise was important, undeserving of all this, the only thing keeping him from giving himself to Aiden as he did in his dreams. It didn't matter that Aiden and Elise's relationship was phoney. Moments like the one in the car made things hard, hard on his conscience and heart.

He walked slowly, passing the familiar cars parked along Glyn Road, including that teal blue Volkswagen up! he wanted. The leaves on branches drooping over fences seemed more fiery than before. The scaffolding was still up across the road, as was the *FOR SALE* sign not much further down. Little had changed within the last two weeks. Not that it should've, just because his life had.

The sight of the silver Hyundai i30 in its usual spot made his heart misbehave. They were home. He stopped at number 54 and took a deep breath. His father was probably in the front room watching TV, his mother in the kitchen preparing Sunday dinner. No one cooked better. Lucky he'd learned how to cook and do other things before his parents threw him away.

Leroy and Viola, not his parents.

Muffled voices made him slow down. Then came rattling.

The door to number 50 opened. That paralysed him. Viola emerged, holding something at diaphragm level, by the base and one of its sides. She was talking in light Jamaican patois then stopped and turned her head towards him. He pulled the hood of his new brown jacket tighter around his face and covered his mouth. Their eyes locked. He broke the gaze as Leroy came out with M&S bags. Leroy locked eyes with him. He tugged his hood just in time; the wind had picked up. He was meant to ring the doorbell. By that time, he would've been ready to face them.

He was anything but ready now.

They were approaching the gate, not taking their suspicious gazes off him. He turned around, light-headedness and lifeless legs making him stumble into the waist-high brick wall separating property 54 from the pavement.

Aiden! Aiden was standing outside his frigging car. He motioned at Aiden, who was probably at number 70, to go back. Aiden hesitated then finally complied.

Leroy and Viola's footsteps were louder. Maybe it wasn't enough that everything he was wearing was new. They were going to confront him and tell him about his nasty backside and to piss off, as if they owned the whole of Glyn Road. He couldn't face them. Should've just gone straight to Eastway. He had to go back to the car.

But they'd probably recognize his walk, the walk they'd admonished him for, since childhood.

He raked his fingers along his former neighbour's brick wall then the gate. He opened the gate and rushed to the door in one piece despite his weak legs.

He'd been followed. Someone stopped at the gate. He turned his head slowly, not too much to reveal his face, but enough to recognize Leroy's posture. His breaths were coming out in fleeting mini clouds as Leroy stood there.

The gate squeaked. It was opening. Leroy was coming to get him.

His heart was trying to break out of his chest.

"Excuse me," Leroy said.

Shannon took out his phone, pretending he hadn't heard.

"Ex—"

Viola called Leroy's name, while Shannon looked all over the house's exterior, as if he'd pressed the bell and was looking for a sign that someone was home.

Leroy told Viola he was coming, then the gate squeaked again.

Shannon turned around, tugging his hood so that it hid most of his face, just as the gate crashed to a throbbing close. Footsteps faded then stopped. Car doors opened, feet shuffled, throats cleared, muffled conversation ensued, doors closed. A car started the moment the wind picked up again. His hood came down just as the car stopped right by the gate.

His haircut. One thing that hadn't changed—the shape of his head. The wind kept him from putting the hood back on. They would recognize him.

They'd probably recognized him earlier. Maybe Viola had called Leroy as a ploy. They were mere feet from him and were going to pounce on him together. That Friday evening all over again.

A patter of footsteps from inside the house.

The car was still there, snoring, no sign it would wake up and frig off any time soon.

Once they saw that the neighbour recognized him, that would be it.

The door clicked open.

The car revved.

He started to turn around so that his former neighbour couldn't see his face. By the time he turned around fully, the car had gone.

"Can I help you?"

He turned his head only slightly. Maybe his former neighbour could see the back of his head and a bit of his goatee at most.

"Sorry," He said in a gruff voice. "Wrong house!" He rushed through the gate.

The door closed when the gate slipped out of his clumsy fingers and crashed to another throbbing close. He stopped for a moment to suck in some air and let it out slowly as speed humps tested the suspension of the Hyundai in the distance. The car kept going straight then turned right before it went out of view.

On the other end of Glyn Road, Aiden was leaning against his Volkswagen. He started approaching. Shannon put his hand out to stop him then headed to number 50.

While he'd been grieving, Viola and Leroy had moved on. Just like that. Maybe Elise was right. Maybe they'd spent years, perhaps most of his life, getting ready for that Friday, getting ready to let him go. Peter had told him things improved over time, that his parents would come round one day. Uncle Lionel had disagreed.

He pulled the catch but didn't push the gate; he vacillated between setting foot on the lawn and staying put. He should've brought his keys with him, though knowing Leroy and Viola, they would've long changed the locks.

His hand was still on the gate, but keys were rattling.

He spun around. No one behind.

The jingling was coming from in front, inside the house. Viola and Leroy had left, but someone was moving on the other side of the door, the two-panelled, glazed glass blurring the person's frame. Before he could retreat out of sight behind the hedge fencing the house, the door opened. A towering man emerged. Didn't recognize him. Besides the grey woolly hat on his head, the stranger was dressed completely in denim, his jeans a darker shade of blue than his fur-collared jacket. The unknown man closed the door and barely stepped away from it when he locked eyes with him and froze.

Couldn't move his feet. His chest must've been the only part of him that was moving because he could see the puffs of smoke his breaths formed.

The man peered at him, hands fidgeting in jacket pockets, scowling as if asking who the frig he was.

"I . . . uh . . ."

The man widened his eyes and shook his head and shrugged his shoulders, getting impatient.

"I think I've come to the wrong house."

The man wasn't buying it, wasn't dropping his guard. His hands were still moving around in his pockets, like he was about to take something out, something sharp, or something with lead.

"Viola . . . Leroy . . . they here?"

The man stopped moving his hands, threat disappearing from his eyes. "Oh, yeah. You just missed them actually. I'm a tenant here."

"What?"

"They're not here."

"No. You're *what*?"

"Oh, a tenant."

Everything inside him plummeted. "You . . ." Strained breathing. Tightening throat. "You . . . live . . . here?"

The tenant came closer to the gate. "Yeah."

The gate was tapping against the stopper. It wasn't the wind. He was holding it, hand shaking.

"You OK?"

A tenant. He'd been a tenant all those years and didn't know it . . . a bombo-frigging-claat tenant?

"I don't think they'll be back for now. I can tell them you came."

"No, don't!" he said, maybe too quickly. He swallowed. "Don't tell them anything. I . . . I'll come another time. . . . Was just passing. . . . Thought I might . . . catch them."

The man, the tenant, was frowning.

He finally let go of the gate, his *bye* almost a whisper.

He turned around quickly, leaving the man's goodbye chasing him in the chilly air, before tears joined his foggy breath in blurring his vision.

27 / Shannon X
Too hot to handle

Aiden and Shannon were approaching Elise and Tempest's building. Shannon was carrying a gift bag in each hand, gloveless fingers cramping. Aiden must've been feeling the same way, not wearing gloves, a bag of drinks in each hand.

"You sure you up for this?" Aiden said.

"It's Elise's birthday. The least I could do."

They'd talked about the new tenant during the drive. Enough tears and cussing for the day.

Aiden transferred a bag to his other hand then took out his phone. He kissed his teeth.

"What is it?"

"Text from the bitch."

Shannon checked his own phone. Three missed calls, a text and a WhatsApp message from the same bitch. "Didn't hear my phone." He frowned at the time. "Not even ten-to-three yet."

Aiden put his phone back in his pocket.

"You're not gonna tell her that we're almost there?"

"Nah. She'll see us when she sees us." Aiden had a devilish smirk. Hot without even trying. "Just remember to be careful."

"I will."

"At least we're together—not like—"

"I know what you mean," he said quickly, hoping he wasn't betraying the butterflies in his stomach. "If he recognizes me—"

"Don't worry 'bout that."

"Don't worry? Have you seen the size of him?"

"Ain't much bigger than me."

"I think he is."

"So, you like man all muscled and shit?"

Aiden had the height and muscle. Clothed or not—he'd only seen Aiden naked in his dreams—Aiden clearly had a body fit for a physique competition. It was obvious from the way he walked, as if he spent hour after hour, and day after day in the gym, everything he wore hugging his chiselled frame.

Something distracted Aiden when they reached the entrance to the residential building. He took his phone out of his pocket again. It was vibrating.

He answered, nostrils flared. "We're outside. . . . What do you mean? . . . Just me and Shannon. . . . Well, we've reached. Buzz us up." Teeth-kissing. "Hung up on me to bloodclaat."

Shannon jumped when the door buzzed. Aiden pulled the door and let him enter first. Something touched his backside. He looked behind, at Aiden.

"What?" Aiden said.

He gave Aiden the once-over. "Nothing." He turned around and proceeded up the stairs.

It happened again, one floor away. A poke this time. He turned around. Aiden was stone-faced.

Tempest and Elise's level. Another poke.

"Aiden, what are you doing?"

"You like it, don't you?"

He hesitated. Aiden smirked.

"Just stop it." No conviction. He might as well have told Aiden to fuck him right there on the dirty stairs.

Aiden was still smirking.

"Go in front of me." He pulled Aiden in front, or maybe Aiden let him.

Tempest was taking long to open the door. Enough time to count the number of balloons on the pink-and-silver *HAPPY BIRTHDAY* banner, which gave vibrancy to a door that looked easy to bust open.

Approaching footsteps stopped on the other side of the door. No sign of activity for a moment. The person must've been looking through the peephole. Tempest—or Muscle Man. Maybe the person was taking so long because it was Muscle Man peeping at them, recognizing Shannon.

The door opened with an unexpected force, like the person wanted to break it from its hinges, the same way Madea opened the door for Helen in *Diary of A Mad Black Woman.*

Tempest, not Muscle Man, stood before them. Besides the Algarve apron she was wearing, any similarities between the gigantic old lady played by a man and the bombshell in front of them ended there. Frigging shame that someone so ugly inside was the complete opposite externally. She stunned in an all-black cap-sleeved dress that almost reached the floor, wearing black lip-liner to match, like she was going on a date with the intention of seducing her lover. Her short hair was styled neatly, her trademark half-fringe covering most of her right eye.

And then she opened her mouth. "Took unu time."

"It's only—"

She twirled like Kenya Moore and sashayed into a room on the left.

One step in, and the aromas from whatever she was cooking accosted him, heat blasting him. Reminded him of his previous and current abodes. They left their shoes in the hallway, while pot covers were slammed, food bubbling and sizzling. Tempest came back to the them, her hands on her hips.

"What's wrong?"

"Get a move on! You need to put up all those decorations," she said, pointing at a bag next to a candle, in its holder, on a square mahogany table.

"Is it just us?" Aiden said.

"Yeah. Carl's gone to get drinks. Don't know what's taking him so long." She sounded distant, as if in a trance.

She snapped out of whatever world she'd been in and picked up the bag. She had a facety countenance.

"What's wrong now, Tempest?" Shannon said.

"Take your stuff off!" she said, tugging at the zip of his jacket.

Aiden snatched the bags from him before they could drop. It was as if she was trying to rip his jacket off, along with everything underneath. He matched her speed before he ended up having to buy yet another jacket.

She handed him the bag of decorations and led him and Aiden to the front room. Balloons of different shades of pink were placed at the four corners of the room, and an assortment of snacks were calling him to the coffee table.

"Put this banner . . ." Tempest interrupted his inspection of the room. ". . . over . . . there."

"You've been real busy." Aiden sounded genuinely impressed.

"I have, but before you know it, people will start arriving. And where is Carl with those damn drinks?

"Take these." Aiden gave Tempest the Blossom Hill and CÎROC Vodka from Shannon, and his offering of Baileys, and Rubicon and KA brands of boxed juice.

"Where are the gifts going?" Shannon said.

"In that corner." Tempest pointed to a space between one of the armchairs and a magazine rack, then she shuffled back to the kitchen.

He whispered, "She's really making an effort. The cooking . . . everything."

"Don't let it fool you," Aiden whispered back, removing cling film from one of the bowls of crisps on the coffee table.

"It's just strange, that's all."

Aiden offered him crisps before they got going with the banner and the rest of the decorations.

J ust gone three. Shannon and Aiden were in the kitchen with Tempest, Shannon preparing salad, and Aiden slicing and buttering hard dough bread. Aiden's muscle fit black shirt was unbuttoned far enough to reveal his rugged chest. Shannon was at an ideal angle to see involuntary pec bounces.

Buzzing made him jump. Had to be Muscle Man aka Carl. Tempest's frantic footsteps out of the kitchen to the passage matched his heartbeat. She wasted no time telling someone they'd taken ages.

He rushed from the doorway to the sink, which wasn't really far. The voices of Tempest and the person she'd let in were joined by rustling bags.

He turned his back to the doorway as footsteps stopped in the small kitchen.

"Guys, Carl's here! Carl, you remember Aiden, and you remember him, too, don't you, Aiden?"

Funny how they were acting, as if everything was fine, unaware he knew what they were doing to Elise. At least he was a step ahead in something.

He turned on the tap and wet his hands. He needed to look busy, needed to buy himself time to act normal. Aiden and Muscle Man greeted each other with a long handshake, the kind that he hadn't yet mastered.

"Shannon." Tempest tapped his shoulder.

A he's-my-man-not-yours look greeted him when he turned to face her.

"This is Carl. Carl, meet Shannon."

As long as they weren't left alone, there was nothing to worry about. There was no reason for them to be left alone anyway. He ripped off a kitchen towel, dried his hands and clenched his eyes shut for a moment before facing Carl properly.

It didn't matter that he'd seen Carl before and knew what to expect—his eyes were probably bulging out. It was the same face, same body . . . same everything, except for the scratch on his left cheek. He couldn't pass up the opportunity to take in the sight up close. He hated that he couldn't deny this cheater looked like good sex. It was all in his stature; broad shoulders that didn't slump; tight waist; muscular arms straining the long sleeves of the burgundy jumper; the rise and fall of his rocks for pecs, nipples poking through . . . If this were a dream, he would've let this cheater have his way with him right on the table top. Everything about Carl's physical appearance was doing something to every part of Shannon, from his wide eyes to his hardening dick, and from there to his curling toes.

The way Carl was staring back, his eyes narrowed, wasn't good. Shannon was busted, either from being caught trying to control his erection, and liking what he was seeing, or from being recognized. If only he knew which.

He glanced at Tempest, who was smirking, then at Aiden, who was snarling, probably his way of telling him to get it together. Could've sworn Aiden's lips trembled momentarily, his gaze ever intense.

He extended his hand. It was shaking too much. He balled it into a fist.

Carl took that as a sign to do the same; he bashed his knuckles into Shannon's. "What's happening."

Voice deep like Barry White's.

"N-nice to m-meet you." Shannon rubbed his knuckles then splayed his fingers.

Carl just stood there staring, pouting as he played with his beard, which wasn't joined to his moustache in a goatee. The same as it had been on the train and in Tempest's photo.

Carl wagged the index finger of his other hand. "Why do you look familiar?"

Maintaining eye contact was a struggle. "I d-dunno know."

Carl was shaking his head slowly.

"Well, Shannon's seen you before."

Shannon snapped his head in Tempest's direction.

"The photo, remember?"

"Oh . . . right."

Tempest was still smirking.

"When you expecting people to arrive? And what about Elise?" That was Aiden, relieving the pressure, to the rescue as usual.

"I told everyone four. Elise is meant to get here with Daddy and Mari-heif—Marietta—at four-thirty."

He would've remained oblivious to Tempest and Aiden's arrangement without the latter's phone. They were acting as if nothing was wrong. Expert deceivers. Yet he was unable to act the same way, always betraying his feelings.

"Looks like everything's almost done," Carl said.

"*Almost* being the key word. Can you and Shannon get the equipment from my room?"

Shannon snapped his head at Aiden, whose slight frown told him his ears hadn't stopped working. He was about to go into Tempest's room with this man he knew was leading a double life, this tower of a man with muscles who would figure out who he was—if he hadn't already.

"Everything alright, Shannon?"

"Huh?"

"The stuff in my room," she said, bobbing her head for emphasis, like she was talking to someone who had no sense. "Can you go with Carl to get them?"

"I'll go with Carl."

Aiden to the rescue again.

"Uh . . ." Tempest was lost for words suddenly.

"Alright then." Carl started out of the kitchen.

Tempest looked surprised then quickly mustered a smile. "If you . . . say so."

Shannon sighed.

Tempest stared at Carl until he was out of sight, then she ripped off a kitchen towel and took two saltfish fritters out of a large container.

"Try one," she said.

Shannon stared at her then at the fritters in the tissue. They looked and smelled tempting, but she couldn't be trusted. He couldn't eat anything she offered.

She moved them around in his face, as if to pull him out of a daydream. He sneezed. Pepper. Probably scotch bonnet.

"I'm worried it might be too peppery."

"No offence, but can I get my own one?"

She frowned like a parent about to go off on her child. "Seriously, Shannon? I used tissue, not my bare hands. My hands are clean anyway."

"Look, it's not about that. I just want a smaller piece."

She wasn't buying it.

Aiden and Carl returned with speakers.

"Where exactly do you want these, Tempest?" Carl said.

"In the corner by the TV."

Shannon and Aiden exchanged glances, Aiden's reassuring, before the muscle-bound duo disappeared into the hallway again.

"It might be too peppery for me. I mean, I did sneeze just now. If it's too peppery, I won't be able to finish it. You have one of those."

"Fine. Pick the one you want."

He took out another fritter as she took a bite of one of the fritters she'd taken out for him.

He watched her mouth and neck slowly—she was chewing and swallowing.

Unless she was a masochist or suicidal, there was nothing wrong with the fritter. He squeezed the grease out of his then took a bite. The second bite was bigger. He bit something crunchy.

Then it hit him. He fanned his tongue and blew, his whole mouth on fire.

Tempest rushed to the fridge. "It's peppery as fuck! I tried so hard not to react. I wanted you to try it." She poured out drinks for them. "I knew it was too good to be true. And look how many I've done." She motioned at the full container.

She barely made it to him before he snatched the drink from her, making it spill over. No break between gulps despite the traces of rum.

"I like my food peppery, but how many scotch bonnet peppers did you use?" Incessant blinking didn't stop his eyes watering.

She went back to the fridge and poured him some more of what tasted like rum punch.

He guzzled most of it down. "Sorry for spilling the drink on you."

"What the fuck was I thinking?" she said, looking at her watch, having downed half of her drink.

Hers was orange. His was watermelon red.

Different drinks.

She followed his gaze to her glass then raised her left eyebrow without raising her right. "I wanted orange juice."

He looked at his near-empty glass, then at Tempest again. "Surprised you didn't have any rum punch. Thought you were a punch kind of girl."

"I am. Had some earlier. Thought I'd let you try it. How was it?"

He nodded. "It's nice." His tongue was still burning.

"Want some more?"

"No!" He mustered a smile which must've looked like a grimace.

"Thought you liked it?"

"I do, but . . . it's alcohol. I'm a lightweight."

"Humph." She looked at her watch again.

Aiden and Carl came back into the kitchen. Aiden and Shannon exchanged glances.

Aiden kept staring this time, lines forming and staying put across his forehead. "Alright, Shan?"

"Yeah."

Tempest looked at her watch again, then she narrowed her eyes at Shannon. "More than three."

Carl nodded.

Aiden furrowed his brow.

"Guys, why don't you take some of those to the living room?" Tempest pointed at bottles of strong and soft drinks by the microwave.

Carl picked some up, practically chucked them in Aiden's arms, picked up some more, then led Aiden out of the kitchen.

Tempest stared at him. She banged on the counter twice out of nowhere, making him flinch.

She darted her eyes as far left as possible, towards the doorway, like she was anticipating something.

She stared at him again, stone-faced. "Sorry about the pepper. I wanted to—"

Grunts and shuffling from another room, wherever Aiden and Carl were. Probably the front room.

Tempest stiffened up, the hollow of her long neck pronounced. She pursed her lips and took a deep breath. Things were falling in the front room, amidst more grunts and thuds.

He headed for the doorway.

Tempest blocked his path.

"What's going—?"

"As I was saying, I wanted them to be peppery—"

Muffled groaning.

"But not that much." She raised her voice, her lips barely moving as usual. She could've passed for a statue.

"Don't . . . worry."

The noises were subsiding.

"They're delicious. Could've . . ." It was getting hot out of nowhere. "Could've . . . given a . . . warning . . . though."

Tempest backed away slowly, still staring, chest heaving, biting her bottom lip.

The room started moving around him, vision getting blurry. He squinted then shifted on his feet.

That sped everything up.

"Shannon?"

Deep breaths. "Yeah?"

"You look a bit strange." She was within touching distance but didn't sound like it.

The speed was becoming unbearable. He shut his eyes.

"Shannon?" Tempest sounded even more distant, as if he were underwater.

He opened his eyes. So intense. This had to be how it felt to swirl in a tornado. Tempest looked smeared like a painting, but it was her voice. Her voice echoed.

She touched him. He backed away, hit the wall hard, like he'd been thrown into it.

She was towering over him all of a sudden, looking down on him.

Everything was spinning around *and* above him. The kitchen light was weaker, blurry, looked like long tiles criss-crossing, but there was meant to be only one.

The same bunched up lights were opposite, not above.

The entire ceiling was opposite, not above.

He was on the floor. He'd dropped. Couldn't move.

Everything kept spinning, became blurrier, darker.

Tempest's black dress was sucking the kitchen light, the beige walls, her lips, and her sepia skin. Her black dress and hair came together like a giant shadow.

Everything was distorted, sucked into that blackness.

Then everything went black.

28 / Elise VI
Sick to the stomach

A chill hit Elise's exposed skin, snatching her out of her thoughts, making her pull her jacket lapel tightly around her neck. Pa had opened the door for her; he'd let the chill in. She thanked him as she stepped out of the car.

"You don't seem yourself," Ma said.

"I'm fine." Elise forced a smile. "Haven't eaten since this morning. Been saving myself for Tempest's food."

Ma averted her gaze abruptly.

Should've known better than to mention Tempest. She sighed regret then took the lead to the flat. She needed to stay ahead of her parents and not say or do anything to make them worry. Hopefully, whatever was waiting for her inside the flat wasn't anything over the top. Twenty-five wasn't as major a birthday as twenty-one or thirty.

The banner on the door was coming off. She set it straight so that *HAPPY BIRTHDAY* could be seen fully. It was quiet on the other side. Too quiet. She turned around. Her parents were struggling to maintain eye contact with her. Pa had made a point of shaving just before they'd left the house, his clean-shaven face knocking at least ten years off his age. Ma had insisted Elise help put her hair in a French roll, and her face was beat, silver drop earrings shimmering with her every movement. She usually wore hoops or studs, hardly ever anything elegant. Then there was the fact that they were dressed as if they were going to an anniversary dinner, Pa's sexy cologne flirting with Ma's sensual fragrance. She sighed then put her key in the latch.

It was obvious what was coming, but she clutched her chest when the lights came on, and party poppers popped and everyone shouted, "Surprise!"

It was like a furnace, so many people packed in, phones aimed at her, recording her as she entered. Carl stood out among the familiar faces, towering over nearly everyone.

Hands free of phones were all over her, but it was hard to tell whom they belonged to, as she was guided further into the flat like a singer making her way past fans to a stage. She caught a whiff of an assortment of cooked food when she reached the kitchen doorway. The small kitchen was packed, so she squeezed past everyone into the front room.

Music came on the instant she set foot inside. Destiny's Child. More familiar faces except for a white guy by the window. Another unknown was sitting in the black leather armchair. They were both staring at her. She was the birthday girl, so all eyes were supposed to be on her. Everyone else was staring at her as well, but theirs were friendly stares. She smiled at them then focused on to the two strangers again. The one by the window was poker-faced, and the other one was sneering at her. She was going to introduce herself, but the guy in the armchair had jarred her. She embraced those familiar to her instead: Kathleen, Aunt Verna, Uncle Frederick, Terrell, Cousin Cynthia, Orville, Charlene . . .

Countless catch-ups later, she finally made it back to the kitchen. She could've sworn it was Aiden standing in the doorway, the arch and thickness, yet neatness, of eyebrows that suggested traces of Middle Eastern or North African ancestry, eyes an unusual shade of brown. The facial hair was different—a goatee instead of a full beard. Aiden had flawless skin; this guy's skin was breaking out. Just as good-looking though. She smiled as she passed him, but his pungent cologne made her clear her throat. She was about to introduce herself to two men who looked familiar—one bald and light-skinned, the other a milk chocolate Rasta, white head wrap keeping his dreads together—and a woman in a form-fitting black onesie by the sink whose back was turned to her, when someone tapped her shoulder. As soon as she turned around, Tempest gave her a one-armed hug, a pack of plastic plates in her other hand.

"Tempest, I—"

She gasped when the woman by the sink turned around. Her heart lost control. Her legs became numb, and she went down, almost bringing Tempest with her; Tempest was strong enough to keep the both of them up.

"Remember my aunt Janice?"

She nodded as she regained her composure.

Janice almost stretched her arms out fully in front of her, then she put them back down. No hug. "Long time, Elise. I love that colour on you."

Elise looked down and tugged at her nude mini dress. Tugging quelled her shaking hands. "Thanks."

"You two have almost the same hairstyle. Bless."

Janice's smile suggested that was a compliment not meant to be shady, but she had to know it wasn't cute.

"Where's Daddy?"

"He's—"

"See me here." Pa was walking in.

That meant Ma was right behind him.

"Janice?" Nothing had ever fazed him, but he didn't know what to do with himself in this moment. He must've thought, for a split second, that his former love had risen from the dead.

Janice didn't hesitate to wrap her arms around him. Tempest put her hand on Pa's back, while Janice still had him in her clutches.

A three-person hug.

Ma just had to walk in at that very moment. She froze at the sight, wide-eyed, as if she'd caught Pa and Sylvia in the act once again, so many years later.

Elise held her ma before she could faint, like she'd almost done. "Ma, this is Jan—"

"Me know who it is," she said quickly.

Janice let go of Pa. "Hi, Marietta."

"Hello."

"Elise, excuse me. . . . Going catch up with Cynthia them." Ma hurried out of the kitchen.

"Soon come back." Pa left the kitchen, glowing. His clean-shaven face made that even more apparent.

It was hard to look at Janice properly. Might as well have been Sylvia's duppy. The thought of that identical twin thing being real, real enough for Janice to have felt when concrete and metal had ensured Sylvia's painful death. Would never forget the strange feeling that had come over her around the time God had taken Grandma, a shrill scream that felt implanted inside her brain and that only she could hear since only she'd grabbed her head, the rest of the family present looking at her as if she wasn't righted. Two generations, or nearly seventy years, separated grandmother and granddaughter.

Mere minutes separated Sylvia and Janice.

"Els, you don't look too good," Tempest said.

"I'm fine."

"You sure?"

She wasn't. Tempest had to know inviting Janice was going to mess with Ma. And Tempest was stealing her thunder; she looked *too* good.

"Els?"

"Just thinking. Can't believe you did all this." She motioned at the counter full of foil-covered dishes.

"Well, I had help." Tempest handed a bowl of something to Janice. "Auntie, take this to the living room please."

Janice finally left the kitchen.

"How did you manage to get everyone here? I haven't seen some of them in ages."

"That was Daddy's doing. By the way, let me introduce you to someone."

The Aiden lookalike put a plastic cup in the bin.

"Ethan, come here a sec. Elise, this is Aiden's brother; Ethan, this is Elise."

"Nice to meet you." He hugged her too tight, too familiarly, squeezing a moan out of her. When he let go, he continued, "You two really favour, especially with the hairstyles."

One of them would have to dye her hair or put in someone else's.

"Could say the same for you and Aiden." She turned to Tempest. "How come you know him, and I don't?"

Tempest looked away, thinking. After a moment, she made eye contact again. "I knew Aiden before you did, remember? I introduced you. . . . Come. Couple more people you should meet."

Tempest took her to the dreadlocked, chocolate and the bald, fair-skinned zaddies sitting on stools. "Elise, this is Lionel, Shannon's uncle, and . . . his . . ." Tempest grimaced.

"Partner." The bald man turned his lips up at Tempest then extended his hand to Elise. "I'm Peter."

The same men in most of the photos in Shannon's new home.

Teeth-kissing sliced through the kitchen.

It was Ethan. He poured himself another drink, his thirst suddenly returning after he'd just thrown a cup away. "Batty man dem," he muttered as he stormed to the kitchen doorway.

If they'd been in the front room, they wouldn't have heard Ethan over Christopher Martin's "Baby I Love You", but nothing went unnoticed in the kitchen. Hopefully, that moment had been an exception and neither Peter nor Lionel—

"Weh you seh?"

Hopes freaking dashed.

Ethan didn't repeat himself, just shot an evil look before he left the kitchen.

"That's why I didn't wanna chat your business," Tempest said. "Can't always be sure how people will respond, as much as society has gotten it together. Still a long way to go."

"That boy's facety," Peter said.

"Need smaddy fi claat him," Lionel said.

Tempest put a hand on Lionel's shoulder. "Sorry about that."

Elise shook off that second bump of the evening and greeted Lionel and Peter.

"Shannon speaks highly of you," Peter said.

She gushed.

"Well want beat some sense into you," Lionel said, his stare intimidating. "For being his beard."

Tempest stifled a laugh.

"Leave her alone, trouble," Peter said.

"Joke me making." Lionel winked.

"So, you're a bit of a jetsetter," Peter said.

"Sort of. Just came back from Las Vegas."

"Nice! We're going on a Caribbean cruise next year."

She gasped. "I'm jealous."

"I'm sure you've seen more places than we have."

"Maybe, but it's really more work than play. I had a little time to shop in Vegas though."

"Go to any shows or casinos?" Lionel said.

"I'm embarrassed to say, but I lost money—won't say how much—in slot machines. And I didn't catch a show this time."

"Elise," Tempest said, as Lionel was about to say something else. "Ready to eat?"

"Yes." She looked into the hallway at family and friends she'd already greeted. "I thought Shan and Aiden would've arrived by now."

Tempest had a distant countenance. "They're here . . . just don't know where. The last time I saw them—"

Carl rushed in. She hadn't noticed the scratch on his cheek earlier. It looked like it wasn't going to heal any time soon.

"Elise, I'll have to love you and leave you."

Her skin crawled to the point that she actually scratched herself. Even *like* was a stretch where Carl was concerned.

"Well, thanks for helping," she mustered, motioning at the front room, as if the wall separating it from the kitchen were transparent.

"You can't leave yet," Tempest said. "You haven't even met Daddy."

Pa came back into the kitchen with Ma, as if on cue. They frowned at Carl.

"Nice to meet you. Sorry I can't stick around to chop it up with you." Carl turned to Ma. "Or you."

Ma snarled. "Don't worry about chopping it up with me. I'm not her mother."

Tempest cut her eyes.

"Did you see what she—?"

"Ma, come with me to speak to everyone." Elise put her arms through her ma's. "You too, Pa."

"Elise, we just came from there."

"Well, let's go again. Help me find my friend and . . . my friends."

"You mean your friend and *boy*friend," Ma said.

"Especially the boyfriend." Pa just had to add that.

She smiled at Lionel and Peter as she left the kitchen.

———

"Tempest, you sure Aiden and Shan are here?" she said, passing the salad bowl to Peter. She'd arrived long ago, and still there was no sign of them.

"If they've gone," Tempest said, "they'll catch pneumonia, because their jackets and shoes are in the passage."

"Me ring Shannon few time; him nah pick up." Lionel sounded worried.

"The last time I saw them, they'd gone to get something from another room." Tempest looked at the time on her watch. "But that was ages ago."

"I'll look for them again."

"Well, you might as well start taking gifts to your room. My gift's under your bed." Tempest looked coy.

"Alright then. Be right back."

She smiled and squeezed her way past the warm bodies of her family and friends. Tempest had given her the sex toy for Christmas. Lord knew what Tempest had in store for her this time.

She reached her bedroom as Ethan came out of the bathroom.

She opened the door. Movement in her mirror-on-wheels made her jump. She looked to the right, to her bed, where the movement was coming from.

No movement now. Just two shades of brown entwined like a fallen sculpture. The bare, muscular leg of the one on top stuck out of the sheets, his foot on the hardwood floor. She clutched her chest, squinted as she stepped closer to the two of them, her head tilted to make sure the one underneath was really . . . It *was* him. The music in the front room wasn't as loud, her room being beyond Tempest's. She could hear her heartbeat in her head.

This had to be a joke. There must've been a hidden camera, maybe behind cosmetics on the dressing table or on top of the wardrobe, everyone in on it.

"Elise."

She made a noise she didn't know she could.

Aiden had called her name.

He looked down at something. She followed his gaze to a trail of underwear, jeans and shirts on the floor. He'd been stepping out to retrieve his clothes the moment she walked in on him.

On them.

Her hand went to her forehead, everything starting to make sense.

Not a simple crush on Shannon's part. The feelings were mutual.

Always had been.

Aiden had never been interested in her, yet he'd been inside her. She'd let him take her. More than once.

"Elise, it's not what it looks like." That was Shannon.

Light-headed, too much going on to speak, legs weak, she staggered backwards into something which darted past her.

It wasn't just a thing. It was Ethan.

"Aiden, what the fuck?" Ethan said.

Aiden moved then froze, pubic hair exposed. It looked frosted, like . . . She covered her mouth with a trembling hand as she retched, muffling her wails. Her head was shaking like a driller, tickling tears zig-zagging down her cheeks.

"Aiden!"

"Ain't what it looks like!"

Shannon moved from under Aiden, pulling the duvet. Aiden pulled it too, exposed more than before. His penis wasn't flaccid.

The two of them had just . . . in her bed.

Shannon got out of the bed from the other side, abandoning the sheets, flashing his own semi-erection then bare backside before crouching down.

Ethan punched Aiden out of nowhere, sent him slamming, heavy penis swinging, onto the bed. Ethan straddled Aiden and kept on punching. Shannon grabbed Ethan, pulled at his clothes to get him off Aiden.

Off his man.

The three of them punched and kicked, one fully clothed, the other two naked.

She screamed into her hand.

"Elise— Oh my God!" Tempest said.

"Tempest! You—"

Ethan cut Aiden off with another punch.

"The drink. . . . *You* did this!" Shannon said through gritted teeth, pointing at Tempest.

"I did what?"

"Elise, listen—"

Ethan punched Aiden again. Aiden fell to the floor. Ethan mounted him, unrelenting in his attack. Aiden punched back. Shannon joined in again, grabbed Ethan from behind. Ethan pushed Shannon into the dressing table.

"You're fucking naked!" Tempest shouted.

Shannon, clutching his penis, got in Tempest's face, his eyes wild. "You did this. You bitch!" He grabbed her half-fringe and pulled it.

"Get the fuck off me!" Tempest thumped, thumped, thumped Shannon until he let go.

Shannon backhanded Tempest, making her hurl into Elise.

"What the hell?" Peter burst into the room, Lionel right behind.

Tempest rained down windmill blows on Shannon before Lionel separated them.

"Shannon, weh di bloodclaat . . . Weh yuh clothes deh, and—?" Lionel spotted something.

Elise followed his gaze, squinted . . . come on Shannon's skin as well.

"So, you're a . . . fucking . . . batty man?" Ethan said, spraying bloody saliva as he wrestled Aiden.

Ashley Joel Osma

The dressing table chair had toppled over, cosmetics were scattered on the floor, and the bed was out of position, sheets messed up.

"That's why . . . nobody could find . . . you two . . . 'cause you . . . were fucking!" Ethan said.

Those words . . . out of someone else's mouth. Confirmation. She tugged at her dress as she staggered backwards into her wardrobe.

Lionel shook his head at her then cut his eyes up and down the nude lovers. "Crosses!"

Her bedroom was suddenly packed, like the party had moved there.

"Elise, I'm so sorry." Tempest's lipstick was smeared. She put her arm around Elise and took her out of the room, away from the fistfight-turned-cussing-match.

The music had stopped at some point.

Ma approached, met her and Tempest in the passage, amidst grunts and hurled curse words and threats from the bedroom. "Darling, what happened?"

"I . . . they . . ." She squeezed her eyes shut and heaved.

"Weh yuh do?"

She opened her eyes. Ma was snarling . . . at Tempest.

"You deaf, bitch?"

"What did you call me?"

"Bitch!" Ma shouldered her way between them.

"Marietta, don't talk to my pickney like that," Pa said, approaching them.

"Your pickney? You say that like she's the only pickney you have."

Pa waved Ma off.

Ma cut her eyes at Pa then pulled Elise and Tempest further away from the commotion, just past Tempest's bedroom doorway.

"Now tell me weh yuh do."

"Get off me!" Tempest snatched her arm out of Ma's grip.

Ma kissed her teeth. "Answer me, gyal!"

"Listen, you stupid bitch, I—"

It happened so quickly. A box so hard that even people witnessing it grunted as loud as Tempest.

It was as if she were suddenly separated from everyone by sound-proof glass, her ma grimacing like one box wasn't good enough; Tempest touching her lip, her hair messed up from being boxed twice, boxed *hard* both times, the sight of her blood turning her expression sinister. Mouths were moving, but there was hardly any sound. Ma's and Tempest's glares were doing all the talking.

Then a shriek seemed to make her hearing return. Tempest charged at Ma, grabbed her French roll and hauled her to the floor.

She shut her eyes to it all, stomach in knots.

Cursing from somewhere else joined the new commotion. She opened her eyes again. Peter was pulling Ethan, face bloody, out of her bedroom, just as Tempest and Ma were clawing and kicking at the space between them, Pa holding Tempest back, and Orville and Uncle Frederick restraining Ma. Separation didn't stop the frantic legs, Ma's tights and Tempest's bare legs exposed.

She turned away, needed to get out of there. Her legs were weak, moving without direction. She stumbled into the passage table. Hands were soon on her, keeping her up.

Janice emerged from the kitchen, a scowl quickly forming on her face as she looked towards the commotion.

"She hurt . . . my pickney! . . . I know it!"

"Is that Marietta?" Janice said.

"Shut you rahtidclaat mouth!"

"So, it's my *fault . . . Aiden and Shannon . . . are fucking?"*

Confirmation again.

Aunt Verna moved in front of her, among those supporting her. Her head became a magnet to her aunt's bosom. Being comforted . . . that was confirmation too.

Ethan cussing Aiden from the open flat door—faggot this, batty boy that—confirmation.

So much confirmation that she'd given her heart and her body to the wrong guy. Yet again.

Charlene stroked her hair as Aunt Verna dabbed her face with tissue.

"Just breathe. Verna, let's get her outside."

"Come on, baby."

"What's going on?"

"Terrell, open the door for us. The poor child needs air."

Someone was in the way despite Charlene saying, "Excuse me, excuse me, excuse me, excuse me."

The mystery guy who'd looked at her funny . . . The other mystery guy next to him . . . They were the ones blocking the way.

"Marvin, allow it," the white one said.

Marvin kissed his teeth at the white guy. "Elise—"

"Not now, young man," Aunt Verna said. "You need—"

"Where's Shannon?" Marvin was staring her down.

"Party's over. Everyone's leaving." Terrell put his hand on Marvin's shoulder.

"If you don't get your fucking hand—"

"Marvin, let's just go!" Marvin's friend started pulling at him.

"Tell Shannon I know what he did, him and his pussyhole man. I'm coming for them."

This Marvin, someone she didn't know, knew more about Aiden and Shannon than she did, knew they were seeing each other.

Another vomiting episode had threatened to return at Ma and Pa's house, just settling as it waited for the slightest disturbance. Everything crashing down in this way was the height of disaster; the vomiting was returning with a vengeance.

"Come on, Marvin!"

Marvin followed his friend out of the flat, but something made them pause. They were still in her way. She summoned enough strength to look where they were looking—Ethan, face bloodied and chest heaving, gritting his teeth at Peter, who was trying to calm him down.

"Ain't him," the friend said. "It ain't."

Their quick footsteps faded along the corridor then down the stairs.

Ethan recounted, every other word a curse word, what he'd walked in on for everyone, near and far, to hear.

"Elise, is that what happened?" Terrell said, his face screwed up.

She barely looked at him, barely looked at anyone or anything, dizziness intensifying, sickness working its way upwards from her stomach.

"Elise!" Shannon scrambled to her, buckling his belt, shirt buttons in the wrong holes.

"Stay . . . away . . . " She took quick breaths through pursed lips as she fanned herself.

"Let me explain what—"

Terrell stepped between them, guarding her. The swimming was getting worse. She closed her eyes as she heard Charlene order Shannon to leave.

"Shannon, make we gwaan!"

She barely opened her eyes. Through slits, she recognized Lionel's head wrap, his dreads sprouting out of it. He was approaching, carrying two jackets and four shoes.

"Uncle Li—"

"No!" Lionel turned to Terrell. "Excuse me."

Terrell sized Lionel up.

"Move, nuh man!"

Terrell kissed his teeth then scowled beyond Lionel and Shannon.

People were holding Pa back, while others pulled Aiden away from him. Aiden was shirtless, bleeding from the mouth and nose.

No amount of pain he was suffering could ever compare to hers.

He rushed to her. "Elise, I'm telling you—"

"Come on, Aiden." Lionel pulled him to the door. "Peter, make sure you keep *him*"—he jabbed his finger at Ethan, hidden from view out the door—"away from his brother."

"Don't touch me, you fucking fag!"

Lionel strode out the door one moment; the next, *"Let go of my fucking neck!"* came out of Ethan's mouth with difficulty before Peter said, *"Lionel, do, nuh kill him!"*

Aiden was blocking the doorway. Terrell proceeded to shut the door, forcing Aiden out. Lionel's booming *"Move to raasclaat!"* was the last thing she heard from the other side of the door before Terrell finally shut it.

"Good. They're gone." Aunt Verna said.

She was going to drop any moment. "I need . . ." She put her hand over her mouth, leaned against the table as Charlene and Aunt Verna held her. The build-up had reached her chest. She braced herself.

"Verna, you go home. I'll stay with her," Ma said. Her make-up and French roll were messed up, made her look like a madwoman. She'd lost an earring too.

"You sure, Marietta?"

"Marietta, gwaan with Verna!"

"Oliver, me nah leave!"

"Get out, bitch!" Tempest said.

Ma hurled curse words as she charged at Tempest, throwing heavy windmill blows. Tempest unleashed windmill hits right back before Pa stepped between the two of them, taking brutal blows not meant for him.

She retched, turned her head away.

"Tempest, grab your coat," Janice said. "You're coming with me."

"This is *my* flat and *my* sister!"

"I won't tell you again!"

"But someone needs to be with Elise."

"I'll stay with her." Pa said. "Tempest, you go with your aunt. Marietta, go with your sister."

"Me nah leave me pickney."

Pa shook his head then fumbled in his pockets. He took out the car keys and chucked them at Ma. "Go to the car! Come back when you calm down."

"Me'll come with you, Marietta," Aunt Verna said.

"Elise." Tempest said, lip busted, dress ripped to reveal her black bra, Pa gripping her arm. "I'm sorry for—"

"Need the . . . bathroom." She broke free of the supportive hands on her arms and shoulders, zig-zagged to the bathroom, lifted the toilet seat, kneeled down as if she desperately needed to send a prayer, and gave into that feeling that had spread from her stomach to her throat. She gripped the toilet bowl, and within moments, someone rubbed her back as she vomited.

29 / Aiden VII
Unfinished business

Ethan was lucky. Wasn't man enough to wait until Aiden had clothes on. Aiden owed him a claat for mashing up his ribs and face, keeping him from opening his left eye properly. He'd seen his reflection. Looked as bad as he was hurting. And those other fuckers, even Elise's dad . . . Punk bitches, the lot of them.

"So, *nothing* happened between the two of you?" Peter said, leaning forward in the armchair closest to the back door.

"It was all Tempest," Shan said, sitting in the other armchair, across the room from Peter.

"And Carl," Aiden added, hardly moving his lips because of the pain.

Lionel came back to the front room and handed him a bag of ice. He put it against his eye, flinched.

"But we see unu naked," Lionel said.

"And what about the come?" Peter said.

If anyone said that one more time . . . "It wasn't come."

"So, absolutely nothing happened?"

"Nothing," Shan said.

"No sex of any kind?"

"No."

"No touching?"

He made eye contact with Shan, letting the seconds pass after Peter's last question. Shan was flustered.

"Did unu touch?"

"Not really."

Lionel and Peter frowned at each other.

"Then you mean *yes*," Peter said.

"But we didn't mean to," Shan said.

"When we woke up . . ."

Shan's cue to say the rest—all he did was shuffle in his seat.

"Yes?"

Shan still wouldn't say shit.

"Tempest and Carl . . . put us like that. When I woke up, I was confused. Thought I was dreaming."

Shan sighed. "Me too, at first. That's why . . ."

"Go on, Shannon."

Shan grimaced. "That's why we *could've* touched each other up."

Peter and Lionel raised eyebrows at each other, then Peter scratched his bald head. "But what about the come on your bodies?"

"It wasn't come!" Pain radiated around his mouth.

"Calm down, Aiden. It's just that considering the situation, how would either of you know that it *wasn't* your come?"

He took the bag away from his eye, flinched when he put it close to his mouth.

"I mean, while you were unconscious you could've had a wet dream. In that case, you couldn't have helped climaxing."

There was no wet dream, but being on top of Shan like that, their dicks touching and growing against each other . . . he could've come.

"Carl and Tempest did something . . . made something that looked like come. Nothing else makes sense," Shan said.

"So, you touched each other. Unintentionally. But I'm gonna ask you two one more time—did you do *anything* else?"

"For the last time, Peter, no."

"No intercourse?"

Shan flinched. "No."

"No oral?"

"No."

"Frot?"

"Maybe a little. Couldn't help it."

"No kissing?"

He paused. So did Shannon.

Peter and Lionel *humphed*.

Hard to piece everything together. The pain wasn't helping. All he knew was that he'd gone from fighting Carl, then Carl *and* Tempest, to feeling something prick his neck before being on top of Shan, who was asleep and stirring. He'd been dying to be that close to Shan. That kind of heaven must've been a dream. He'd had Shan dreams before, never knowing when, or if, he would ever have them again. He had to take advantage before waking up.

In the dream, he kissed Shan awake, went crazy with his tongue. Would've been cool if Shan had rejected him because it was a dream and at least he managed to give Shannon his tongue.

But Shannon didn't stop it. He gave tongue back, lick for lick. Maybe he'd been dreaming too, wherever he was in the real world, desperate to suck Aiden's tongue before waking up.

Then Shan ripped his tongue from Aiden's out of nowhere. Something was off, from the distant Spice song beating out conversations, to the room they were in. And then the sting in his neck that wouldn't go away. The moment he realised he hadn't dreamed shit.

He'd been on top of Shan, the two of them naked, kissing, hard, in some room he didn't recognize until he noticed the mirror-on-wheels.

Elise just had to walk in the moment he stepped out of the bed to get his clothes, no memory of anything between the struggle with Carl and waking up naked with Shan, just before the kiss.

Couldn't remember anything because he'd been unconscious.

The sting in his neck . . . itchy where it stung. He scratched. That part of his skin started peeling. He pulled and pulled, till skin came off completely.

"Weh dat plaster come from?"

Plaster, not skin. He turned it around. A spot of blood on the white part.

An injection.

The fucker had injected him with something.

"Never seen a plaster that matches brown skin tone before," Peter said.

Lionel took the plaster from Aiden, put it against Aiden's neck. "Brown, but not Aiden's shade of brown."

"Can't tell from here." Peter was squinting.

"More Shannon's complexion."

Shannon got up, approached Lionel.

"What is it, Shan?"

Shan took the plaster, put it against his skin.

"Me nuh tell yuh! It match him skin more than fi Aiden."

Peter took the plaster from Shannon for a closer look. "You're right. The plaster . . . it's a russet brown . . . like Shannon's skin. Aiden's skin tone is more sepia."

Shannon shook his head. "No wonder."

"No wonder what?"

"I wasn't meant to stay in the kitchen with Tempest. That's why she was surprised when Carl agreed to go with Aiden. I was meant to go with Carl so that he could inject *me*. I'm not built like him or Aiden. I would've been easier to subdue."

Tempest and Carl had set them up real good. Would've been worse if Elise had walked in during the tongue-kissing. That would've been hard to explain. But her walking in on them while they were still naked . . . Tempest must've told her to go to her room, timed it perfectly.

The look on Elise's face . . . Ethan's too . . .

He'd done everything the bitch had demanded. His secret should've been safe with her, but it wasn't. Maybe it never was. She'd been fucking him over all along.

Naked. In front of Elise, Ethan, all those people. Left eye hard to keep open, swollen cheek, busted lip, nose feeling like it was about to fall off. He let the bitch reduce him to *this*.

"We believe you," Lionel said. "But me confuse to backside."

"Yeah. Why would Tempest do that?"

"Because she's a twisted bitch." Shan cut his eyes like he was watching everything play out on the massive flatscreen swallowing the front room. "It's got something to do with her mum's death. She blames Elise for it." He shook his head. "Can't believe I let her do something I promised I'd never let her do."

"What's that?" Peter said.

"Get the better of me. The bitch is really smart. The fritters, the drink . . . she planned it all. She *drugged* me." Shan shook his head.

"I know Tempest is a piece of work, but did you have to go along with it, Aiden?" Peter said.

"Look at my face."

Peter nodded. "That boy . . . I swear I was on the verge of . . ." Peter grimaced and punched his palm to fill in the blank.

"Shannon, make you nuh tell Elise wha'gwaan?"

Shannon looked at Aiden, cut his eyes as he looked away, then said, "That one next to you convinced me to tell her *after* her birthday."

"I'm in fucking agony right now, so don't—"

"Alright, alright, Aiden," Lionel said.

Nothing was said for a while, then lines formed in Shannon's forehead. There was something in the distance, beyond the cabinet full of pictures of Lionel and Peter, only he could see.

"Shannon, ah wah?" Lionel said.

"She's been up to no good for a while, right?"

"Yeah," Aiden said.

"We haven't known each other that long, so that stunt of hers must've just been planned."

He stared ahead at Jamaica-shaped clock, African art hanging either side of it, until they became a blur.

"Think about it, Aiden. She wanted us there early. . . . What if she *did* know I knew what was going on?"

"You were set up, but . . ."

"But what, Uncle Lionel?"

"You both thought you were dreaming?"

"Yes."

"Yeah."

"Dream or no dream, you kissed each other, made each other hard . . ."

His dick was swelling.

Shannon got up.

"Shannon, where you going?" Peter said.

"Getting my phone. I need to speak to Elise."

"No, no, no, no, no," Peter wagged his finger.

"For all we know, Tempest could have a lot worse in store. Elise isn't safe."

Lionel dashed to the doorway, blocked Shan's path. "The girl's in shock, feels betrayed. If you ring her, she probably nah go answer."

Aiden got up, clutching his sore ribs. "Never imagined Tempest would do shit like this, as long as I did what she wanted. She has no limits."

Lionel stood there, in Shannon's way, contemplating. "Fine. Phone her."

Once Lionel let Shannon pass, he motioned for Aiden to sit back down, sat next to him then said, "You outta order."

"What?"

"You hear weh me seh."

"We were set up!"

"Me know, but ah nuh that me mean. You and her did *deh*."

"You deceived her, made her think whatever feelings she had— or has—for you were mutual," Peter said.

The two of them had him fucked up. *He'd* been set up. *His* life was fucked-up now. Life had already been fucked-up. Now it was fucking fucked-up. His bloodclaat brother and old dude fucked his face up. The sooner he got home, the better—so that he could fuck Ethan up. Elise though . . . Nothing but fucked-up-ness for everyone—except for fucking Tempest and Carl.

"I'm not trying to make you feel any worse."

Jamaican patois gone just like that.

"Yes, me deh ah England long enough fi know how fi chat good." Lionel kissed his teeth to top it off.

Peter shook his head, smiling.

"Look," Lionel continued. "I've hurt some women, too."

Aiden narrowed his eyes.

"Me did always like man, but me did have few girlfrien'. Me take them virginity and— Ah wah?"

He rested his elbow on his thigh and his chin in the palm of his hand.

"What is it, Aiden?" Peter said.

He looked up, at Lionel, then at Peter, then at Lionel again. He clenched his jaw. "I was her first."

Lionel leaned away, looking at him with his head bent and eyes almost disappearing up his head. Peter kissed his teeth.

Shannon stormed back in, making leaves of plants flanking the doorway shake. "No answer. I tried three times. The first two times, it just rang, but it went straight to voicemail the last time. I left a message. She probably won't listen."

"We should go over there."

"Not a good idea, Aiden." Peter said. "If she's not picking up the phone, I doubt she wants to see you."

"We can't let them get away with it."

"You need to rest, heal up. Stay here if you want. That's a sofa bed you're on," Peter said.

"Thanks, but I have to go home."

"Suppose you and that bwoi kill each other?"

"I *wanna* kill him."

"Look at you. You're in no fit state to fight."

"I've got to go." He got up.

Lionel held his shoulder firmly. "Mind you make me claat you. And nuh look pon me like that. You young and big and strong, but me big and strong and not righted."

"Look, I won't do shit to him."

"You sure you want your grandparents to see you like that?"

"Ethan don't look good either, but he's probably home. My grandfolks can handle seeing me like this."

His grandfolks.

Ethan knew. He was no snitch, but they would see something was off. Aiden would have to tell them. There was nothing to tell anyway. He'd been set up.

But then he would have to tell them *everything*.

He rang the house.

"Good evening," Grandma said, starting deep, ending high.

He opened his mouth. No words, just exhales that sounded like quiet burps.

"Hello?" she said, deeply.

He swallowed. "It's me, Grandma."

"Aiden? Weh you deh? You alright? Ah wah do Ethan? Lord Jesus, him nah tell we how him mouth mash up so. Make the two of unu nuh come home one time?"

He took a deep breath, crackling the connection.

"I'm just . . . I'll be home soon."

Shan looked at him with wide eyes, asking if he was sure.

"Alright. Me'll dish out food fi you, leave it in—"

"Don't, Grandma. I ain't hungry."

"Yuh eat something?"

"Yeah. Belly full," he lied.

"Fine. See you soon."

"Bye, Grandma."

"What did she say?" Shan said. "How did she sound?"

"She's fine, but I've got to go." He writhed until Lionel let him go.

"How you ah go reach yuh yard?"

"I'll drive."

"That bwoi really beat all the sense outta yuh. Your face mash up. Your eye swell up. Yuh can't drive."

"Lionel's right. I'll drop you in your car, and Lionel and Shannon will follow in our car."

"Aiden, are you sure you want to be around Ethan?"

Shan still gave a shit about him.

"Ethan can't mash ants."

"But look what he did to you." Shan pointed at his face.

"And your brother's really strong. You don't know what it took to get him off you," Peter said.

Enough of the watch-out-for-Ethan shit. "He surprised me. I was naked. Cunt got lucky."

"What if he tells your grandparents?" Peter said.

He shrugged his shoulders. "At the end of the day, I know what happened. He don't."

Lionel sighed. "We better get going then."

———

ight was flickering in the bay window next to the front door of his house. Someone was messing with the net curtains. Ethan showed his face. Must've heard the cars pulling up. The look he was giving, he was begging to lose some teeth. He closed the net curtains like he was trying to rip them off.

"Aiden, I really don't like this," Peter said, getting out of the driver's side. "That boy's a homophobe."

"I can handle him."

Aiden hugged and thanked Peter and Lionel.

He paused.

He'd just hugged man without first checking to see who was watching.

Shan was inches away. Maybe waking up naked, dick on dick, was enough closeness for one day. They made eye contact, Shan blinking constantly, in his usual fight to keep his composure, no end to the fog from his breathing. They'd really seen each other naked. They'd been set up, but if nothing happened between them ever again, at least they'd been close like that.

Throat-clearing.

It was Lionel.

Aiden shuffled. "Catch you later, Shan."

Shan broke the eye contact—probably the longest he'd ever held it with him—and started playing with one of his jacket buttons, then he wrapped his arms around Aiden out of nowhere. Aiden exhaled long and hard, from the shock and the pain, but squeezed Shan anyway, like he would never see him again. Shan moaned.

Shan, Peter and Lionel waited inside Lionel's double-parked, grey Kia Sportage as Aiden manoeuvred past the plants then opened the front door and stepped inside the house.

"God in heaven!" Grandma said when she met him in the passage. She touched all over his battered face.

Ethan emerged from the front room, mouth busted, left eye swollen and red where it should've been white. "I did it."

Grandma clutched her chest. "Jesus have mercy! Why?"

He scowled at Ethan. "Because he's desperate for a claat."

"Let's go, you prick!"

"That whole thi—" Shit, the pain. He'd moved his mouth too much. "I was set up."

"The two of unu, stop it! Ethan, why you beat your brother so?"

"Ain't my brother." Ethan was snarling.

Aiden clenched his fists, keys digging into his hand. "Your ears too hard." He chucked the keys at Ethan, aiming for his face.

Ethan stumbled as he dodged.

"Wah wrong with unu?" Granddad came out of the front room. "Stop the foolishness."

Granddad slammed his forearm into Ethan's as Ethan threw the keys back at Aiden. The keys missed, landing inches from Aiden's feet.

"It was a set up!" Moved his mouth too much a-fucking-gain.

"I know what I saw. Always wondered about you anyway."

He held Ethan's gaze. "What?"

"Ethan, you come back in here with me!" Granddad said, motioning at the front room as he grabbed Ethan by the arm. "Cora, take Aiden to the kitchen."

"No, Grandma, don't. I have to go."

"Go? Go where?"

"Su'um I need to sort out."

"You soon come back?"

"Yeah." He clutched his ribs as he picked up his keys and went through the front door before his grandfolks could stop him.

His heart plummeted when he reached the gate—the Kia Sportage hadn't gone.

Lionel wound his window down as the car rolled to a stop. "Wha'gwaan?"

"Um . . ."

Lionel's eyes went to the car keys in Aiden's hand, then he screwed up his face before thumping the dashboard. "Aiden, your ears too hard!"

He grimaced through the pain as he rushed to his car. He unlocked it, adrenalin beating the pain, then got in. By the time he turned on the ignition, Peter was standing in front of the bonnet, arms folded.

Lionel knocked on the window. Aiden rolled it down. He and Lionel had a staring contest. Didn't take long for the mad Rasta to win.

"He really wants another claat, Lionel."

He beeped at Peter. "Move out the way, man!"

"Coo yah!" Lionel said.

Aiden kissed his teeth.

Shan emerged next to Lionel. "I wish I'd followed my mind and told Elise everything ages ago. If I'd done that . . ."

Lionel looked at Shan then Peter, who shrugged his shoulders.

"Aiden and I want to see Elise *now*, not later, before Tempest does anything else."

Lionel sighed. "Cho! Come outta the car, Aiden."

"No!"

"Come out. All ah we going deal with the shithouse gyal."

30 / Tempest VII
Auntie's intuition

Elise's humiliation was supposed to be a victory, but Tempest couldn't celebrate. Lip busted, hair messed up and dress ripped, she was sitting at the kitchen table in her childhood home, her daddy's house, a house she couldn't stand being in because it also belonged to Mari-heifer, and all she wanted to do was pick up where she'd left off at the flat—fuck the heifer up.

Mari-heifer was glaring back at her, nostrils flared, hair fucked-up, just as eager for round two, glass of apple juice in front of her hardly touched. Tempest's glass of water was about three-quarters full.

Daddy was to Tempest's left, between them, running his fingers up and down the neck of a Heineken bottle. Auntie Janice was to her right, a mug of peppermint tea in front of her.

No one had anything to say. They'd all been sitting at the table long enough for Tempest's batty to hurt. Everything else spoke: sips, swigs and gulps; the tick-tocking clock with various hot beverages representing the hours of the day; the rain pounding the window and back door; the toilet where Elise had been sobbing and vomiting; and the fucking phone making noise in Elise's handbag, which was hanging over the back of the chair Tempest was sitting on, her back to the door.

The vomiting had stopped and recently started again, Elise's regurgitations making everyone cringe. Hard to tell if tampering with Elise's food had finally kicked in or whether the sight she'd walked in on had caused the vomiting. The only other possibility . . . Seemed too early to be that.

Auntie Janice was staring at Tempest like she was eager to tell her something in private. Tempest drank some more water, an excuse to stop staring back.

Shannon wasn't meant to be a factor. He'd actually been growing on her—until he put his hands on her. He was lucky his batty, fake Rasta uncle stepped in. Served Shannon right for pretending to be Aiden on the phone. They were going to snitch on her to Elise. She couldn't go down without taking them with her. Aiden and Elise could've done with more time, more fucking, to increase the chances. Only time would tell.

It would've been so easy for Elise to walk in on Shannon and Aiden when they'd already woken up, put their clothes on and wiped the faux-come off. Carl had been right about the timing. Elise had been humiliated, on her birthday at that. Everyone knew her business. Had to come up with an explanation for Daddy before Aiden and Shannon got to Elise. They were probably trying to call her right now. Elise's phone needed to disappear, like her passport.

Phone or no phone, those pricks knew how to get to the flat, were bound to go back. Elise needed to put on that cheap Virgin Atlantic uniform come Monday morning. More time for Tempest to figure shit out that way and be convinced her mission had been completely accomplished. If the last part of the plan worked, Elise finding out would be no big deal. Same for Daddy.

That was a big *if*.

She jumped out of her thoughts when Mari-heifer got up. Daddy asked the heifer where she was going. She ignored him, kept moving, towards Tempest, staring at her. Auntie Janice shuffled then drew her chair out.

"Stay in your seat, Auntie."

Auntie Janice didn't get up, but she didn't draw her chair back in.

Tempest tightened her grip around the heavy glass of water, ready to smash it into Mari-heifer's cheekbone.

The bitch stopped right in front of her, her frame sucking the light. Bashing her face in for Daddy to see wasn't ideal, but there was no other option. She had to do it before she ended up shattering the glass with her tight grip.

She shut her eyes, bracing herself for what she was about to do then lifted the glass off the table.

"I just wanted to— Gimme your hand."

She opened her eyes.

"Please, Tempest, your hand."

She looked at her daddy. His expression mirrored what she was feeling. She turned to her aunt, who raised her eyebrows.

"I'm serious." Mari-heifer must've been reading everyone's minds. "Give me your hand, Tempest."

"Give *you* . . . *my* hand?"

"Yes."

"Bitch, please!"

Daddy rubbed his face in one fell swoop.

"Tempest!" Her aunt slapped her hand. "Tell her you didn't mean that."

"Oh, I meant it, Auntie. I'm waiting on this bitch to—"

"Tempest!"

"It's fine, Oliver. She nuh haffi gimme her hand if she nuh want to. Me'll just come out with it." Mari-heifer looked at her again, her expression soft. A first. "It was—this is hard for me, but me just going say it. I . . . Lord have mercy—" She clutched her chest.

"Marietta?"

"It's alright, Oliver." Mari-heifer took a deep breath and stood up straight. "I was wrong to . . ." She squeezed her eyes shut, screwed up her face as if water had been thrown in it. "I shouldn't have blamed you earlier."

Daddy exhaled like it was his first breath in years. Auntie Janice put a hand over her mouth.

"What—?" Tempest cleared her tight throat then put the glass down and let it go. "What—?" Still croaky.

"You heard."

She'd been waiting for a reason to maim the heifer. This was an unexpected turn, after a lifetime of being disrespected and despised, after all the pain and humiliation, after years of hating the woman. Couldn't turn off the hate just like that. Couldn't be nice back. Didn't want to be nice. Wanted to have a reason to keep hating her.

"Because of you, Elise had a wonderful birthday. The food, the decorations, the planning . . . everything. I'm just sorry those boys ruined it." Mari-heifer touched her shoulder. "Thank you."

She couldn't let Mari-heifer see her cry. She clenched her eyes shut, womaned the fuck up, opened her eyes, made eye contact with her daddy again. He was catching flies, his eyes glistening. He closed his mouth when he realised it was open, and he wiped his eye corners with his fingers, his lips twitching.

"There's something I don't understand," Marietta said.

"What?" Tempest said.

Marietta stared her dead in her eyes, as she let the question linger before finally saying, "Are they that stupid?"

"Who?"

"Those boys."

"What do you mean?"

Marietta brought a finger to her mouth. "Are they so fool that they would do their business in Elise's bed, on her birthday?" She narrowed her eyes.

Tempest narrowed her eyes back.

Marietta started sneering.

Then it hit her.

The apology . . . too good to be fucking true. Just an act. The bitch had tricked her.

The way she was staring at her was nothing new. It was the same look she'd given her when she'd caught her playing with Elise's dolls. "Play with the dolls your nasty mother give you, you likkle wretch," her mum's sorry replacement had said. Marietta had always waited for her to fuck up, like the time she'd figured out she'd started fucking early. Fucking bitch couldn't wait to tell Daddy.

"Tempest, why would they be so stupid?" Marietta—no—Mari-*heifer* said.

"What the hell is this?"

"Watch your mouth."

She cut her eyes, nearly cussed off her father.

"Your ears hard, likkle girl?" Mari-heifer leaned over her.

Unless she could ram into the fat heifer like a bull, she was trapped. She knocked her knuckles against something. The glass. She wrapped her fingers around it again.

"Marietta—"

"Me not going do anything, Janice," Mari-heifer blindly pointed at Auntie Janice. "Just tell me, Tempest, something else ah gwaan?"

"I think there's something going on with your medication. Either you need to take more, or less."

Mari-heifer waved off that shade as if she'd heard worse.

"You must have amnesia."

"Gyal, don't ramp with me. Why would they . . . ?"

"Fuck in your daughter's bedroom, the same room Elise probably let one of them fuck her in?"

Mari-heifer buckled for an instant, those words punches to her gut.

"Watch it, Tempest!"

"No, Daddy, I won't! You know what she's put me through." *All because Mum was a better woman than she could ever be.*

It took everything to keep from adding that.

"My sister is crushed that two people she loved and trusted betrayed her, and you're blaming me?"

"It nuh make sense. Me *know* you had something to do with it."

"Fine, pretend I'm Aiden. Pretend I'm the one who took Elise's virginity and cheated on her with Shannon."

Mari-heifer clutched her chest, her face tight.

Yes, bitch, your daughter got fucked before marriage. She's fast like me.

A piss-take not knowing whether Elise's pre-marital sins ended there.

Something clicked. They all snapped their heads at the doorway, as if nothing had happened since the last time Elise had gone to the toilet. Mari-heifer rushed to meet Elise at the door. Tempest and her daddy made their chair legs scream against the tiles and scrambled behind.

"My poor child!" Mari-heifer looked at Elise as if she were reunited with her after years apart, not recognizing this version of Elise, this impostor.

Elise looked like shit, her upsweep an ugly downsweep, her make-up streaked, and her bland, nude dress creased all over. She turned her head gingerly in Daddy's direction, like moving it was painful, eyes vacant.

Mari-heifer rubbed Elise's back as she sat her down in the nearest empty seat, the one that Tempest had been sitting on, Tempest's phone right in front.

The thought of Mari-heifer being in the same state, pregnant belly in tow, when she'd found out that her rival had had her husband's first child. The mother of Daddy's first-born was more worthy of being Mrs Oliver Cunningham. The wrong woman was dead. For that, Elise could fuck herself.

"We need to call Virgin," Daddy said.

"Call . . . Virgin?"

"They need to know you can't travel."

Elise sprang to life suddenly. "I have to go."

"Not in this state," Mari-heifer said.

"I have to. . . . That passport mess . . . they weren't happy."

"But you're not well," Tempest said. "The vomiting, the betrayal. We're talking about a physical sickness *and* an emotional sickness."

"I'll feel better in the morning. I just need to rest—"

A phone started vibrating. It was coming from Elise's handbag. Now that she was sitting on the chair her handbag was hanging on, her phone was within reach. Elise looked at everyone like she needed permission to answer.

"Maybe it's someone else calling you."

Auntie Janice needed to shut the hell up.

Elise took her phone out of her bag. She braced herself, looked at the screen, snarled then dropped the phone on the table as if it had burned her.

Tempest grabbed the phone and looked at the screen.

Shannon Horne.

She answered. "Shannon, she doesn't want to speak to you."

"Gimme the phone!" Daddy stretched his arm to take the phone from her.

She distanced herself from him.

"Answer the door. We know you're there."

She yelped, covered her mouth immediately.

"Hurry up, bitch!"

She was about to peep out of the kitchen to the front door when she remembered where she was and where she was not.

"Look, *bitch*, you've fucked up. She's done with you—"

"Elise! Elise!"

She moved the phone from her ear and cut off Shannon's shouts with a jab.

"What the brute haffi say for himself?" Daddy said.

"Looks like they're back at our place. He thinks we're there and won't open the door."

The phone rang again. It was Shannon. Rejected. So many fucking alerts. Must've been messages from Shannon and Aiden. Didn't have to open them to know what was in them.

"Why won't they stop ringing me?"

"Maybe you should hear what they have to say for themselves," Mari-heifer said.

"What?" Tempest said too quickly.

Mari-heifer gave her a facety look. "Don't you think they owe her an explanation?"

She had to watch her words, "Yes . . . but not now. Elise needs to . . . She can't face them yet."

"This might help her get to that place. She needs closure." Mari-heifer was enjoying this.

So determined to get Shannon and Aiden that she didn't think hard enough to make sure nothing could be traced back to her. Aiden wasn't supposed to know anything about her mum's death. Shannon wasn't meant to know shit. Everything coming out wasn't meant to be a bad thing, was meant to happen *after* she got Elise in the worst way. Maybe she had, but she didn't fucking know. Had always thought she could handle Daddy's anger.

If the main thing didn't work out and Daddy found out everything that had happened was her doing . . .

It had to work out. She would see months from now, see it was all worth it.

"You're right, Ma. They owe me." Elise motioned for the phone.

Tempest gripped it as if it were a stack of £50 notes.

"Tempest . . . phone please."

Everything worked out.

"Give her back the phone," Mari-heifer said.

Everything worked out. It really did.

Positive affirmation wasn't fucking working, wasn't doing anything about her pounding heart and clammy hands. Sweat was tickling her face and chest, settling between her titties.

"Rest yourself first." Daddy to the rescue with something constructive.

"My phone's been making noise non-stop."

Tempest fingered her way for the power button, her eyes nowhere near the phone, and pressed and held.

"Give it to me, Tempest."

"Looks like it needs charging." She showed Elise the black screen. "Let me go upstairs and charge it for you."

"Fine."

She couldn't get out of the kitchen, with Elise's phone, any faster.

She raced up the stairs to her bedroom for the night, and shut the door and leaned against it, cussing.

She turned the phone back on.

Pattern required to unlock it. She cussed some more, close to hurling the shithouse phone to the floor.

She turned the phone back off. A Samsung lead was hanging out of Elise's overnight bag. She went to it.

Noise from downstairs halted her. She opened the door to shouting. It was Elise.

She hauled up her torn dress and raced downstairs, to the kitchen. Elise was saying something about erections.

"You really expect me to believe that my sister did all that?"

Tempest's wide eyes met Mari-heifer's suspicious gaze. Elise was holding a phone to her ear—Tempest's phone.

She grabbed the edge of the granite counter top to steady herself.

"Shannon . . . Shannon, I'm hanging up." Elise hung up. "Those two must really think I'm that stupid."

"W-what . . ." Her fucking breathing . . . "What'd he say?"

"Something about how you drugged him, and Carl injected Aiden, and the two of you stripped them naked, and—"

"*What?*" Hopefully, that reaction wasn't over the top. She drew closer to Elise and put her hand out for the phone.

"Exactly."

She shook her head, sensing Mari-heifer still staring at her. She was off her game, not ready to stare back.

"My head . . . I . . . I'm going to bed."

"I think I'll get going," Auntie Janice said once Elise left.

"I'll walk you out."

"No, Daddy, I will."

Tempest followed her aunt to the front door. When Auntie Janice opened the door, a gust of wind chucked rain at her. She cussed.

Her aunt glared at her.

"What?"

Auntie Janice peeped behind her into the house. "Pull the door in and come out here."

"It's rain—"

Her aunt pulled the door in herself and yanked her away.

"What . . . are you . . . doing?" Couldn't snatch her arm out of her aunt's grip. "My hair!"

Her aunt's face was close to hers, their exhales creating fog between them.

Auntie Janice gritted her teeth, her cigarette-blackened gums exposed. "I can't believe you."

"What you . . . talking 'bout?" She managed to free herself from her aunt and rush to the porch, out of the rain.

"Girl, you're not too old for a clap."

Auntie knew better; even she could get clapped back.

"That woman"—she jabbed her index finger into the air, pointing at the front door—"was right. Those boys nuh look 'tupid to me. It *was* you, wasn't it?"

Anyone else, and she could've lied, but this was her mum's identical twin. She couldn't take the eye contact any longer.

"God almighty, Tempest!"

"I had to."

"What else have you done?"

She looked away again.

Her aunt grabbed her by her cheekbones, fake almond nails marking skin, to make mutual eye contact again. "Tell me!"

She pushed Auntie Janice's hand away. "The less you know, the better. Even if I tell you . . ."

"My God!" Auntie Janice shook her head as she looked her up and down, then she turned away and headed to the gate.

She scurried after her aunt, withstanding the rain, so cold that her dress might as well have been made of cling film.

When Auntie Janice stopped, hand on the open iron gate, and turned to face her, Tempest whispered, "What happened to Mum was no accident. Elise knew what she was doing when she went into the road. She timed it, waited for the fucking cab to get close enough so that by the time she ran into the road, the cab couldn't stop or slow down fast enough. I heard her say it."

She rushed back to the door, opened it a crack, peeped inside. No one was within earshot, eavesdropping like she'd done all those months ago. The weather kept their voices from reaching the kitchen anyway. She pulled the door in again, as her aunt closed the gate and drew nearer.

"That bitch baited Mum, and Mum took the bait."

Auntie Janice gritted her teeth. "You . . . fool!"

"Auntie!"

"You have no idea."

"I'm not lying. I heard it out of her own mouth. I was stuck with that cunt all those years because her child killed my mother. Bitch has the nerve to smile in my face, knowing what she did."

Auntie Janice shook her head. "I can't believe it. Can't believe it's come to this."

"What?"

Her aunt scrunched up her face, looked close to tears. "Me read it long time . . . did vow fi never show you."

"You've lost me."

"Me know something did wrong when you tell me 'bout her birthday party. Something tell me all that sweetness was too good to be true, so me dig it out after all this time and bring it with me, just in case."

"What is *it*?"

"Something you need to read as soon as you go back in."

"You're not making sense."

Her aunt dug into her handbag for something, pain etched on her face. She sighed as she took out an envelope. Wind blew rain their way; raindrops battered the envelope in no time.

Auntie's lips were quivering. "Lord have mercy."

"What is that?"

Her aunt was holding the envelope so tightly that she could've hole-punched it with her thumb and index finger. "Lord knows what you've done to that girl and what else you're up to."

"For the last time, Auntie, what is it?"

Her aunt handed over the wet envelope. "It's a letter. Before you do anything else to that poor girl, make sure you read this, and nuh make anyone else see it." She raised one eyebrow. "I mean it."

"Who wrote it?"

Rain getting heavier and the wind howling, Auntie's lips quivered some more, lines creasing her forehead. She shut her eyes for a few moments, creating thick fog with deep breaths.

She opened her eyes again. "You'll see when you read it. Promise me you'll read it tonight."

"OK."

"Swear it, Tempest." Auntie closed her eyes again, like she was praying, about to get into the spirit. "Swear on your mother's grave."

Tempest clutched her chest.

"Do it, Tempest. Please."

"Fine. I swear."

"On Sylvia's grave."

She swallowed.

"On. Your. Mother's. Grave."

"On my . . . mum's . . . grave."

Auntie Janice, her eyes glossy, caressed Tempest's cheek, stared a moment then turned around as soon as a tear was about to fall. She scurried through the gate, heels clacking, her back arched and her forearms a pathetic substitute for an umbrella, then disappeared behind the hedge to her car.

"Sorry, Auntie," she whispered into the chilly night air, as a car door closed.

She looked up, eyes barely open because of the rain. "Sorry, Mum. I'm not reading this tonight."

MONDAY

31 / Elise VII
Coming to light

The three o'clock news had just finished on the radio, and Elise was still awake. Painkillers hadn't worked. Still felt as if something was trying to burst out of her head. Being in bed did little to ease the wooziness. Her old bed. Her old room.

Tempest, laying next to her, had asked after her long ago, hadn't said anything since the two o'clock news. The moonlight had crept through the curtains and scattered onto the steady rise and fall of Tempest's chest, an age between each breath. The wrong sister had received the gift of sleep.

Shannon and Aiden refused to get out of her head, kept rolling around in her brain, like they'd done in her bed. They'd wanted each other so badly that they'd done it in her bed on her freaking birthday, unable to wait until they were somewhere else.

Good thing they hadn't waited though, or else she would've remained in the dark and continued to let Aiden touch her, eat her, stroke her. She would've fallen for him.

She *had* fallen.

Freaking idiot for not following her mind about him. Aiden knew she didn't have a problem with gay people; he could've told her the truth. He'd deceived her instead, made her orgasm.

Multiple times. He'd climaxed too. She must've pleased him somehow.

Unless he'd imagined she was Shannon during their intimate moments. She covered her mouth to stifle a shudder.

A blessing they'd used the condoms Tempest had given her, after the first time.

And Shannon . . . After all the proof, he was still lying, lying on Tempest and Carl. He knew how she felt about Aiden, knew they were intimate, yet he couldn't help himself. She'd never betrayed him, so there was no reason . . . His parents.

Maybe that was it—he blamed her for losing his parents. It was payback. Always something with her and people's parents. First Tempest and Sylvia, and now Shannon and his parents.

But he knew she hadn't outed him on purpose. His actions were intentional. He knew what he was doing.

She shook her head, too quickly, worsening the pain. Tears were accumulating. She blinked quickly until they escaped, had to cover her mouth to keep from waking Tempest.

Tempest must've been horrified when she'd found out about Aiden and Shannon. If not for Tempest—poor thing, the way she'd vouched for Aiden—she probably would've followed her instincts about him, maybe even played matchmaker between him and Shannon. Dummy.

Of all the times for her to be awake. Not even an hour of sleep to relieve her of the headache and the heartache. Not long before she had to get up. Reporting sick wasn't the best move but was still an option. She was sick anyway, slightly better than before, but still not back to normal. Couldn't be sure the vomiting was behind her. If it was just to avoid hearing from, or seeing, *them*, she would've gladly thrown her phone away, but she needed it. She needed to contact Virgin. Funny how the battery had died so quickly.

She dried her eyes, shifted closer to the edge of the bed, freeing herself from the duvet, just as Tempest changed position. The moonlight was straining to light up Tempest's forehead. She was facing Elise fully now. Something fell out of Tempest's hand and disappeared under the duvet. No clue what it was, but it landed quietly enough to keep Tempest from stirring. Elise lifted the duvet slowly. Something light in colour stood out against Tempest's crushed black dress. The crushing was nothing compared to the rip. There really was no changing Ma's mind. It was that deep for her to take Shannon and Aiden's side over Tempest's. Maybe that fight needed to happen. They'd both been carrying years of baggage. Their fight emptied it out, maybe not fully, but it was a start.

That light-coloured object . . . just as she'd suspected. Her phone. Tempest probably hadn't charged it.

She crept out of the bed and tiptoed to her overnight bag, guided by the light that had snuck through the slit between the curtains. She crouched then brushed her hand against the bag until the cable tickled her fingers.

Shuffling. Tempest was turning again. Still fast sleep.

She snuck out of the room. One thing she missed about being back home with her parents—hardly any squeaking and creaking.

She crept down the stairs to the front room, squinted as soon as she turned on the light, then she connected the charger to her phone and plugged the charger in the socket behind one of the two kentia palm plants. The light that came on at the top of the phone was green. Almost fully charged. Tempest must've charged it after all.

She turned on the phone, snaked her finger from one dot to the next, completing an hourglass pattern to unlock it, then turned off the light coming from the shimmering candle chandelier.

The phone's light guided her to the beige fabric armchair next to the other kentia palm plant, by the bay window. A barrage of missed calls and unread texts. Some WhatsApp notifications too. She started with the texts.

No surprises. Shannon's and Aiden's names kept showing up as she scrolled down. She rolled her eyes, jabbed at an earlier message from Aiden. Tempest did this, Tempest did that. Tempest set them up . . . Pure bull— She paused.

Then she went back to the beginning of the last message.

> *I dunno the deets of TEMPEST'S MUM'S DEATH,*
> *& how U WERE INVOLVED,*
> *but TEMPEST KNOWS about it.*

She clutched her chest. *Tempest's mum's death . . . how u were involved . . . Tempest knows . . .* She got up and started circling the glass coffee table as she brought up the next message.

> *Tempest HATES U. She always knew about me.*
> *Threatened 2 tell my fam my secret if I didn't pursue u.*
> *Been calling u. Ur not answering.*

Aiden was lying.

But Sylvia . . . Aiden wasn't supposed to know that much about her.

> *She took ur passport. Don't know what she did with it. Trust*
> *me. We need 2 talk.*

She continued circling the coffee table, exited Aiden's messages, went into Shannon's.

The same things . . . over and over again . . . things she'd never told him. . . . Two phones?

She had to speak to one of them. She was about to call Shannon when the sight of the time stopped her.

382

They'd been sending her messages up until something to two though.

She called him, hung up after countless rings then tried Aiden.

"Elise?" His voice was groggy.

"Aiden, *what's going on?*"

"I'm glad you—"

"The texts!"

"Good. You've seen 'em."

"Aiden, I—"

"Where are you? Tempest with you?"

"She's upstairs, sleeping."

"You ain't safe with her."

"How do you know what happened to her mum?"

He sighed. "Ain't saying you're a killer, but she blames you for her mum's death. That's why— Elise, chill."

"I . . . I . . ."

"Come on, Elise."

"I . . ."

"I know her mum was run over, but—"

"How do you know that?"

"Forget how I know. Tempest blames *you*. Dunno how long she's known, but she knows something, more than I know. She hates you."

Tempest didn't know. They were close. If the roles had been reversed and Elise knew, she would've been done with Tempest. Aiden was trying to save himself.

But Sylvia . . .

"Elise?"

She squeezed her forehead, no ease from the pain.

"Elise!"

"Why are you saying these things?"

"What?"

"Why lie like this?"

"I ain't lying! She set us up!"

"How do you know about Sylvia?"

He told her he and Tempest had fought in his car, and that Tempest had blurted out she blamed Elise for Sylvia's death.

She stretched out an arm, searched the darkness for the armchair closer to the door, then collapsed into it.

"She planned all of it—me and you together, you falling for me, getting me to . . ."

"What?"

He muttered curse words, kissed his teeth.

"Tell me, Aiden."

"Be your first."

She paused.

"She knew . . . about me . . . wanted me to make you fall for me . . . so you'd give it up to me. Then I was meant to leave you hanging, make you regret being with me."

Strained breathing came out instead of words.

"Elise?"

"You . . . I wasn't . . ."

She'd started out young, like Tempest, but maybe it was a good thing, better than if she'd actually saved herself for Aiden. Good thing she hadn't told Tempest, or let guilt get the better of her when Ma and Pa found out about Tempest's teenage sexcapades.

"You weren't what?"

He didn't need to know he was the fourth wrong guy.

"You weren't what, Elise?"

"Nothing. . . . She would do that to me?"

"She *did* that to you."

She shut her eyes, pulled her hair, head still pounding. They were sisters, for heaven's sake. They were blood. She'd known Tempest longer than she'd known Shannon and Aiden. She *knew* her. She knew them.

Or so she'd thought. This had to be their way of saving themselves. She hadn't imagined seeing them naked in her bed. Those times she'd slept with Aiden, had he already been sexing Shannon?

"I'm telling you, Elise, we were set up."

"But the two of you—"

"It wasn't what it looked like."

"Your penis wasn't soft, Aiden. Neither was Shannon's. And the come—"

"It wasn't come! It . . . Look, who introduced me to you?"

Who'd introduced them? What was he talking . . . ?

Tempest.

Tempest had been obsessed with the idea of them being together . . . right from the start. So determined. So angry that Sunday when Aiden didn't show up for dinner.

Too angry.

"And your passport. . . . Think about it. You said you put it in your handbag, that it was just the two of you."

She was searching for something, fragments of a memory stuck in the depths of her aching head, as if she were on the verge of discovering wreckage in the Bermuda Triangle. Tempest had been concerned that morning, which was odd, because nothing ever fazed her. Tempest had been unusually caring and helpful. That still didn't explain what her old passport was doing in her handbag. She'd put it in the top drawer—that was a fact—but Tempest wouldn't have known . . .

She shot out of the armchair. As it came back to her, she fought through the pain for a clear picture . . . Tempest returning her perfume to her in her bedroom . . . around the same time she put her old passport in the top drawer.

She wasn't going mad at all.

"Whatever went down with you and her mum . . . that's why she's on some evil bitch shit."

385

More tears were coming. "You're . . . right." Hand to mouth to muffle sobs again. Other hand on stomach.

"Elise! Elise!"

The phone was in the hand she was clutching her tummy with.

She collapsed back into the armchair, hand moved to her heaving chest, nose running. She blinked tears away, collected herself.

"Elise, say su'um!"

She used the phone's light to find the tissue box on the coffee table, snatched out a few tissues, blew her nose, said, "I'm here."

"Stay away from her. Probably up to more fuck-shit."

She rubbed her stomach then stopped. She and Tempest both did the cooking, maybe Tempest slightly more. She'd made her a plate of avocado, rice and shrimp earlier. She'd specifically asked her if she was ready to eat.

"You said she's upstairs?"

"Yes. We're sharing a bed for the night."

"Sleep somewhere else." He kissed his teeth. "Fuck that—don't sleep!"

"Too much on my mind to sleep."

"I'll stay awake with you."

They did nothing but breathe into their phones awhile until she spoke again.

"How could you go along with it?"

He sighed. "Had no choice."

"You did."

"Look at my brother."

Ethan, the way he'd behaved, the things he'd said about gay people . . .

"And my grandfolks . . . I couldn't take that risk. They're all I got. Can't lose anyone else, and . . ."

"Anyone else? Who—?"

"Forget it."

"But—"

"Forget it!"

She flinched.

"Sorry for snapping—"

"I should be the one snapping."

"I know. I just can't go there. That shit ain't even important right now."

She hadn't told him about not being a virgin. She probably never would. "Fine."

Sighs into the phone from both ends.

"There's something I need to know though."

"What?"

"How did the two of you even meet?" Saying Tempest's name might have woken her up, even though they were on different levels. Her superstitious ma had always said uttering someone's name, no matter where they were, would make their ears ring.

Aiden knew whom she meant. Tempest had visited the gym where he worked, and after a free training session, they hit it off well enough to exchange numbers. As their friendship quickly blossomed, he became comfortable with her, glad to have someone to confide in regarding his sexuality, then out of the blue, Tempest turned on him, using a recording to blackmail him into making Elise his girlfriend.

"You still there, Elise?"

"Yes, I just . . . can't find the words." Her first impression of Aiden had been spot on, but her own sister?

"One minute, she was fine, the next she was bawling."

"Why?"

"Because of su'um she found out about *you*. She wouldn't tell me what. Just said you'd pay."

"When was this?"

"Probably a few months ago."

"What month?"

"Dunno . . . maybe August . . . September."

They'd moved in together in September. Tempest had come up with the idea in August, around the time she'd given Elise the fright of her life, walked into the front room when the truth about Sylvia's death came up.

August made sense. Or late July.

Aiden spoke again, snatching her away from the fragments of her memory. "Thought she was shitting me the first time she told me what she wanted me to do. Realised soon enough she wasn't."

"Go on."

It looked as if nothing would go beyond kissing, but the passport disaster ensured it would.

"So, she took my passport so that I would have sex with you?"

"Dunno. Think she just wanted to fuck with your head, your money. Anyway, she showed up at my house pressuring me to . . ."

"Fuck me?"

Words were caught in his throat.

"Let's just say it for what it was. It wasn't lovemaking. There was no love, not really."

Breathing crackled the silence.

"I was . . . so low that day . . . all because of her . . . fucking . . . reescleet . . . bitch."

She hadn't cursed in a long time. It felt good.

Cursing like that wouldn't have brought her passport back, but it would've been better than crying non-stop. Would've gone ham like Angela Bassett's Bernadine. Wouldn't have called Aiden.

Wouldn't have let Aiden . . .

"Jesus."

"I know."

"No, you don't. I'm talking about you. You actually went through with *fucking* me?"

"Elise, don't make it sound so—"

"So what, fucked-up?"

He exhaled as if frustrated, crackling the line some more.

"You tricked me into thinking you were straight."

Silence again.

"She really wanted *you*—a gay guy—to . . . take . . . my virginity?"

"I ain't *gay*."

"Come on, Aiden."

"I ain't."

"It's all out now. No need to keep lying."

"I ain't lying!"

"Are you trying to say you're—?"

"Ain't saying I'm anything. I . . . like females . . . and males."

That explained his ability to please her. Suddenly, it was as if he were inside her again. Heat settled between her legs.

She sat forward in the armchair, squeezing her thighs together to overcome the sensation. "What did Tempest have to gain from us having sex?"

"Like I said, she wanted me to make you fall for me—couldn't have taken your virginity otherwise—and then . . . dump you."

She squeezed her eyes shut, trying to keep the pain in her head at bay while figuring out Tempest's intentions. All those lengths to make her lose her virginity to the wrong guy. There had to be other things Tempest could've done.

Maybe Tempest had done other things no one else knew about.

Or maybe losing her virginity years ago made it hard to make sense of Tempest's stunt.

"Elise, you still there?"

"Yeah."

More line-crackling from him.

"Aiden, we kept fucking. One time was bad enough. How could you?"

"I feel like shit because of it, but that day when we . . . the first time . . ."

"Go on."

"You . . . initiated it."

She sprang from her seat. "Don't you put this all on me. You knew I was vulnerable. You had no business doing everything you did to me. You . . . really went to town. Shit!"

"Wasn't just about being the first to hit it."

He must've felt like *the man* thinking he was her first. Maybe bursting his bubble wasn't a bad idea.

No. That secret was all she had.

"Then what was it about?"

"Honestly, I . . . felt sorry for you."

"*What?*"

"Didn't know what else to do. You were in a bad way and all up on me. Rejecting you would've made you feel worse. I needed to get Tempest off my back anyway. Wasn't gonna let her tell my fam about me."

Shannon's parents had abandoned him. Then there was Ethan's reaction.

"But your family knows now. Your brother saw you and Shannon—"

"They don't know shit."

"Have you seen your brother since . . . ?"

"Yeah."

"And he hasn't said anything to anyone?"

"Don't matter if he's said anything to them. He don't know shit."

"But he saw the two of you—"

"We were set up!"

"But—"

"No *but.*"

"The erections and the come—"

"It was all her and Carl."

"So, nothing at all happened between the two of you?"
Silence again.
"Aiden, did anything happen?"
He kissed his teeth.
"Yes or no?"
"No!"
"Don't sound sure."
"Like I said before, we were set up."
"Aiden, you better not be keeping anything from me. I want to know everything."
"Nothing happened."
She sat back down and continued to scour memory lane for things that could've been lies. "Aiden?"
"Yeah?"
"You and Shannon didn't really meet at the gym, did you?"
He hesitated. "No."
It was easy to lie over the phone. Maybe something did happen between them. They could have been intimate before her birthday, before that meal at TGI's—maybe during. They could've been *playing* with each other under the table, right under her nose.
If Shannon and Aiden had messed around while she and Aiden had . . . If the same penis that had been inside her had been inside Shannon . . .
If it had been the other way round . . . If she'd been penetrated by someone who'd been penetrated . . . She screwed up her face.
Then she paused.
Didn't matter who did whom. Didn't make Aiden more or less into men.
If he was telling the truth—and he had to be—then Shannon hadn't betrayed her after all. *Shan.* She *did* know him.
But Shannon didn't know about her and Aiden until that day in Westfield Stratford. That look on his face . . . Something could've really happened between them prior.

"Elise, you listening to me?"

"What? . . . Sorry, Aiden. The line was bad just now. . . . Tell me how you met him."

Aiden hesitated again before telling her about the first time he saw Shan, Lionel and Peter. Nothing Shan had gone through was funny, but his mum's assumption that he and Aiden were seeing each other, saying the Lord's name in vain, was. Drama queen like Ma.

"Do you think he's attractive?"

"Come on now, Elise."

"Tell me."

"I . . ."

"Yes or no, Aiden?"

"Come on, man."

"I'll take that as a yes."

He kissed his teeth. No denial.

She'd been right about Shan's feelings for Aiden. She could've lived with it because—Shan being Shan—he would've forced himself to get past it. And until hours ago, Aiden was her straight boyfriend. Shan wouldn't have been a threat.

Silly her for not knowing Aiden liked Shan back.

"If you want him, have him."

He sighed what sounded like gratitude then said, "Can't explain why I . . ."

"Fell for him?"

He sighed again; that question stressed him out. "When I saw him that day, he looked down and out. I just wanted to do su'um good for him. Sounds wack. Never knew him. First time seeing him. I'm used to people being thirsty, all up on me. I figured out he liked me, but he was shy about it, respectful."

"I think I understand. He *is* attractive. If only he knew it, or even felt it. If he were straight . . ." She sighed then chuckled as she remembered being crushed out on Shan.

"What's funny?"

"Nothing. Just thinking about him."

"Yeah."

"You'd be lucky to have him."

His silence let her know her approval overwhelmed him.

"You said Lionel and Peter were there with him?"

"Yeah."

"That must've been when he moved."

"Yeah, when Shan moved."

Shan, not *Shannon*.

They fell silent, except for their breathing and position changes. Nearly four o'clock. Still pitch black outside.

She sighed then said, "Aiden, something's still bothering me . . . The *fluid* on your bodies . . . your penis . . . I've seen it flaccid. It wasn't flaccid when you were with Shannon."

Aiden told her about the struggle he'd had with Carl, and Shannon's spiked drink. "Nothing happened with me and him."

"But Shannon's penis looked sort of . . . hard as well."

"Elise, we were naked, on top of each other. Dicks are sensitive. Waking up with a boner, and sometimes come, is normal."

"Alright, Aiden, I get it."

"Wasn't even come. Those fuckers made something that looked like it."

"Carl is a surgeon, knows medicine. Knowing what I know now, I guess I can't put anything past her. I always knew there was something about him, but I can't believe her."

"Well, you better believe it."

Silence again. Opportunity for another time check. Almost ten past four.

"Aiden?

"Yeah?"

"I let you enter me more than once. Why didn't you dump me after the first time?"

"Tempest wanted it to continue."

"But you said she wanted you to dump me."

"When she found out about the first time, she decided to take it to another level of bullshit, wanted it to continue."

She grimaced. "Why?"

"Dunno. . . . Maybe she wanted to make sure you really fell for me."

"Aiden, it shouldn't have happened more than once. Shouldn't have happened at all."

"That's what the bitch wanted."

"I know that, but there has to be more to it than just Tempest."

"I don't get you."

"I know she was blackmailing you, but for someone to have that much power over you . . ."

He crackled the line with his agitation. "I guess a part of me needed to know that I can still have sex with a female. And like I said before, you initiated it sometimes. I couldn't reject you."

"Bullshit!"

"Bullshit my ass!"

"Maybe the first part was true. Don't make it seem like I was pushing up on you. I'm not fast."

"Have it your way."

"I will."

Another sigh tickled her ear. "There's something I nearly told Tempest when I thought we were cool. No one else knows."

"Go on."

"Can't believe I'm doing this . . . Feel like I owe you though."

"OK . . ."

"This whole thing . . . my feelings for . . . liking . . ." His voice was almost a whisper.

"Men?"

He exhaled deeply. "When I was little, I . . . did things . . ."

She bent her legs so that both feet were tucked under her thighs in the armchair, resting her right side on the part of the armchair where her back should've been. "Things?"

"Yeah, *things*."

"What things?"

"Things with my cousin."

"Things like what?"

"Shit, Elise! I'm talking 'bout sex!"

She grimaced. "Oh."

"He—"

"He?"

"Yeah, *he* did stuff to me. I did stuff back. Stuff we shouldn't have known how to do. We were kids."

"How old were you?"

"He was nine. I was seven."

"God! Are you trying to say that's why . . . ?"

"You know what's funny?" He gave a dry chuckle.

"I don't."

"Not ha-ha funny. Fucked-up funny."

"What?"

"For ages, I blamed Craig for making me . . . this way."

"Craig?"

"Shit."

"That's the cousin?"

He kissed his teeth. "Pretend you didn't hear the name."

"OK."

"Anyway, I blamed him for . . . the way I am . . . But now I know—guess I always knew—that he did those things to me 'cause he knew he could."

"What do you mean?"

"There were other cousins, and he had a whole heap of friends, but he chose me. He knew I was . . . different."

"I . . . don't know what to say."

"Like I said before, Tempest made me sleep with you, but a part of me needed to know I could still make a female come, that I could come for a female—"

"Aiden, stop!"

"What I'm trying to say is I needed to feel like a real man."

"That's what a real man is to you, a man who can please a woman? Look at Peter and Lionel. They're real men, as real as real can get, for loving each other all these years in a world that hasn't been kind to them . . . people like them . . . and Shan . . . and you."

Silence, besides breathing, for a few moments.

"Aiden, how did it end?"

"What?"

"You and . . . Cr—your cousin?"

"I . . . I . . ." Distressed breathing from his end crackled the line.

"You don't have to tell me."

"It's a long story. Don't think I can go there. Just know it ended."

"That's the main thing. Seven though, Aiden? No one's supposed to even know about that stuff at that age."

"Fucking knew because of him."

She was going to ask how Craig knew anything sex-related at nine, but she'd been exposed to things—not sexual thankfully—when she was around that age. Wouldn't have had the mind to lure Sylvia otherwise.

"Haven't seen him since then. Probably won't see him ever again. Lives in America."

"Must've been confusing, traumatic. That could ruin a person. You're here though. You made it."

"Suppose."

He kissed his teeth, not prolonging it as usual. "Elise, I *am* sorry. For everything."

She took a moment to take in his apology, this side of him she had no idea existed.

"Elise, you're going all quiet on me again."

"Just something that came to me. I asked shortly after our first time, and I'm asking you again . . . do I need to worry about your sexual health?"

"I already told you I'm clean."

"Don't be so defensive. It's just . . . the first time . . ." Her stomach tingled. ". . . and we didn't use protection when we . . . God . . . when we—"

"I'm clean. Get tested anyway. Peace of mind."

"I will."

"Sorry for taking your virginity."

She rolled her eyes. "What's done is done. I forgive you."

But forgiveness wasn't that simple. She'd backtracked after vowing to be celibate until marriage, to make the man earn her body. Aiden was just like the others, a guy she'd mistakenly trusted, another example of bad judgement.

Four guys out there had a part of her she couldn't reclaim. Four instead of freaking zero.

After talking to him, after getting all the puzzle pieces from him, she was close to forgiving him, closer than she'd thought possible before the phone call. He wasn't completely out of the woods, but hopefully accepting his apology meant no further mention of her 'virginity'.

"Whatchu thinking now, Elise?"

"Oh . . . just . . . everything."

"I wish I could take back me and you . . . *you know*. I'm mad at myself for doing that to you."

"There's a Syleena Johnson song . . . "My First", I think. . . . It's about how she considers her current man to be her first, even though there were other men before him. Her man, her true love, is *truly* her first. . . . Guess I haven't found my *true* first yet."

"That's deep."

"Sure is."

"Elise?" He sounded serious.

"What is it?"

"Watch your back."

The problem upstairs.

She looked around in the darkness, let her phone illuminate pictures on the wall. She was in a few. There were none of Tempest.

Ma had been right all along. Ma was right without knowing how right she was.

"What she did to me and Shan, she must've figured out he was onto her. Stay away from her. I've only known her for months, but I know she has no limits when it comes to fuck-shit."

"I don't know her at all. The sister I thought I knew is . . . troubled."

If not for being motherless at a young age, and being rejected and ridiculed by Ma, maybe Tempest would've turned out differently.

But to be that vengeful, to go that far . . . "I'm done with her."

"You should make her pay."

She grimaced. "Make her pay? I don't have it in me to think like that. Too fool, I guess."

"I can make you learn."

"It's just not me."

"Look what she's done!"

"If she's really doing this because she blames me for . . . her mother . . ."

"What actually happened?"

"Sylvia . . . I . . . No, I can't do this. Not right now."

"If it's bothering you that much, you need to do something."

"I . . . I will."

"Is it really that bad?"

She didn't answer. Instead she said, "I better let you go. You must be tired. We've been on the phone for ages."

"I needed this."

"More than holding and kissing Shan?"

"Elise, come on."

"Just joking." *Not.*

"When can I see you?"

"I don't know. I'm flying out tomorrow—well today."

"For true?"

"Yeah. I thought about calling in sick, but I'd rather go away. Don't want that bitch anywhere near me."

"I feel you."

"This didn't go how I thought it would. Thought I was going to go *in* on you, but you opened my eyes."

"Least I could do."

"Feels like I'm getting to know you for the first time."

"I feel you."

"Anyway, I'll go now."

"Catch you later, Elise."

"Bye, Ai—"

Shuffling from behind made her turn around swiftly.

The phone's light illuminated swaying leaves of the plant by the door, then some of those leaves were swallowed by darkness. She moved the phone around.

Feet were under that darkness.

Her heart rate shot up.

She brought the phone higher, stopped when its light hit the torn bust of a dress.

She gasped and squinted when light from the candle chandelier washed over the front room.

"What's going on, Elise?" Tempest said.

Elise swung her legs round, planted her feet on the carpet, squinting. She flicked her tousled hair. "W-was just sitting in here for a bit. Couldn't sleep." She was looking at Tempest one second, then taking her eyes off her the next.

Tempest stepped closer to Elise, whose puffy eyes were adjusting to the brightness. "I'm not surprised you're awake. Then again, I wouldn't be awake. I'd be dead . . . would've done myself in." She just had to include that last part.

Elise gave her a look she'd never given her before. Her expression went back to normal quickly, but not quick enough.

Something had changed.

From the moment she awoke, phone and Elise gone, it was obvious what the score was.

She swallowed. "Shouldn't have said that. Sorry." She sat on the armrest.

Elise scooted to the other end, clinging to the other armrest, like dust that refused to be sucked up by a vacuum cleaner, stiff from wanting to get up, but knowing that getting up would've looked suspicious.

Elise was going to snitch, and there was still no certainty everything had worked out.

She turned her head away from Elise to grimace then turned back around. "Anymore texts from you-know-who?"

"N-no—I mean, yes . . . same old lies."

Elise was a shit actress. No wonder she was so close to Shannon.

Maybe Tempest was giving a shit performance too, too many thoughts swirling. "I heard you talking."

Elise shielded the phone in her lap like a mother protecting her baby, thoughts of what to come up with contorting her face, then her puffy eyes became animated. "It was just Virgin."

Don't want that bitch anywhere near me. . . . Feels like I'm getting to know you. Some fucking conversation with Virgin.

Keeping up with her breathing and heart rate, making sure she was controlling them instead of the other way round, was becoming impossible. Everything was going to come crashing down if she didn't do something.

She pressed her eyes shut. Never imagined experiencing anything worse than the childhood she'd had after her mum's death, always coming second to Elise. The fallout after everything came out would be worse. Elise would be favoured over her yet again, and perhaps she would lose Daddy forever. No mother, no father. This couldn't be what everything had come to. After all she'd done, invested . . . still unsure if the real damage had been done, if Elise and Aiden had had sex often enough or at the right time, that Elise had reached a point of no return. Losing Daddy's trust and respect had always been a risk, but to lose him *and* fail to achieve the ultimate revenge . . . Elise and Aiden could've done with more fucking, and Shannon shouldn't have been a sneaky bitch.

She opened her eyes. "So, you'll be off work again—?"

"No, I'm flying out later this morning. I need to get away, even if it's just work."

"Really?"

"You sound happy about it."

"I just . . ."

The bitch was testing her. Of course Elise going away was the best thing. More time to decide what to do next. Just had to watch Elise's every move until she was out of the country, even if it meant being in the back seat while Daddy or that bitch drove.

"Getting away is a good idea, that's all."

Elise narrowed her eyes for a moment then forced animation into them as she smiled. The way Elise was sitting, there was space for one more person in the armchair.

Tempest took it.

Elise moved away, or tried to; the armrest was in the way. She started shaking.

Tempest grabbed Elise by her stiff wrists. "What's wrong?"

"N-nothing."

"Poor thing." She put her arm around the lying bitch's shoulder then pulled her head to her chest.

Bitch was close to having rigor mortis, her stiffness betraying her unwillingness to be embraced. Tempest had learned ages ago how to fake it, ever since she'd discovered Elise's betrayal.

And now Elise knew everything, fresh from a conversation with Aiden or Shannon.

She pressed her arm against the back of Elise's neck, not much short of a chokehold.

A necessary head start for someone in a ripped, crushed maxi dress against someone in turquoise satin pyjamas. Elise tried to free herself as Tempest talked about no good men and learning lessons.

Talking whatever bullshit came to mind wasn't helping take the focus off Elise as she tried pushing Tempest's arm away and turning her head to free up her airway.

She couldn't hold Elise like that much longer, but she wasn't ready to let go. She could've continued squeezing the life out of her, but something like that had to be planned. The glass coffee table was in front of them, one of its corners glinting under the candle chandelier and pointing right at them. She could've hurled Elise right into it. People died from accidents all the time. Anyone could accidentally hit their head on a blunt or sharp object and die.

But if that didn't kill Elise, Tempest was going to have to finish her off, creating another hole to escape from, making everything she'd done pointless. Rumbled or not, there was still a chance that everything had worked. That would be better payback than a dead Elise.

She squeezed her eyes shut, bracing herself, then opened them. "What time's your flight?"

Elise mumbled as she thumped Tempest's arm.

Tempest grimaced as she let go of Elise.

Elise coughed, chest heaving, staring at Tempest, her wide eyes asking what the raas she'd just tried to do.

"Daddy taking you to the airport?"

Elise rubbed her throat and cleared it some more.

"Is Daddy taking you?"

"No."

"You all packed?"

Elise exhaled like she was irritated. Again, she caught herself too late. "I'm going back to the flat. Will sort myself out and leave from there."

"That's a shitty journey. You sure you'll be OK?"

"I've done it before."

"Where are you flying to?"

"Antigua."

"Lucky bitch."

Elise screwed up her face.

"Sorry." She wriggled her hips from between her side of the seat and Elise. Yawning, she continued, "Coming back up?"

"No!"

She might as well have asked Elise to jump off Devil's Bridge. "I'm not tired."

"But you need your rest. How will you—?"

"I'm fine!"

The real Elise, finally.

Elise grimaced then took a deep breath. "Sorry about that. I just can't sleep."

She was sorry alright. A sorry, lying, murdering bitch. "It's OK. I'll stay up with you."

"No, don't!" Elise's animated eyes betrayed her. She laughed it off. Wasn't even her usual laugh. "You have work in the morning. *You* should be sleeping right now."

"Annual leave till Wednesday."

Elise had nothing to say to that.

"How are you feeling? You still feel nauseous?"

"Well . . . I'm OK, right now."

Key words: *right now*. Hopefully a different story in a few weeks. "Good."

"I'll see how tomorrow goes, and the days after. I think the situation brought it all on."

"Maybe."

Silence, until Jill Scott broke it.

It was probably Carl calling. He had some explaining to do, leaving her there to deal with the fallout. She couldn't have been sure at the time that everything had been done the way they'd planned. All she could've done was hope for timing to work in her favour.

Another awkward smile from Elise. "Not answering?"

She told Elise she'd be right back, went into the kitchen, and was getting ready to ask Carl what the fuck he'd been thinking, bailing on her, but it wasn't him. It was Auntie. She let it ring until it stopped.

Jill Scott started again moments later. She scraped her finger across the screen. "Auntie Janice, do you know what time—?"

"You haven't read it, have you?"

That blasted letter.

"I can't believe you!"

"Why are you up so early?"

"Why haven't you read it?"

"Auntie, it's a really bad time."

"Bad time, my backfoot."

"For God's sake, what's in this letter?"

Auntie Janice was breathing heavily. "How could you? . . . On Sylvia's grave— That's it, you're reading it *right* now."

"I can't."

"Yes, you can, and you will. I'm outside."

"What?"

"I drove back, had waited up to get a call from you, hoping you'd read the letter. I know you though—your ears too hard."

"Auntie, go back home."

"No!"

"What's the big deal about the letter?"

Auntie took a deep breath then said, "Your mother wrote it."

She reached for something, anything, to stay on her feet. The fridge handle kept her up.

"Wrote it days before she . . ."

"I can't."

"You have to. Whatever you've done to that girl, whatever you're planning on doing, it stops now. Get that letter, bring it outside. Read it make me hear. That way, you'll have someone to cry to as you read."

"Auntie, you're scaring me."

"There's no other way. Go and get the letter, Tempest. Bring it to the car. Right now."

33 / *Aiden VIII*
Release

ack of sleep and pain all over had taken a toll on Aiden. He'd gotten out of bed like his grandfolks probably did. Couldn't go to work. Had to reschedule training sessions. A day off meant that he could get a blood test. He was still alive, but he needed to be sure that the shit Carl had injected into him wasn't deadly. He'd skipped breakfast; fasting blood tests were meant to be more accurate. He'd waited ages at Homerton Hospital, but he'd expected to get home before Ethan.

One of the first things he spotted when he reached home— Ethan's main jacket draped over the banister.

The front room light was on, and murmurs from the TV reached the passage. He took off his jacket and trainers, then braced himself before going to the front room. He stopped in the doorway.

All of them were in the room. His grandfolks turned their heads to him at the same time. Ethan didn't shift.

"Yo."

His grandfolks responded, then his grandma added, "We eat done, but your food in the microwave."

"Thanks."

"The two of unu too mash up fi go work today," Granddad said. "What a trial!"

That explained it. Ethan had been home all day. Good to know the prick was too mashed up to go to work.

"We soon come fi talk 'bout what happen," Grandma said.

No sooner than he brought his piping hot plate of stewed fish, plain rice, and plantain to the table than his family filed into the kitchen, his grandma in front, and his granddad in front of Ethan. He'd opened his mouth for the first forkful of food, steam kissing his lips. He stayed like that while his grandma slapped herself into the seat to his left and his granddad took the seat on her left. He put the fork down and glanced at the only empty chair then scowled at Ethan, who was leaning against the door frame, his left eye looking like he'd put eye shadow around it. He stretched his right leg until the ball of his foot was touching a leg of the empty chair. He pulled it in.

Grandma slapped his arm.

Granddad was fidgeting. He kicked that same chair back out. "Ethan, sit here so."

"Feel like standing."

"Yeah, he's fine, Granddad."

Granddad clutched his chest as he repeated himself, grimacing. Ethan dashed to him. So did Aiden.

"Granddad! Should we call the am—?"

"No, Aiden." Granddad caught his breath. "Just wind."

Looking convinced that everything was cool with Granddad, Grandma said, "We need to talk." She looked at Aiden. "We know what happen yesterday."

His eyes darted to Ethan. Ethan didn't look back, but he snarled at the memory. Fucking dickhead.

Meeting Grandma's knowing gaze was like looking directly at the sun. He looked at his granddad, who was staring into space. He looked at Ethan again; Ethan turned his head, cutting his eyes.

"Eat before the food get cold," Grandma said.

He sat back down, gulped some orange juice, and dove into his food.

"From you was down there"—his grandma brought her outstretched hand level with the table—"me know you was different."

He choked, got himself together.

"Take time eat." Her voice was deep.

He paused.

"Your father did think you too soft, but me tell him fi leave me grandpickney alone. Me tell him ah nuh soft you soft, just . . ." She sighed. "Arthur, me one son." Her voice was trembling. "Anyway, you were my special grandpickney—you too, Ethan— but after . . . after Craig . . ."

His heart started fucking with him and his fork slipped out of his hand, dropping to his plate with a piercing clang.

"We know what happen," Granddad said.

"Know what?" Ethan grimaced. Moving his mouth a certain way must've hurt. "Who's Craig?"

"Lord have mercy." Grandma closed her eyes and covered her trembling lips with her hand.

"Grandma—" That wasn't supposed to come out high-pitched. He cleared his throat. "What you talking 'bout?"

"Me never know it would come to this. When me find out 'bout it, when your mother tell me what happen, me think she couldn't be righted, just making it all up, excusing what she did to your father."

He swallowed.

As if talking to herself and seeing something for the first time, Grandma said, "Didn't think Arthur could really beat him own likkle pickney so."

He clenched his fists to stop his hands shaking.

"Grandma, what are you saying?" Ethan said.

"Lord, forgive me." Her eyes were glistening.

Granddad sighed. "Your mother tell us your father catch you and Craig . . ." He peered at Aiden.

Aiden looked away.

All the years he'd spent mastering his poker face couldn't have prepared him for this.

His heart was racing and belly churning. "You've known all this time?" he said quickly to mask his unsteady breathing.

"Me see her in Holloway long time."

"*What?*"

"Aiden, calm down. Make your grandmother finish."

He couldn't keep from bouncing his right leg. He wasn't looking at his grandma, but he could imagine her expression, so he had to avoid eye contact. "When did you see her?"

"A few months after Arthur leave this earth." She grabbed something from under the table, a kerchief, probably from her skirt pocket, and whimpered into it.

Granddad said, "We wanted her fi tell we why she kill him. We never really dash her weh. We did love her, but . . ."

"I'm confused," Ethan said, squinting like he was having a headache.

"Bear with us, son." Granddad squeezed Ethan's shoulder, swaying him. "She tell your grandma why she did it, then your grandma tell me."

Aiden clenched his fists, unclenched them, clenched them again, then unclenched them before putting his elbows on the table and burying his face in his palms, his stomach still churning as it started coming back, the night Craig had slept over.

They'd been playing their secret game. Of all the times for his daddy to catch them, Aiden's hard little seven-year-old *janny* in Craig's mouth. One moment, Aiden was enjoying what Craig was doing to him, eyes closed, and the next he jumped out of his skin, disconnected from Craig when Daddy burst into the room. Daddy was like a monster, screaming at them, mouth open wide like he was going to eat them up.

As soon as Daddy dragged them off the bed, he clapped them all over with his big, rough hands, until Mummy appeared and pulled Daddy off them. Mummy shielded the bawling cousins as Daddy tried to get to them. When Daddy told Mummy what he'd walked in on, Mummy gave them one look, like she was going to beat them too, but she didn't. She continued to protect them from Daddy.

Before he knew it, Mummy was carrying Craig out, Craig's bawls fading, and he was the only one being punished by Daddy. He was being held down on the bed by Daddy, as Daddy beat bawls and screams out of him with the belt—buckle end.

Mummy came back, managed to get between him and his daddy. Daddy threw himself into them. Mummy ended up taking the blows from the belt buckle

"Move!" Daddy yelled at her.

She didn't budge, just kept yelling at him to stop, while he shouted and went wild. Everything seemed to be happening so fast until the thump. Felt like slow motion when Daddy's fist struck Mummy's cheek so hard that she spun in the air like an ice-skater.

Except Mummy didn't land on her feet.

Couldn't forget how Mummy looked once she hit the floor, like Craig's sister's rag doll that time she threw it at Craig but missed. Couldn't forget thinking that Daddy had killed Mummy and how he charged at Daddy, thinking he could hurt him with his seven-year-old feet and fists, and just like that, he was on the floor, Daddy claating him with his bare hands.

He was going to end up like Mummy—dead.

The first time he'd been called *chi-chi*, *batty boy* and *dick-sucker*, no clue what they meant, but they had to be bad, the way Daddy's face screwed up as he said those things, spit dripping.

Didn't feel like the beating was going to end—until he was dead. All he could do was bawl and beg Daddy to stop. Craig and Ethan's bawls joined in from the other bedroom.

And then everything stopped.

Daddy's face directly above his, Daddy went from looking frightening to frightened, eyes bulging, mouth open, tongue out. He was frozen like that while he *k-k-k*-ed.

Mummy was behind Daddy, her mouth and eyes wide open.

Something dripped on Aiden's neck. Another drip hit his chin. The dripping wouldn't stop. He looked to see where it was coming from. Something on Daddy's neck.

Something sticking out of Daddy's neck, blood all over it. Blood dripping from it.

Then whatever was sticking out of Daddy's throat disappeared inside his neck, Mummy making sounds like someone trying to scream with a sore throat. Daddy put his huge hands around his neck, like he was choking himself, *k-k-k*-ing some more, then blood squirted between his fingers, spraying Aiden's face and pyjamas until he fell to the floor next to him. Daddy's body shook like the floor was going to collapse under his weight.

Daddy finally stopped *k-k-k*-ing, started gurgling blood. Then something in his eyes changed; the fear was disappearing, his eyes not about to pop out after all. His body stopped shaking and his hands fell to his sides. His chest stopped moving.

Something fell close to Daddy—scissors covered in blood.

Aiden looked at his mummy. Blood was all over her hands, and her hands were covering her mouth. She was shaking, crying, wide-eyed, then she screamed into her bloody hands.

Another look at Daddy, a look he never knew would be the last—Daddy's eyes were closed.

Ethan was shaking his head, muttering like he was watching everything play out, eyes as wide as Mum's and Arthur's had been that night.

"For a long time, we never believe her. And then we find out 'bout Craig engagement."

Aiden squinted at his grandma. "Engaged?"

"Yes."

"To a woman?"

Grandma turned up her lips. "Of course!"

No point saying anything about same-sex marriage.

"We never believe Valerie, because she did deh with man besides Arthur. Him play away first though. Me give him one box when me find out. Then when she do the same thing, me coulda did wring her neck. She did ah carry on fi a long time. If she could lie 'bout that, she could lie 'bout anything."

"But we know it's the truth now. Ethan tell us what happen at that girl's birthday. Wah wrong with you? In her bed, on her birth—?"

"You really told them?"

"Don't chat to me!"

Aiden kissed his teeth and threw the rest of his orange juice in Ethan's face. He punched Ethan off his chair before Ethan could recover. Ethan writhed on the tiles, while Aiden kicked him repeatedly. Strong arms pulled him back, hurling him into the cooker.

"I'll fuck you up!" Ethan charged at him, but their grandfolks were in the way.

All of them were bunched together, as if the kitchen had shrunk.

"I'm sick of your mouth!"

"Aiden, stop it! The two of unu, stop the nonsense! This kitchen ah fi me! This yard ah fi me!"

"Grandma, calm down!"

She hit Ethan in the chest.

Aiden smirked, and then a box left his cheek prickling.

"Me nuh know wah sweet yuh." Granddad had him by the collar. "Ethan, sit back down! Cora, sit with him. Me'll stay here so with Aiden."

"After Ethan tell—"

"Grandma, what he told you . . . that ain't how it happened."

"Really?" Ethan said, fresh blood inking his lips.

"Yeah!"

Ethan kissed his teeth.

"Make me finish."

"Sorry, Grandma."

Grandma sighed. "After what Ethan tell we, the two ah we talk 'bout what Valerie did tell me. You did ah cry fi she, at the cemetery, nuh true?"

He turned his head, still in his granddad's clutches.

"Shoulda did know it was too good to be true. You hate yuh puppa."

"Grandma—"

"So, your mother was really telling the truth? Your father did catch you and Craig . . . *playing* with each other . . . and him claat you?"

"Grandma . . ."

"Tell the truth, Aiden." There was more bass in Granddad's voice than usual. His granddad let go of his collar, gripped his shoulder instead.

"It's true," he whispered.

Granddad muttered something.

"And your—" Grandma's voice was shaking again. "Your mother—oh, God in heaven. She really . . . did what she did . . . to save you?"

His throat was tight. He sucked in his trembling lips.

"Aiden?" Granddad said.

Grandma put her kerchief over her face as tears streamed.

He shut his eyes. Wasn't going to be like his grandma and let tears escape. He nodded.

"Make we hear you say it."

"It—"

The tears were determined as fuck, pushing through. Before he knew it, his eyes were flooded and tears were breaking out of his eye corners like prisoners escaping during a riot.

"It's true," he said before he broke free from his granddad, and sniffed and heaved as he gripped the counter top.

Everything that had happened started hurtling towards him. All the fuck-shit because Craig had seen his mum naked, sitting on his dad's face, wining, his dad's big janny bouncing up and down, stringy fluid coming out of it, and then his mum bringing her face down to put the janny in her mouth.

Fuck knew what else Craig had seen and how long he'd been watching. Same for Tammy, his sister.

If not for that fuck-shit, Arthur wouldn't have become *Arthur*; he would've kept on being *Daddy*. They would've stayed together, or divorced after getting tired of stepping out on each other. His grandfolks would've been just that, instead of being burdened with Mummy and Daddy duties. His mum wouldn't have ended up in prison—though he'd seen Arthur thump her before and she'd promised to kill him if he ever did that to her again.

"Come on, son." Granddad shook him gently away from the past, brought him to a chair.

Role reversal. Aiden had become the frail one.

He wiped his face. "Do Craig's parents know?"

"No. Not what you and Craig did, not why your mother did what she did. Them think it was self-defence, which is true, me suppose; them nuh know she was defending *you*."

"How did you find out about Craig's engagement?"

Grandma's face lit up as she sniffed and blinked quickly. "Your auntie tell me."

"She told you? Ain't she in America?"

"Ee-hi. She did phone the other day. Nearly most me have heart attack when me realise ah did she. She tell me seh she find our number and had to ring it. Me never say anything, not even to your grandfather at first. We wash our hands of Valerie and her family long time." She rubbed her hands the way she rubbed flour off them whenever she was baking.

"Knowing what we know now, it was a blessing to hear from Ingrid, nuh true, Cora?"

"Yes, Clyde. Your auntie is doing well. She and her husband marry thirty years now. What a blessing one of you turn out alright."

"What?"

"You beyond fixing."

"Beyond fixing?"

"After what Ethan tell us, you too far gone." His granddad muttered something else.

"Tell us what happened at that girl's birthday."

He repeated what he'd already told Elise, Lionel and Peter. "It's the truth."

"Me know Temptation was a likkle wretch," Grandma said.

"Me too," Granddad added.

Grandma snapped her head at Granddad. "Ah lie!"

"But the two of you came."

He squinted at Ethan. "What?"

"Your dick . . . I know you ain't hung like that."

"It was all Tempest. And her man."

"The way homeboy was fighting me . . . it was like he was protecting *his* man."

"You went crazy on me *and* him."

415

"I guess." Ethan smirked then grimaced. Must've remembered his lip was busted. "So, there's nothing going on between you and homeboy then?"

He wasn't ready for that question.

"Aiden!"

"I . . . I . . ."

"Why ain't you saying *no*?"

He couldn't look Ethan and his grandfolks in the eye. He kept opening his mouth, but his words were trapped. Didn't take long for his grandfolks' sighs to fill the silence. Ethan just kissed his teeth.

His grandma and granddad clasped each other's hands, eyes glistening. Grandma's other hand was on her chest. The wrong fucking place for her hand to be. He'd never forgive himself if something happened to either of them. He almost reached out to grab her arm, to hold her, but he didn't know how she'd react. As soon as tears started running down his grandfolks' faces again, tears blurred his vision. He clenched his eyes shut, kept the tears to a minimum.

"God is a healer." Granddad sniffed long and strong, and his face brightened up. "Maybe if you find the right woman, like Craig did . . ."

Craig's engagement, to a woman, was bullshit. Had to be. Couldn't say that though.

He exhaled hard. "If that's how things turned out for him . . . then whatever." He held his head down, got his folks' pained expressions out of his sight.

"It ain't right. He . . . molested you . . . made you this way, and he's still straight."

Ethan defending him . . . that was some shit.

"He didn't molest me, Ethan, and he didn't make me anything. I still like girls . . . I just . . ." No need to tell them that he probably liked dudes more, that he was falling for Shan.

416

"But Craig made you like this."

"I was already looking at boys." Shit, he wasn't supposed to say that.

Grandma chuckled, face still wet.

"Wah sweet you?" Granddad said.

"Me jus' ah consider the times when Aiden look 'pon man."

"What you talking 'bout?"

"Ah true," Granddad said. "All them times me catch you ah look 'pon man. We did always know, but we did think you woulda grow outta it."

Grandma wiped her cheeks.

No one said shit for a while. Granddad's throat-clearing, Grandma's sighs, and Ethan's tapping feet filled the silence.

"What now?" he finally said.

Ethan shrugged his shoulders.

Grandma reached for Aiden's hand then grabbed it, like she was trying to keep him from falling off a cliff. "You're still our grandpickney. And the two of unu are still brothers." Her head turned from side to side, from grandson to grandson.

"We still love you," Granddad said.

That put Aiden's stomach in knots. He made a sound like he wanted to shit.

"But the Bible is the Bible. Me nuh know what to tell you 'bout that."

He frowned. "Dunno what to tell you either, so . . . when should I move out?"

His grandfolks snapped their heads at each other.

"Move out?" Grandma said, her voice deep.

"Yeah. I know I can't stay here now—"

"Bwoi, mind me clap you again!" Granddad said.

"But nothing's changing."

"Maybe, maybe not," Grandma said. "But this is your yard."

Pointless trying to convince his grandfolks there was no going back. Maybe they would realise one day, maybe they wouldn't. What was for certain was no one was about to have a heart attack over it, and this was still his yard.

Blackmailed by Tempest for nothing; taking Elise's virginity for nothing; his mum going down for nothing, no one believing her self-defence story, the story she'd stuck with for fear that telling the truth would get her son and nephew in trouble; the shit on his back all those years . . . for fuck all. Just Ethan to deal with, which was cool. Nothing a claat here and there couldn't sort out.

"Moving out," Granddad muttered then kissed his teeth.

"Shan's folks kicked him out when they found out 'bout him."

Grandma covered her open mouth with her hand. "Poor pickney. Him homeless?"

"Nah. Staying with his uncle."

"Thank God," Granddad said.

"We nuh want you with man, and we want great-grandpickneys from the both of unu." Grandma shook her head. "But . . . this is hard. . . . You is a hardback man. Can't tell you weh fi do."

"Mum said the same thing," he thought aloud. *Fuck.*

"Beg your pardon?"

He looked down at the table until he could bring himself to look at his folks again. "Saw her the other day. Been visiting her for a minute."

They all looked at each other, Ethan squinting, his grandfolks wide-eyed, before Grandma finally asked how she was doing.

"Alright, I guess. She should be released soon, early next year."

"For true?" Ethan widened his eyes then caught himself, shrugged, made his face return to normal. He didn't want to look hyped about it.

"Yeah."

"Sounds right. Twenty-odd-year sentence," Granddad said.

"What a blessing," Grandma said, her voice high.

FRIDAY

34 / Shannon XI
Friend & lover

"**W**ish I were there with you," Shannon said, changing position on his new bed. He grimaced at the echo of his voice as it reached Elise via WhatsApp.

"No, you don't," Elise said. "This flight delay's taking the piss."

He smiled and sighed. He had his friend back, and she finally knew the truth about Tempest. She was across the pond for now, but she would be back in London, hopefully by Saturday morning.

"What you gonna do about that sister of yours?"

She exhaled deeply. "Not a clue."

"You can't let her get away with it."

"I know. And the thing is . . ."

"What?"

"I think she knows I know."

He sat up in his bed. "How?"

"Hours before I flew out, the same night—well, morning—I was on the phone to Aiden. Just as I was telling him bye, there she was, standing in the doorway. Scared the frig out of me. I thought she was sleeping. When she asked me who I was talking to, I told her it was Virgin."

"Did she believe you?"

"I think she pretended to. Could've sworn she was trying to . . ."

"What?"

"Nothing. She knows."

"When you come back, you can stay with me. Or just move back in with your parents."

"I'll see. . . . You know what was strange?"

"What?"

"Her phone rang and she met someone outside. She was gone long enough, then when she came back, she went straight upstairs. When I went back up to the bedroom, I caught her crying. I guess she didn't hear me coming up the stairs. Maybe she feels guilty—"

"Doubt it. She was probably crying because she knows you know."

"Dunno. She was on the phone to someone, and she had a piece of paper in her hand. She hid it when she realised I was there."

"Whatever that's all about, you have to stop being flatmates."

"There's still a lease and—"

"Forget the lease!"

Moments passed with neither one saying anything. Distant beeps followed by an airport announcement came through from Elise's end.

As if an idea came to her out of nowhere, she said, "Maybe I could help her. Maybe she wants me to acknowledge my part in her pain."

"I don't get it . . . her mum being hit by a car . . . what's that got to do with you?"

Another airport announcement was all he got from the other end.

"Elise?"

"Sorry. Was just thinking, remembering."

"What happened back then?"

"If you knew, you'd think I'm just as bad as Tempest."

"No one could be as bad as Tempest."

"Not so sure about that."

"Even if you did something so terrible, at least you feel bad about it. She has no conscience. She's pure evil."

"If that's the case, it's because of me, and maybe Ma." She suddenly sounded as distant from him as she was physically. "Ma was never nice to her. All because of what Pa and her mother did. Who wouldn't end up resentful? I basically killed . . ."

"Elise, what are you trying to say? You were a child and—"

"I can't talk about this right now, not like this."

They let their breathing and background noises do the talking long enough that it made sense to change the subject.

"Think you'll be too tired to see me tomorrow?"

"Course I want to see you. Then again . . ."

"What?"

"You've probably made plans . . . with Aiden."

His heart started racing. He pressed his fist against his chest and sprang up from the bed. He'd been dying to talk about him.

About them.

"Why the silence?" she said, mock seduction in her voice.

"Uh . . . I just . . ." His breathing misbehaved with his heartbeat.

"It's obvious you want each other."

"But he was with *you*. You were in love with him."

Her turn to be lost for words.

"What kind of friend would I be, being with my friend's ex?" He rolled his eyes.

Only yesterday, he'd met up with Aiden, talking about being together. No kissing. No touching as such. Just fingers caressing fingers in Aiden's car, and long-lasting eye contact. Their eyes had been doing the kissing, touching, fucking, love-making . . . The idea that an affair could be non-physical—besides finger contact—finally made sense.

"This is different though. If Aiden were straight and you were female, then it would be a problem. But Aiden likes men. He's not interested in me, and he never will be."

"But you fell for him. And he's not totally off females."

After crackling the connection with a deep sigh, she said, "I had strong feelings for him, but it wasn't love. I think we—no—*I* was heading in that direction. Maybe I was dicknotised."

Aiden's semi-erection on Elise's birthday . . . he *was* hung. The thought of it at its hardest . . .

He shook naughtiness away. "That's another thing. You two were intimate. More than once."

"Still can't believe that happened, knowing what I know now."

"Well, it did happen, and I know you wouldn't sleep with just anyone. He was your first. That's probably the worst part."

She didn't respond.

"Elise?"

"I'm still here." She sighed. "Do I wish we never slept together? Yes. Do I wish he wasn't . . . my first? . . . Of course. But I can't change anything. Probably worse guys I could've given myself to, but you should be with him, Shan."

"It's too soon after everything that's happened."

"I'm not telling you to sleep with him as soon as we hang up from each other. Just give things a go with him. He's in a better place now. His family knows the truth about him. And things aren't as bad as he thought they'd be. He's free. You're free."

Not quite. The pep talks Aiden had given him didn't change the fact that the frigger who'd died in Mabley Green had been claated in the head. No stab wounds. Shannon was a killer, had killed in self-defence. The longer he didn't do anything about it, the worse it would get. He wasn't strong like Aiden, couldn't move on, couldn't pretend he hadn't killed someone, couldn't continue avoiding the news, was tired of fretting whenever he heard sirens.

He had to settle this once and for all.

The police would have to see his side. He would try his hardest to keep Aiden out of it. Needed to do it before footage of the whole thing appeared on *Crimewatch* or *Watchdog*, his face zoomed into, the presenter saying, *"If anyone recognizes this man, please call—"*

"Did you hear me, Shannon?"

"What? . . . Sorry." He shook Mabley Green out of his mind.

"Thinking about Aiden?"

He chuckled, and then his smile remained at the memory of Aiden telling him that his grandparents were alright—not great—with his revelation. The two of them trumped Ethan, who was struggling the most. Still a good start. If only his own parents were like Aiden's grandparents. He had Uncle Lionel and Peter though. Maybe they were enough. But the prospect of going through the rest of his life without Viola and Leroy—fuck it—his parents . . . That just couldn't be it.

"Shannon?" Elise sang.

"God. Sorry, Elise. No more thinking. I promise."

"Shannon." Her tone was serious.

"Yeah?"

"You and Aiden better be official by the time I get back."

Together. Strange and beautiful at the same time. Butterflies came to life. "I'll bear that in mind."

"Forget about my history with him. What we had was nothing. It was just part of Tempest's scheme. I was fooled. None of it was real. You and Aiden, on the other hand . . ."

"Thanks, Elise."

"See you some time this weekend."

"Alrighty. Safe flight, hopefully sooner than later."

"Thanks."

He let Elise hang up first. He stayed in the same spot, staring ahead, beyond furniture, guilt over his fast-approaching date with Aiden disappearing.

The date had gone better than expected, though Aiden *and* Shannon needed to work on not caring what other people thought, the two of them looking around Levi Roots Caribbean Smokehouse to see who noticed Uncle Lionel and Peter holding hands.

Aiden had opted not to go along with Peter and Uncle Lionel to Lolita's wife's birthday party, saying he needed to get up early, but he probably wasn't ready to be around potentially so many non-straight people. Peter and Uncle Lionel had headed straight there, not due home for hours.

Aiden and Shannon were shivering at the front door, no words exchanged as the wind howled over the distant traffic. Aiden's eyes were as devastating as usual, a stunning shade of brown that had nothing to do with contacts. Penetrating gaze. Could barely look into those eyes, even when foggy breath obscured them.

"Had a good time?" Aiden said.

Shannon took his keys out of his pocket. "Yeah. You?"

"Yeah."

More silence.

"I know you have an early start tomorrow . . ." Shannon let out a deep breath, waited for its evidence to almost disappear then continued. ". . . but . . . do you . . . wanna . . . come in?"

"Yeah!" Aiden said quickly, his golden-brown eyes glinting as much as his tiny hoop earrings, before his usual intensity took over.

Shannon smiled, battling butterflies, then turned the key in the latch, his hand shaking. Hopefully, Aiden thought it was the cold's doing.

No sooner than he let Aiden in and turned on the passage light than his body was enveloped by Aiden's from behind. He writhed to free himself. Aiden was having none of that. The shaking he was desperate to be free of was at full force. The tightness of Aiden's arms around him, combined with the shaking, left him trembling all over, to the point that he could hardly stand.

But Aiden wouldn't let go.

"Ai . . . den."

"Can't help myself." Aiden's breathing was heavy, tinged with excitement and impatience, as his hands found their way underneath Shannon's jacket and all over the front of his upper torso.

Could've sworn he'd blacked out for a moment. The dreams he'd been having about Aiden were one thing, but this was another.

He grabbed Aiden's hands, making him stop. The strength had been transferred. Aiden's hold was no longer firm, his hands slipping away. He was about to back off, but Shannon reached behind, for his face, until Aiden's breathing and beard tickled his nose and lips. He turned his head to lock eyes with Aiden's then brought Aiden's face closer to his. Aiden parted his lips. Shannon did the same. They closed their eyes, Aiden starting it off. Facial hair prickled lips, then one pair of freshly-licked lips found another. Not much movement. Just pressing and muffled moans and a distressed heart, or two.

Aiden spoke. "I . . ." Something was taking over him, making him lose control of his breathing. "I . . ."

"I feel . . ." Shannon swallowed ". . . the same way."

Their lips came together again, not as clumsily as before, but harder. Another momentary blackout. Then lips stretched lips, making the kissing sounds they were supposed to. Then the two of them stopped, caught breath.

Aiden became firm again as he moved Shannon away from the door, stepping on the back of his Vans. They bumped into the banister. Aiden let out impatient grunts and teeth-kissing as he fumbled with the zip of Shannon's jacket from behind. Shannon helped Aiden. Aiden moaned his appreciation and eagerness as he yanked off his own jacket. Something fell on the floor as Shannon threw his jacket over the banister. Aiden shocked different parts of Shannon's body as he felt him up with his powerful hands, frisked him as if he were carrying a dangerous item hidden deep inside his muscles and bones. Tremors lingered and became magnified.

Aiden found what he was looking for in the front of Shannon's trousers. He let out a satisfied breath. They both froze. It seemed they'd both stopped breathing.

Then Aiden did it. He squeezed Shannon's hard dick, their moans creating a haunting melody. Shannon tried to squirm his way out of Aiden's clutches, doubled over until his chin met the banister, desire and fear at war inside him.

His horny side was winning, had him gyrating against Aiden like he was doing the batty rider, Aiden getting hard while grinding against him. Too much happening to think straight. He wanted all of it like he'd never wanted anything before. A line— no—*lines* were being crossed with every second and with every grunt, moan, squeeze and grind, to the point of no return. Lines would keep being crossed until . . .

He grew more surprised by everything Aiden was doing to him. He got a whiff of fabric softener as Aiden bent over him. He was trapped between the banister and solid muscle, ragged breaths and beard warming and tickling his ear, tongue all over his cheek, the two of them wining against each other.

Aiden brought him back upright. He fumbled for Aiden's head, lowered it to his. They side-head-butted each other, trying to find each other's lips blindly, before lips found facial hair then lips. Connected lips quelled desperate breathing.

Aiden's tongue broke through lips and teeth and invaded Shannon's mouth. Shannon sucked traces of Levi's punch from Aiden's long tongue, swallowed that taste like he needed it to stay alive. His inhibited side had long gone, replaced by the part of him that needed pleasing, had dreamed this moment of being taken by a man . . . by a sexy man . . . by Aiden. He was experiencing something more meaningful than porn, less lonely than masturbation, the real thing.

Tongues, then lips, finally parted. Shannon turned around to face Aiden straight-on. He gasped. The only thing Aiden had on from the waist up was a black string vest, pecs and shoulders busting, a pointy, 2p-coin-sized nipple exposed.

They stared at each other, chests heaving, lips glistening. He searched Aiden's face and demeanour for a cue to continue. He was looking at the wrong thing. Should've looked at Aiden's hands, hands which started yanking off his jumper then his vest. He did the same with Aiden's string vest. One shirtless chiselled upper torso, with a T-trail of hair from perky nipples to D'Angelo groin, put the shirtless torso opposite it to shame.

Aiden pulled Shannon to him and lowered himself until their denim-bound boners made contact. Their foreheads touching, they started to grind against each other, as they'd done before, when they'd been front to back. He rubbed all over Aiden's hard, strong back, Aiden doing the same to him as their dicks swelled and hardened even more. Aiden's countenance was sinister as he muttered curse words. Making eye contact was dangerous. The danger was hot. Shannon flinched when Aiden snuck his cold hands into his underwear, then grunted and trembled when Aiden started pinching all over his backside like he owned it. Couldn't keep from moaning and shuddering.

"Sorry," Aiden said.

"For . . . what?"

"Sounded . . . like I . . . hurt you."

"No . . . complete . . . opposite."

Only had to say it once. He grunted and held onto Aiden for dear life as Aiden continued owning him, as if using his hands to feel into his soul. Nothing to do but take it and curse and call for God . . . speak a new language . . . *Shanglish*.

Aiden must've been feeling the same way, making up his own language . . . *Aidish*.

Shannon bit his bottom lip as Aiden's lips trembled, dicks continuing to strain through cotton and denim. He squeezed Aiden's dick. Aiden shuddered, his mouth and eyes wide open as he grunted, the control he'd had from the start transferring in that moment. He was giving in, his face contorted like he was in distress. More grunts. More Aidish. Aiden upped the ante as he felt up Shannon's private areas some more and damn near choked him as he brought them both to the hardwood floor.

They rolled around, dicks intent on being skin to skin. They rolled right, left, right, left, right, then stopped with Shannon on top. Pre-come was trickling out. He wiggled to lessen the sensation. Aiden had other ideas, kept him from repositioning, his countenance like that of a starved lion. Aiden's sneaky hands became a barrier between Shannon's underwear and skin. Aiden pinched his backside some more, squeezing him into him. They groaned in unison, the remnants of their groans making a haunting harmony. He buried his head in Aiden's chest, as he lost the battle to keep in meek, submissive sounds, hiding as if they'd an audience. As Aiden cupped Shannon's backside and raked his hairy crack with a finger, Shannon rubbed against Aiden, his perineum getting sore. He removed his face from hiding. Aiden's eyes were closed, his mouth open like he was letting out a silent scream, as he wined.

"Fuck me."

Aiden's eyes opened, the widest he'd ever seen them.

He grimaced, the non-sexual part of him cussing off his horny side for being so nasty.

Horniness made him continue simulating the act of riding dick, the prudish killjoy in him frigging off.

Aiden licked his lips. Then came the dreaded snarl and lines-between-eyebrows combination.

Shannon quivered, begging the tingles in his body for mercy and ruthlessness at the same time. He ran his fingers over Aiden's lips before allowing him to suck one.

"Mmmmm . . ."

He added another finger then surprised Aiden, replaced his fingers with his tongue. Aiden gave tongue back, shoved it in his mouth.

As they tongue-flicked, they sped up the grinding, Aiden kneading Shannon's backside, Shannon feeling up Aiden's muscles, hard all over, from shoulders to biceps to chest to abs. Couldn't get enough of the hardness, the involuntary pec bounces. He felt Aiden up as if he would never live this moment again, as Aiden did the same to him. He rubbed up and down Aiden's hairy pebbles for abs with one hand and pinched hard nipples with the other, amidst the fondling and tingling and being tongue-fucked in the mouth.

He yanked Aiden's trousers down. Aiden introduced his backside and thighs to the cold, taking him to a place so good it scared him, hands as devastating as electrical massagers. He was humming, squirming and speaking more Shanglish, embarrassment, excitement and eagerness taking over all at once.

Aiden flipped him over, becoming the one on top. Shannon's left shoe had slipped off and his left leg was bare, while his right foot was lost in a leg of his jeans. He wrapped his legs around Aiden, running his trembling fingers up and down Aiden's moist, hairy crack. He gyrated as the pre-come from his and Aiden's erections seeped out like pus. Aiden had that devilish look on his face as he squeezed Shannon's hard dick, more pre-come flooding the tip. Aiden wouldn't let go, just squeezed tighter as he jerked, had Shannon arching his back and thrashing his head. More embarrassing whimpers. Watery eyes. And this was only the beginning.

He fumbled for Aiden's erection as Aiden brought his face to his. The ridges all over Aiden's dick tickled his hand. Foreheads touching, they jerked each other.

He ran his tongue along Aiden's lips. "I can't"—peck on the lips—"believe"—lips pressing against lips—"I'm"—lips forming a tower with four levels, Shannon's being the ground and second floors—"pre-"—tongues reuniting, adding two more levels—"coming."

Tongues were at war again, each frantic to come out on top as unbidden moans left mouths, dicks dabbing ink of love and lust on skin and pubic hair, that ink blending with sweat.

He sucked Aiden's long, lethal tongue like his saliva could quench his thirst, like he wanted to swallow it. Couldn't wait to do the same to Aiden's dick. He took his mouth away from Aiden's, unable to keep from throwing his head back and forth, and side to side, like someone fast asleep on a rickety train as Aiden ran his soggy dick head along his perineum, taunting his hole.

"*Aiden.*"

"*Mm-hmm?*"

"*Ai . . . den.*"

Aiden muttered some more in Aidish.

"*Hurry . . . up . . . and . . . fuck me.*"

Aiden growled and became firmer with him, frantically running his fingers around his sweaty sphincter. Shannon closed his eyes, raised his hips and brought his knees to his chest. His cheeks were spread and his tight hole blown and prodded, Aiden's deadly dick, curved upwards like an arm of a cactus, in his periphery. This was the night. This was Aiden. It was going to be Aiden's big dick filling him up. Completely worth the pain if there was going to be any. He tried to keep his balance as he ran his hand up and down

Aiden's jagged, thick, long erection, pre-come and sweat lubricating it, while Aiden's fingers went deeper inside him.

Jingling.

He froze, then winced, tightening around Aiden's fingers, eyes wide open.

Scratching against the door.

"Shit!" Aiden wiggled his fingers out.

The two of them struggled to their feet, Aiden's erect dick springing with his desperate movements, a string of pre-come stopping just above his knee.

The door clicked open. Shannon, shackled at the ankles by his underwear, could only manage to shuffle to the door.

The door opened a few inches before he pushed it shut. Teeth-kissing was the response.

"What the fuck are they doing back?" Aiden hissed as he struggled to get his underwear past his low-hanging balls and thick dick.

"No fucking idea!" Shannon leaned against the door, one foot on the floor, the other up as he tried to get one jeans leg past his ankle.

Not strong enough to keep the door shut, especially standing on one frigging foot. Someone from the other side hurled into the door, flinging him into Aiden, whose erection was still exposed and leaking pre-come.

"What the . . . Shannon? . . . Aiden?"

"Weh the rahtidclaat ah gwaan?"

Tingles tormented him everywhere, heart pounding, bare backside still out, dick nowhere near flaccid. He couldn't face his uncle or Peter. Aiden's head was down, nothing but pisstivity on his face as he failed to get his jeans up to his waist.

Someone spun Shannon around. His pubic hair and part of his dick were still exposed. His uncle was holding him firmly.

"Don't know what the two of you are trying to hide," Peter said, smirking as he looked Aiden up and down then did the same to Shannon, Uncle Lionel keeping Shannon in position to give him a better look. "Not like we haven't seen you two naked before."

He wrenched himself out of his uncle's clutches then stumbled closer to Aiden, kept his back turned to the dick blockers.

"Yes, we see the front, now the batty."

He clenched his backside to get his pants up more easily.

"Your turn, Aiden," Peter said. "Show us those cheeks."

Aiden's lips trembled.

"What a way your body hot, Aiden. If me was single and younger . . . Shannon, you ah gwaan with *tings*!"

"The two of them ah gwaan with tings!"

Would've probably laughed at hearing patois come out of Peter's mouth if not for the frigging embarrassment.

"We came back too damn soon, Lionel. Missed opportunity to see them climax."

Aiden made a throaty exhale. Shannon doubled over as his perineum tingled and dick shifted.

Finally covered up, albeit clothes twisted, Shannon said, "Why are you back so soon?"

"We haffi explain weh we ah do ah we yard?"

"We just came back to get something," Peter said.

"We soon leave though, so unu can carry on."

"Preferably *not* right by the front door." Peter looked at them out of the corner of his eye. "Hope you two had condoms ready."

"Haffi disinfect the whole floor ah morning."

"Shannon, I'll see you around," Aiden said, shouldering past him to the door, head down.

"You're leaving, Aiden?"

Aiden bit his bottom lip, barely making eye contact with anyone.

"Shannon, kiss him goodbye before him leave, nuh? Aiden, turn round. Kiss him make we see." Uncle Lionel pushed Aiden closer to Shannon.

Aiden's widened his eyes like Uncle Lionel's strength surprised him.

"Kiss, kiss, kiss, kiss . . ." Peter said.

Aiden closed his eyes like he was doing a woosah in his head, then he opened them and broke into that hot smirk of his, one side of his mouth lifted higher than the other.

Butterflies.

"Kiss, kiss, kiss . . ." Uncle Lionel joined in with Peter.

Shannon gave Aiden a peck on the lips.

"They can do better than that, can't they Lionel?"

"Ee-hi. Make we see unu tongue?"

"Yes. Tongue, tongue, tongue . . ."

Aiden smirked again. Shannon smiled. Aiden tilted his head to the left, as his left eyebrow twitched. Shannon closed his eyes, put his arms around Aiden's waist, while Aiden held the back of his head firmly. Then their lips connected, Shannon opening his mouth wide for Aiden's tongue. Applause encouraged them as they tongue-flicked and moaned into each other's mouths, movement in their pants.

The applause had stopped at some point, or maybe Shannon was so gone that he'd stopped hearing it. Aiden's hands, strength, presence, lips and tongue had him floating.

Aiden had him floating to a place he never wanted to come down from.

35 / Tempest IX
Lioness vs. tigress

Elbow on dressing table, hand under chin, Tempest was staring at the discoloured paper folded in four. Another try at convincing herself that everything she'd done was justified, that the letter her mum had written meant something else.

Maybe Auntie Janice had written it, pretending to be her mum. Her aunt knew she hated Elise. Maybe Auntie Janice had written the letter to fuck up her plans.

Auntie Janice would've made a damn good actress though, crying the way she had. The paper was yellow on the edges from age anyway.

She unfolded the letter for the thousandth time and read it again. No hidden meaning, no exaggeration, no metaphors. The same fucking words. She closed her eyes and pulled at chunks of her hair as she rocked on the dressing table chair.

By the time you read this, I will have ended it all . . .

Years of coming up with reasons, besides the obvious, why her mum's wrists were bandaged that day. It never mattered, never had anything to do with what Elise had done, but after reading the letter again and again and a-fucking-gain . . . The truth, her mum's truth, was claating her soul. Her closed eyes were flooding. She squeezed them even tighter, but tears pushed through her sticky eyelashes. She opened her eyes and blinked rapidly as tickling tears became a torrent.

She'd spent the last few months plotting ways to fuck Elise's life up, only to find what had been her ultimate goal for so long had become her biggest fear. Would have to wait months to notice changes in Elise to know the true outcome. Would've been better if she'd given Elise a claat and called it a day. Having Elise lose her virginity to a gay guy was fucked-up, but at least she finally knew how dick felt, how to please a man, a gay man even.

A door squealed open then yawned to a close, then another did the same.

Elise had gone from the room next door, her bedroom, to the bathroom.

The bathroom. Elise was back in there again, even though the food-tampering had stopped. It couldn't have gone that far, now that Tempest knew her mum had intended to die.

And Elise knew what the deal was. It was obvious from the way she'd been acting since her birthday, barely making eye contact, hardly speaking to her, avoiding her, staying in her bedroom.

Or the bathroom.

A knock on the flat door made her jump and cuss. Carl. Finally. He must've timed it right, must've reached the door to the flats the moment someone opened it, no need to be buzzed up. She needed him, more than she ever had, just to hold her, squeeze her. Where he'd been and why he hadn't contacted her for over a week didn't matter. What was important was that he'd come.

She folded the letter, stuffed it inside her jeans pocket, and wiped her cheeks as she stumbled to the flat door, ready to collapse into Carl's strong arms.

That desire shrunk to nothing the instant she opened the door.

Some tall, thirty-something-looking woman was within arm's reach in the doorway. She was about to ask the woman who she was when features teased her memory: her braids in a bun half the size of her head; her black thigh-length jacket; and facetiness in her frown, snarl and flared nostrils. The visitor had on a pair of tiger-print leggings.

It came to her. That facety woman near Aiden's house that evening . . . the hat . . . the camera.

The woman had taken a picture of her.

The woman must've realised that Tempest recognized her—maybe Tempest's demeanour was betraying her—because she barged into the flat.

"Oi! You can't—"

"Shut up!" The woman chucked her black Chanel handbag on the entrance table like she owned the place, knocking the candle out of position, then she hung her jacket on the coat rack, over Elise's navy jacket.

She stepped to Tempest, stopping inches from her.

Tempest backed up, raising her hand, index finger pointed upwards.

The woman stepped closer, her exhales hitting Tempest's finger before swatting Tempest's hand, muttering something in another language.

The letter had drained Tempest, but being touched was waking her the fuck up. "Whoever you are, I'm not the one to fuck with."

The woman snarled at her as she adjusted her tight white EleVen tee with purple cap sleeves.

"Look, if it's your hat you came here for, it's right—"

"Fuck the hat!" This time, the woman's purple-stiletto-nailed index finger was in Tempest's face.

"Get your bombo-bloodclaat hand out of my face."

"Make me, bitch!" Finger so close that it scraped her nose.

436

Tempest transferred most of her weight to her left leg and shook the right. She grabbed the woman's hand and forced it to her side. "Like I said, *heifer*, I don't know who you are, but your hat is hanging up right there." She pointed to the hat on the coat rack. "Now get it and . . ."

This heifer knew where she lived.

She scanned the floor, from the furry slippers on her feet to her five-inch-high-heeled boots drooping under the coat rack. Those boots were closer to the woman. The woman had on Nikes, white with flecks of red. Her ankles were exposed between Nike ankle socks and the hems of her tiger-print leggings.

The woman choked her, face contorted in effort and psycho bitch-ness. Both hands. Nails digging into her skin. She clawed at the woman's face, struggling to breathe, but scraping skin and cotton was all she could do, the assailant moving her head about, not easing up on the choking.

"Can't stand . . . bitches like you."

The woman had her dangling on her toes and almost her knees, slippers coming off.

"You have . . . no respect . . . for marriage."

She dug her nails into the woman's hands until the woman yanked them away.

She gasped for air as she backed into the flat door and got to her feet. "Mad . . . bitch!"

The woman clenched her teeth, charged at her, slamming her into the door, and clawed at her face.

Cheeks on fire, Tempest flailed her arms about as she tried to tear up the woman's cheeks, but her assailant dodged. She threw desperate punches, cheeks feeling like they were being peeled off. Her fist connected with the bitch's mouth. It was as if the bitch had ripped off chunks of flesh when she stumbled backwards from the punch. Nothing could extinguish the flames. She was going to tear the bitch's face up for that.

A kick in the chest drove her into the door.

She lunged at the bitch.

The woman came for her, short purple stiletto nails primed to create more fire.

Tempest grabbed her bun. The enemy clutched her half-fringe, had her by the cheek with the other hand. They were trying to rip each other's scalps from their skulls as they spun each other around, shoes stepped on and kicked around. The fire was spreading from cheeks to scalp. She made sure the bitch was feeling the same thing.

Thumps to her face out of nowhere. She thumped right back.

"Homewrecking slut!"

Haphazard footwork had them taking turns with their backs to the door. When the bitch's back was to the door again, Tempest kicked her in the stomach, into the door. The woman threw herself into her again as if the kick had been nothing. They ended up on the floor, on their sides, thumping and kicking each other like they wanted to break bones.

"What"—she kneed the bitch in her belly—"the fuck"—the woman's wayward fist got her in the neck—"is wrong"—she grabbed the woman's braided bun again—"with you?"

They were writhing on the floor, limbs flailing. Bitch was having a hard time grabbing Tempest's hair, desperate for Tempest to let go of hers. Tempest grabbed more chunks of braids as she withstood hard, swift blows to her face and body.

"I'll kill you, heifer!"

Wasting energy on words. The reason her scalp suddenly felt like it was roasting again. The bitch had grabbed a big chunk of her hair, playing tug of war with it.

Tempest shuffled on her hip to get closer to her high-heeled boots. They were somewhere behind her. Shuffling, grunting, and playing tug of war with braids, all at the same time, while kicks from the bitch made her thighs, shins and stomach suffer. She tried to give as good as she got, tried to rip the bitch's scalp off, her head twisted, as the bitch did the same with her scalp. The bitch wasn't going to give up. Neither was she.

"You fuck . . . my motherfucking . . . husband . . . and don't expect me . . . to claat you?"

The enemy let go of her hair and put all her energy into blindly unleashing with thumps intended to knock out teeth and rupture organs.

She lost her grip on the enemy's hair, the heifer's speed and strength keeping her from hitting back like she really wanted to. She hit back like she couldn't mash ants.

"He's the . . . fucking . . . problem!"

"So are you . . . you . . . come-guzzling . . . trick!"

She took the gamble, gave the heifer's fists more access to her face. Couldn't dodge for shit as she fumbled for one of the shoes digging into her back. Thumped in the neck, forehead, nose, mouth, jaw . . . She couldn't take anymore. Had to grab hold of something quickly. Her nose was running, lips stinging. She tasted blood.

She had it . . . something in her hand. . . . Grip tight. . . . Bitch drawing more blood from her. She was going to make blood pour out of the bitch like a fountain.

The toilet flushed.

That paused them both.

She was the first to get going again, picking up what was in her hand—a boot. Blowing through pursed lips, she pounded the enemy with it. The bitch blocked, blocked, blocked, blocked, blocked. Had to change things up, throw blows from different directions, make the enemy's blocks pointless.

Then the bitch shrieked, withstood wicked blows from the boot heel to her face as she frantically unleashed thumps and kicks.

A door opened.

Neither of them stopped this time.

"What the . . ." Quick footsteps were approaching.

She screamed, blood from her nose and mouth mixing with her sweat, her cheeks burning, blood boiling as the bitch thumped and scratched blood out of her. She windmilled and kicked and spat, getting the bitch in every way, giving what she was getting. The bitch spat back, getting her chin and neck. She hawked up and spat at the bitch again.

"Stop it!" Elise said.

Elise got in the way, ended up getting hits not meant for her, then she backed into the woman as she pushed Tempest away.

Tempest was gasping for air. "Come on . . . fucking heifer!" She swallowed blood from her busted lip. "Fuck you up some more!"

Elise snatched the boot from her.

"You come on!" The woman was squirming past Elise, managed to get another kick in, blood underneath her left eye, blood running from her nose and her lip busted, only a few strands left of her braided bun, the rest all over the place. "You wanna . . . take him from me? . . . He's my husband . . . motherfucking slut!"

The bitch kicked past Elise again. Tempest grabbed her foot, twisted it. The bitch wailed, went down.

"Tempest . . ." Elise put her hand over her mouth, her widened eyes confirming Tempest's face looked as horrific as it felt, then she turned to the woman. "What are you talking about?"

"That *puta* . . . is fucking . . . my bastard husband." The woman shuffled backwards, towards the front door, on her elbows and flat batty.

Tempest pressed her trembling hands against her burning cheeks, the agony at another level with the fight over, adrenalin waning. "You fucking psycho!" She went for the woman, but Elise kept her back.

"You'll pay for this. When you see your reflection . . . you'll wish you were ugly." Bitch got to her feet. "If you think I'm finished tearing your face up . . . you have another *fucking* thing coming!"

Tempest sucked her busted lip, withstood the stinging, swallowed more blood. "Bring it, you pussyclaat heifer!"

"You've got this all wrong." Elise had her arms stretched out, made Tempest her shadow.

The bitch stared at Elise then shook her head, breathing hard. "You really . . . favour this whore. . . . Sorry for the messages. . . . They were meant for her."

Tempest paused.

"What messages?" Elise said.

"About how you were sleeping with my husband, and you'd be sorry. But I know now that it wasn't you. . . . It was that *puta*." Pure evil in the bitch's bloody eyes. "Different complexions, more different than I realised, but you really favour. You both have short hair now. That's what threw me. . . . Bitch had braids before."

Adrenalin was depleting faster; burning cheeks were growing more un-fucking-bearable, strands from her half-fringe irritating the scratches. If Elise wasn't between her and the bitch . . . "Just hurry up and fuck off, hoe!"

"I'm not going any-fucking-where! I've been watching my shithouse husband for weeks. This ends now."

"The vows were between you and him, not me and you, you stupid bitch!"

The woman rummaged through her handbag, making Tempest and Elise back up. Before they had a chance to pounce, the bitch took something out of her handbag, her hand shaking, a black LG smartphone with scratches on it.

Tempest gasped.

"What is it?" Elise said.

"That's . . . Carl's."

"Of course it is. You sent a message to this phone earlier—and *I* responded."

Her stomach dropped.

"You've probably seen the scratch on his face." The woman sounded like she was talking about artwork she had on display in The National Gallery. "I told him to stop seeing you, but he couldn't help himself. I showed him. I don't like being taken for a poppyshow. Don't know if it's the Cuban or Jamaican in me, or both."

Cuban? That explained the Spanish.

Spanish.

Carl on the phone that morning, speaking Spanish.

Not to his sister.

To this . . . damn . . . trashcan heifer!

Fucking liar, fucking liar, fucking liar.

"You really thought he was done with his wife, that he was going to leave me for you? You haven't seen enough shows, or read enough books, to know that it never ends well for the side piece?"

"Don't *you* know it never ends well for the wife whose husband wants someone else?"

"What, you expected him to leave me for you and put a ring on it? Bitch, you were just available pussy to him."

"Well, my pussy must be sweeter, tighter and flier than yours, or else he wouldn't be fucking me every chance he gets, drowning in my juices while I fuck his face."

The bitch's expression was stuck between hurt and rage.

"That's right, heifer. My pussy owns him. Same for my titties, batty crack, in between my toes—"

"Stop it, Tempest!"

"Elise . . ." She kissed her teeth, instead of telling Elise what was on the tip of her tongue—to suck her mother.

She turned back to Carl's wife. "He craves every part of me, bitch."

The bitch started chuckling, and looked psychotic doing it, like she was about to start round two, but she did something on the phone instead then handed it to Elise. "Read it."

"Read what?"

"You'll see. Just read it."

"What is it, Elise?"

Elise ignored her, started reading something, eyes narrowing, mouth widening, head shaking slowly.

"Elise, for fuck's sake, tell me!"

The bitch with braids was smirking.

"Fucking hell, Elise!"

Elise kept scrolling and reading, her chest starting to heave.

She snatched the phone then scrolled and read. Messages between her and Carl about Elise . . . about everything.

"That fucking bastard and this bitch have been plotting against you. Then there's the passport she threw away."

Her stomach dropped again, heart sprinting all over her chest.

"Wait a minute." Elise furrowed her brow then widened her eyes slowly, as if she were solving a mystery.

She had to regain control. Elise didn't need to hear anything else. She chucked the phone at her enemy. "Leave, heifer!"

Elise cut her eyes at her then turned to the enemy. "What passport?"

"Elise, this bitch is crazy."

"I might be crazy, but I'm no liar. Passport's in here, sweetie." The enemy fumbled through her bag again, took out the passport, handed it to Elise.

"Elise, let me—"

"Shut up, Tempest!" Elise moved away from her, closer to the enemy.

Two against one.

"The post-it at the back with a number written on it . . . could've been anyone's. Tried it anyway. Good thing I fucking did."

Elise kept opening and closing her mouth, her eyes slits as she turned to stare at Tempest.

"Elise, what's this bitch talking about?"

"That time . . . I changed my number . . . wrote the new one down. . . . Didn't remember I'd stuck it in my passport."

She clutched the living room door frame, legs weak.

"Something else that confused me . . . I searched your name on the electoral roll. The address I found . . . I went there, but when I kept seeing the same man and woman coming out of the house, I couldn't believe that woman was Carl's whore, someone so much older and . . ." The heifer screwed up her blood-streaked face. "She's just not his type." She peered at Tempest, her face contorted more than before. "This *trash*, on the other hand, is."

Elise's hand went to her mouth.

"You alright, sweetheart?"

"Tell me how you got the passport."

Carl's wife explained how she'd started following him then Tempest. She followed her to an address—Aiden's house—waited for her to leave and saw her throw the passport into a bin. "I'm the cleanest person, so you can imagine my desperation when I put my hands in some fucking bin to get more info on this bitch." She looked at Tempest. "I saw you looking for me. Thought you'd found me when you stopped beside my car."

Tempest frowned. There was a whole heap of cars, some moving, some parked, but nothing that was . . .

"The BMW."

"Bingo." The heifer took out her compact. She gasped at the reflection of her mashed-up face and jacked-up braids.

"It really was you."

"Prank calls too. Saw that in the texts." The bitch ran her fingers through her messed-up braids. "Can't believe that motherfucker had the nerve to not only cheat, but also plot with his slut . . . just up and tossed me aside to play away with some flat chest skank . . . did more for her than he ever did for his own wife."

Tempest clutched her stomach then stumbled backwards, tripping over her own feet and ending up on her batty. She rushed to her feet before the two of them could jump her.

Elise shot her a murderous look. "You really did it . . . Shannon . . . Aiden."

"I know those names too."

"Shut up!" Tempest picked up one of her slippers and threw it right in the woman's parted mouth.

The cunt wiped her mouth, felt her teeth as if to make sure they were still intact then pressed her lips in, picked the slipper up and threw it back. It was like wind cutting past Tempest's neck. The bitch missed. She scanned the passage. Her gaze fell on the candle, in its holder, on the entrance table. She picked the whole thing up and threw it at Tempest. Too slow to dodge it. It tore into the left side of her forehead then came apart on the floor, the candle rolling away. She scrambled for the candle holder, but Elise pushed her and picked it up.

The bitch snatched up her hat and jacket.

Elise was shaking and blinking quickly, eyes shimmering. "You really want to destroy me." She rushed to her bedroom, sobbing.

"Elise—"

The flat door opened.

The bitch cut her eyes up and down Tempest, hat in one hand, handbag in the other, jacket slung over her shoulder. "One last thing. Now that I know what my husband's been doing, unless you can come up with over £3,500—which I'm sure you can't—for the rent you owe me, you need to pack your *shit* and get the *fuck* out of here within a week. I own this whole building, bitch." She cut her eyes at Tempest one last time, then she slammed the door behind her.

Elise stormed back out of her room.

"Elise, listen."

Elise yanked her Virgin jacket off the coat rack and jammed her feet into flats.

She grabbed Elise. Elise boxed her, adding another level of burning to one of her scratched cheeks, then stormed out of the flat.

Tempest slipped on the first pair of shoes she could find then snatched a jacket off the rack. Something wasn't right about it. It was Elise's navy one. No time to take it back off and put on another one. She raced down the stairs, caught up with Elise, reached the building entrance door before her.

"Move, Tempest!"

"No!"

Elise was breathing like her chest was about to explode. "Move!"

"No! We need to talk first."

"You really hate me."

"I don't."

"Tempest, for the last time, get out of my way."

"We both know what's going on."

"You did this whole Aiden thing, nearly ruined my friendship with Shannon and tried to lose me my job, tried to drive me crazy."

"I thought you'd killed my mum!"

Elise's lips quivered as she held her head up.

"But I found out the truth. It wasn't you. She was . . . suicidal."

"Su—" Elise swallowed. "Suicidal?"

Tears stinging her cheeks, she told Elise what she'd heard those months ago.

"But when we went back to Daddy's house after your birthday, Auntie Janice gave me this letter." She took the letter out of her pocket and handed it to Elise. "By the time my mum wrote this, she was already cutting her wrists, and . . ." She heaved. ". . . and tried to get herself run over . . . two separate times . . . before she . . . before you—"

"Stop! Just stop!" Elise doubled over like she'd been kicked in the gut.

"Read it, Elise. She was called the whore of Hackney, as if she'd gone from dick to dick. Can you imagine? And she loved Daddy so much that she was done when he stayed with your mum."

She slumped down against the door as Elise clutched her chest and her shiny eyes moved from side to side. Those eyes sucked her into a trance, took her back to that hot July day in Regent's Park.

Daddy had taken them there. They were throwing a tennis ball around. Elise was the only one who couldn't catch.

No one knew her last attempt to catch the ball was going to be her last.

When she didn't catch it that last time, it bounced far away then rolled even farther. Mummy must've followed them since she turned up out of nowhere, her dress as yellow as the sun, and picked up the ball. Elise started acting stupid, kept calling Mummy a monster. Mummy wouldn't give the ball back. Daddy marched over to her, started telling her off. Couldn't hear him, but he was pointing at her, face all screwed up. Then Daddy said something that made Mummy look like she wanted to cry. Mummy suddenly threw the ball so high, so far, it ended up in the road. Elise was the closest to the road, so she ran to get the ball.

Mummy ran after her, then Daddy ran after them.

Screams soon followed, then screeching tyres and thuds at the same time, thuds like the noise the bigger kids at school made with their feet at the end of the last assembly before the summer holidays, only this noise didn't last as long. Then something crunched as people screamed some more. Tempest ran to the road to be with her mummy, daddy and sister.

A crowd was forming. People were staring at something, shock on their faces, some with hands over mouths. When Tempest followed their gazes to something yellow on the ground blown by the wind, Daddy grabbed her, pressed her face to his belly. His body was shaking. He sounded like he was choking. Could've sworn something wet her forehead. When he wiped it, she had a chance to see what he didn't want her to see. She took it, got a peek of something red spreading around braids. Then Daddy turned her head, squeezed it into his belly again, tighter than the first time.

"If the car never killed her, she would've killed herself somehow." She shook her head, blinking back tears rapidly. "I know that now."

Elise was clutching her stomach, cheeks wet. Tempest reached for her.

She jerked away then pushed past Tempest to the door.

"Elise!"

She opened the door.

"Wait!"

"Stay away from me!"

"Things are different now. I don't blame you anymore."

"I don't care!"

"Don't say that." Tempest struggled to her feet, body sore, face burning all over.

Elise shook her head. "I mean it."

"But—"

Elise nearly let the heavy door trap Tempest's fingers as she scrambled out of the building.

This was the beginning of the end, worse than whatever damage Carl's wife had done to her face and body.

She'd gotten it completely wrong. She should've gone after Mari-heifer instead, or cut ties with Elise. Should've never come to this.

Her cheeks throbbing, she ran her fingers over the parts that stung. She hissed. If she ever saw that bitch again . . . As for Carl . . .

She grimaced until those cunts shrunk in her mind. They were the least of her worries. She had to catch up with Elise, because there was only one place she was headed—their daddy and that other bitch's house.

36 / Elise VIII
Ambush

Running for the bus was pointless. Not only had Elise missed it—the next one wasn't due for another fifteen minutes—but her insides couldn't take the jerking. She raised her head then closed her eyes to everything spinning around her as something sickly rose from her abdomen to her chest. The nausea was meant to be behind her, but it was back, for whatever reason. Her tummy was pushing something upwards as she breathed through pursed lips. Rapid breaths made no difference. Her insides were erupting. As if snatched out of a deep sleep, she opened her eyes and staggered to a filthy spot next to the bus stop and let it all out.

She collapsed onto the bus stop seat when she was done. A little relief. She closed her eyes as she took quick, short breaths, fighting to keep from vomiting again.

Feeling guilty all those years over something she wasn't responsible for. What had she been thinking anyway, luring Sylvia to a busy road? It really hadn't been to kill her, only to hurt her, because Ma had been hurting. But the violent thud of the cab hitting Sylvia, her body tumbling and rolling over it, and the crack of body against concrete, was as audible now as it had been back then.

The reason Tempest had done the things she'd done.

If she'd really been a virgin, gone to great lengths to save herself for the right man . . . She grimaced and shook it off. None of that mattered now. There was no way back, back to the day Sylvia died, back to their father's double life, back to her courtship—or whatever it had been—with Aiden and the times they'd had sex. Good thing they'd used protection. It was as if Tempest had hypnotised her, said the right things, to make her give Aiden a chance.

Her lips were trembling. Pressing her eyes shut would only keep her tears at bay for a little while until the pressure became too great. She opened her eyes and let the tears flow freely.

Her own sister. All that hatred.

Her parents. Tempest could've done things to them, without anyone knowing. Maybe—

"Elise!"

She jumped. Someone wearing a burgundy hoodie was approaching.

"Should've done this long time." He grabbed her.

Unapproachable countenance. Sunken lips. Familiar face.

Her birthday.

"Where the fuck's Shannon?"

"Let . . . go of me. I don't even know— Aargh!"

He was pressing his thumb into the part of her arm where her forearm and biceps met. "If you ramp with me, I'll fuck you up. Gender don't mean shit to me."

"You're . . . hurting me." Twisting . . . writhing . . . no relief.

"Come on!"

"Marvin, what the fuck are you doing?"

Someone had come to help her, someone wearing a beige cardigan and black New York Yankees hat.

"Shut the fuck up, Callum!"

This Callum had been at her birthday too.

He was no help at all.

Marvin pushed Callum out of the way, not easing his grip on her one bit. "Come on, bitch!"

She grimaced when his saliva sprayed her face.

"Where are you . . . taking me?"

They were approaching Wick Road. As fast as he was walking, he might as well have been dragging her along. She was tripping over herself trying to catch up with him; if not for the way he was holding her, she would've fallen flat on her face. The traffic, buildings, the ground . . . everything was starting to spin again. More vomit was coming.

"I ask the questions."

"Not too rough, Marvin!"

"We have to get her in the car. Taking no chances."

"Car?" she said.

Marvin shook her. "You're taking us to that batty man."

Her insides were merciless, the dizziness worsening. She almost completely shut her eyes. She stumbled some more then lost her footing. She was about to fall on her hip when Marvin yanked her back to her feet.

She covered her mouth, as if that were enough to keep the vomit down.

He shook her again.

"You'll be alright . . . long as you don't do stupid shit," Callum said.

Marvin had referred to Aiden as Shannon's man on her birthday. She hadn't asked Aiden about these guys. They were after Shannon for some reason. Capable of anything. Couldn't just take them to him.

Only one thing to do now that they were on Wick Road.

"Help! Help! H—!"

Something dug into her side, something Marvin was holding. Didn't need to see it to know what it was. The dizziness couldn't mask his countenance. This face of a madman, his eyes as fiery as his complexion, forehead lines abundant, told her what would happen to her if she didn't cooperate.

Pedestrians and vehicles were bouncing around. People were looking her way. They'd heard her shouts. One wrong move and she'd be . . . No. Couldn't think like that. She forced a smile to convince them she was safe. Between maniacal Marvin and the imminent vomit, she must've looked peculiar.

The vomit was coming, flooding her throat. She stopped fake-smiling.

"Already told you. For your sake . . ."

She turned her head gingerly, tripping over her feet towards Callum. He was on her other side, holding her right arm. He didn't like what was happening, but his loyalty was to his friend, his leader. Maybe he was her only way out though.

". . . don't do anything stupid."

Marvin shook her again. "Better listen to him."

Spinning accelerated. Traffic bounced faster. She couldn't take it. Her stomach couldn't take it. "Gonna . . . be sick."

"I swear I'll stab you!"

The way they were holding her, she couldn't double over. It was going to go all over her, unless . . . She turned to Marvin, the knife digging into her even more, and then it came out.

"For *fuck's* sake!"

They both let go of her, backed off.

She ran as fast as the dizziness allowed, screaming. That got people's attention again. Everything was probably spinning faster than she was running. A vehicle beeped. Hard to tell if it was intended for her. Maybe she was heading into the road. Or maybe it was road rage between two drivers. She fought the disorientation, kept going, veered right, further inside the pavement, then straightened up. It was no good, the spinning making what was ahead one moment, almost behind her the next.

Her insides were rolling like a washing machine in its spin cycle. She memorised the swirling sight before her, marking the kerb most of all, as she approached the first of two bridges, then she closed her eyes for relief, quick breaths making her mouth and throat dry. Everything was louder: the wind, the constant flow of steady traffic, footsteps . . .

Footsteps from behind.

Quick footsteps. Louder, closer.

Vomit was burning its way up.

The scrape of fabric joined the footsteps trampling the ground.

She opened her eyes a slit too late. She couldn't slow down fast enough. She crashed into something hard. She opened her eyes fully. A fence. Someone crashed into her, bringing her to the ground.

"Look what you've done!" Marvin lifted her to her feet and slammed her against the fence.

The nausea had stolen all her strength. She was so gone. Marvin might as well have knocked her out.

He boxed her, shocking her into alertness. "Look at me, you bitch!"

She didn't have to look; the wind was blowing the scent of her vomit from his burgundy hoodie to her nose. She lifted her hand to sooth her cheek. He shook her, jerking her insides around. Her lips quivered. Everything was blurry, from dizziness and tears.

"What did I tell you, Elise?" That was the other one. "Wrong fucking move."

She wasn't going to tell them where Shan was. Even if she wanted to, she couldn't; speaking would make her feel worse and bring up more vomit.

"You've fucked this up, not taking us to Shannon. He took something from me. I'm taking something from him so that he knows how it feels to lose someone. Your blood's gonna be on his hands."

He clamped her by her jacket collar with one hand, the other hand holding the knife pointing to her throat.

The spinning was unrelenting. Vehicles were bunched together, slowing down, stopping. People were watching and approaching. They were going to save her, or at least try. Keeping an eye on them worsened the dizziness. Staring into the distance was better.

She winced when Marvin shook her again. His firm hold kept the swaying to a minimum, forced eye contact. His mind had been made up. His eyes were telling her he couldn't care less about witnesses as he scraped the knife's edge against her skin. She couldn't break free, too weak from the dizziness and the vomit building up. She was pinned.

"Ain't worth it, mate!"

"Lord have mercy on our young people."

"God in heaven, have mercy on this poor child. Save her, Lord Jesus!"

"Put the knife down!"

"Don't do it, young man!"

"Marvin! You dare! I'll fucking kill you!"

She turned her head slowly to keep the spinning at bay until someone in a navy jacket identical to hers came into view, battered face attracting stares.

If not for the jacket and the half-fringe—albeit a mess—it would've taken longer to realise it was Tempest.

Tempest. The one who'd invited these strangers to her birthday party.

She'd put Marvin up to it. Even now she was pretending.

God, that was it.

Tempest wanted her dead.

It had all started with the mental torture. And now it had come to this—the grand finale.

Tempest was finally about to get what she'd wanted all along.

There was nothing the witnesses could do to stop Marvin.

She closed her eyes. The undertakers wouldn't have to force her eyes shut. A death like this would take the victim by surprise, shock all over the face. That wasn't going to happen to her. She swallowed. She would look good in her casket. Her parents would—

God, her parents. Christmas was only a few weeks away. She wouldn't make it. Her throat was heavy and hard. Tears flooded her eyes and her lips trembled. That bitch had her right where she wanted her. She was going to give Tempest the satisfaction of seeing her at her lowest, especially with the toothless shit taking long to finish her. She bawled.

"Marvin, wait!"

"No!"

"Listen!"

"No!"

"It was me!"

"What was you?"

"Jason."

No one spoke for a while. She kept as still as a statue, eyes still shut, tensed as she waited for Marvin to send her to her granny and grandpa, and maybe Sylvia.

"I did it."

That made her jump, kept her heart in distress, as she anticipated the knife bursting the veins in her throat.

Marvin took pressure off the knife against her neck, and his grip on her collar wasn't as tight.

She didn't dare move. The prick was toying with her, delaying things. She couldn't take the bait and open her eyes. Dying with eyes open in horror . . . That couldn't happen. She clenched her eyes tighter, until they hurt. No good for the undertakers. She tried to relax her face. Still wobbly, even in the blackness.

"It was me."

She jumped. The end was still delayed, the torture continuing.

"Callum, what the fuck you on about?"

Callum didn't respond.

Sharp pressure from the blade again made her scream. Her heart was pounding in her chest and head, and her chest was heaving. She wanted to swallow, but she couldn't; the slightest neck movement would draw blood.

Then the knife started boring into her neck. Her face tightened as she shook and more tears fell. This was it.

"I did it!"

Marvin decreased the pressure again. *"Did. What?"*

She wailed.

Callum muttered something.

Hardly pinned now.

She raised her arms gingerly, unable to straighten them completely. All she was clutching was air. She couldn't open her eyes though. Marvin was still toying with her.

She stepped sideways, over her own feet, opened her eyes as she fell.

Marvin was approaching Callum. Callum was backing away. She crawled away from them, limbs shaking as someone grabbed her, helped her to her feet. People all around her on the pavement, and drivers standing next to their cars, blocking vehicles behind them. Beeps in the distance. Sirens too. People gasped, started to look away from her, some with their hands over their mouths. She followed their gazes.

Callum had swapped places with her; Marvin was stringing him up, the knife at his throat as it had been at hers.

"You did what?"

People were creeping up behind Marvin. The closer they got, the more Callum's head went back to relieve the pressure from the knife, hat coming off to reveal brown hair at the top of his head, the sides shaved clean.

"You're lying, Callum."

Callum's eyes were wide. *"N-no, I ain't."*

"What?"

"He had something on me, and—"

"You killed Jason?"

Two men were mere footsteps from Marvin.

Callum was crying hard, his words unclear.

Marvin said something she couldn't hear.

Then someone in her periphery diverted her attention. By the time she took a good look, the person was gone, hidden behind the two men closest to Marvin and Callum. She knew what she'd seen though—the navy jacket lapel, facial injuries and half-fringe.

Two footsteps away, in position to grab Marvin.

Callum made frantic shakes of the head.

"Tell me!"

"Marvin, please—"

"Tell me, you cunt!"

"OK! OK! The drug money. . . ."

She didn't hear the rest of what Callum said.

The men were about to grab Marvin.

But they were too late. A line of red formed across Callum's throat.

Marvin gritted his teeth as he applied more pressure.

People screamed. Blood sprayed. She turned her head too late. She'd seen enough to make her want to vomit some more.

Vomiting drowned out Callum's gargles.

Or maybe everyone else's groans and screams did.

37 / Elise IX
The plan all along

Another week off work pretty much over for Elise. At least the time off had been for good reason, as proven in the folded *Hackney Gazette* on her parents' glass coffee table. So close to being murdered.

And Marvin would've killed her if Callum hadn't decided to own up to the killing in Mabley Green.

To think that Shan had something like that hanging over him. He and Aiden had lied; he'd been attacked in Mabley Green, not Dalston. Their way of keeping her out of the mess and protecting themselves.

The two of them were happier now; they deserved it. She prayed they would stay that way despite . . . She clutched her tummy.

Maybe it was a blessing, or at least it would be, months or years down the line.

Just a big freaking mess, all because of Tempest. No clue how she'd managed to pull it off. Tempest had gone above and beyond to destroy her. And succeeded. It didn't matter that Tempest felt bad now that everyone knew Sylvia had been suicidal. The damage had been done. By her. The prank calls, the passport, tampering with her food and drink, setting her up with someone she knew wasn't straight . . . it was all sick. If not for what Tempest had made everything come to, maybe forgiveness would've been possible. Granted, Tempest had had a difficult childhood, always playing second best, her toys and clothes never as good as Elise's. Same for her hair. Pa couldn't plait properly, but he'd tried. He had to try because Ma had no intention of ever touching Tempest's hair. And then the rampant teenage sex and subsequent pregnancy. Tempest had been through a lot growing up, always the black sheep.

And now her sick stunts ensured that title would be passed on to Elise. Tempest's idea of getting even.

They weren't even though. Tempest could move on. Things would never be the same for Elise.

Being evicted from the flat couldn't have come at a better time. If circumstances hadn't been so dire, she would've laughed when she'd found out Carl's wife owned the flat. The cheap rent had been too good to be true. There wasn't a twenty-five year-old as eager to move back in with her parents. Tempest had her aunt to stay with. Lucky bitch, though not so lucky in love.

Mistress or not, Tempest was hurt by her break-up with Carl, crying living tears, as if she were the wife losing her husband to someone else.

Still so freaking sympathetic. She needed to cut that out if she wanted revenge of her own. Tempest deserved the claat from Carl's wife . . . Damn shame it hadn't been one-sided.

Too much thinking, procrastinating. She grimaced as she tapped *Aiden Gordon* on her phone, then she quickly stopped the call when the gate came to a throbbing close.

Movement through the net curtains made her look that way. Familiar black jacket with the furry lapels. Supermodel walk of someone who thought she ruled the world. After all the chaos she'd caused, the bitch had the nerve to show up.

Elise stormed out of the front room, hurled the front door open then stood in the doorway, arms crossed.

Tempest, a footstep away, gave attitude back with cutting eyes. Her half-fringe was to the left this time, hiding the gash caused by the candle holder Francesca, Carl's wife, had thrown at her. Her complexion was lighter. Hadn't quite found the right shade of foundation to hide her injuries and keep her from looking like she was trying to bleach her skin. Bitch had done a good job with the lipstick unfortunately, considering how mashed up Francesca had left her lips.

"Elise, it's freezing."

She peered at Tempest through the fog their exhales created.

"He's my daddy too."

True. Unfortunate, but true.

Tempest tried to get past.

"I don't think so, bitch."

Tempest leaned back, looking like she was considering pouncing. She thought better of it, huffed instead.

"I want to see my daddy."

"He's not here."

"Then let me wait inside."

Elise didn't budge.

Tempest narrowed her eyes, leaned to her left and shook her right leg. "You bitch!"

"Bitch?"

"Yes! Bitch!"

"You're the bitch!"

Tempest cut her eyes as she looked away, leaned again, shaking her left leg this time. "Heifer, you're not about that life, so stop."

"Try me, *heifer*."

Tempest sighed then made eye contact. "Look, I came here—"

"To what, see if I've said anything to Ma and Pa yet?"

Tempest fluttered her eyelashes as she looked away again, then she peered at Elise through the corner of her eye. "Have you?"

"No."

"Will you?"

If not for that one thing . . . "If I do, I do. If I don't, I don't."

Tempest released a stressed exhale, her fog quickly lost in a sudden gust of wind.

When the wind died down, Elise said, "They know about Sylvia's letter."

"*What?*"

"Didn't tell them you overheard the conversation all those months ago. Told them about Aiden and Shan, that they were set up."

Panic took over Tempest's face.

"Couldn't let them go on thinking Shan and Aiden betrayed me."

"You told them about that?"

"Yes. Told them they were set up."

"By me?"

"By Carl."

"And me?"

"Just Carl. He's not in the picture anymore. Oh, they know he's married."

Tempest widened her eyes.

"Be glad that's all I told them."

"I bet your shithouse mum is lapping it all up."

"Don't talk about her like that."

"She is a *shit*house."

"What about your mother? She slept with a married man. *She* was a shithouse, a nasty one at that."

She didn't see the box coming; it was as hard as it was fast. She grabbed hold of the door frame. She formed a fist and drove it into Tempest's left cheek on her way back up. Tempest would've ended up on the ground if not for the bare branches of the hedge she clutched. Elise pressed her stinging left cheek against her shoulder, while Tempest flicked her half-fringe back in place and rubbed her left cheek.

Tempest came closer to her, teeth gritted. Elise gave a cutting look.

Tempest stopped, stamped the ground. "I didn't come here for a fucking fight."

"That's a shame."

"Girl, please!"

"Just—"

Vibrations in her pocket. She took her phone out, one of her fingers feeling odd. Aiden. She grimaced, caught herself to keep Tempest from noticing, then stuffed the phone back in. That strange sensation hadn't gone. She splayed her fingers. Nail broken off the middle one. The pissing door frame.

"What about your passport?"

She squinted at Tempest.

"Does Daddy and that . . ." Tempest caught herself, was going to call Ma out of her name, gestured with her hand instead. ". . . know what I did with it?"

Elise rolled her eyes.

"Do they?"

"No!"

Tempest exhaled deeply, her eyes clenched like she was saying a silent prayer of thanks. A gust of wind messed up her half-fringe. She took a pin out of her pocket and pinned most of the fringe to the left side of her head. Seemed she'd forgotten about the gash.

"They don't know you set me up with a gay—a guy you knew wasn't straight."

Tempest smirked. "How did they take the fact that their angel was busy getting *fucked* by Aiden, out of wedlock at that?"

She clutched her stomach then quickly removed her hand. That was the last thing she needed to think about right now. She needed to save that thought for when she saw Aiden.

"Humph. The innocent daughter lost her virginity outside of marriage, to a gay guy no less."

The bitch was still smirking.

"Not many people could wait till they were almost twenty-five." Her smirk faded as her countenance became distant. "I certainly couldn't, with my fucked-up teenage self."

Elise turned her head, gave the wind more of her left cheek.

"I did some dirty stuff to you."

She snapped her head back towards Tempest. "You think?"

"You were no better."

"Your mum committed suicide."

"Maybe, but it doesn't change the fact that I overheard you and Daddy and . . ." Again she refused to say the name. "You actually knew that black cab was coming, knew that my mum was going after you to save you, and you timed it so that she'd push you out of the way and get killed."

"I didn't want her dead."

Tempest kissed her teeth.

"I just wanted her hurt, didn't think it would kill her."

"So you're not an evil bitch after all, just a dumb bitch."

"Definitely dumb, never suspecting you were the one behind those stunts. Everything you did to me, to Shan, to Aiden . . . *you* are the evil bitch. Humph, guess you're a dumb bitch too, fucking a married man. Picked up right where your mother left off."

Tempest stepped to her.

"Try me."

Tempest stopped herself, grimaced. "Look, you hurt me, and I hurt you. We're even."

That pissing word—*even.*

"I could've done a lot worse. I wasn't meant to do Shannon and Aiden like that on your birthday, but Shannon found out, so I had to do it."

"It wasn't part of your plan?"

"No. You were meant to keep having sex with Aiden until . . ."

"Until?"

"It doesn't matter now. It didn't get that far, and I'm glad it didn't."

She grabbed Tempest. "How far?"

"Let . . . go of me!"

"Tell me!"

Tempest tried to free herself, teeth gritted, pulling Elise away from the doorway. Elise pulled Tempest back.

"I said . . . let go!"

"Tell me!"

"The fucking condoms I gave you!"

She froze.

Tempest slipped out of her clutches.

"What?"

"Like I said . . ." Tempest caught her breath. ". . . things ended between you and Aiden before . . . I'm glad that messing with the condoms was for nothing. I'm glad that things ended between the two of you when they did— Elise, you're shaking. What—?"

"You need to leave."

"What's wrong?"

"Go!" Her voice echoed, scared birds away from nearby trees.

Tempest backed away, squinting. "But—"

"Leave, bitch!"

Tempest jumped, scurried away, the mostly leafless hedge hiding her. Her frenzied footsteps faded quickly.

———

"Elise?" He sounded different.

Maybe it was because of the wind and traffic along Wick Road.

"Hi, Aiden. I need—"

"Elise, it's Shannon."

"Oh." She looked at her phone screen; she hadn't called Shan by mistake.

Her throat tightened. She put the phone back to her ear as Shan kept calling her name.

"Sorry, Shan." She swallowed. "I'm back now."

"No worries. Aiden's making me cut his hair every week."

"Really?"

"Yeah." Animation left his voice. "Everything go well with the doctor?"

The lump returned with a vengeance.

"Elise?"

"I'm here. . . . It was Tempest. . . . She . . ." Aiden needed to know first. "She tampered with my food."

Couldn't tell if Shan gasped or sighed. "I'm so sorry, Elise. At least you know."

"Y-yeah. What about you? Got your test results?"

"Yeah. Whatever Tempest put in my drink wasn't dangerous. Some funny name."

"Thank God."

"Yeah. I know you called for Aiden, but I have something to tell you."

"You do?"

"Yeah. Guess what I did?"

He sounded so happy. He was the last person she wanted to make unhappy, but it would all come out eventually. Everything had to work out somehow. It wasn't as if she wanted Aiden. Then again, that would make the situation a bit better.

"Still there, Elise?"

"Uh . . . yes. Sorry. Tell me."

He paused. "I walked along Glyn Road."

She stopped at a zebra crossing, even though it was clear on both sides. "What?"

"You heard correctly."

"Did you see them?"

"Yes. And they saw me."

"Really?"

"Yeah. They were looking at me through the front room window. It was hard . . . awkward . . . but I stared back. They looked away first."

"That was so brave of you, Shan. Maybe one day things will get back to normal between you and your parents."

He sighed. "Who knows? I don't even know if I want that, not after everything that's happened."

"Can't say I blame you."

"Besides, Uncle Lionel and Peter, they're everything."

She smiled.

A car beep made her jump. The car was stationary at the crossing, its driver, a woman, giving her an aggressive gesture. She scurried across the road.

"Anyway, here's Aiden."

"Thanks, Shan."

"Bye, Elise— Wait, before I go, we're still on for tomorrow?"

After what she had to tell Aiden—tell them both—her guess was as good as anyone else's. "Yes."

"Alrighty." Shan handed Aiden the phone.

"What's good, Elise?"

"Hi, Aiden. I won't keep you long."

"OK."

She lowered her voice. "Are you on loudspeaker?"

He hesitated. "No."

"I need to see you."

"O . . . K."

She lowered her voice. "Without . . . *my friend.*"

"Without your—?"

"Don't repeat what I said. I need to see you—and only you."

"Oh . . . right." Shan must've still been close by.

"I'm near Victoria Park. I'm guessing you're in Dalston."

"Yeah. Was gonna leave soon. Maybe we can meet in Victoria Park."

"That would be great. Is thirty minutes too soon?"

"No."

"Well, I'll wait here. Not too far into the Wick Road entrance."

"Fine. Later."

"Bye." She clasped the post attached to the flashing yellow beacon to keep from crumpling to the ground.

There Aiden was, swaggering towards her, head tucked in the furry hood of his camouflage jacket. She started towards him and he sped up before they met at a bench.

He hugged her.

She barely hugged him back.

"What's wrong, Elise?"

Too late to wish things were different, that he were straight. Things were too far gone. Well, not really, but changing something like this would go against everything she believed in.

She sat down on a part of the bench that didn't have any traces of bird mess. "I'm . . . I don't know how I am."

He sat down. "Why not?"

"I'll get to that in a minute. How's everything with you and Shan?"

"Alright?"

"Just alright?"

"Good, really good, but . . ."

"But what?"

468

"Remember the cousin I told you 'bout?"

She paused, then it came to her. "Craig, the one who . . . ?"

"Yeah."

"What, did you tell Shan?"

"No, he doesn't know."

"Will you tell him?"

"Dunno yet, but the fam know."

"Really?"

"Yeah. If they didn't know, then it wouldn't be so bad."

"What do you mean?"

"He's coming back to England."

She clutched her chest.

"Exactly. He was engaged—"

"Engaged?"

"Yeah, but they've split up."

"God . . . don't know what to say."

"My grandfolks might be cool with him, but I ain't. Don't want shit to do with him."

"Don't blame you. I'd be mortified."

"And Ethan's worse."

"How is he taking you and Shan?"

Aiden looked away, shaking his head.

"Sorry."

"Could be worse."

Things were worse.

"What about you and Tempest?"

"Let's not go there."

Aiden put up his hands defensively.

"Didn't mean to snap. We're done, that's all."

"For true?"

"Yeah."

"Must be relieved, knowing everything."

"Suppose."

"You sound off, Elise."

She took a deep breath as a cyclist sped past them.

"What is it?"

"I haven't been well."

"Yeah, Shan said it's 'cause of Tempest."

She was going to tell him that wasn't true, but it actually was.

"Elise, you know I ain't with the suspense shit."

She took a deep, hitched exhale, her fog lingering and her heart racing. "I . . . I . . . don't know . . . how to say this . . ."

Aiden was stone-faced, his silence telling her to hurry up.

"We all know what Tempest did, as far as you and me, right?"

"Yeah."

"But there's something else."

He shrugged, raised his eyebrows to hurry her up again.

"The vomiting stopped, but it came back again recently, and I've gained weight."

He frowned.

She broke the eye contact, looked ahead at cyclists in the distance, wind making dead leaves swirl.

If only the wind could sweep her away.

Aiden waved right in her face.

"Sorry. . . . When the doctor told me what she told me, it didn't make any sense, but when Tempest revealed what else she'd done . . ."

His frown grew sinister, made her skin crawl.

She looked away. "When we . . ."

"What?"

"When we slept together, we used condoms."

"I know, except the first time."

"Right."

"Yeah, but you took the pill."

"Y-yes."

She hadn't, but that wasn't when it happened, based on the calculations. She'd climbed off him before he'd climaxed anyway.

She summoned the strength to look at him. "The thing is . . ."

"What?"

"The condoms we used . . . she gave them to me."

"Tempest?"

"Yeah."

"OK . . ."

"No, it's not OK."

One of his legs was bouncing. He put his elbow on his right thigh, his hand cupping his cheek and chin so that part of his top lip squashed into his nose. "Why not?"

She was really going to have to spell it out for him. "The vomiting, my tight clothes . . . my missed period, and—"

"You said all of that, and— Hold up. Missed period?"

She nodded, her pounding heart making her weak.

He licked his lips; they trembled.

"Tempest . . . she . . ."

"Tempest *what*?"

"Th-the condoms . . . when you came out of me . . . and the condom was wet on the outside . . . and we thought it was from me . . ."

He was sitting upright now, his lips pursed, his stare deadly.

"She . . . tampered . . . with the condoms."

He kept opening his mouth. No words. Just fog.

He swallowed and tried again, his eyes closed, teeth gritted. "Tampered with them *how*?" He was bracing himself for what he already knew.

"She *tampered* with them, Aiden."

He leaned back, his arms stretched over the top of the bench, his head all the way back, mouth open, like death had taken him by surprise.

471

He took a while to finally lock eyes with her, nostrils flared. His lips were moving, but no words were coming out, just fog. His expression . . . it was new to her, hard to read. There was a war in his honey brown eyes, the desire to kill someone on one side and desperation to be struck down by God on the other. The devil lines between his eyebrows were coming and going.

Something crunching leaves from the right made them look that way. Two women, arms interlocked, one of them pushing a pram with a baby inside. Perhaps sisters, friends or cousins.

Maybe even a couple taking their baby for a stroll.

Could be Aiden and Shan, if Shan decided to stick around after the news.

The baby dropped something, a rattle. One of the women went to pick it up as the other one stopped pushing. If Elise stretched out her arm, she would've been able to touch the baby's gloved hand. Her heart sped up as she locked eyes with the baby boy's—it looked like a boy—big ones.

Then the baby smiled at her.

MONTHS LATER

EPILOGUE / Shannon XII
Journal interrupted

2nd August 2016

I should be continuing my job search right now, checking my emails to see if anyone's willing to hire me, or polishing up my CVs and covering letters, but there's only so much rejection I can take. I got a distinction in my master's, but that seems irrelevant right now.

I am happier than I've been in a long time. I have Uncle Lionel, Peter—officially Uncle Peter now that he's Uncle Lionel's husband—Aiden, and Elise. I didn't make anyone feel a certain way when I had to choose a maximum of two people to attend my graduation ceremony; Aiden and Elise thought it was only right that my uncles attend. Elise wasn't well anyway, in her state, and who better than Aiden to spend time with her, cater to her? I'm even getting used to not having my parents like I used to. As much as I hate to admit it, I still think of them—probably even miss them—but I'm not ready to let them back into my life. Maybe one day, as stubborn as they both are, they'll come around somehow. But I'm not ready to take that step yet. If that step is taken, they should be the ones to reach out to me. I know they're alright *though. I sometimes go to Glyn Road and watch them from afar. I know they know I'm watching them. They pause then pretend nothing gave them pause, making sure not to look my way, but the pauses are long enough to let me know they see me.*

Aiden's mum's a blast. I'm glad she's out of prison. When Aiden told me she'd killed his father, I wondered why they were letting her out, but he says it was self-defence. I get the feeling there's more to it, but I won't push the issue. She's Aiden's mum, and she accepts him and me.

But I've been in a frigged-up frame of mind for the last day, as long as Elise has been in labour.

I thought I would've come to terms with everything by now, but I'm petrified. Aiden is my first man. It still feels weird calling him that. I guess it's because of the residues of shame, misunderstanding and ignorance concerning gay love over time. Most people don't go through life having had just one lover, but here I am thinking I can't be with anyone but Aiden. I've given him my body and my heart, things I can't get back. No need to break up and end up giving someone else those two things.

There's really no one like him. He's opened up to me in ways that I don't think he has with anyone else. Most people see the muscular, reticent giant with a gaze that's sharp enough to cut someone's throat, or the teeth that are sometimes gritted behind barely-moving lips when he talks, but he's different with his nearest and dearest. For a long time, I thought he couldn't help looking at people the way he does, but that's just how his eyes are. What really takes me over the edge is the look he gives me when he's horny. That look takes me to the point of no return. He's always concerned whenever he's inside me—with good reason, as hung as he is—but I've learned how to let him in and keep the pain to a minimum. I'm actually involved with someone intimately.

Now that I think about it, that tough exterior is his armour in a world that's tough on people like him, and me.

I don't know what I would do without him—I don't ever want to know—but once the baby is born, who knows what will happen?

Things would be perfect if it wasn't for that bitch. Yes—bitch, heifer, shithouse, wretch. This is for my eyes only. I might as well get it out on paper if I can't cuss her for Elise to hear. I still can't believe Elise has forgiven her. If she can do it, I suppose I should too. After all, she's the one Tempest fucked over the most. Even Aiden has found a way to tolerate her. I'm going to have to get over what Tempest did, for Elise's sake.

For what it's worth, Tempest has been helping Elise through the pregnancy as much as Aiden and I have. I can't pretend she hasn't changed. She's actually nicer, especially since Elise set her up with Aiden's cousin. Craig has had some effect on her. Even her voice isn't so gruff. It's as if the main thing that has helped Elise through the pregnancy has been the progress in Tempest and Craig's relationship. I hope they last, even though I get weird vibes between Aiden and Craig. It's probably nothing. Aiden isn't fussed about the relationship. He's just letting them get on with it. I guess

Jill Scott's "Not like Crazy" played out of nowhere. Shannon jumped, took in one of his favourite songs, then froze, the pen in his hand hovering over his unfinished journal entry. No need to look at the phone to know it was Aiden. That song was just for him. Any other time, he would've been eager to answer the call, but not now.

The call meant only one thing—Elise and Aiden were officially parents.

Acknowledgements

Mum, it'll be interesting to see what you make of this novel—presuming you're not too delicate for it—and especially if you can relate to a particular character (or two). Thank you for all you've done for me from birth till now.

Grandma, you lived long, but you were taken too soon. I wonder how you would've felt about the similarities between yourself and a character (or two) in the novel. Words can't describe how much I miss you.

Kharima, you were one of the first people—if not the first—I told that I was writing a novel. You were the first person to read any part of it. You encouraged me to keep at it and gave me a heads-up on opportunities to submit my work and attend writing events. And I pestered you for feedback on cover design. For all you have done, thank you.

Paula, one of the first people I told I was working on a novel. You encouraged me to go for it. You didn't read any part of my novel while it was in progress, because you said you'd prefer to read the published version—talk about putting it into the universe—but you read a short story I wrote, and I appreciate your feedback on that.

Reneice, you gave me hope that I was onto something, just by reading a proposed back cover for the novel. I remember you telling me that if you saw a novel with that blurb, you would buy it. Thank you for your support and being a listening ear.

Alistar, when I was reluctant to put myself out there, you forced the issue by having me correspond with someone in order that I may write more. That didn't work out, but I appreciate your good intentions. I haven't forgotten your feedback on the cover design. I'm forever grateful for your encouragement.

Adenike, you never knew the details of my novel, but when you found out I was writing one, the excitement that came over your face was enough to let me know you were behind me. Many thanks for your encouragement and for your feedback on the cover design. (Sorry to disappoint you in my choice of author name.)

Sam, one of the first people I told I was working on a novel. Your excitement, without even knowing the premise of my story, did more for me than you can ever imagine.

Shadae, you read a part of my novel while it was a work in progress, and you gave me feedback on the cover design. Your excitement for, and interest in, my work was invaluable.

Kamara, I'm unsure how much of the story you read, and at what stage, but your encouragement and excitement meant a lot to me, especially since I know you're an avid reader.

Lisa, you didn't know anything about my novel, but you read a short story of mine. Your feedback meant a great deal.

Acknowledgements

Tara and Jizan, I told you both I was writing a novel without giving much detail. Jizan, your intrigue when I told you I was working on a novel, as well as informing me your husband had self-published a book, was motivating. Tara, I appreciate you sharing your experiences as a scriptwriter with me and for your advice.

Alina & Laura, you didn't know much about my novel, but you encouraged me. Laura, I know you were keen to spread the word, so thank you for keeping quiet about it. Alina, thank you for the message you sent that you couldn't wait to read my book.

Mustafa, you didn't know much about the novel, but you were interested in its progress, which I'm grateful for. Thank you also for the cover design feedback.

My Big Three: Eric Jerome Dickey, whose recent passing still hurts; E. Lynn Harris, whom I still miss dearly; & Marlon James, whom I'm thankful to have met. Three very different authors, but three authors whose works I marvel at most of all and who are among my greatest inspirations.

Most of those mentioned have helped me throughout my life (i.e. in a non-writing capacity), but so have MANY others. Naming you all would turn this into an essay, but please know how grateful I am for you and all you've done for me.

Last but not least, I thank YOU, the readers of *Cold Hearts, Troubled Souls*. I hope you enjoyed this novel.

Printed in Great Britain
by Amazon

44419425R00273